MY NAME IS RYAN TYLER . . .

. . . and people say I killed twenty-seven men. The fact is, I killed just ten, every man jack of them in a stand-up, fair fight. And that goes for Indians as well, though nobody counted Indians in those days.

Some people say I was all bad. That I killed without reason. That I was an outlaw. They say that no man has a right to kill another man. That's why I'm writing this all down—so you can judge for yourself.

Nowadays, the know-it-alls say it wasn't really wild back in the years when I grew up. Well, records show one hundred and two murders around Alder Gulch before vigilantes hanged the outlaw killers. Feuds in Texas, New Mexico and Arizona killed at least five hundred more. There were a hundred and ten killings in a small town named Alta. The records go on and on.

My feeling is my guns and some other guns made it easier for those who came later. The cattle roam fat and lazy now, people sleep well at night. The guns are hung up—and I think they've got people like me to thank for it.

BENDIGO SHAFTER
BORDEN CHANTRY
BOWDRIE
BRIONNE
THE BROKEN GUN
BUCKSKIN RUN
THE BURNING HILLS
THE CALIFORNIOS
CALLAGHEN
CATLOW
CHANCY
THE CHEROKEE TRAIL
COMSTOCK LODE
CONAGHER
CROSSFIRE TRAIL
DARK CANYON
DOWN THE LONG HILLS
THE EMPTY LAND
FAIR BLOWS THE WIND
FALLON
THE FERGUSON RIFLE
THE FIRST FAST DRAW
FLINT
GUNS OF THE TIMBER-
    LANDS
HANGING WOMAN CREEK
THE HIGH GRADERS
HIGH LONESOME
HONDO
HOW THE WEST WAS WON
THE IRON MARSHAL
THE KEY-LOCK MAN
KID RODELO
KILKENNY
KILLOE
KILRONE
KIOWA TRAIL
THE LONESOME GODS
THE MAN CALLED NOON
THE MAN FROM
    SKIBBEREEN
MATAGORDA
MILO TALON
THE MOUNTAIN
    VALLEY WAR
NORTH TO THE RAILS
OVER ON THE DRY SIDE
THE PROVING TRAIL

THE QUICK AND THE
    DEAD
RADIGAN
REILLY'S LUCK
THE RIDER OF LOST CREEK
RIVERS WEST
THE SHADOW RIDERS
SHALAKO
SHOWDOWN AT
    YELLOW BUTTE
SILVER CANYON
SITKA
THE STRONG SHALL LIVE
TAGGART
TUCKER
UNDER THE SWEET-
    WATER RIM
UTAH BLAINE
WAR PARTY
WESTWARD THE TIDE
WHERE THE LONG GRASS
    BLOWS
YONDERING

Sackett Titles by
Louis L'Amour

1. SACKETT'S LAND
2. TO THE FAR BLUE
    MOUNTAINS
3. THE DAYBREAKERS
4. SACKETT
5. LANDO
6. MOJAVE CROSSING
7. THE SACKETT BRAND
8. THE LONELY MEN
9. TREASURE MOUNTAIN
10. MUSTANG MAN
11. GALLOWAY
12. THE SKY-LINERS
13. THE MAN FROM THE
    BROKEN HILLS
14. RIDE THE DARK TRAIL
15. THE WARRIOR'S PATH
16. LONELY ON THE
    MOUNTAIN
17. RIDE THE RIVER

TO
TAME
A
LAND

Louis L'Amour

BANTAM BOOKS

TORONTO • NEW YORK • LONDON • SYDNEY • AUCKLAND

All characters in this book are fictional
and any resemblance to persons living or dead
is purely coincidental.

TO TAME A LAND

*A Bantam Book / published by arrangement with
the Author*

Bantam edition / January 1984

ISBN 0-553-23860-4

Published simultaneously in the United States and Canada

*Bantam Books are published by Bantam Books, Inc. Its trademark,
consisting of the words "Bantam Books" and the portrayal of
a rooster, is Registered in U.S. Patent and Trademark Office
and in other countries. Marca Registrada. Bantam Books, Inc.,
666 Fifth Avenue, New York, New York 10103.*

PRINTED IN THE UNITED STATES OF AMERICA

O   0 9 8 7 6 5 4 3 2

1

It was Indian country, and when our wheel busted, none of them would stop. They just rolled on by and left us setting there, my pap and me.

Me, I was pushing a tall twelve by then and could cuss 'most as good as Pap, and we both done some cussin' then.

Bagley, the one Pap helped down to Ash Hollow that time, he got mighty red around the ears, but he kept his wagon rollin'.

Most folks, those days, were mighty helpful, but this outfit sort of set their way by the captain. He was Big Jack McGarry.

When the wheel busted, somebody called out and we swung back. Big Jack had no liking for Pap because Pap never took nothing off him, and because Pap had the first look-in with Mary Tatum, which Big Jack couldn't abide.

He swung that fine black horse of his back and he set there looking at us. We had turned to and were getting that wheel off, fixing to get it repaired if we could.

"Sorry, Tyler. You know what I said. This is Indian country. Goin' through here, we keep rollin' no matter what. We'll wait a spell at the springs, though. You can catch us there."

Then he turned his horse and rode off, and nobody else in the wagons said by word or look that they even seen us setting there.

Pap, he didn't waste no more time. He looked after them, his face kind of drawn down and gray like, and then he turned to me and he said, "Son, I don't mind for myself. It's you I'm thinkin' of. But maybe it'll be all right. You take that there gun, and you set up high and watch sharp."

So that was the way it was, and Pap aworking to fix that wheel so we could go on. He was a good man at such things, and he had built many a wagon in his day, and had done some fine cabinetwork, too.

He worked steady and I kept my eyes open, but there was mighty little to see. It was a long rolling grass plain wherever a body looked. Here and there was draws, but I couldn't see into them. The wind stirred that tall grass, bending it over in long rolls, the way the sea must look, and it was green-gray and then silver in the changing light and wind. Overhead the sky was wide and pale blue, with just a few lazy clouds adrifting.

We had us a good Conestoga wagon and six head of cattle, good big oxen, to haul it. We had two horses and two saddles, and inside the wagon was Pap's tools, our grub, bedding, and a few odds and ends like Ma's picture, which Pap kept by him, no matter what.

Pap had swapped for a couple of Joslyn breech-loading carbines before we left Kansas, and we each had us a handgun, Shawk & McLanahan six-shooters, caliber .36, and good guns, too.

Like McGarry said, this was Indian country. Not two weeks ago the Indians had hit a wagon train, smaller than ours, killing four men and a woman. They hit it again a few miles west, and they killed two more men.

Ours was a big train, well armed and all, but Big Jack, I seen the look in his eyes when he sat there watching Pap aworking. He was just figuring to himself that he wouldn't have to worry any more about Pap, and by the time the wagons got to Californy he'd be married up with Mary Tatum. Her and all that silver her old man carried in the big box under his wagon.

When it was almost dark, Pap called to me. "Son, come on down. You ride your horse, scout around a little. If the wagons get to stop at the springs, we'll catch 'em."

But cattle don't make no speed with a heavy wagon. Their feet spread wide on turf and they pull better, day in, day out, than any mule or horse, but they can't be called fast.

Night came, and we set a course by the stars, and we rolled on west all through the night. When the first gray light was in the sky, we saw the gleam on the water. Least, I saw it. Pap, he was still too far back.

I seen the water where the pool was, and the cottonwood leaves, but no white wagon covers, no horses, and no breakfast fires acooking.

When the wagon came up I saw Pap looking and looking like he couldn't believe it, and I seen his Adam's apple swallow, and I said, "Pap, they've gone on. They left us."

"Yes," he said. "I reckon that's so."

We both knew we had to stop. Cattle can stand so much, and these had a tough night and day behind them. "We'll water up, son," Pap said. "Then we'll pull into a draw and rest a while."

So that was how it was, only when we got to the springs we saw the wagons had not stopped there. Big Jack McGarry had taken no chances. He pulled them right on by, and nobody to know he'd promised to wait for us there. Nobody but him and us.

We watered up and then we pulled out. Maybe three miles farther on we found a draw with some brush and we pulled into it for a rest. Pap unyoked the oxen and let them eat buffalo grass. He taken his Joslyn up on the ridge and bellied down in the grass.

Me, I went to sleep under the wagon, and maybe I'd been asleep an hour when I felt someone nudge me, and it was Pap.

"Here they come, boy. You get on your horse and take out." He was down on one knee near me. "Maybe if you hold to low ground you can make it safe."

"I ain't agoin' without you."

"Son, you go now. One can make it. Two can't. You take Old Blue. He's the fastest."

"You come with me."

"No, this here is all we got, boy. I'll stay by it. Maybe they'll take what sugar we got, and go."

"I'll stay, too."

"No!" Pap rarely spoke hard to me after Ma died, but he spoke sharp and stern now, and it wasn't in me to dispute him. So I loosed the reins and swung into the saddle.

Pap passed me up a sackful of cartridges and such, then caught my arm. There were tears in his eyes. "Luck, boy. Luck. Remember your ma."

Then he slapped Old Blue on the rump and Old Blue went off up the draw. Me, I was in no mind to leave him, so when we rounded a little bend I put Blue up the bank and circled back.

I heard a rifle shot and saw dust kick near the wagon, then a whole volley of shots. Along with the rest I heard the sharp hard sound of Pap's Joslyn carbine.

Tying Blue among some brush in a low place, I grabbed my Joslyn and went back, keeping low down.

Maybe a dozen Indians were out there, and Pap's one shot had counted, for I saw a free horse running off. As I looked the Indians began to circle, and Pap fired again. An Indian grabbed at his horse's mane and almost slipped off.

The sun was out and it was hot. I could smell the hot, dusty grass and feel the sun on my back, and my hands were sweaty, but I waited.

Boy though I was, and Pap no Indian fighter, I knew what I had to do. Night after night I'd sat by the fire and heard talk of Indian fights and such-like from the mountain men we met, and a couple of others who had been over this trail before us. I soaked it up, and I knew there was a time for waiting and a time for shooting.

Pap was doing right good. He downed a horse and

the Indians pulled off and away. I lay quiet, having a good view of the whole shindig, me being no more than a hundred and fifty yards off.

Sudden-like, I saw the grass move. They were crawling up now. Did Pap see them?

No, he couldn't see them from where he lay, but he had guessed that was what they would do, for I saw him worm out from behind the wheel where he'd been shooting and ease off into some rocks not far from the wagon. They were coming on and right soon I could see four of the Indians.

Pap waited. I give him that. He was no Indian fighter, just a good wheelwright and cabinetmaker, but he was smart. Suddenly he came up with his carbine and fired quick. I saw an Indian jerk back with a busted shoulder. Then two of them ran forward. Pap fired and missed, and fired again and hit.

And then I heard a whisper in the grass and saw four Indians walking their horses careful behind him. Behind him and right below me. They weren't thirty yards off from me, at point-blank range.

This here was what I'd waited for. My mouth so dry I couldn't spit or swallow, I ups with my Joslyn. I took steady aim the way I'd been taught, drew a deep breath and let it out easy, and then I squeezed her off. The rifle jumped in my hands, and that first Indian let out a grunt and went off his horse and into the grass. I'd shot him right through the skull.

Pap turned quick, fired once, then swung back as I shot again.

My second shot took an Indian right through the spine, and the other two went to hellin' away from there.

My shooting had caught them flat-footed, as the fellow says. They'd figured the man at the wagon was the only one, and now I'd killed me two Indians, and all in less than a minute.

Another shot, and I turned quick.

Two Indians had rushed Pap and now they were fighting with him. At the same moment the two I'd run off circled back. I shot and missed, too excited, and

then I saw Pap go down and saw a knife rise and fall,
and I knew it was too late to do anything for Pap.

I hustled for Old Blue, jumped into the saddle, and
rode out of there.

But I didn't head for no settlement, or try to catch up
with the train. That wagon was ours, and the stuff in it
was ours. I circled around, walked my horse a couple of
miles in a creek, then brought him out of the water
onto rock and cut back over the hills.

It was full dark when I got back there. All was quiet.
There was no fire, nothing.

I studied about it some, then decided those Indians
would never figure on me to come back, and once
they'd taken what they wanted from the wagon, they'd
not stay around. So I went down, taking it easy. Finally,
when Old Blue began to get nervous, I tied him to a
bush and went on alone.

When I got close I could smell the burned wood. The
wagon had been set on fire, but it was still there.

I crawled up closer, and I found Pap. He'd been shot
through, then stabbed. And they'd scalped him.

Using a match, I hunted through the wagon. They'd
looted it, throwing stuff around, taking most of what
they could use. I knew where Pap had kept the forty
dollars in gold he had, and with my knife point I dug it
out of a crack in the wood Pap had puttied over.

They'd set fire to the wagon, all right, but only the
cover had burned. The hoops were some charred, and
the sideboards, but most of the stuff was intact. Pap's
tool chest had been busted open, and most of the sharp
tools were gone. The chisels and like that.

There was a few cents change in Pap's pocket, and I
took it. He'd be wanting me to have it.

Then I got the shovel and dug out a grave for him on
the hill, and there I toted his body and buried him,
crying all the time like a durned girl-baby. Me, who
bragged it up that I never shed no tears.

On the grave I piled some rocks and on a piece of
board I burned out Pap's name with a hot iron. Then I
rustled around amongst what was left to see what I
could find.

There was little enough, but I found Ma's picture. Miracle was, it hadn't burned. But it was stuck down in the Bible and only the edges of the leaves had charred a mite, and the cover. I put Ma's picture in my pocket and went back to Old Blue.

The cattle were gone. They'd drove them off and somewhere now they were eating real big.

Eating . . . eating too much and maybe sleeping. Eating too much and in their own country, and they wouldn't be keeping a guard, maybe.

The nearest water was where they would head for, and the nearest water was the springs. I got up on Old Blue and started walking him back.

Maybe I was just a fool kid, but those Indians had killed Pap and stolen our cattle. I was going to get me an Indian.

One more, anyway.

2

The night smelled good. There were a million stars in the sky, looked like, and I could feel the soft wind over the grass. And on that wind I smelled smoke; wood smoke, with some smell of buffalo chips, too.

Old Blue seemed to know what I was about. He walked real light and easy on the grass, his ears pricked up. He could smell the smoke, and from the uneasy feel of him between my knees, I knew he could smell Indian.

After a while I got down and tied Old Blue. Then I crept along, all bent over, and got up close.

They had a fire that was almost dead, and I could see their horses off to one side. They were all asleep, expecting nothing. I could see four oxen still standing, so they had only eaten two, or most of two.

Take white men a week to eat an ox, but not Indians. They gorged themselves one day, starved the next; that was the way of it. Well, one or more had eaten all he was ever going to.

First off I crawled around to where their ponies

were. Working up close through the grass, I got up and walked casual-like among them. Maybe because of that, maybe because I was just a boy, they didn't fret much until I had my hand on a tie rope. Then one of them blew loud through his nostrils.

And when he done that, I slashed the picket ropes with my pocket knife, first one, then another. Then I yelled and two of the horses done what I'd hoped. They ran full tilt into that Indian camp. I held my fire until I saw Indians scrambling up, and then I shot.

I shot three times as fast as I could trigger that Joslyn. Then I hauled out my old Shawk & McLanahan .36 and, running up close, I fired three times more.

Two Indians were down, one of them holding his belly. Another was staggering with a bullet through his leg. But that was enough. I turned and got out of there almighty fast. When I was a distance away, I circled around to Old Blue.

Once in the saddle, I headed off across country. Twice I came up to Indian ponies from the bunch I'd stampeded and started them moving again.

All night I rode on, heading west along the track of the wagons. Come day, I found a place high on a hill where there was a sort of hollow. I picketed Old Blue and stretched out on my back.

The sun woke me up, shining right in my face. I got up on Old Blue again and headed west. Next day I killed a buffalo calf. Here and there I found some wild onions, and I ate the buffalo meat without salt.

It was like that for a week. Finally I got so I rode mostly at night, using the stars to travel by, as Pap had shown me. Indians don't travel by night much, and they don't like night fighting, so it was safer. By day I'd hole up and keep out of sight. Twice I saw Indians, but not up close, and none of them saw me.

Twice I found burned wagons, but they were old fires of wagons burned long ago.

I rode west. I saw the grass plains left behind and high mountains roll up, and sometimes I saw buffalo, and lots of antelope. I was sparing of my ammunition, and I never tried any long shots. Usually I'd work in close and try to cut out a buffalo calf. The old cows were mighty fractious, and sometimes I'd kill one of them, usually with the pistol, at close range.

But there was meat, and there were always onions. Once I caught me a mess of fish and fried them in buffalo fat for my meal.

There were beaver streams, and more and more trees on the mountains, and the country became rougher.

It was two weeks before I caught up with the wagon train, even though I could travel faster than they. Two weeks because I'd taken time out to hunt grub, and because they had a good two-day start on me. Also, I was riding mighty careful. I didn't want my hair hanging in no Arapaho wickiup.

When at last I saw the wagon train it was in South Pass. Old Blue carried me down out of the hills and I took him at a lope across the grassy valley that lies between the Sweetwater Mountains and the Wind River Range.

The wagons stretched out, white and long, the horsemen rode alongside, and a lump came up in my throat when I thought of Pap and his wagon. He could have been here, too, if they'd stopped to wait. Right then I hated every one of them, but most of all I hated Big Jack McGarry.

It was Bagley I saw first. His face went kind of white when he saw me. "Rye!" he said. "Where's your Pap?"

Wagons drew up and several riders started toward me. McGarry started back from the head of the wagon train.

"He's dead," I told them, tears starting into my eyes. "He's dead, and you all killed him. You could have waited."

"Waited? Where?" Bagley was angry. "Risk our families? What you talkin' of, boy?"

"McGarry said you'd wait at the springs. He told Pap that. We got to the springs right quick, and you all didn't even stop."

There was a slim, wiry man in buckskins setting a black horse there, and he looked at me. "Boy, are you sure Big Jack promised to wait at the springs?"

"I'm damn sure!"

Big Jack came up then and pushed his horse through the circle. "Here! What's this? You're holdin' up the . . . Oh, it's you."

You didn't need to look close to see he wasn't happy to see me. His face showed mighty plain that he had never expected us to come through . . . and only one of us had.

The slim man in buckskins looked over at Big Jack. "Jack, the boy says you told his pap you'd wait at the springs."

"He lies!" McGarry said angrily. "The boy lies. I told him nothing of the kind."

"You did so." I put my hand on my Shawk & McLanahan. "You say I lie and I'll shoot you sure."

The man in the buckskins shook his head at me. "Sit quiet, boy. We'll get the straight of this." He turned back to McGarry. "I never did understand why we passed up the sweetest water in a hundred miles. It was early to stop, but with that wagon left behind . . . ?"

"I told him no such thing! What would I do that for?"

"Because Pap wasn't afeared of you. And because you were shinin' up to Mary Tatum."

That man hated me. I could see it in his hard little eyes. "Boy, you shet that mouth! You shet up or I'll blister your hide!"

"You'll blister no hides, McGarry. You've a question or two to answer." The man in buckskins turned and looked at Mary Tatum. "Ma'am, I reckon we all know McGarry's been wantin' to court you. You been talkin' with him some. Did you set out with him so much when Tyler was with us?"

Mary was a right pretty girl and she had spunk. I knowed Pap set a sight of store by her, and he had asked me once what I'd think of her as a mother. I told him that seeing as how my own ma was buried back East, there was nobody I'd like better.

Now she lifted her chin and said quietly, "I was thinking a lot about Mr. Tyler. He was a good man and an honest man. I believe he was in love with me."

"I know he was," I said.

She looked at me, her gray eyes wide and full. Then she said quietly, "I am a single girl and I want a husband. I hoped to marry Ralph Tyler. I have never even considered marrying Jack McGarry, and will not now."

McGarry's face went red, then white. He started to speak.

The man in buckskins interrupted. "We don't know the straight of this, and I reckon we'll never know exactly. If you told him we'd wait at the springs, we should have waited. We should have stopped there, anyway. I wondered why we didn't. I think you're guilty."

I expected McGarry to grab for his gun, but he didn't. There was something about that slender man that didn't look very safe.

A solidly built man in a black coat and flat black hat spoke up. "We'll be having an election. We'll be wanting a new captain."

Big Jack McGarry looked over at me and there was nothing nice in his eyes. He looked mighty mean.

Mary Tatum saw it, and she walked over to my horse. "Rye," she said gently, "I'm very sorry about Ralph. Will you ride with us now?"

"No, ma'am," I said, "but I thank you. I don't figure to stay with this outfit." I looked over at Bagley. "There's some folks here won't feel right as long as I'm about."

"But, Rye, you're only a boy!" she protested.

"I killed me three Indians," I said. "I've come across the plains these last days all by myself. I'll go on by myself."

She smiled at me. "All right, Rye, but will you eat with us this night?"

"Yes, ma'am. I'll be obliged."

It was mighty good, setting up to a civilized meal again. Mary Tatum was a wonderful cook, and she even managed some cookies, and most of them she gave to me. Night came, and when I got my buffalo robe she brought me blankets from her own wagon.

"Ma'am," I said, "I'd have liked it, having you for a ma."

She put her hand on my head then and pulled it

against her, and I guess I cried, though I ain't much to brag on that.

That shamed me, the crying did. When I got to my feet I was some taller than Mary, and I brushed those tears away, and felt worse about crying than anything else. So I took my blankets and went away to the edge of the circle and started to spread them out.

Something moved out there in the dark, and I took out my Shawk & McLanahan, for those two weeks had put me on edge. Whoever was out there went away.

The next morning when I was saddling up, Big Jack McGarry came by. He looked down at me and his eyes were mighty mean. "Figure you're a big man now, don't you? I'll slap some of that out of you!"

Right then I was some scared, but the pistol was in my belt and I knew if he started for me I'd pull iron. I didn't want to, but I would.

"You got my pap killed," I told him, "just like you figured on. If he was here you'd not talk about whuppin' me. I notice you never tried to come it over him."

He started his horse at me and raised his quirt, and just about that time a gun clicked behind me and I heard a voice say, "Go ahead, hit him. This wagon train can wait long enough to bury a man."

McGarry sat there with his quirt raised up and had the look of a fool.

It was that slim man in the buckskin shirt. He had a six-shooter in his hand and he was not fooling. "McGarry," he said, "if anything happens to that boy while I'm with this wagon train, even if it's an out-and-out accident, I'll kill you."

McGarry lowered his quirt and rode off to the head of the column. Only he was not there officially any more. They had voted him out of the captain's job.

The man in the buckskin shirt walked over to me and looked at me thoughtfully. "Boy," he said, "you're mighty young to be packin' a gun, but you'd better keep it handy."

"All right, sir."

"My name is Logan Pollard." He studied me a minute.

"Tell me what happened back there. When your father was killed."

So for the first time I told the whole story.

He questioned me right sharp, then he knocked out his pipe and told me, quiet-like, "You'll do, boy. But don't use that gun unless you have to."

He went away then, and the next morning when the column moved out he came by on horseback. He motioned me to follow and I went with him and we rode out away from the wagons.

It wasn't until we were over the hill that he said, "We'll get an antelope or two, and we'll start your education same time."

"I can read. I been to school."

"Not that kind of education." He looked at me from that narrow brown face that never seemed to smile. "The kind you'll need. I'm going to teach you how to read sign, how to tell an Indian's tribe from his moccasins, and where to find game. Also, how to use that gun. I'm going to teach you things you need to know. So don't think of riding off by yourself just yet."

We rode on a ways farther, and then he drew up, indicating a plant about four feet high. It had a prickly look, with sort of white flowers shading off to violet.

"Indian thistle," he said, "and the roots will keep a man alive if there's nothing else to eat. Don't forget it."

He rode on, leading the way, pointing out things as we rode. Toward evening we circled back and we had two antelope.

"Back home," he said, "we had almost two thousand books. I read most of them. But this,"—he swept his arm wide to take in the country—"this is the book I like best. You can always learn. There's always something new on the page."

When he left me, he said, "Don't despise the Indian. He's lived here a long time, lived well. Learn from him."

3

The second day it was different. That morning he came for me right after the wagons started, but we rode fast, rode on ahead. As we rode, he told me things. They were things to remember, and Pollard did no aimless talking.

"Stalking a deer," he said, "you remember you can move as long as he has his head down, feeding. Just before he looks up he'll start to switch his tail. Stop moving then and stand right still, or sink down and wait until he starts to feed again.

"Indians often smoke their bodies in sage to kill body odor when going on a hunt. Mint will do the same thing, or any grass or plant that smells."

We were several miles ahead of the wagon train and far off to one side when we drew up in a grove of aspen. Ever seen aspen growing? Most times they grow in thick clumps, grow straight up, their trunks almost all of a size.

Logan Pollard swung down and I followed him. Then he paced about fifty feet from an aspen about four inches in diameter. "Take out your gun," he said, "and hold it down by your side."

He faced the slim young aspen and drew his own gun. "Now," he said, "lift your gun in line with that aspen trunk. Just keep lifting it at arm's length until your gun is shoulder high."

When I had done that a few times he had me take the shells from my gun. For over an hour we worked. He kept me at it, lifting that six-shooter and sighting along the barrel. Lifting it straight up from the base of the tree trunk until it was at eye level, always sighting along the barrel and keeping it in line with the trunk. Not until I'd been at it a few minutes longer did he start me snapping the gun when it reached shooting position.

"Every day," he said, "you'll practice that. Every day we'll ride out here."

"Will you teach me to draw real fast?" I asked him. That was something I wanted to know. I'd heard talk of Jack Slade and others who were mighty good that way.

"Not yet." He squatted on his heels. "First you learn how to use a gun. The draw isn't so important as it is to hit what you shoot at. Learn to make that first shot count. You may," he added dryly, "never get another."

He taught me to look where I was shooting and not at the gun, and to shoot as a man points a finger, and how to hang my holster so my palm came to the gun butt naturally. "No man," he said, "ever uses a gun unless he has to. Don't hunt trouble. Sooner or later you'll always find more than you want. A gun is a tool, mighty handy when you need it, and to be left alone until you do need it."

Beyond the shining mountains there was desert, and at its edge we left the wagon train.

"We'll be in California, Rye," Mary Tatum said. "If you want to come, you're welcome."

"Another time, ma'am. I'm riding south with Pollard."

She looked past me at Logan, who sat slim and straight on the black horse he rode. "Take care of him, Logan. He might have been my son."

"You're a child yourself, Mary. Too young to have

had this boy. Maybe when he comes, I'll come with him."

She looked up at him and her cheeks were a little pinkish under the tan. "Come, then, Logan Pollard. There's a welcome for you, too."

So we watched them start off toward the Salt Lake and the distant Pilot Butte, beyond the horizon. "If she couldn't marry Pap," I said, "I'd rather it would be you."

Pollard looked at me, but he did not smile. Only his eyes were friendly-like. "Rye," he said, "that was a nice thing you said."

South we rode then, and he showed me Brown's Hole, where the trappers used to rendezvous, and we rode through the rugged country and down to Santa Fe. Only it wasn't all riding, and it wasn't all easy. Every day he drilled me with the gun, and somehow I began to get the feel of it. My hands had always had a feel for a gun butt, and the big six-shooter began to handle easier. I could draw fast and shoot straight.

We lived off the country. Logan Pollard showed me how to rig snares and traps for small game, how to make a moose call, and what to use for bait when fishing. He showed me how to make a pot out of birch bark in which a man could boil water as long as the flame was kept below the water-level in the pot. He showed me how to build fires and he taught me to use wood ashes for baking powder in making biscuits.

Sometimes we would split up and travel alone all day, meeting only at night, and then I would have to rustle my own grub, and often as not track him to where we were to meet.

When he would ride on ahead and have me track him down, I would practice with the gun while waiting to start out. It had a natural, easy feel in my hand. I tried drawing and turning to fire as I drew. But Logan Pollard told me to respect a gun, too.

"They make them to kill," he said, "and you can kill yourself or somebody you love just as easy as an enemy. Every gun you haven't personally unloaded that minute

should be treated as a loaded gun. Guns aren't supposed
to be empty."

Santa Fe was a big town to me, the biggest since the
wagon train left Missouri, and bigger than any town I'd
seen up to then, except St. Louis.

There in Santa Fe I took a job herding a small bunch
of cattle for a man, keeping them inside the boundary
creek and out of the canyon. It was lazy, easy work
most of the time. He paid me ten dollars a month, and
after two months of it Logan Pollard came around to see
me.

"You need some boots," he said, "and a new shirt."

He bought them for me from a pocketful of gold
coins, and then went to a Mexican place he knew and
ate a good Mexican meal, chicken with rice and black
beans. Only he made me tuck my gun down inside my
pants, and I wore it like that when I was in Santa Fe.

One day when I was with the cattle he rode out to
see me and he took a book out of his saddlebags.

"Read it," he said. "Read it five times. You'll like
it better each time. It's some stories about great men, and
more great men have read this book than any other."

"Who wrote it?"

"Plutarch," he said, "and you can read it in the saddle."

It was warm and pleasant in the sunshine those days,
and I read while I sat the saddle, or loafed under a tree
sometimes, making an occasional circle to hold the stock
in. And then one day two Mexicans rode up with a
mean look in their eyes, and they fretted me some,
looking over the cattle like they did.

One of them rode out and started to bunch the cattle,
so I put Plutarch in the saddlebag and got up on Old
Blue.

He walked out there mighty slow. I figure Old Blue
knew more than me, and he could smell trouble making
up before it hit.

We were halfway out there before they saw us, and
they hesitated a moment, and then, getting a better
look, they laughed.

"*Niño*," he said, and kept bunching the cows. And as

I drew nearer they started them moving away from me, toward the creek.

"Leave those cows," I said. "Get away from here!"

They paid me no mind and I was getting scared. I'd been set to watch those cows, and if anything happened to them it would be my fault. They were driving them toward the creek when I raced Old Blue ahead and turned them back.

The big Mexican with the scar on his face swore at me in Spanish and raced at me with a quirt. He raced up and I pulled Old Blue over and he swung, lashing at me. He struck me across the face, and I pulled the Shawk & McLanahan out of my pants.

His eyes got very big, and me, I was shaking all over, but that gun was as big in my fist as his.

He began to talk at me in Spanish and back off a little, and then the other Mexican rode over to see what was happening. When he saw the gun he stopped and looked very serious, and then he turned away from me as if to ride off, but when he turned he suddenly swung backhanded with his rope and the gun was torn from my hand and sent flying. Then he came at me, and he hit me across the face with the rope, and then lashed me with it over the back, and the half-coiled rope struck like a club and knocked me from my horse.

Then he spat on me and laughed and they drove off the cows, taking Old Blue along with them, and I lay there on the ground and could do nothing at all.

When I could get up I was very stiff and there was blood on me, but I walked to where the Shawk & McLanahan lay and picked it up.

It was ten miles back to town, but I walked it, and asked around for Pollard. When I found him he was playing cards. He waved at me and said, "Later, Rye. I'm busy now."

The place was crowded with men and some of them stared at my bloody face and the dirt on me, and I was ashamed. They would laugh at me if I told them I'd been knocked off my horse and had my cattle run off. So I went and borrowed a horse and took out after those Mexicans.

It was not only the cows; my mother's picture was in the saddlebags, and the Plutarch. And the Joslyn carbine was in the boot on Old Blue.

That night I didn't come up with them, or the next, but the third night I did.

They were around a water hole where there were some cottonwoods. It was the only water around and I was almighty thirsty, but I looked for Old Blue and saw him picketed off to one side.

It was dark and I was hungry, and they had a fire going and some grub, and I shucked the old Shawk & McLanahan out of my pants and cocked her.

The click of that gun cocking sounded loud in the night, and I said, not too loud, "You sit mighty still. I've come for my horse and cows."

"*El Niño*," the scarred Mexican said.

I stepped into the light with the gun cocked.

"Kill him," the scarred Mexican said. "Kill him and they will think he took the cattle himself. Kill him and bury him here."

The other Mexican was sneaking a hand toward a gun

"Stop!" I said it loud, and I guess my voice sounded shrill.

He just dived at the gun, and I shot, and the bullet knocked him rolling. He sprawled out and the other Mexican lunged at me, and I tried to burn, but before I could shoot there was a shot from the edge of the brush, and then another.

The Mexican diving at me fell face down, all sprawled out, and then he rolled over and there was a blue hole between his eyes, and the first Mexican, the one I shot, had another bullet that had torn off the side of his face after it killed him.

Logan Pollard stood there with a gun in his hand, his face as still and cold as always.

"You should have told me, Rye. I didn't realize you'd had trouble until one of the men said you were bloody. Then I started after you."

We walked over and looked down at the Mexican I had shot. My bullet was a little high . . . but not much.

Pollard looked at me strangely, then caught up Old Blue and we started the cows toward home.

The next day he told me to quit, and when I collected my money I had thirty-two dollars, all told. With that in my pocket, and the money from my Pap, which I'd never touched yet, I felt rich. We started northwest into the wild country around the San Juan, following the old Spanish Trail.

"We're going to California to see Mary Tatum," he said, "and then maybe you can go to school. You're too willing to use a gun."

"They stole the cows," I said.

"I know."

"And Ma's picture."

He glanced at me. "Oh, I see."

It was a wild and lonely land of great red walls and massive buttes. There were canyons knifed deep in the rocky crust of the earth, and cactus with red flowers, and there were Indians, but they seemed friendly enough, and we traveled on, me riding Old Blue.

The sun rose hot and high in the mornings, and sometimes we took all morning to get to the bottom of a canyon, then all afternoon climbing out. We crossed wide red deserts and camped in lonely places by tiny water holes, and my face grew browner and leaner and I learned more of the country. And one morning I got up and looked over at Logan Pollard.

"Today I'm fourteen," I said.

"Fourteen. Too young to live like this," he said. "A man needs the refining influences of feminine companionship."

He was a careful man. Careful of his walk, careful of the way he dressed, careful when he handled guns, and careful in the care of his horse. Every morning he brushed the dust from his clothes, and every morning he combed his hair.

And when we rode he talked to me about Shakespeare and the Bible, and some about Plutarch and Plato. Some of it I didn't set much store by, but most of it made a kind of sense.

From Virginia, he'd come. Educated there, and then he'd come west.

"Why?"

"There was a man killed. They thought I did it."

"Did you?"

"Yes. I shot him fair, in a duel."

We rode on for several miles. I liked watching the shadows of the clouds on the desert. "I was to have married his sister. He didn't want me to."

And in California I went to school.

Logan Pollard stayed around for a while, and then he rode away. I did not believe Mary Tatum wanted him to go.

Yet he was gone no more than a week before he came back, and when I came riding in on Old Blue I saw them talking, serious-like, on the porch. "It has happened before," he was saying, "and it may happen again."

"Not here," she told him. "This is a quiet place."

"All right," he said finally. "I'll stay."

The winter passed and all summer long I worked, felling logs for a lumber mill and holding down a riding job on a nearby ranch the rest of the time. In the fall and winter I went to school and learned how to work problems and something of history. Most of all, I liked to read Plutarch.

Logan Pollard rode out to see me one day. I was sitting on a log, reading my nooning away.

"Third time," I said. "I read slow."

"This is a book to be read that way. Taste it, roll the flavor on your tongue."

It was not only school and reading. I was growing, too, and some part of every day I went out into the woods and practiced with the gun. I'd a natural gift for guns, and my skill had increased rapidly. Pollard never mentioned guns to me now, and was no longer wearing his. Not in sight, anyway.

These were good months. Work never worried me. I enjoyed using my muscles, liked feeling strong, and there was always a little time for riding in the mountains, tracking stray cattle or horses, hunting varmints that preyed on the stock.

It was spring again and Old Blue kept looking at me, and I knew he expected me to saddle up and ride. It was spring, and I was fifteen years old, close to six feet tall, but thin. Only my shoulders and arms were strong, and my hands.

"What happened to the gun?" Logan asked me.

So I reached down in my pants and brought it out, that old Shawk & McLanahan .36 Pap had given me.

"Ever shoot it?"

"Yes," I said, and turning the muzzle, I fired. It was all one easy move. Sixty yards away a pine cone shattered into bits. Pollard looked at me and nodded. "You can shoot. I only hope you never have to."

He was married that next Sunday to Mary Tatum, and I stood up with them, feeling awkward in a store-bought broadcloth suit and a stiff collar, the first I ever owned. And when it was over and we ate the cake, Mary said, "We want you to stay with us, Rye. If you can't be my son, be my brother."

So I stayed on.

When two months more had passed I mounted Old Blue and rode down to the store. It was mighty pretty that morning, and the sun was bright, and every leaf was like a tiny mirror. The water of the stream rippled and rollicked over the stones, and it seemed the world had never been so nice.

I was wearing my broadcloth suit because I was going to a pie supper before I came home.

At the store I bought some crackers and cheese and went to the steps to eat, and there I was sitting real quiet when a big man rode up on a white horse. He was thick in the middle and his vest was dirty with food stains, and when he saw old Blue he fetched up short and stopped.

He got down from the saddle and he walked slow around that horse. He glanced over at me, only my head was down and he couldn't make out my face, and I was eating.

"Who owns this horse?"

He said it real loud, his voice mighty big and important-like. There were two men settin' up on the porch and they said nothing, so he looked over at me. "Who owns this horse?"

Stuffing the last of the cheese and crackers in my mouth, I got up. "I own him, McGarry. You want to make something out of that?"

His nose was blue-veined and bigger than I'd remembered, and his eyes were even smaller and more piggish. He was a wide man, the sleeves of his dirty white shirt rolled halfway to his elbows, his big boots scuffed and worn. His hat was too small for his big head and he was unshaved and dirty.

"You? You, is it?"

"It's me," I said, and suddenly I knew I hated this man. I was wondering, too, if he realized Mary Tatum was in town. Or that she was married to Logan Pollard.

"It was you made all that trouble," he said. "I ain't had no luck since. You an' that little skirt your pap played with."

Right then I hit him. I hit him on the mouth and he staggered back two steps and almost fell. Blood started to come and he grabbed for his gun.

Then something bucked in my hand and he stepped back and sat down as my gun bucked again, and he was settin' there dead almost half a minute before he rolled over on his face and stretched out, but in that last split second of life I saw shocked surprise on his face. And there I stood with that old Shawk & McLanahan in my hand and Big Jack McGarry dead at my feet.

4

Mary Tatum was feeding the chickens when I rode into the yard. She looked up and I saw her eyes widen a little, and she came up to me as I got down.

"Rye, what is it? What's happened?"

So I stood there, feeling a sinking in me, hating to tell her, yet knowing I had to.

"Mary," I said, "I killed a man."

"Oh, *no*!" She caught my arm. "Not you, Rye!"

"Yes, ma'am. I killed Jack McGarry."

That stopped her, and she held my arm a minute, her gray eyes searching mine. "Jack McGarry? *Here*?"

"Yes, ma'am. He said words. . . . He reached for his gun after I hit him."

"Words, Rye?"

"Yes, ma'am. He spoke slighting of you and Pap."

"Oh. We had better tell Logan."

Somehow Logan did not seem surprised. He listened to me and I told it plain and simple, holding nothing back. "I reckon," I said honestly, "it was partly because I hated him."

There was something else on his mind. "He touched his gun first?"

"Yes, sir. He had it almost out when I shot him."

Nothing more was said and Mary went about getting supper. She was never one to take on when it was past time for it to do any good. We ate some, although I didn't have much appetite, and kept seeing how McGarry looked, lying there on the ground with that shocked expression on his face. I didn't hate him any more, I didn't feel anything about him except maybe sad that he had pushed me into it. I didn't want to shoot anybody any more.

We went out on the porch and Logan began to talk. First off, it seemed like he was just telling us about his boyhood and his travels, and then it came to me that this was something special, for me. It was a lesson, like.

He had killed a man at nineteen. The man was a riverboat gambler. Then he killed his sweetheart's brother, because back there, them days, if a man called you out, you went, or you left the country wearing the coward brand.

Afterward he left the country, anyway. He had killed four men in gun battles, he said, and he told me he hoped never to kill another, and then he said, "Rye, you're a hand with a gun. Maybe the best I ever saw. You've a natural skill, a natural eye, and you judge distance easy and fine. That's a responsibility, Rye. This is a time when all men carry guns. Naturally, some are better than others, just like some men can use an ax better, or make a better wheel, like your pap. But a gun is different, because with a gun you can kill."

He paused a minute, looking down at his fine brown hands, the sort of hands you might expect to see on a violinist. "You'll have to use a gun, from time to time. So be careful that you use it right. Never draw a gun unless you mean to shoot, never shoot unless you shoot to kill.

"Back there with the Mexicans you were too slow to shoot. If I hadn't been there you might have been killed. Yet I'd rather have you shoot too slow than have you too ready to shoot. Never kill the wrong man or it will punish you all the days of your life."

He was right about that, and I knew it. I was no fool kid who thought a gun made me a big man. Right then I didn't ever figure to kill anybody else, anytime.

Morning came, and when I walked out to saddle up there was a big, rawboned roan coming into the yard with a man on his back. The man had a shock of uncut hair and a big mustache. His hat was small and he looked sort of funny, but there was a badge on his chest that was not funny, and he wore a pistol.

Logan came to the door, and Mary. She looked white and scared, but Logan was like he always was, quiet and sort of stern.

The man on the roan wore a checked shirt and it was untidy. He wore suspenders, too.

"Name of Balcher," he said, and he took some chewing tobacco from his shirt pocket. "Carry it there," he said, sort of smiling, "so nobody will mistake I'm reaching for a gun. I'd sure hate," he added, "to be shot by mistake."

"What's your business, Mr. Balcher?" Logan stepped down off the porch.

Balcher looked at him thoughtfully. "My!" he said. "For a quiet man I sure run into a lot of you folks. You're one of them, too, sure's shootin'."

Logan stood quiet, waiting. Balcher turned his big head and looked at me, chewing slow. "How old are you, boy?"

"Fifteen. Going on sixteen."

He rolled his squid in his jaw. "Young," he said, "but you handle a gun like a growed man. You killed that feller yestiddy."

"Yes, sir."

He studied me carefully. "You know him before?"

Logan Pollard interrupted, and quietly he told the story of what happened on the trail, leaving out nothing. He made it plain that I had reason to feel as I did, and that McGarry had opened the trouble, not I.

Balcher listened, looking from Logan to me with lonesome hound-dog eyes.

"Reckon I'd feel like shootin' him myself." He turned in his saddle. "Don't blame you, son. Understand that. Don't blame you a bit. But you got to go."

"Go?" Mary said. "But he can't, Sheriff! He's like my own brother! This is his home!"

The way she said it made a lump come in my throat and I was afraid it was bringing tears to my eyes. I reckon there was nobody quite so nice as Mary.

" 'Fraid so." Balcher said it regretfully. "I ain't much hand with a gun, myself. Reckon either one of you could shoot me dead before I could touch iron, but the way I keep the peace about here is to send all gun folks apackin'.

"Now don't get me wrong. I got nothin' against you, Tyler, but folks know you're handy with a gun now. Some rambunctious youngster is liable to want to find out if he's better. So I reckon you better ride."

The sun was bright on the hard-packed earth of the ranchyard. It was warm and pleasant, standing there, a trickle of water falling in the trough, the smell of coffee from the house. This was home for me. The only home I'd had for a long, long time. And now they were telling me to go.

"And if he doesn't?" Logan asked the question, his voice low and hard.

Balcher shrugged. "Well, I can't shoot him. Folks down to town say they never saw anything as fast as this Rye Tyler. He shucked his gun so fast nobody scarce seen it. An' he didn't miss once he got it out. I reckon if the bullet hadn't killed McGarry, the shock would have, he was that surprised."

Balcher turned in his saddle. "Look, Mr. Pollard. I got to keep the peace. She's my job. I reckon I'm too lazy to farm, and nothing much grows for me, anyway. But, four years now I kep' the peace. I hope, folks, that he'll ride out quiet. If he don't, I got to go back down to town and round up eight or ten of the folks with shotguns to start him movin'. To do that I'd have to spoil a day's work for a lot of folks. Now, you wouldn't want that, would you?"

"I reckon not, Mr. Balcher," I said. "I reckon I can go."

"Rye!" Mary protested.

"Got to, Mary. You know I got to. It's all right. I been sort of itchin' to see more country, and Old Blue, he's been downright disappointed in me."

Daybreak I taken the road out to Surprise Valley, across the mountains and north. I figured I might hunt a little, then maybe get a riding job before I headed south. Right then I had twenty-six dollars of my own money, and I was still carrying the forty dollars Pap left me.

Saying good-bye to Mary was worst of all. She clung to my sleeve and she kissed me, and I reckon it was the first time since I was a mite of a baby I'd been kissed. It was kind of sweet-like, and the feel of it stayed on my cheek all the way across the mountain.

Logan rode a ways with me, then he shook hands and said, "Come see us, Rye. This is home, always."

Two miles down the trail I saw a man on a roan horse setting out there in plain sight. He was setting sideways on that horse when I came up to him, and he grinned at me, sort of sly. It was Balcher. He put his hands on the pommel and said, "Boy, I wish you luck. You take it easy with that gun. You're a fine boy, so don't you start to shootin' less you have to."

Then I rode down the trail, and a lump was in my throat and in my heart, too, and my stomach was all empty. This was the second time I'd lost folks that loved me. First Pap, by Indian guns, and now Mary and Logan, by my own gun.

Was that the way it was going to be?

Do you know that Western land? Do you know the far plains and the high, snow-crested ridges? Do you know the beaver streams, the water laughing in the bright sun? Do you know the sound of wind in the pines? The cloud shadows on the desert's face? Have you stood on a high ridge and looked fifty miles across the country, country known only to Indians, antelope, and buffalo?

Have you crawled out of your bedroll in the chill of a spring morning with the crisp air fresh in your lungs and the sound of running water in your ears? Have you started a fire and made coffee, and broiled your vension over an open fire? Have you smelled ironwood burning, or cedar?

That was how I lived for a whole year after I left Mary and Logan. I lived away from men, riding, drifting, and reading Plutarch for the fourth time.

Washington, Oregon, Idaho, Montana, Wyoming, and down to Colorado.

Beside campfires under the icy Teton peaks, I read of Hannibal and of Cato. I smelled the smoke of a hundred campfires, as I drifted.

Rarely did I find a white man's fire, and only occasionally one left by an Indian. I saw the country of the Nez Percés and the Blackfeet, of the Crows, the Shoshones, and the Sioux. I wandered up the lost red canyons of the La Sal Mountains, and through the Abajo Range.

The only sounds I heard were the sounds that the wilderness makes. The slap of warning from a beaver's tail on water, the sudden crash and rush of an elk, the harsh, throaty snarl of a mountain lion . . . the wind, the water, and the storm.

The shelters I had were caves or corners among the trees, or wickiups I built myself. All that Logan Pollard had taught me came in handy, and I learned more.

And so after many days I came again to a town where there were people. I rode to the edge of the hill and looked down, a little frightened, a little uncertain. And I knew that I had changed. Some of the stillness of the mountains was in me, some of the pace of the far forests, but there was also the old thing that lived in me always. But I could be alone no longer. It was time to return to the world of people, and so I started Old Blue down the slope.

5

My shirt was buckskin. My breeches were buckskin. My boots had long since worn to nothing and been replaced by moccasins. I still carried the old Joslyn carbine, and I still carried the Shawk & McLanahan .36. So I rode into town to sell my furs.

Right then I was nigh seventeen. I was an inch over six feet and I weighed one hundred and seventy pounds, and no bit of fat on my bones. Lean and tough as any old catamount, wearing a torn and battered hat, I must have been a sight to see. Into that town I came, riding slow.

Old Blue was beginning to feel the miles. He was getting some years on him, too. But he loved the life as I did and he could still run neck and neck with a buffalo while I shot.

The town was a booming mine camp, the street lined with a jostling crowd of booted, belted men. Leaving Old Blue at the livery-stable hitch rail, I walked up the street, happy to be among people again, even if I knew none of them. Yet I walked aloof, for I hesitated to meet people or to make friends. There was always in the back of my mind the thought of the gun, and I did not wish to fire in anger at any man.

Oddly enough, in those long wilderness months I had no trouble with Indians. I had wandered their country, shared their hunting grounds, but evaded contact with them. A few times I had gone into the Nez Percé villages to trade for things I needed.

It was warm and sunny in the street. Leaning against an awning post, I watched the people pass. Tents and false-fronted stores, a long log bunkhouse that called itself a hotel, and a bigger log building that was a saloon. Down the street a man sold whisky from a board laid across two barrels, dipping the whisky with a tin cup.

And it was good to be there. These were tough and bearded men, a rough, roistering, and on the whole friendly crowd. They were men, and I was a man among them. My face was lean and hard, and my body was lean, too. Only my shoulders were wide, my chest deep, my arms strong. Those long months in the mountains had put some beef on me, and tempered my strength.

A man came up the street wearing a badge. He had a broad brown face with strong cheek and jawbones, the skin of his face stretched tight. His eyes were deep-sunk and gray to almost white.

He looked hard at me, then looked again. It was a long, slow look that measured and assayed me, but he continued to walk. Farther down the street he stopped and I saw him standing alone, watching me.

Finally he moved on, but when he did a slim young man walked over and stopped beside me. "Don't know you, friend, but watch yourself. Ollie Burdette's got his eye on you."

"Trouble?"

"He's the marshal, and he shoots first and asks questions later. Killed a man last week."

"Thanks."

"My name's Kipp. Got a little spread out east of town. Come out, if you've a mind to."

He walked on away from me, a quiet young man with quick intelligent eyes. But maybe too quick to warn me.

For a while I loafed where I was, thinking about it. Right now I should ride on, but I'd just come into town and had done nothing, nor did I intend to get on the wrong side of the law, ever. Sometimes the law can make mistakes, but usually it's right, and it's needed to regulate those who haven't yet learned how to live with their fellow men.

Walking across the street, I went into the hotel. The dining room was only half full, so I found a table and sat down.

After I'd ordered, I picked up an old newspaper and browsed through it. I was just getting to the last page when a voice said, "Please? May I have it?"

Looking up from the paper, I saw a slender young girl. She could have been no more than fourteen, but she had beautiful eyes and a nice smile.

I got to my feet quickly, embarrassed. "Yes, ma'am. Of course. I just finished."

"It was Papa's paper. I put it down on the table and forgot. He would be just furious if I didn't have it. He loves his newspaper."

"Sorry, ma'am. I didn't know."

Suddenly someone was beside us. Glancing around, I looked into those gray-white eyes of Ollie Burdette's. They were cold and still. "This man botherin' you, young lady?"

His voice was harsh, commanding. There was something almost brutal in its tone and assurance. It was the voice of a man not only ready for trouble, but pushing it.

"Oh, no!" She smiled quickly. "Of course he isn't! He just gave me my newspaper. I'd have lost it otherwise."

"All right." He turned away almost reluctantly, giving me a hard look, and I felt the hairs prickle on the back of my neck, and my mouth was dry. Yet it angered me, too. Burdette was very ready to find trouble.

"Are you looking for a job?"

My eyes went back to her. She was looking up at me, bright and eager. "Papa needs a man to break horses."

"I'd like that. Where's your place?"

She told me, then added, "I'm Liza Hetrick. You ask for me."

When she was gone and my dinner finished I sat there thinking. What Kipp had said might be true. There were gunmen who deliberately hunted trouble, some because of an urge to kill, some because they wanted to stop trouble before it began, some who were building a reputation or whose only claim to recognition was a list of killings. But why pick on me? Because I was only a boy and wore a man's gun?

Yet I was no longer a boy in Western consideration. At seventeen and younger, a boy wore a man's boots and a man's responsibilities. And was the better for it, I thought.

Yet it would be a good idea to ride out of town. Avoiding trouble was the best thing. I wasn't trying to prove anything to anybody. I wasn't so insecure that I had to make people realize I was a tough man, and no man in his right mind hunts trouble.

Walking to the door after paying my check, I looked down the street. Burdette was a block away, standing in front of the barbershop. Stepping out of the door, I walked down the street to my horse. As I gathered the reins I heard his boots on the walk.

"You, there!" His voice was harsh. "Don't I know you?"

When I turned around it was very slowly. I could feel a queer stillness in me, something I'd never felt before. His cold eyes stared into mine.

"Don't believe you do, Mr. Burdette. I'm new here."

"I've seen you somewhere. I know that look."

I sat my horse and looked at him. "You've never seen me, Mr. Burdette. I'm only a boy and I've lived most of my life in the hills. But I think the look is one you've seen before."

With that I touched my spurs and started away. But he was not through. "Wait!"

Drawing up, I looked at him. All along the street

movement had stopped. We were the center of attention. That strange, cool, remote feeling was in me. That waiting. . . .

"What d'you mean by that?" He came into the street, but not close. "And where did you get my name?"

"Your name was told me," I said, "and also that you killed a man last week." Why I said it I'll never know, but it wasn't in me to be bullied, and Burdette was making me angry. "Don't ride me, Burdette. If you want to kill a man this week, try somebody else!"

And then I rode out of town.

The trail wound upward into the tall pines. The grass smelled good, and there were flowers along the way. At the fifth turning, just four miles from town, I saw a rail fence and back of it a barn bigger than any I'd ever seen, and a strongly built log house.

A dog ran out, barking. Then a tall, rough-hewn man with a shock of white hair came to the door. "Light and set, stranger! I'm Frank Hetrick."

"My name is Ryan Tyler. I was told to ask for Liza."

He turned. "Liza! Here's your beau!"

She came to the door, poised and pretty, her cheeks pink under the tan. "Papa! You shouldn't say such things. I told him you'd give him a job."

Hetrick looked at me from keen blue eyes. "Do you break horses, Tyler?"

"Yes, sir. If you want them broke gentle."

"Of course." The remark pleased him. "Get down and come in."

At the door I took off my ragged black hat and ran my fingers through my hair. There were carpets on the floor and the furniture was finished off and varnished. You didn't see much of that in pioneer country.

It was the first time I'd been inside a house in over a year, and I'd never been in one as nice as this before. Not, at least, since Pap and I left home. There was a double row of books on shelves across the room, and when Hetrick left the room I walked over to look.

Some of them were books Logan Pollard had talked about. Tacitus, Thucydides, Plato, and a dozen others that were mostly history.

Hetrick returned to the room and noticed my interest. "I see you like books. Do you read a lot?"

"No, sir. But I had a friend who talked about books to me."

After supper we went out on the porch to sit and Hetrick built a smudge to fight off the mosquitoes. We sat there talking for a while and watching the black shadows capture the mountains. But that smudge was almost as bad as the mosquitoes, so we went in.

Liza sat down beside me and started asking questions, and the first thing I knew I had told them about Logan Pollard and Mary, and how Pap died. But I didn't tell them about the Indians I killed, or about the Mexican rustlers, or about McGarry.

It wasn't that I wanted to hide anything, but I wasn't the kind to talk, and that was over and done. The one thing I did not want was a gun-fighting reputation, and besides, I liked these people. Somehow, I felt at home here. I liked Hetrick, and Liza was a mighty nice girl, even if she did look so big-eyed at me sometimes that I was embarrassed.

The next day I went to work at forty a month. There was one other hand on the place, a Mexican named Miguel.

Hetrick came out and watched us that first day. And from time to time in the days that followed he came around and watched, but he had no comment and made no suggestions. Only one day he stopped me. "Rye," he said, "I like your work."

"Thanks, sir."

"You're working well and you're working fast."

"You've good stock," I said, and meant it. "Breeding in these horses. It shows."

"Yes." He looked at me thoughtfully. "Breeding always shows through." He changed the subject suddenly. "Rye, Liza told me you had words with Ollie Burdette."

"It was nothing."

"Be careful. He's a killer, Rye. He's dangerous. You've known horses like that, and I've watched Burdette. He's got a drive in him, a drive to kill."

"Yes, sir."

Twice during the following month, Kipp came over. He liked to talk and he liked Mrs. Hetrick's pies. So did I. He was over for my birthday, too, the day I was eighteen.

He looked at my old Shawk & McLanahan. "You should have a Colt," he said. "They're a mighty fine gun."

"Heard of them," I admitted. "I'd like one."

The next morning when we went out, nine of Hetrick's best horses were gone. Stolen.

The story was all there, in the tracks around the corral where we held the freshly broken stock. Moving around, careful to spoil no tracks, I worked it out. "There's two, at least," I said. "Probably one or two more."

Kipp had stayed the night, and when I went to the barn for my saddle, he followed along. "I'll go with you," he said. "Three is better than two."

Reading their sign was no problem. I'd been living too long like an Indian. The three of us rode fast, knowing as we did that they were going clear out of the country. We could tell that from the direction they took. There was nothing that way, nothing at all for miles.

Hetrick had a fine new rifle, and Kipp was well armed. As for me, I still had the old Joslyn .50, although it was pretty nigh worn out now. But I knew that old carbine and could make it talk.

The thieves took the horses into a stream and followed it for miles, but that isn't the trick some folks think it is, and it didn't wipe out their trail the way they expected. A horse makes a deep track in wet sand and sometimes the tracks don't wash out very soon.

So water or not, we held to their trail until they left the stream and took out across a sandy flat. From that they reached some prairie, but the dew was wet on the grass and the horses had knocked the grass down and you could follow it at a trot.

On the fourth day of trailing the thieves had slowed down. We were coming up fast until we smelled a wood fire, and then we started walking our horses. We were

going down a long slope covered with pines when we
saw the branding fire.

We bunched a little as we neared the fire and they
were busy and didn't see us until a horse whinnied.
One man dropped his branding iron and a thin trail of
smoke lifted from the grass where the iron fell.

There were four of them, four to our three. They
stood waiting for us as we walked our horses nearer,
four tough looking men from the rough country. One of
them was a lean, hatchet-faced man with hair that curled
over his shirt collar. He had gray-striped trousers tucked
into his boot tops.

"Reckon you got the wrong horses," I said.

The big man with the black beard looked nervously
at the one with the hatchet face. I was watching him,
too. He had a bronco look about him that spelled trouble,
and I could see it plain. He wore his gun tied down and
his right hand was ready. And they were four to our
three.

"You think so?" Hatchet Face was doing the talking.

One of the others was an Indian or a breed, a
square-jawed man with a wide face and a beaded vest.

"The horses belong to Hetrick, here. I broke them
all. We're taking them back."

"Are you, now?" Hatchet Face smiled and showed
some teeth missing. "You're a long ways from home,
boys, and we've got the number on you. That means we
keep the horses."

Kipp and Hetrick were forgotten. I could feel that
lonely feeling again, the feeling of trouble coming, and
of being poised and ready for it. It was the something
that happened to me when something was coming up.

"No," I said, choosing my words careful-like. "You
are four to three, but with us it's just one to one."

Hetrick had a wife and daughter, and I knew he was
no fighting man, although he would be right with me
when the chips were down. I wanted to keep this short
and quick, and I had an idea that I might do it by
keeping the fight between the two of us. The others
didn't look ambitious about a shoot-out. Black Beard
would back up quick if he had the chance. The man I'd

called was number one and if there was to be a fight, he would make it.

His face thinned down, seemed to sharpen. He had not expected that. There was a quick calculation in his eyes.

Old Blue walked forward two steps, then stopped. I was looking right down the muzzle of his courage.

"Yes." I said it low and straight at him. "You have this wrong, Bronco. I'm the man you think you are."

He measured me, not liking it. "What's that mean?"

"It means we take our horses. It means if you reach for a gun, I'll kill you."

Never before had I talked like that to any man. Nor did I know where the confidence came from, but it was there, as it had been when Logan Pollard stopped McGarry that day when he would have quirted me.

Bronco was bothered, but he was still confident. So I gave him time. I wanted his sand to run out. Maybe it would. And there was an even better chance it would not, for whoever Bronco was, he had used his gun; I could sense it, feel it.

That feeling sharpened all my senses, set me up and ready for what would come. Yet there was no hanging back. The horses were ours, and no man would dare walk away from such a situation and still call himself a man. Not in the West, not in our day. And we weren't about to walk away. Hetrick and Kipp would have got themselves killed, but this time they had the difference, and I was the difference.

"Mr. Hetrick," I said, "you and Kipp gather up the horses."

"Like hell!" Bronco flared.

Shorty nervously shifted his feet, and that did it. Maybe Bronco thought Shorty was starting something. Anyway, his hand swept back and I shot him.

The bullet cut the Bull Durham tag hanging from his shirt pocket. The second bullet struck an inch lower and right.

His gun was half drawn, but he seemed to shove it down in his holster and he started to take a step, and then he was dead.

A crow cawed out in the trees on the slope. A horse stamped. The other men stood flat-footed, caught that way, unmoving, not wanting to move.

And there was no more fight. Even if they had wanted one, it was too late. My gun was out and they were under it, and few men have the stomach to buck that deal.

"I'll get the horses," Kipp said, and he started for them.

Hetrick got down from his saddle. "Rye," he said, "we'd better collect their guns."

"Sure," I said.

Shorty stared at me. "Rye," he said thoughtfully. "I never heard that name. Know who you killed?"

"A horse thief," I said.

"You killed Rice Wheeler," he said, "the Panhandle gunman."

"He should have stayed in the Panhandle," I said.

6

Returning was only a two-day trip. We had no trail to find, and we could cut across country, which we did. Nobody had very much to say that first day out.

Late on the second day, when we were walking our horses up a long canyon, Kipp said, "That Wheeler, he killed six or seven men." Nobody said anything to that, and he went on. "Wait until I tell this in town! It'll make Ollie Burdette turn green."

"Don't tell him!" Hetrick said angrily. "Don't say a word about it. I got back my horses and let's let it lay."

"But why not? It isn't every day a man kills a Rice Wheeler!"

"You don't know gunmen," Hetrick said testily. "It will start Burdette hunting the boy all the more."

Reluctantly Kipp agreed, but only after I said, "I don't want that kind of talk about me, I'm not making any reputation."

All the way home I was thinking it out. I had killed another man. This was two. That Mexican . . . My shot might have killed him, but it was Pollard's shot that did kill him. No doubt about that. And I didn't want to claim any more than I had to.

Liza ran out to meet us as we came up. "You got the horses!" She was excited. "Did you catch the thieves? Where are they?"

Later, I guess she was told, or she heard about it, because for several days she was very big-eyed around me. But she didn't say anything to me about it, or to anyone else. And it wasn't even mentioned for a long time.

Sometimes at night we would sit over the table and talk, and I'd tell them stories about living in the mountains alone, and of some of the places I'd seen. And once when we were talking I went to my saddlebags and got out Ma's picture and showed it to them.

She was a pretty woman. Only twenty when the picture was taken.

Mrs. Hetrick looked at it for a long time, then at me. "Do you know anything about her family?"

"No, ma'am. Pap told me that when they were married her family sort of got shut of her. I mean . . . well, the way I heard it, they didn't think Pap had money enough. But Pap and Ma, they were happy."

Mrs. Hetrick put the picture down thoughtfully. "That dress she had on . . . that was expensive."

I knew nothing about women's clothes. It looked just like any dress to me. Women, I guess they know about things like that. One time, a few days later, I heard her telling Hetrick, "Real lace. I never saw a prettier collar. It's a pity the boy doesn't know her family."

Sometimes of an evening Liza and I would walk down to the spring and talk, or out by the corral. Always in plain sight of the house. She was a mighty pretty youngster, but just a youngster. Me, I was eighteen, headin' on for nineteen.

We'd talk long talks there by that corral, leaning on the bars close to Old Blue. We'd talk boy-girl talk, even though she was younger than me. About what we wanted to do, the dreams we had, and where we wanted to go. We both wanted to be rich, but I guess that wasn't very important to us, either. It was just that we both wanted more things, and to see more.

Liza would listen, all wide-eyed and excited when I talked about the mountains up in Wyoming. Or the Blues over in Oregon, or those wild, empty canyons that cut down through the southwest corner of Utah.

Twice I went to town, but only once did I see Burdette. The other time he was out of town chasing down some outlaw. He brought back his horse with an empty saddle.

The time I did see him I was coming out of the store with some supplies to load into the buckboard. He came down to the walk to watch me load up.

"Breaking horses for Hetrick, I hear."

"That's right. Nice stock."

"Hear you lost some."

"Found 'em again."

"Any trouble?"

His eyes were searching mine. It gave me the feeling he might have heard something, but either wasn't sure or didn't believe what he had heard.

"Nothing to speak of."

"Lucky. I heard Rice Wheeler was working these hills."

By that time I was up on the seat, turning the team. Liza was there beside me and she looked up at Burdette. "He isn't any more," she said, and before he could question that, I got the team started out of town.

"You shouldn't have said that," I told her. "Now he won't rest until he digs out the story."

"I don't care," she said pertly. "I don't like him."

It was nice driving along over the trail, talking to Liza. We always had something to say to each other and it was hard to realize she was growing up, too.

And my time to leave was not far off. Hetrick had much to do yet to make his place pay. He would have a fine bunch of horses to sell, and he had some good breeding stock. So he had a good chance of building something really worth while. It made me see what a man could do. When all the rest of them were hunting gold or silver, running saloons or gambling houses, he was quietly building a ranch and a horse herd. It was something stable, something that could last.

But once the horses were broken he would need me no longer, and it was time I started to find a place for myself in the world. And a ranch was what I wanted, too. My own ranch, somewhere back in some of those green valleys I'd seen during my wandering.

When I had broken the last horse, a sorrel with three stockings, I went to Hetrick.

"Finished," I said.

He opened a drawer in his desk and took out some money. He paid me what he owed me. Not counting what I had drawn on my wages, I had seventy dollars coming to me. And I'd still not touched the forty dollars Pap left me. I still had that, sewed into my gun belt.

"Wish I could keep you on, son. There just isn't work enough."

"I know."

"Come around whenever you like, Rye. We enjoy having you." He pushed his desk drawer shut. "Got any plans?"

"Yes, sir. I thought . . . well, I heard tell of some placer diggings down on Willow. I figured to try that. Maybe . . . well, I don't aim to ride aimless all my life long. I had an idea that if I could get a stake I'd start ranching."

"That's wise." Hetrick hesitated, then he said, "Son, be careful around town. Kipp got drunk the other night and Burdette got the story out of him. He knows you killed Rice Wheeler."

"I'm sorry."

"So am I. But Liza told us she had said something to him about it."

"It was nothing. I don't blame her."

"It started him asking questions. You'll have to be careful." He took out his pipe and filled it. "Rye, you watch him. He's killed three men at the Crossing. He's . . . well, he's tricky."

"All right, sir. But I don't expect to be around there."

The next morning after breakfast I rode away. Liza did not come out to say good-bye, but I could hear her in the next room. It sounded as if she was crying. I sort of felt like crying myself. Only men don't carry on.

When I was turning into the lane she ran out and waved. I was going to miss her.

It was thirty miles to Willow Creek, and it was far away from anywhere. Once there, I scouted along the creek and picked a likely-looking bench. It was my first time to try hunting gold, but I'd heard talk of it, and around Pollard's place in California they had taken thousands from the creeks.

The work was lonely and hard. The bench was on a curve of the Willow, and I found a little color. I sank a shaft to bedrock, which was only eight feet down, and I cleaned up the bedrock and panned it out. After two weeks of brutal labor I had taken out about ninety dollars.

Not much, but better than punching cows. It was harder living alone now than it had been in the mountains before I met the Hetricks. They were good people, and I'd liked staying there with them, and I thought a lot about Liza. It was Liza I kept remembering. The way she laughed, how she smiled, and the warm way her eyes looked sometimes.

The next week I cleaned out some seams in the bedrock and took out more than two hundred dollars in twenty minutes.

It was spotty. There was a lot of black sand mixed in with the gold and it was hard to get the gold out. Twice in the following week I moved upstream, working bars and benches to the tune of a little color here and a little more there.

My grub ran short, but I killed an elk and jerked the meat, then caught a few fish from time to time. Living off the country was almost second nature to me by this time.

Nobody came around. Once a couple of Utes came by and I gave them some of my coffee. When they left, one of them told me about a bench upstream that I should try.

Taking a chance that they knew what they were talking about, I went upstream the next morning and found the bench. It was hidden in the pines that flanked both sides of the stream, and it was above the water.

There was an old caved-in shaft there, a shovel with the handle long gone, and a miserable little dugout in the bank. I found some arrowheads around. Whoever had mined here must have been here twenty years ago. This was Indian country then.

When I cleaned out the old shaft I panned some of the bottom gravel and washed out twelve dollars in a few minutes. The second pan was off bedrock and ran to twenty-six dollars. Working like all get-out, I cleaned up a good bit of dust. Not enough to make a man rich, but more money than I ever had before.

When I finished that week I loaded my gear and saddled up. Old Blue was fat and sassy, so we drifted back to the Crossing.

The old black hat was still on my head, and I was wearing buckskins. It wasn't trouble I was looking for, but I remembered Hetrick's warning. Outside of town I reined in and got out the old Shawk & McLanahan and belted it on.

When I swung down at the bank, Burdette was coming down the street, and when they had finished weighing out my gold they counted out my money and it came to just $462. And I still had $50 of my wages from Hetrick.

"Doing well," Burdette said.

"Not bad."

"So you killed Rice Wheeler?"

"Uh-huh."

"That was what you meant, then? When you said I should know the look of you?"

I shrugged. "Read it any way you like."

He watched me as I walked out to my horse and stepped into the leather. When I rode toward Hetrick's, he was still watching. I could feel his eyes on me and I'll admit I didn't like it. At a store on the edge of town I bought some ribbon for Liza, and I'd also saved her a small gold nugget.

She ran out to the gate to see me, recognizing Old Blue from far down the road. She stepped up in my stirrup and rode that way up to the house. Mrs. Hetrick was at the door, drying her hands on her apron, and Hetrick came up from the corral, smiling a greeting. I felt all choked up. I guess it was the first time anybody felt good about seeing me come back. Most of my life I've been a stranger.

It was good to walk around the place again and to see the horses. One of them, a tall Appaloosa, followed me along the fence, whinnying at me, much to Old Blue's disgust.

While we waited for dinner and talked about the horses, Hetrick suddenly asked, "Did you see Burdette?"

"I saw him."

"Bother you?"

"No."

"He wanted to buy a horse from me, but I turned him down. I've seen the way he treats his horses."

That gave me some satisfaction, but it worried me, too. I wouldn't want any of the horses I had broken so carefully to get into the hands of Ollie Burdette, who was, as Hetrick said, a hard man with a horse. But it worried me because I knew that Hetrick, a stiff-necked man and stern about such things, would not have hesitated to tell Burdette what he thought.

It was pleasant inside the house, and Mrs. Hetrick put on a linen tablecloth and had the table fixed up real fancy. When I had my hair slicked down as much as it would ever slick, which isn't much, I sat down to the best supper I'd had.

Kipp rode in while I was there, all excited about the gold I'd panned out, but I knew he wouldn't be so much excited by the work. It was a good supper and there was good talk around, and had I been their own son, I couldn't have been treated any better.

"That Burdette," Kipp said suddenly, "I don't think he's in your class. He's fast, all right, but not as fast as you."

Hetrick frowned. He never liked talk about gun fighters, but Kipp was always talking of Clay Allison, the Cimarron gun fighter, or the Earps, Bill Longley, Langford Peel, or John Bull.

"You'd match any of them," he said, his excitement showing. "I'd like to see you up against Hardin, or this Bonney feller, down in New Mexico."

"Why, Kipp." Mrs. Hetrick was horrified. "A body would think you'd like to see a man killed!"

He looked startled, and his face flushed. "It ain't that," he said hurriedly. "It's just . . . well, sort of like . . . I don't know," he finished lamely. "I just like to see who's best."

Talk like that worried me some, and I didn't want any more of it. Loose-talking folks have promoted more than one fight that would never have happened otherwise.

Kipp wasn't the only one. When I was around town I'd heard some talk, folks speculating on who would win, Burdette or me. The talk excited them. It wasn't that they were bloodthirsty, just that they liked a contest, and they just didn't think that a man would have to die to decide it.

Or maybe they did. Maybe they figured the sooner we killed each other off, the better.

It nagged at a man's mind. Was he better than me? I didn't want to be better than anybody, not at all. But it worried me some because I wanted to live.

Even nice people warned me, never realizing that even their warnings were an incitement. It was on their minds, on all their minds, so how could it be different with me? Or with Burdette? The sooner I got out of town, the better.

"I'm taking out," I said suddenly. "I figure to go East. Have a ride on the cars, maybe. I want to see St. Louis or Kansas City. Maybe New Orleans."

"Will you look up your family?" Mrs. Hetrick asked.

"I reckon not. They never tried to find me."

"You don't know," she protested. "Maybe they think you're dead. Maybe they don't even know about you."

"Just as well. They didn't set much store by Ma, or they'd not have thrown her over like that."

"Maybe they were sorry, Rye. People make mistakes. You have some money now, why don't you look them up?"

No matter about that, I was getting out of here. I didn't want to hear any more talk about Ollie Burdette, or whether he was faster than me.

So we talked it out, and I made up my mind to leave Old Blue behind. He was all of eleven years old, maybe even older. It was time he had a rest. I'd ride one of Hetrick's horses over the mountains to the railroad and sell him there. We agreed on that.

Hetrick wanted Old Blue. He was gentle enough and would be a good horse for Liza to ride, and she liked him. I said I'd rather see her have him than anybody else, and she flushed a little and looked all bright-eyed. She was a nice little girl. And I was going to miss her. I was going to miss her a lot.

Come daylight, I saddled up.

Burdette was standing on the street when I rode into the Crossing with Hetrick. He saw the bedroll behind my saddle.

"Leavin'?"

"Going East," I said. "I want to see some country."

"Better stay shut of Dodge. They eat little boys down there."

It rankled, and suddenly I felt something hot and ugly rise inside me. I turned on him. "You hungry?" I said.

It surprised him and he didn't like it. We were close up, and he didn't like that. We weren't four feet apart, and neither of us could miss. Right then I stepped closer. It was a fool thing to do, but right at the moment, I was doing it. I crowded him. "You hungry?" I repeated. "You want to eat this little boy?"

He backed up, his face gray. He wasn't scared. I knew he wasn't scared. It was just that nobody could win if the shooting started. It was too close. It was belly to belly. He wasn't scared, he just wanted to win. He didn't want to get shot, and he was older than me, old enough to be cautious. Later I would have better judgment, but right then I was mad.

"Any time," I said. "Just any time."

Those gray eyes were ugly. He hated me so bad it hurt, and he wanted to draw. He wanted to kill me.

But he laughed, and he made it sound easy, though it must have been hard to do.

"You got me wrong, kid. I was just foolin'."

But he was not fooling. It just wasn't the right time, and Ollie Burdette figured he could wait.

"Sure," I said. "Forget it."

So I left him like that and I rode out of town and down the trail.

Maybe I would look up my relatives, after all.

When I looked back, Ollie Burdette still stood there, but Hetrick was gone.

Right then I had a hunch. "I'll see you again, Ollie Burdette, I'll bet on it."

And there was an unspoken thought that it would be the last time . . . for one of us.

7

Market Square in Kansas City was hustling and booming when I first walked down the street. To me it was a big town, all crowded with people, all seeming in a big hurry.

I liked seeing the beer wagons with their big Percheron or Clydesdale teams, and I liked watching the fancy carriages with their fine driving horses all neck-reined up and prancing along. And right away I noticed that nobody carried a gun where you could see it, so I stashed mine away behind my waistband.

For hours I just walked the streets, looking at all the things I didn't want. I never saw so much I could do without, and never so many people. Right away I saw I'd have to do something about my buckskins. Even the new black hat I'd bought looked shabby, so I went to a tailor and had him make me up a fine gray suit and one of black, and I bought a fine white hat, some shirts with ruffled fronts, and some black string ties. When I'd found some boots of black calfskin I began to feel mighty dressed up.

Almost nineteen, I could pass as several years older. I was weighing one hundred and eighty now, and no ounce of fat on me. Once in a while I'd pass some girl who would look at me, then turn to look again. And I always saw it because I'd usually turned to look myself.

The old Shawk & McLanahan was still with me, but seeing some of the Bisley Colts, I longed for a new and more efficient gun. Several times I almost went in to buy one, but each time I hesitated. Right now I needed no gun and there was a lot I wanted to see on the money I had left.

One day on Market Square I saw a bunch of men sitting or standing around a bench. Some of them looked Western, so I walked over, and when I got there they were talking about shooting. It was warm, and most of them had their coats off. One tall, finely built man with long hair to his shoulders and a mustache interested me. He was wide across the cheekbones and had gray eyes.

Several times I saw him studying me, and whenever I was around, I noticed he knew where I was.

There was a young fellow standing near me and he whispered out of the corner of his mouth, "Wild Bill's trying to figure out who you are."

"Wild Bill? Is that Hickok?"

"Sure thing. He's a fine shot."

This fellow stood there listening to the talk of guns and shooting, and then he turned to me. "Have you eaten yet? I'm hungry."

We walked along together. He was a buffalo hunter, he told me, and he had come into Kansas City with nearly three thousand dollars from his hides. "My name's Dixon," he said. "Billy Dixon."

"I'm Ryan Tyler . . . lately from Colorado."

We ate together, then went to see a show. Later we met a strong-built man, older than us, whom Dixon had known on the prairie. His name was Kirk Jordan.

Several days we hung around town, but my money was running short and I'd begun to think about leaving. When I was sitting on the Square one day, a sharp-faced man in a black coat stopped near me. Several times he looked me over carefully. Me, I'd hunted a good bit myself, and knew how a hunter looked. This man was hunting something.

He sat down near me, and after a bit he opened a conversation. After a while he mentioned poker . . ,. a friendly game.

Now, I'm not so smart as some, but Logan Pollard had taught me a sight of poker. And he taught me how to win at poker, and how a cardsharp works. Pollard was good. He knew a lot, and being naturally clever with my hands, I had learned fast.

Moreover, poker isn't a very friendly game. If you play poker, you play for money, and beyond a certain point there is nothing friendly about money. So when a stranger suggests a friendly game of poker . . . well, you figure it out.

This fellow had me pegged right. He figured I was in from the hills, had bought some fancy clothes, and was carrying a stake in my pocket. Only the last was a wrong guess.

"Don't really play cards," I said cautiously, "but if you're going to play, I'd enjoy watching."

"Come along, then."

We started off, and glancing back, I saw Hickok and Jim Hanrahan and some others looking after us with amused smiles. They were thinking that I would learn a lesson, and every man has some lessons to learn for himself.

There were five men in the game and one of them looked like a buffalo hunter. The others . . . well, I didn't know about them. But after a while, I sat in.

They let me win three out of four times. Each time the win was small, but it was enough to double what I had to begin with.

I played a blundering, careless game, sizing up the others. The way I saw it, all but two were cardsharps. The buffalo hunter was named Billy Ogg, and there was a man who had been a stage driver in Texas. A mighty fine fellow.

On the fifth hand they built the pot pretty strong and I stayed with them, and lost.

It was my deal then, and clumsily I gathered in the cards, having a hard time getting them arranged, but in the process I got two aces on the bottom. Shuffling the cards, I managed to get another ace to the bottom, and then I dealt the cards, taking my three aces off the bottom as I needed them. That is, I dealt myself two of them to begin; then when I drew three cards, one of them was the third ace.

Woods, the man who had roped me into the game, raised five dollars. I saw him and raised again. Woods raised and I went along, and at the showdown my three aces took the pot.

Woods didn't say anything, but he looked angry, and one of the others, a fat, dirty man, growled something under his breath. It was a good pot, more than seventy dollars, as I recall.

We played for two hours, and I was careful. When a hand looked too good to be true, I wouldn't go along or played it so badly that I lost little, and when I dealt or could hold out a card or two, I won. At the end of that time I was four hundred dollars ahead, and Woods was getting mighty ugly.

Right about that time I decided enough was enough. There had to be a break, and I wanted to make it when I was ready, not have Woods or one of the others make it and catch me off balance. Pushing back my chair, I said, "Got to get some sleep. I'm quitting."

"You can't quit now!" Woods protested. "You've got our money."

My smile didn't make him any happier. Nor did what I said. "And that wasn't the way you planned it, was it?"

Woods's face went red and the fat man's hand dropped to his lap. Only I'd seen the gun under the napkin almost an hour before. My old Shawk & McLanahan was out and covering them and I sort of stepped back a little.

"You," I said to Ogg. "You've been taken. So's he." I indicated the stage driver. "You two pick up the pot."

"Like hell!" Woods started to get up.

My gun muzzle swung to him. "I'd as soon kill you," I said pleasantly. "Don't make it necessary."

Ogg and the stage driver scooped up the money. Both of them had been in twice as deep as I could have gone, and most of the money was theirs. They gathered it up and went to the door, but at the door Billy Ogg shucked his own gun. "Come on, Tyler. I'd as soon kill one of them my own self."

The three of us walked out together. The stage driver was Johnny Keeler, and they split a thousand between them and insisted I take the two hundred that remained. I refused.

Ogg glanced skeptically at the old Shawk & McLanahan. "Does that thing shoot? I didn't think they made them any more."

"It shoots."

"I'm beginning to get this now," Keeler said suddenly. "You're Rye Tyler, the Colorado gun fighter."

"I'm from Colorado," I said.

"You killed Rice Wheeler?"

"He stole horses from my boss."

Billy Ogg looked me over thoughtfully. "Now, that's mighty interestin'. T'other day down to Tom Speers' place, Hickok said you were a gun fighter. Said he could read it in you."

"You'll have to come around and meet the boys," Keeler said. "Wyatt Earp's in town, too."

"I'm going to New Orleans," I said.

Next morning early I woke up, bathed, shaved, and got slicked up. Just as I was starting to pack there was a knock on the door. When I opened it there was a man standing there with a box in his hands, and a rifle.

The rifle was a new .44 Henry repeater, the finest made. And in the box were two of the hard-to-get Smith & Wesson Russians, the pistol that was breaking all the target records.

Behind the man came Billy Ogg and Johnny Keeler. "A present from us," Ogg said, grinning at my surprise. "You saved our money. This is a present."

Long after I was on the river boat, headed downriver for New Orleans, I handled those guns. Yet it was with something like regret that I packed away the old Shawk & McLanahan. It had been with me a long time.

For two weeks I loafed in New Orleans, seeing the sights, eating the best meals, sometimes playing cards a little. But this was honest playing, for I played with honest men, and I lost a little, won a little, and at the end of two weeks had won back half what I'd spent around town.

New Orleans was a lively place, and I liked it, but I was getting restless to leave. The West was my country, and I had to be doing something. Nowhere in the world was there anything that belonged to me, nor did I have any place to call home. Also, I kept thinking about Liza. She would be sixteen now, and girls married at sixteen. The thought of her marrying somebody made me feel kind of panicky and scared, as if I was losing something I needed.

Finally I packed to go, and then while I was waiting for time to leave, I went to a gambling hall called the Wolf Trap. As soon as I was inside the door I saw Woods, and with him a local tough known as Chris Lillie. Wanting no trouble, I turned at once and went out.

The streets were dark and silent. It was very late and few people were about. Walking swiftly, I was almost to the end of the street when I heard someone running behind me. Quickly I ducked into a doorway.

Nobody passed, and nobody came near. Yet I had heard those feet. Suddenly I remembered that at this point another street, a very narrow one, intersected the one on which I had been walking. It would be on that other street that I'd heard the running.

Deliberately I crossed the street away from the corner. Cities were new to me, but the hunting of men is much the same anywhere. In the blackness of a doorway I waited, watching the point where the two streets came together.

Several minutes passed and then I saw Chris Lillie come out of the alley and peer down the street up which I had come. The street was, of course, empty.

All was dark and still except under the few misty

street lights. Fog was beginning to drift in from the bottoms, and the night was ghostly in its silence.

Then a second man emerged, and this was Woods. They stood there together, whispering and peering around. My disappearance worried them. And then I stepped out into the street. "Looking for me?" I asked.

Woods had a pistol in his hand. He whipped it up and fired, but he shot too quickly, and missed. I felt the bullet whip past me as I steadied my aim and fired. Woods turned back, starting in the direction from which he had come, and then fell dead.

Lillie sprinted for the alley, and I let him go. Waiting only a minute longer, I turned away and walked back to my hotel. By daybreak I was riding a rented horse west of the river. And I had killed my third white man.

But this time with the Smith & Wesson .44, not the old Shawk & McLanahan.

8

In 1872 much of Texas was still wild. In eastern Texas there were vast thickets of chaparral, and some good forests. It was lonely country, dangerous for a stranger. It was feuding country, too. The Lee-Peacock and Sutton-Taylor feuds had left the country split wide open. Neither of them was really settled, and much of the bloodiest fighting was still to come.

Every ranch in some sections of eastern Texas was an armed camp, and few men rode alone. There were old enmities that had survived the fights of the Regulators and the Moderators, and the fighting and general lawlessness had brought into the country some bad men from the Indian Territory and elsewhere. But Texas had enough of her own.

In Marshall I bought a horse. He was a fine dappled gray, the fastest walking horse I ever saw. He was seventeen hands high and could really step out and move, ideal for such a trip as this.

Some nights I camped out, and at times stayed in wayside inns or at ranches. It was good riding, and new country for me. In the back of my mind all the while was the thought that I was heading for Colorado, where I'd stay a while before riding on to California to visit Logan and Mary. Meanwhile I was young and restless, and the country looked good.

For a month I rode, drifting south and a little west, and one day I came on a man with a herd of cows.

He had six hundred head and he was short-handed. He was a big man with a blunt, good-natured face. He looked me over as I came along the road, then called out, "Hunting a job?"

"Use one," I said, and swung my gray alongside him.

"Thirty a month," he said. "I'm driving to Uvalde. Selling this herd to Bill Bennett. He's going up the trail to Kansas."

"All right."

"Can't promise you Kansas, but the job is good to Uvalde. My name is Wilson."

The gray was quick, intelligent, and active. He became a good cow horse, and learned fast. Mostly, though, I rode one of Wilson's horses.

Nobody asked questions in those days. Every man was judged by what he did. Lots of men had pasts they did not want examined, and if you minded your own business and did your work, nobody bothered about anything else.

Riding jobs always suited me. I liked to think, and a man could follow along with a herd of cattle and do a powerful lot of thinking. In my jeans I had over a thousand dollars. Here and there along the trail I'd gambled some, and I'd won and lost, but I had a stake. And I wanted more.

The beef Wilson had was mostly young stuff, and it looked good. In Kansas City I'd heard a lot of talk about the rich grass of the northern prairies and how cattle could actually fatten while on the trail. This stuff Wilson was driving was young, rawboned, and would fill out.

The third day I made up my mind. Wilson was riding point and I drifted alongside the herd until I pulled abreast of him. After we'd passed the time of day and talked about the weather and how dusty it was, I started in. "Got a little money," I said. "Mind if I buy a few cows and drift them with yours? I'd be a partner in the herd then, and you'd have a free cow hand."

"Go ahead!" Wilson waved a hand. "Glad to have you!"

· Leaving the herd that night, I rode on ahead and began to check the ranches. And right away I began to wish I had more money.

Cash was a scarce thing in Texas in those days. Men had cattle, horses, and hay, but real cash money was mighty hard to come by for the average rancher. Moreover, he had to gamble on riding anywhere from thirty to a hundred miles to market with maybe no sale when he got there, or a niggardly price.

I rode into a ranch yard and drifted my horse up to the trough. Looking around at the cattle, I saw they were mostly good stock, with a few culls here and there such as you'll find in any cow outfit. But this stock was big, like your longhorns are apt to be, and rangy. Given a chance, a longhorn could fill out to quite a lot of beef.

Grass was not good and most of the range was overstocked. Most of the ranchers had not begun to realize that there was a limit to the amount of stock the range could carry. Their great argument was a buffalo. They had themselves seen the range black with their millions. I had seen it, too, but what I remembered that some of them seemed to forget was that the buffalo never stopped moving. They gave the grass a chance to grow back. It was a different thing with cattle. They were confined to one range, once men began to herd them, and they ate the grass to nothing.

My horse walked up to the trough and started to drink, and a long-geared man in boots with run-down heels walked over from the corral.

"Light an' set," he invited me. "Don't get many visitors hereabouts."

"Riding through," I told him as I swung down. "I'm going to Uvalde."

"What I ought to do," he said, biting off a chew, "I should drift me a herd up to San Antone. But that takes hands, and I ain't got 'em. I'd like to drift a herd to Kansas."

"Risky," I said. "Indians, herd cutters, an' such-like."

His wife came out to look at me, and two wide-eyed children in homemade dresses.

"Might buy a few myself," I said thoughtfully. "I'm ridin' through. Shame to make the trip for nothin'."

He glanced at me. My rig was new and looked good and prosperous. "You could do worse," he said. "Fact is, if a man had him a little cash money he could buy cows mighty cheap."

"Don't know," I said doubtfully. "A man could lose a sight of money thataway. Stampedes . . . Men have made money goin' over the trail, but they've lost it, too. Lost their shirts, some of 'em."

"Young fellow like you," the rancher said, "he should take a chance if anybody should. Got your life ahead of you. I reckon you could double your money."

"Well," I hesitated, "I have got a little money, but gold is scarce in this country and I hate to get shut of it." I let that settle down through his thinking for a few minutes, and then added, "Why, a man can buy most anything for gold in this country!"

"Gold?" He looked at me again. "Mister, if you want to buy cows with gold, you don't have to go any farther. They pay ten dollars a head in San Antone. Now I—"

"More'n I'd pay. A man's got risks, driving to Kansas. He has to hire riders, get a chuck wagon, grub, a string of horses. Takes a sight of money."

The rancher chewed slowly, looking thoughtful. "Might sell a few," he said. "Could use some cash money."

Cattle bred like rabbits and his range was overstocked. He would have been a fool not to sell, if only to save grass for the other cows.

"Give you five dollars a head?"

He was astonished. "*Five?* You're crazy."

I gathered my reins and moved to mount. "Maybe I'd better forget it, anyway. As it is, I'm drawing cow hand's pay. If I own cows, I stand to lose. I'll just forget it."

"Might let a few go for eight dollars?" he suggested hopefully.

"No," I said, "I've got to ride on. Enjoyed the talk."

He put a hand on my saddle. "Now, look—"

A half hour later we compromised at seven dollars a head, his men to round them up, and no culls. I bought a hundred head. And when Wilson came along, I swung them into the herd. A neighbor boy who wanted to see San Antonio came along for the ten dollars I promised him to make the drive.

It was a good feeling, seeing those cattle, knowing they were mine. They were good stock, and would bring a good price whether I sold them in San Antonio or at the end of the trail in Kansas.

William J. Bennett was waiting in the plaza at Uvalde when I rode my horse into the square with Wilson. Wilson gestured to me. "Ryan Tyler," he said, "a good hand."

"Glad to know you." Bennett cut the end from his cigar. "Got any cows?"

"A hundred head."

"I'll buy 'em."

As easy as that I could turn a profit, maybe double my money, and in only a few days of work. I might go out again and buy more cattle and sell them, too. If I worked hard and used my head, I could build a business for myself. But the trail to Kansas was north, and it was closer to Colorado.

"Ten dollars a head," Bennett said. "Take it or leave it."

"No," I said, taking my time. "I don't want to sell. I want to make the drive with you." I leaned on the pommel. "Mr. Bennett, I want an outfit of my own. I know a little valley out in Colorado that's just what I want, but I need money. If I can sell those cattle in Kansas, I'll be well along toward having my stake."

He rolled his cigar in his teeth and looked around the plaza. Finally he took the cigar from his mouth. "Have you any more money?"

"Just a few hundred dollars."

"You want to buy more cattle?"

"Yes, sir."

He looked at the end of his cigar. "All right, Tyler." He reached in his pocket and took out a small sack. "There's a thousand dollars in that. Buy cattle for me, too. We want to leave here by the fifth."

As I started to swing my horse, he spoke again, only just loud enough for me to hear. "You the man who killed Rice Wheeler?"

For a moment I sat very still in the saddle. Then looking around at him, I nodded.

"Knew him," Bennett spoke abruptly. "He killed my saddle partner at Red River Crossing four years ago."

Riding out of town, I felt the weight of that sack of gold. It was the first time anyone had ever trusted me with money, and he had merely turned and tossed it to me. Yet it was more than trust of money. He was trusting my judgment to buy well. It gave me a good feeling.

A week later I had bought few cattle. The areas close to San Antonio had been swept clean, and all I had been able to send in were thirty head, all good stock but nothing like what we wanted for the drive. So I pushed on, hoping for better luck.

The country was wild and lonely, occasional chaparral, but mostly open country, broken and rugged. Ranches were scattered, and some of the small ones were merely rawhide outfits without enough cows to bother with. The air changed and it began to look like rain.

By nightfall the clouds were hanging low and they were spitting a little rain, so I started the gray to moving along and dug my slicker out of my bedroll. I'd taken to wearing both guns, but only one in its holster. The other I tucked behind my waistband, the butt out of sight under the edge of my coat. It was added insurance, because I was carrying another man's money and was never one for trusting to luck. I'd helped bury a few men who did.

This was rough country in more ways than one. During any day's ride a man would come up to several horsemen, mighty hard-looking men. Most of them, by the look of them, had been up the creek and over the mountain.

The wind was blowing, splattering rain ahead of it, and I was thinking of something to crawl into when I heard cattle. Just the restlessness of a good-sized bunch, and some lowing from cows. Then I saw the hard outline of a roof gable, and just off the road loomed a large house. In a flash of lightning it showed itself square and solid, built of sawed lumber.

To one side there were corrals and a lean-to, and beyond, in an open place that was walled on three sides by bluffs, was the herd. Catching glimpses by the heat lightning, I saw the steers were big and rangy, and they looked like young stock. It was a herd that might run to six hundred head.

And then the rain hit. She swept in with a roar, the solid sheets of water striking like blows on a shoulder, and I raced the gray to the lean-to and swung down. Here, partly out of the storm, it was quieter except for the roar of rain drumming on the roof. The lean-to was partly faced, and there was shelter for several horses. I found a place and tied the gray, and then I slopped, head down against the rain, to the house.

There was a light gleaming faintly behind a shutter, so I banged on the door.

Nothing happened.

I was standing in the rain, as there was no porch, only a slab of rock for a doorstep. Dropping my hand to the latch, I pressed it and stepped in, closing the door. I was about to call out when I heard voices. I heard a man saying, "You pay us now or we take the herd."

"You've no right!" It was a woman's voice, protesting. "You were to be paid when the herd was delivered and sold."

Outside rain drummed on the roof. I hesitated, feeling guilty and uncertain of what to do, but the conversation held my attention. It was also my business. This was cow talk and I was looking for cows.

"We done changed our minds."

In the tone of the man's voice there was something hard, faintly sneering. It was a voice I did not like, and quite obviously the voice of a man talking to a woman with no man standing by.

"Then I'll simply get someone else to handle the herd. After they're sold, you'll be paid."

"We ain't gonna wait." The man's voice was confident, amused. "Anyway, who would you get? Ain't nobody gonna handle them cows if we say they ain't."

I felt mighty like a fool, standing there. But this woman had a herd to sell, and it looked mighty like I'd be doing her a favor to buy it right now. But it was not going to make me any friends among those men.

"Anybody to home?" I called it out loud and there was silence afterward, so I walked through the door into the lighted room.

There were two women there. One—I guessed it was the one who had been doing the talking—was standing. She was young, and, in a plain sort of way, an attractive woman. The other woman was older. She looked frightened and worried.

There were three men, a rough-looking outfit, unshaved and dirty. All of them were looking at me.

"You didn't hear me knock," I said, taking off my hat with my left hand, "so I took the liberty of coming in out of the rain."

"Of course. . . . Won't you sit down?" The young woman's worry wasn't making her forget her hospitality. "We haven't much, but—"

"He won't be stayin'," the big man said abruptly. "We got business to talk. Nothin' for strangers to hear."

Before she could speak up, I took the issue by the quickest handle. "Heard some talk of selling cattle," I said. "I'm buying. How many and how much?"

The big man had heavy shoulders and a blunt, powerful jaw. There was a cross-eyed man and one in a gray shirt. They didn't like it. They didn't like me.

"You heard wrong." The big man did the talking. "We're selling in San Antone."

Ignoring him, I looked at the young woman. Her eyes were wary, but hopeful. "I take it you're the owner. I'll buy the cattle here and save you the drive.

I'm buying for Bennett, and he's the only one buying i
San Antone now."

From an easy steal it was beginning to look to th
three men like a total loss. The big man was getting re
around the gills and the others were showing thei
anger. So I took the play right away from them.

"Ma'am, coming in like I did, I couldn't help over
hearing some of the talk. Seems you hired these men t
round up the cattle, to pay them when the cows wer
sold. That right?"

"It is."

"Now you look here!" The big man stepped towar
me, his lips thinned down.

"I'll buy your cattle," I said to the young woman. "I'
buy them as they stand according to your tally. I'll pa
cash."

"I'll sell."

I swung one foot just enough to face all three c
them. "The cattle are sold to me," I said. "You'r
fired."

"You—"

"Shut up!" I took an easy step toward the big man
"I'm paying you off right now. You worked for wages
and I'm paying your wages. Want to make somethin
out of that?"

It had them flat-footed. I was no defenseless woman
and while I might look young, that gun on my hip wa
as old as his.

"We got no argument with you. You didn't hire us
you can't fire us."

My eyes stayed right where they were, on him. But
spoke to her. "Ma'am, will you sell me those cows?"

"You just bought them," she said quietly.

"The price," I said, "will be mutually agreeable."

The man in the gray shirt was inching his hand down
Some signal seemed to pass between them and the bi
man started to move. So I shucked my gun and laid th
barrel across the side of his jaw. He went down as
he'd been hit with an ax, and my gun muzzle droppe
on the other two.

"The fewer there are," I said, "the fewer I have to pay."

They wanted to try me. They wanted it so bad they could taste it. Maybe if they both tried, they might take me, but somebody had to make a move—and nobody was anxious to die. And there is something about a man who knows what he intends to do, who knows what he can do. Burdette had seen it in me, and Logan Pollard had seen it long ago. These men could see it now, and they hesitated.

The man on the floor groaned. Slowly the gray-shirted man let his hand relax.

"Pick him up," I said, "and get out."

The man in the gray shirt hesitated. "What about our money?" he asked.

"They were to get thirty a month," the young woman said. "They worked about three weeks."

With my free hand I counted out twenty-five dollars per man. "Pick it up, and if one of you feels lucky, start something."

They could see I was young, but this was John Wesley Hardin's country, and he had killed twenty men by the time he was my age. They didn't like it, but I was too ready, so they picked up their money and got out.

I followed them to the door and watched them get their horses.

"Don't get any ideas about those cattle," I said. "If anything happens to them, or to any part of them, I'll hunt down all three of you and kill you where I find you."

Waiting in the doorway, I listened to them move down the road, then went back inside.

The two women were putting food on the table. The young woman turned on me. "Thanks," she said. "Thanks very much."

It embarrassed me, the way they were looking at me, so I said, "Seven dollars a head?"

"All right." She pushed the tally sheet across the table. It was for 637 head. "How will you get them to San Antone?"

"Hire riders."

"There's nobody. Those were the Tetlow boys. Nobody wants trouble with them."

"Rona, we might get Johnny," the older woman suggested, "and we can both ride."

"All right, Mom." Rona turned to me. "I've been riding since I was six. We can both help."

So it was like that, and I took the herd into San Antone with two women and a boy of fourteen helping me. But I had an old mossy-horn steer leading and he liked to travel. He was worth a half-dozen riders.

Bennett paid Rona himself, glancing at me from time to time. When he had paid her off, the two of them turned to go.

Rona held out her hand to me. "Thanks," she said. "They were all we had."

One of Bennett's hands came in. "Tyler," he said, "you want those cows—"

Something stopped him. I guess it was the way everybody looked. Everybody but me, that is. Bennett's face went kind of white, and both the women turned back again to look at me. We stood there like that, and I was wondering what was wrong.

And then Rona said, "Your name is Tyler?"

"Yes, ma'am," I said.

"Not *Ryan* Tyler?"

"Yes, ma'am."

She looked at me again, and then she said quietly, "Thanks. Thanks, Mr. Tyler." And then both women walked out.

Bennett took his cigar from his teeth and swore softly, bitterly. Then he put the cigar back in his mouth and he looked at me. "You know who they were?"

"Who?"

"That was Rice Wheeler's widow . . . and his mother."

9

We pointed them north across the dry prairie grass, three thousand head of them, big longhorns led by my tough old brindle steer. We pointed them north and took the trail, and it was a good feeling to be heading north and to know that I owned part of the drive; that at last I had a stake in something.

After the first week the cattle settled down to the pattern of the drive. Every morning at daybreak that old mossy-horn was on his feet and ready, and the first time a cow hand started out from the chuck wagon he turned his head north and started the herd.

It was a hard, tough life, and it took hard men to live it. From daylight to dark in the saddle, eating dust, fighting ornery cow stock, driving through occasional rainstorms and fording rivers that ran bank-full with tumbling water. But we kept them going.

Not too fast, for the grass was rich and we wanted them to take on weight. Sometimes for days at a time they just grazed north, moving the way buffalo moved, taking a mouthful of grass here, another there, but moving.

Two hundred and fifty head of that stock were mine,
wearing no special brand. Depending on prices, I could
hit the other end of the trail with between five and
seven thousand dollars, and that was a lot of money.
And it was real money, not gambling money.

New grass was turning the prairies gray-green, and
there were bluebonnets massed for miles along the way
the cattle walked, with here and there streaks of yellow
mustard. The grazing was good, and the stock was
taking on weight. If we got through without too much
trouble, we would both make money.

Nothing was ever said about Rice Wheeler. Sometimes I wondered what they thought when they heard
my name called and knew who I was. Bennett ventured
the only comment, about two days out.

I'd cut out to head off a young steer who was getting
ornery and trying to break from the herd. Bennett
helped me turn him back, then turned in alongside me.

"Don't think about Wheeler," he said abruptly. "He
was no good. Best thing ever happened to Rona, when
he took off and never come back."

"Leave of his own accord?"

"No. Folks caught him with some fresh-worked brands
in his herd. He killed a man and left ahead of the
posse."

It was a good crew we had. The oldest of the lot, not
speaking of the boss or the cook, was twenty-six. Two of
the hands had just turned sixteen. And we had fourteen
cow hands in all, seventeen with Bennett, the cook,
and me.

We crossed the Red at Red River Station and pushed
on into the Indian Territory, heading for Wichita.

Twice groups of Indians came down and each time
we gave them a beef. Each time they wanted more, but
they settled without argument.

After crossing the North Canadian we lost a hand in a
stampede. We buried him there, high on a hill where
he could listen to the coyotes and hear the night singing
of the herders. He was seventeen the day he was killed.

The Osage drums were beating, and we held the
herd close. We weren't looking for trouble, but we

knew it could come. Nighttime we slept away from the fire, and we kept two men on watch near camp. We missed a lot of sleep, them days. But we were getting on toward the Kansas line, and things looked good.

When the first cows were coming up to the Cimarron we were attacked by a party of Osages. They came sweeping down on us from a wide-mouthed draw, a bunch of young bucks with more nerve than sense. And they hit us at the wrong time.

Me, the boss, and a tough hand called Mustang Roberts were riding drag. As though by command, we swung around, dropped to the ground, knelt, and took steady aim. Then we waited.

They came on fast, very fast, riding low down on their horses' sides. On signal, we fired.

An Indian fell, his horse catching him in the head with a hoof as he went over him. A horse went down, throwing his rider wide where a bullet from Kid Beaton's Sharps nailed him.

They lost three men and two horses in a matter of seconds, and drew off, deciding they'd had it.

Two days later Mustang went out after antelope and didn't come in. I was in the saddle, so I swung around and picked up his trail. When I'd followed him maybe five miles I heard the boom of a rifle.

It was far off in a bottom somewhere. Taking it fast, I headed toward the sound with that fine new Winchester of mine ready for action.

There were six of them, all Kiowas, and they had Mustang pinned down in a buffalo wallow with his horse dead and a bullet through his leg.

There was no chance for surprise. They would have heard my horse's hoofs drumming on the sod, and they would be ready for me. So I went in fast, the reins looped on the pommel and shooting as I came. I wasn't hitting anything, but I was dusting them some, and they didn't like it.

Maybe I did burn one of them, because he jumped and yelled. Then I went down into that buffalo wallow, riding fast, Mustang covering me. He nailed one of them just as I swung down to the wallow, and then he came up and I slid an arm around his waist as he put a boot in my stirrup.

Surprising thing was, we got away with it. We got clean out of there, with Mustang shooting back at them. Five of us came back later and picked up his saddle. We scouted some, and found a lot of blood on the grass at one point, a little at a couple of others.

"Killed one," Kid Beaton said. "Killed one sure."

And then there were days of dust and driving, and the grass thinning out a little. So we swung wide, taking a longer route, ducking the main trail, finding richer grass to keep the stock up. Twice we stopped and let them loaf and graze two days at a time. Bennett knew cattle, and he knew the markets.

We moved on. Crossing the Kansas line we found a long, shallow valley with good grass and a creek. We moved the herd into the valley and made camp near the creek, upstream from the herd in a bunch of willows and some cottonwoods, big old trees.

We were just finishing chuck when we heard the beat of horses' hoofs and four men rode up.

Mustang put his plate down and glanced over at me. "Watch yourself," he said.

Three of them got down. The leader was a small man with a thin face and quick, shifty eyes. The two backing him were tough, dirty men, one of them a breed.

"My name's Leet Bowers," the leader said. "Come daylight we're cutting your herd."

" 'Fraid you might have picked up some of our cattle . . . by mistake," another man said, grinning.

Bennett was quiet. He was standing there with his feet apart, holding his coffee cup. "Nobody cuts my herd," he said flatly.

Bowers laughed. He had a laugh with no smile in it. "We'll cut it," he said.

When they came up I'd been standing over the coffee pot with a fresh-filled cup. Now I stepped a little away from the fire, still holding the cup. "I don't think so," I said.

Bowers turned to look at me. He turned his head straight around and looked at me out of both eyes, the way a snake does. He had his gun tied down, and it was a Bisley Colt. I remember there was a patch on his vest, sewn with lighter material. The patch was below the heart.

"We've got twenty-five fighting men," he said, and he was measuring me. "We'll cut it, all right."

"You don't need twenty-five," I said, stepping out a bit more from the fire. "You only need one if he's good enough. Otherwise twenty-five couldn't do it, nor fifty. The boys here," I added, "like a fight. Ain't had much fun this trip."

He kept looking at me. Mustang Roberts was off on my right. He had his leg bandaged but there was nothing wrong with his gun hand. Kid Beaton was a little farther over.

"Who're you?" he asked softly.

"My name is Ryan Tyler," I said, "and I own some of these cows."

Leet Bowers's eyes glinted and his tongue touched his lips. He was laughing a little now. "Rye Tyler," he said, "who killed Rice Wheeler and then let Burdette run him out of Colorado."

It was poor shooting light, with only the fire flickering, and the shadows uncertain and strange.

"Burdette never ran me out of anywhere," I said, "but that's no matter. You ain't cutting this herd."

"Burdette ran you out of Colorado," he repeated, a taunt in his tone. "You're yellow!"

My first bullet cut the top of that white patch on his vest, my second notched the bottom of the hole made by the first.

Leet Bowers fell with his head in the fire but he didn't feel it. He was dead.

It happened so fast that nobody had a chance to do anything, but no sooner had the sound of the shots died than Kid Beaton threw down on them with his Sharps. "You boys drag it," he said, and gesturing toward the body, "Take that with you."

"Now," said the cook. He was holding one of those old Colt revolving shotguns. "Or we can bury all of you here."

They dragged Leet Bowers out of the fire and slung
him over his saddle. None of them looked so very spry
and I'd say they'd lost some wind.

Bennett walked toward them. "Don't come near my
herd. If so much as one cow is missing, we'll hunt down
every man jack of you and hang you to the highest tree.
And if there isn't a tree, we'll drag you."

They rode off, drifting mighty quiet.

Mustang Roberts looked around at me, drinking coffee.
"See that? With his left hand, yet. And never spilled
his coffee!"

Bennett turned around to me. "Nice work, Tyler.
I've heard of this man. He killed a rider two months
ago and since then has had everything his own way."

For once I didn't feel bad about a shooting. In Leet
Bowers's eyes there had been something vicious. The
flat, mean look of a man who kills and wants to kill.

Outside of Wichita, bunching the herd, Roberts rode
over to me. "Goin' back to Colorado?"

"Uh-huh."

"Who's this Burdette? Heard something of him?"

"Gunman. Mighty salty, they say."

"Have trouble?"

"Words." I headed a steer back into the herd. "He
had his chance."

"Seems he's talkin'."

"Well," I said, "I'm not hunting trouble. But I am
agoing back."

"Maybe I'll ride along."

"Welcome."

In Wichita Bennett decided to hold his herd for a
better price, and advised me to do the same. "It's down
from what it's been, but there's only a few cows around
and no herd within miles. The price will go up."

"I'm selling," I told him. "I want to go to Colorado."

He nodded, chewing on an unlighted cigar. Then he
took the cigar from his lips and looked at it. "You stay
with me," he said. "We'll make a good thing of this,
then bring another herd from Texas. A few years and
you'll be a rich man."

"Maybe. . . . I don't want to kill a man for every herd, though."

"Won't have to." He gestured south. "By now every herd cutter on the trail knows what happened to Leet Bowers. There'll be no more trouble."

It was there for me. And I liked cattle drives. It was hard, brutal work, but it was strong work, and good work, and a man was doing things. There was talk of taking cattle to Wyoming and Montana, and there was open country up there. New country, fresh country.

But there was a girl in Colorado I kept thinking about. She had been only a youngster then, but by now . . .

"No," I told him. "Thanks anyway. I'm going back."

"Burdette?"

"No. I hope I never see him. It's . . . well, there's somebody there I want to see. And there's that ranch I want."

Two days later I sold for a nice price and left there with more than seven thousand dollars. Some I carried in gold, some in a draft on a St. Louis bank. Mustang Roberts rode along with me.

It was late fall, the air turning crisp and sharp. I liked the feel of it because it reminded me of the high country. We rode west, heading for Dodge.

The new town was at the end of the tracks, and crowded with hide hunters, the buffalo men of the plains country. We crowded up to the bar for a drink, something I rarely did, but I wanted to see how things went in this wild town.

The first person I saw was Billy Dixon, whom I'd known in Kansas City.

"Come with me," he argued. "I'm going out west of here and shoot in the big herd. We can make a fortune in a few months."

"Not me. I don't like to kill."

Dixon glanced at me. I guess Mustang Roberts did, too. My face started getting red, and I told them, "I mean that. I kill for food or if somebody pushes me. Not otherwise."

"Reminds me," Dixon said. "Billy Ogg told me that

gambler we knew, that Charley Woods—Billy said he was killed."

"That so?"

"Must have happened when you were in New Orleans. Chris Lillie was telling the story around that Woods tried to murder some Western man."

"Probably deserved what he got."

I wasn't telling anybody anything. Four men I'd killed now, not counting Indians. It was nothing to be proud of. Nobody but a tinhorn ever scratched notches on his gun, and I never would.

Nor was I wanting to be known as a killer. So far nobody knew about Jack McGarry. That is, it was known in California, but there wasn't too much traffic between the cow and mining camps. The bad men of one group weren't much known to the other.

So far as the public was concerned, I had killed but two men—Rice Wheeler and Leet Bowers. So far, not so many knew about me, although the reputation of the two I'd killed had been such as to make folks believe me a dangerous man.

No man in his right mind wanted such a reputation, which immediately made a man a target for half the would-be gun slingers in the country. And if I were to be known for something, I wanted it to be something of which I could be proud.

"Thinking about you the other day," Dixon continued. "Didn't you tell me you worked for a man named Hetrick? Out in Mason Crossing, Colorado?"

"Uh-huh. Fine man."

"Then you'll be sorry to hear this, but you'd better know it now. He's dead. Ollie Burdette killed him."

10

It took a while for it to sink in. Hetrick almost never carried a gun, and he was a man who never got angry with anybody. He did not believe in killing. He was a stern but gentle man. Yet he was also a man who would not compromise his principles.

Even so, there seemed no way he could have come to trouble with Burdette. He was rarely in town, and he did not loaf when he was there, or drink. He did what business brought him there and left. He was a man who preferred his own family, his own home.

Then I began to think. Hetrick had stood beside me when I made Burdette take water.

To Burdette it would be a galling thing to know that even one man lived who had seen him back down, who had seen him refuse an issue.

That must have been it. Burdette could not rest easy as long as one man knew. And it might even be that Hetrick had heard Burdette's story of running me out of the state and had told the true version of what happened that day on the street.

A thing like that would ride Burdette. His reputation as a dangerous man was all he had. He was an empty man. But he was a killer.

"When did it happen?"

"Four, five months ago."

"I see."

The glass in my fingers still held whisky. I had never cared for it, and suddenly I cared less for it now. Right now I had only one idea: I was going back to Mason Crossing.

Yet it was not Ollie Burdette that I thought of, it was Liza. What about Liza? Where would that leave her?

"You like this town?" I asked Mustang.

"I lost nothing here."

"All right. We're riding."

Billy Dixon went out on the walk and watched us get in the saddle. "You take care of yourself," he warned. "That Burdette's a bad man."

Me, I just waved a hand.

Country slid away behind us. Big, open, grassy, wonderful country. Two days out we saw the big herd, black sea of shifting buffalo as far as the eye could reach. Never saw anything like it. Made my gray plumb skittish, but we circled and come sundown we followed a stream bed through the herd and away.

Country began to get rougher, all cut up with ravines and some high mesas. I was getting so I liked the smell of buffalo-chip fires, although it brought back memories of Pap and the wagon train.

Someday I wanted to go back and find his grave and put a stone marker on it. He would have liked that. But I wouldn't move him. He was always one to say, "let the chips fall where they may." He had fallen there, and he would like to lie there, right in the middle of the West. He could have built himself a good life, Pap could. Sometimes I wondered what would have become of me if he had lived. Probably I'd never have used a gun. I'd have gone to school to be a lawyer or something. A man never knows.

Bennett had tried to tell me one night before I left Wichita that men like me were needed, that the country had to grow up, and it had growing pains, and that all the guns must not be on the bad side. There had to be guns for the right, too.

That I knew. Yet it was a hard thing to be sure one was always on the right, and sometimes there wasn't a chance for figuring out the right and wrong of it when guns started smoking.

We rode on, into rougher, wilder country. One time we had a brush with Comanches. Nobody killed. Mustang downed one of their horses a quarter of a mile away with his Sharps. They didn't figure to like that sort of shootin' and they went to hellin' across the country.

"Never forget you saved my bacon that time," Mustang said, shoving a shell into the breech.

"What time?"

"Them Kiowas. They had me, cold turkey. Horse dead, bullet in my leg, and just three rounds of ammunition left. Then you come arunnin'. Mighty fine sight you made."

"You was late for supper."

Mite of snow came time and again. The country was high now, the weather crisp, the nights cold. There was more brown than green in the grass now, and the cottonwoods looked like tall feathers of gold with their yellow leaves. In the morning there was fog in the low ground, and sometimes it was noon before a man rightly began to feel warmth in the air.

The gray was growing his winter coat. He didn't look so pretty any more, but mighty ragged and tough. He was all horse, that one.

This was a man's country—wide open, big as all creation, and as far as you could look, nothing but rolling miles. Antelope bounded up and away, giving queer jumps. Sometimes a rabbit scurried out of the way, and at night there were coyotes calling the moon.

Once we sighted an Army patrol and went out of our way to get some tobacco and talk a bit. It was a routine patrol. Somebody had seen some Cheyennes, but they turned out to be Shawnees, peaceful, hunting buffalo from the fringe of a small herd.

"We goin' to Denver?" Mustang wanted to know.

"Uh-huh."

"I want to get me a sheep coat. This here wind cuts a man."

All I could think of was Burdette, shooting Hetrick. Time a man like that was sent packing.

I wasn't going to kill him. I was going to do worse. I was going to break him. I was going to bust him right in front of people. I was going to ruin him as a gunman.

The one thing a gunman can't stand is to lose face. Too many men hunting them. Too many men wanting to make a cheap kill. Once they get shown up, it's only a matter of time until they áre killed . . . unless they leave the country.

We reached Denver in late September with snow sifting out of a lead-gray sky. We reached Denver and headed for a hotel. I had money, so we went to the best.

That night I lay in bed thinking, staring wide awake at the ceiling. What did a man come to? Where could a man get, drifting like this? I had a little stake now, and the thing to do was to go someplace and light. Get some roots down. Maybe I should marry.

That thought stopped me a bit. I didn't like to think of being tied down. Not when I might have to ride on at any time. But Logan Pollard had stopped. Good old Logan! I'd sure like to see him. I told myself that and it was true. By now they probably had a family. No time at all since I'd seen them, but it seemed a long while. I was going to be twenty soon, and I'd been through the mill.

Getting up, I went to the washbowl and poured some water and bathed my face. I picked up a towel and dried it and looked at myself in the mirror.

Ryan Tyler, I told myself, there you are. What looked at me was a smooth brown face without any mustache, curly hair brushed back from the forehead, but always inclined to fall over it. A brown face that had strong cheekbones, and a strong jaw, but the eyes were sort of green and there wasn't any smile around the mouth.

That wasn't good. A man should smile. And there

was something a little cold around the eyes. Was I
cold? I didn't feel cold inside. Not a bit.

Never had many friends, but then, I'd drifted too
much, and the few friends I'd had were good ones.
Logan Pollard, Hetrick, and now Mustang Roberts.
Yes, and Billy Dixon, Ogg, and Bennett. Good men
they were, all of them.

But where did that leave me? The one thing I could
do better than most men was the one thing I did not
want to do. Maybe, as Bennett had said, the West
needed its gun fighters. Maybe in a land where there
was no law, some restraint was needed for the lawless.
But I didn't want to be one of them.

What did it get a man, twenty years old and no
smile? Twenty years, and four dead men behind him,
and eyes that were always a little cool, a little remote, a
little watchful. I wanted no more of it. I wanted to get
away, to make an end of it.

But a man does what he has to do. That's why a man
is a man.

I walked back and got into bed and tried to sleep.
When it was daybreak I did sleep for an hour or so.

Outside the ground was two feet deep in snow. In
the streets men were shoveling walks, their breath
smoky in the cold air. It was no time to travel, but it
was no time to stop, either.

"Hetrick's been dead a few months," Roberts argued.
"Take your time. Burdette ain't going nowhere. If he
does, maybe so much the better."

That made sense, and crossing those mountains in
the winter would be no picnic. Even if a man made it,
and the old-timers were smart enough not to try.

Denver was booming those days and gambling was
booming right along with it. Maybe I'd played poker a
mite, but I was no gambling man. Just the same, those
places were wide open and mighty exciting. Maybe,
too, it was because I was still just a boy, although I'd
been caring for myself for a long time now.

So Mustang and me, we made them all. The Morgue,
the Bucket of Blood, the Palace, the Chicken Coop,

and Murphy's Exchange. All of them wide open. Crowded, too.

Soapy Smith was there, a fellow we were to hear a lot about later. Young Bat Masterson was in town, and Doc Halliday drifted through, bound for Texas. Kit Carson was there for some time, and one of the Bents from down New Mexico way.

One night after we got back to the hotel Mustang and me were having supper when he nudged me.

"Rye, there's a dude got his eye on you. He's been studying you for some time now. You ain't been in no trouble back East, have you?"

Mustang, he was a blond fellow with a lean, tough face. No gun slinger, but a mean man to face in a fight, and game as they come. He was also a man very sharp to notice things, so when I could, I glanced around.

This tenderfoot sat across the room. He was a tall man with black hair, gray at the temples, and mighty handsome. Maybe he was fifty years old, but dressed real fine. When I looked around he saw me and our eyes held for a moment, and then he got up and started across the room.

I wasn't duded up as I had been in New Orleans. My fancy clothes were all packed away. Nonetheless, I didn't look so bad, I guess. I had on those black calfskin boots, a gray wool shirt with a black string tie, and a black, braided short coat that I'd picked up in Texas. It was cut Mexican style. And I had on my gray pants, tucked into my boots.

Without looking again, I tried to place the stranger. He might be a gambler, but somehow that didn't fit, either. And at a quick glance my guess was that he wasn't packing a gun.

He paused alongside the table. "I beg your pardon. My name is Denison Mead."

I got up. "I'm Ryan Tyler," I said, "and this here's Mustang Roberts. Will you sit down?"

"Thank you." He sat down and motioned for his bottle of wine to be brought to our table. "I'm a lawyer," he said, "representing a mining company. I've been looking over some gold properties."

"Sounds prosperous. I've been dealing in cows."

"Texas?"

"Lately."

We talked a mite, just casual conversation. He had nothing to say about his reason for joining us. He was pleasant enough, yet I had an idea he was fishing for something, something he wanted to know. He didn't ask many questions, but he had a way of getting a man to talk. But I hadn't played poker for nothing. I wasn't going to tell him anything more than I wanted to. On the other hand, I'd nothing to conceal.

"This country your home? Or is it Texas?"

"I'm drifting," I said. "No home, properly speaking, but I aim to get a little home over in the mountains. A ranch, I've got in mind."

He looked at me thoughtfully. "About twenty? Or twenty-one?"

"Twenty," I said.

We talked some of cattle, and he gathered I'd recently been in Kansas City and New Orleans.

"Were you born out here?"

It came quickly, but it slid into the conversation in such a way that I became suspicious. Something about the way he said it made me believe this was what he had been planning to ask all the time.

I was getting uneasy. That shooting in New Orleans, now. That was off my home grounds, and they looked at things different there than out here. Unless somebody had stolen the gun, they would have found Woods with a pistol in his hand, but no telling what Chris Lillie might tell the law. Still, he was apt to tell them nothing. Not his kind.

"No, sir," I said finally, "I was born in Maryland. Or so my pap told me. Lived in New York when I was a boy, then in Missouri and Kansas."

"You've traveled a good bit." He paused, and me, I'm good at reading sign. I can read it on faces as well as on the ground, and that's why I play a fair game of poker. And right then I had a feeling this was another question he'd been building up to.

"You've no home," he said. "Wouldn't you say your home was where your parents were?"

"Ma died on the way West," I explained. "Pap was killed by Indians when I was twelve."

"So. I've heard of such stories," he commented. "I guess they're a part of the West. Men have to die to build any country strong. All of them don't die in battle, though."

"Pap did," I said, and then I told him about it. Mustang had never heard the story, either, but he heard it now. How Ma took sick and didn't really have no decent care, though Pap did the best he could. Then she died and when she was buried we started on West. I told him all that, and I told him about the last few hours, about the wagon train leaving us, about the fight in the ravine. But I didn't tell them about what I did to the Indians, or about Jack McGarry.

He was a pleasant man, easy to talk to, and he was friendly. I told him about Logan Pollard, and about reading Plutarch.

"And did you read it five times?"

"Only four, so far. But I'll get to it."

"And this place you're going to . . . Mason Crossing? Do you intend to stay there for a while?"

"Prob'ly," I said, "but I might move on."

After he left us I did some thinking about it. No law that I knew about was looking for me. Woods was killed in self-defense, and he was no account, anyway. Those days, men like him didn't attract much notice when they died. Everybody figured the country was saved a hanging. Nevertheless, this talk worried me some.

Tired of hanging around gambling joints, I bought a dozen books and lay on my bed in my room through the long cold days and read. Outside the wind blew a lot, and every other day or so it snowed. All the passes were closed and nobody was traveling. The streets sounded with the jingle of sleigh bells and the stoves in the saloons glowed cherry red.

At night sometimes we sat around a big stove in the lobby and yarned. I didn't talk much, but I liked to listen. There were mining men and cattlemen there, gamblers, drifters, and businessmen. There were drummers and cattle buyers, and men just looking for something to put money into. Most of them had been around a lot and they talked well.

Up in my room I read a couple of books by an English writer named Dickens, and I read the *Scarlet Letter*, by Hawthorne. There was some poetry, too, by an English writer named Byron. This I liked a mighty lot.

One day when I came back to the hotel that lawyer was waiting for me. Mustang was out somewhere, but this fellow was sitting in a big leather chair in the almost empty lobby.

He seemed anxious to talk private, so we went upstairs, and when my room door was closed, he turned on me. "Tyler, I've been hearing some talk. Don't go back to Mason Crossing."

This stopped me flat-footed, but I waited a long minute and then said, "Why not?" And I was pretty cool, for I want no stranger butting into my affairs.

"Burdette will kill you."

"I doubt it. Anyway," I looked him right in the eye, "I'm going back."

He said no more about that, walking up and down the room a couple of times. Then suddenly he stopped and looked at me. "How many men have you actually killed, Tyler?"

"None of your business."

He looked at me for a long time, his eyes sort of searching my face. Yet there was something friendly about it all, and something worried, too. Almost as if he had an interest.

"Of course," he agreed finally, "you're right. It is none of my business. Only . . . well, no matter."

He crossed to the door. "Whatever you do, take care of yourself. And you may hear from me."

He went out and the next day I heard he had taken the stage for Cheyenne. Nobody in town knew much about him except that he had been investigating the titles to some mining claims, and he had looked over some prospects. At least, looked them over as much as he could with the weather what it was.

Two days later the cold spell broke and I shook Mustang out of a sleep.

"Pack up, man. We're riding."

He didn't argue any. I expect town was getting on his nerves, too. Anyway, within the hour we were riding out of town, headed west.

The route we had taken swung south by way of Durango, and as the thaw was on, we made good time.

We reached Durango late at night and the next morning I found a squaw who had been making buckskin breeches, and I bought some. I was beginning to feel as if I belonged again.

This was my country. I liked the largeness of it, the space, the sharp, clear mountain air, and the riding. When I had a ranch it was going to be a horse ranch.

While we rode west I told Mustang about this Denison Mead, and what he had said about staying away from Mason Crossing.

"Mighty good advice," Roberts agreed, "but what's he takin' on so about?"

"Can't figure that—unless he knows Burdette."

"Ain't that. But he was askin' a lot of questions about you."

We forgot about that during the day, for we were coming up to my old country again, and somewhere ahead was the ranch, and I'd be seeing Liza again. To say nothing of Old Blue. And Mrs. Hetrick was almost like my own mother. It had been a long time. Too long. And Hetrick was dead.

Those last few miles before we reached the ranch sure fretted me. Finally I started the gray into a trot, and Mustang, he came right along with me. When the town came in sight I cut around back of it toward the ranch. I could hardly wait to see the place, and to see Mrs. Hetrick and Liza.

The gray was almost at a run when I rounded to the gate. We went through, and then I pulled up.

Grass grew in the dooryard and there were tumble-weeds against the fence. The porch was sagging and the door banged on loose hinges. A low wind moaned among the pines and around the eaves, and I stood there looking around, a big empty feeling inside me.

I got down from the saddle and walked slowly through the house. She was empty. The folks were gone, and from the look of things, they had been gone for a long time.

Inside I felt as empty as the house, and when a long wind with a touch of snow on it came down off the mountain, I shivered. The gate at the garden creaked and banged, and I stood there, sick and empty. Liza was gone.

11

The Crossing was built up some. I could see that as we rounded into the main street. It was built up, and Mason's Store was bigger. There was a long awning in front of the rooming house and it had become a two-story hotel.

Thinking suddenly, I turned aside and rode around to the cemetery. Mustang, he trailed along, never leaving me.

At the cemetery gate I got down and went in. It was like so many of those Western cemeteries, a high knoll outside of town with the wind blowing across it and tumbleweeds racked against the fences.

And I found what I was looking for, and more. Hetrick's grave, and beside it the grave of his wife, who had died just four months later.

Both gone.

And Liza? She might still be in town, although somehow I was sure she wasn't.

"Mustang," I said, "I got to get me a man. But I don't aim to kill him, not unless I have to. I want you to go down to town. You be careful, because this Burdette is mighty mean. But you listen around and find out if he's still there, and where he is. I want to come on him unexpected-like. I want to get the jump."

Sitting under some cedars there by the graveyard, with the gray grass alongside me, I waited. Maybe I slept some. Anyway, lights were coming on in town before Mustang came back.

The chill had awakened me, and when I sat up I heard his horse. He rode up to the gate and got down, then he walked over and squatted on his heels and began to build a smoke.

"Burdette's there, all right. Mighty mean, like you say. The folks got no use for him, but he's still marshal and they're scared. Ever' night about this time he makes his rounds. Then he goes to the saloon and sits until everybody turns in. He makes another round, then he turns in himself.

"Come morning, he goes up to the restaurant for breakfast, and he sits around some. He killed another man about two weeks ago, and I got an idea the town would like to get shut of him."

"You eat?"

"Uh-huh."

"I ain't hungry. I think we'd best bed down right here. I want to get him in the morning at breakfast."

"Good. The restaurant has a back door, too. You want I should come in and get the drop?"

"No. You leave it alone unless somebody tries to butt in. This is my branding. I'll heat my own irons and make my own mark."

When we were all rolled up in our blankets and lying there listening to the town sounds, he said, all of a sudden, "That girl? Liza Hetrick? She left town six, seven months ago. And she only had sixty-three dollars. Took the stage out. West."

"You should have been a Pinkerton."

Mustang drew on his cigarette. "Maybe I will be." He chuckled. "But first we find your gal."

Morning found us with our beds rolled and ready. We took the trail down into town and went through

streets and alleys until Mustang could show me the
back door to the restaurant. Then we rode past it.

"We may have to leave fast," I said.

Mustang chuckled dryly. "You leave. I'll be right
behind you, maybe ahead of you."

We got down and tied our horses and went inside.
Mustang went through the door first with me right
behind him, my head down.

There were four people in the restaurant: the woman
who ran it, old Mason, who sat at a table alone, and two
cow hands in from the forks of the creek.

Four people besides Burdette. He was sitting behind
a table facing the door.

When we got three steps inside the door Mustang
sidestepped and I was looking into those mean, slate-
gray eyes of Ollie Burdette's.

He was surprised. That was plain. And he never got a
chance to get over it. I walked right up to his table
because he didn't like it close up. I walked right up,
and I had only two steps to make to get there, and then
I spoke up, loud and clear.

"Burdette, you murdered Hetrick. That old man never
packed a gun in his life. And you told it around that you
had run me out of town. That's why you killed him,
because he knew you were a liar. He saw you take
water that time."

He hadn't no time to get his mouth open. Me, I just
kept shoving it at him, and when he started to drop his
hand, I slammed against the table and smashed him
back against the wall. And then I slapped him twice
across the mouth, once with each hand.

Suddenly I was mad. I was mad clean through, but
not killing mad. I just wanted to destroy everything he
was or thought he was.

It had been a complete surprise, shocking to Ollie
Burdette, and my lunge against the table had pinned
his gun holster.

But suddenly I jerked the table away and stepped in.
He grabbed for his gun, but I hit him. He staggered
and I swung a boot from the floor and kicked his gun

loose. It fell, and as he grabbed for it, I hit him in the face.

He put his hands up and rushed at me, but he was a man who had trusted to guns. Big as he was—and he was heavier than me—he was no fighter. I hit him in the belly, then on the side of the face. That last blow cut deep and knocked him around, smashing his head against the edge of the table.

He got no chance at all from me. No more than he had given some of the men he killed. I grabbed him by the collar and back-walked him to the door, slapping him across the face at every step. Then I shoved him out of the door and into the street.

He fell in the dust, and fell hard. Then he lunged to his feet, but he didn't know which way to turn. He was caught without a gun, and without a gun he was nothing. He started to back up, and I went after him.

Walking him back across the street, I slapped him. He tried to fight back, striking at me, trying to knock my hands down. A time or two he hit me, but he had been sitting around taking it easy while I had been riding, working, roughing it.

In front of the saloon, with fifty men looking on, I knocked him down. He got up and rushed me, and I hit him in the mouth, smashing his lips into his teeth. He backed up, bloody and beaten. I walked up to him and, throwing one from the hip, knocked him down again. Then I picked him up and tossed him bodily into the water trough. Then I fished him out and stood him up against it.

"You murdered Hetrick. You might as well have murdered his wife. You bragged around that you run me out. You're just a two-bit bad man in a four-bit town."

He couldn't talk. His wind was gone and his mouth was all blood and torn lips.

"You got a horse?" I looked around at Old Man Mason, who had followed us. "Where's his horse?"

"I'll get it." The voice was familiar, and I looked around. It was Kipp.

Burdette stood there, soaked to the hide and shivering.

He shook his head like a wounded bear. It had all
happened so fast that he hadn't no time to get set for it.
Right then I don't think he had realized yet what was
happening to him. Too long he had lorded it around,
doing it all on the strength of his gun. And now he had
no gun.

When Kipp came up with the horse, I told Burdette
to get into the saddle. "Now ride. And don't stop riding
until the week is gone."

"I got property," he protested, able to talk at last. "I
got stuff at the house."

"You lose it," I said, "like Hetrick lost his ranch."

He stared at me, and those poison-mean eyes were
shocked and dull. "Don't I get a gun? Without a gun
my life ain't worth a plugged nickel."

"No more than the lives of some of those you killed.
You get no gun."

He never said anything more. He just walked his
horse off down the street and out of town. Somebody
gave a halfhearted cheer, but not much of one. Trouble
was, they were shocked, too.

"Kipp," I said, "where'd Liza go?"

"Don't know, Rye. She wouldn't take any help. After
her ma died she aimed to take care of herself. She
didn't get much out of the ranch. After Hetrick was
killed, the horse thieves stole them blind. All I know is,
she bought a ticket for Alta. She would have had about
forty dollars left when she got there."

Mustang and me, we mounted up and rode out of
town that night. There was nothing at the Crossing for
me now, and Mustang, he just seemed to want to stay
along with me. And no man had a better friend.

We never talked any about being partners. We never
said much of anything to each other. We just rode
together and shared together, and that was the way of
it.

Alta was a boom mining town, half across the state of
Utah. It wasn't a Mormon town, being populated mostly
by gentile miners from Nevada or Colorado. Many had
been working on the Comstock Lode and some had
come down from Alder Gulch, Montana.

Enjoy the best of Louis L'Amour in special volumes made to last as long as your pleasure

As a reader of Louis L'Amour's tough and gritty tales of the Old West, you'll be delighted by <u>The Louis L'Amour Collectio</u> a series of hardcover editions of Louis L'Amour's exciting Western adventures.

The feel of rich leathers. Like a good saddle, these volumes are made to last—to be read, re-rea and passed along to family and friends for years to come. Bound in rugged sierra-brown simulated leather with gold lettering, <u>The Louis L'Amour Collection</u> will be a handsom addition to your home library.

<u>*Silver Canyon*</u> opens the series. It's the memorable tal of Matt Brennan, gunfighter, and his lone battle against du ling ranchers in one of the bloodiest range wars the West had ever seen. After <u>*Silver Canyon*</u> you'll set out on a new adventure every month, as succeeding volumes in the Collection are conveniently mailed to your home.

Receive the full-color Louis L'Amour Western Calendar FREE—just for looking at <u>*Silver Canyon*</u>. Like every volume in <u>The Louis L'Amour Collection</u>, <u>*Silver Canyon*</u> is yours to examine without risk or obligation. If you're not satisfied, return it within 10 days and owe nothing. The calendar is yours to keep.

Send no money now. Simply complete the coupon oppo site to enter your subscription to <u>The Louis L'Amour Colle tion</u> and receive your free calendar.

The newest volume...

The newest volume I placed on the shelf of my 8000-volume home research library was very special to me—the first copy of _Silver Canyon_ in the hardcover Collector's Edition put together by the folks at Bantam Books.

I'm very proud of this new collection of my books. They're handsome, permanent and what I like best of all, affordable.

I hope you'll take this opportunity to examine the books in the Collection and see their fine quality for yourself. I think you'll be as pleased as I am!

Louis L'Amour

Send no money now–but mail today!

☐ **YES!** Please send me _Silver Canyon_ for a 10-day free examination, along with my free Louis L'Amour Calendar, and enter my subscription to <u>The Louis L'Amour Collection</u>: If I decide to keep _Silver Canyon_, I will pay $7.95 plus shipping and handling and receive one additional volume per month on a fully returnable, 10-day free-examination basis. There is no minimum number of books to buy, and I may cancel my subscription at any time. The Calendar is mine whether or not I keep _Silver Canyon_.   85019

☐ I prefer the deluxe edition, bound in genuine leather, at only $24.95 each plus shipping and handling.   87015

Name _____ _(please print)_

Address _____

City _____ State _____ Zip _____

In Canada, mail to:
Bantam Books Canada, Inc.
60 St. Clair Avenue East, Suite 601
Toronto, Ontario M4T 1N5

THE BETTMANN ARCHIVE   1J

BUSINESS REPLY MAIL

FIRST CLASS   PERMIT NO. 2154   HICKSVILLE, NY

Postage will be paid by addressee:

The

Louis L'Amour

Collection

Bantam Books
P.O. Box 956
Hicksville, New York 11801

I'd been hearing about Alta. It was a sure-enough mean town, where they killed men every night and mostly every day. The mines were rich and the town was booming. It was wide open and ararin'.

Never before had I had much of any place to go, or any purpose in life. Now I had one. I was going to find Liza. I was going to make sure she was doing all right. It wasn't right for a girl of seventeen to be traipsing around rough country on her own. No telling what had happened to her.

Right then I thought some mighty fierce thoughts, and I angered up some, just thinking things that might have happened to her.

It was snowing when we rode into town and stabled our horses. The first thing to do was to find a place to sleep, but I left that to Mustang and started for a saloon.

The saloon was the club, the meeting place, the clearing house for information. In a mining camp or a cow town the same rule held true, and often enough the company would include many who drink little or nothing at all.

The snow was falling fast, and except in the street, churned into mud by the passing of men, horses, and heavy wagons, the ground rapidly grew white. Huge ore wagons dragged by, their shouting drivers bundled up against the cold, their huge horses or oxen leaning into the harness as they strained against great loads.

A music box was going up the street, and in the feeble light of a lantern behind a saloon a man was splitting wood.

When I pushed open the door of the Bucket of Blood I was met by a wave of hot air, thick with tobacco smoke and the sour odor of bad whisky. At least a hundred men crowded the small room, standing three deep at the bar. Bearded men loafed along the walls, leaning or squatting and watching for a favorable moment to grab a chair.

This was a familiar scene, and I had known it before, in other towns. There were even familiar faces, men whose names I didn't know, but whom I had seen in

Denver, Santa Fe, or Mason Crossing. There was even
one I knew from New Orleans.

Moving through the crowd, I was lucky enough to
get close to the bar. Beside me two men talked
Norwegian, and down the bar I heard a man order in
German, and the bartender replied in the same language.
This was the West, a melting pot, a conglomeration.
These were hard, tough, reckless men from all over the
world, following the lure of a wild new country and
quick riches in the mines.

No telling what had happened to Liza here. Maybe
she had seen the place and what it was like and had
gone on. Certainly this town was no place for a pretty
girl alone.

Two hours later I was no closer to finding her. True,
I wasn't asking questions. I was listening, drifting from
place to place, keeping my eyes open. The stage station
was closed, so I couldn't check there.

Snow kept falling. The Gold Miner's Daughter was
jammed when Mustang found me there.

"Got a place," he said, "and it wasn't easy. This town
is crowded."

We drifted around the tables. We had a drink, and I
played a little roulette and lost fifteen dollars, then won
five of it back.

Turning toward the door, I saw a man stop and take
another look at me, then walk on. He knew me from
somewhere.

All of a sudden, somebody swore, men jammed back
out of the way, and a gun blasted.

It was that quick, and all over. A man in digging
clothes was backing up slowly, both hands holding his
stomach. He sat down and rolled over, moaning softly.

The gambler with the gun in his hand walked around
the table and stood over him. Coolly he lifted his pistol
for another shot.

Me, I don't know why I did it, but I stepped from
the crowd.

"He's dying. Leave him alone."

The gambler was in his shirt sleeves and vest. He
was a tall, pale man with a mustache. His eyes held

uch cruelty as I've never seen before. He looked coolly
t me.

"You're making it your business?"

He held a derringer in his hand. It was one of those
hort guns with two barrels, each holding a .44 cartridge.

"I am."

He looked at me. His gun was in his hand, half lifted.
Mine was in my holster. Yet he had one shot left, and if
he did not kill me with that shot, he was a dead man.

He shrugged. "He'll die, anyway. No use to shoot
gain."

The man on the floor coughed heavily and stared at
he gambler. "Cheat . . . You cheat . . ." and then he
agged back on the floor and died.

He wore a gun, all right, but it was buttoned under
his coat. He'd had no chance at all.

"He lies," the gambler said contemptuously. "He just
ouldn't take losing."

"He sure didn't have that gun where he could use
t," I said.

The gambler was turning away, but now he swung
round to face me, his face livid. "You keep your mouth
hut!" he shouted. "I've taken all I'm going to."

"If I was the law in this town," I said, "you'd be on
he first stage out. And you'd never show your face in
own again. This was murder. He had no chance, none
t all."

The derringer started to lift, coming up slowly. And
ust when I was going to take my chance and draw, I
heard Mustang's voice.

"His gun ain't drawed, mister . . . but mine is!"

And it was. The gambler didn't like that big six
ooking at him. He shrugged and turned sharply away.

"You push your luck, stranger," a miner said quietly.
That's Key Novak. He's killed three men in the past
wo months."

With Mustang at my side I turned away and walked
ut, leaving the Gold Miner's Daughter and starting up
he street. We had taken only a few steps when a door
losed behind us and we heard footsteps on the walk.

Flattening into a doorway with my gun in my hand, I

watched three men coming down the walk. Mustang was standing on the other side, half behind a water trough and an awning post. A frozen water barrel offered added protection.

The men drew abreast and in the light from a nearby window I recognized the man who had appeared to recognize me in the saloon. They stopped, and this man spoke. "Tyler, you don't know me, but I used to see you around Kansas City. Heard about you from Billy Dixon."

"So?"

"I heard you were the man who killed Rice Wheeler? And Leet Bowers?"

"That's right."

"Tyler, we want a marshal in this town. One who will clean out the crooked gamblers and the thugs. We had two knife killings last night. We don't know who did them. We had a miner killed last week. The crooks are running the town. We'll give you two hundred and fifty a month to clean up for us."

This was a surprise. I'd never fancied myself as the law before. On the other hand, there would be no better way to look the town over for Liza.

"All right," I said, "but I want Mustang as deputy."

"As you like." He hesitated. "My name is Murdock. I own the general store. This is Eph Graham, agent for Wells Fargo. Newton here has the hardware store and the mining supplies. We're the town council."

"All right."

"One thing . . . the present marshal is John Lang. He's the Texas gunman. He has to be fired."

My eyes went over the three of them. A wagon was passing in the street and the clop-clop of the heavy hoofs in the stiffening mud was loud. "I fire him?" I asked. Newton looked uneasy, and Murdock shifted his feet, but Graham nodded.

"He's dangerous . . . and we think he's with the crooks."

Gesturing toward the crowded saloons, I said, "This won't be easy. Suppose somebody gets hurt?"

"We'll back you. Organize vigilantes if you want them."

"We won't need them."

Murdock took some badges from his pocket and handed hem to me. I shook my head. "These are all right, but want a signed paper, appointing us. Signed by all hree of you."

They gave it to me and I was the new marshal of lta, with Mustang Roberts as deputy.

They walked away and we stood there getting used to he idea. Mustang, he looked over at me and grinned. Like 'em tough, don't you?" Then he added, "Now we an really look for your girl."

"What I was figuring," I said, "so let's get busy."

He hitched his guns. "What's first?"

"We fire the marshal. Rather, I fire him. You stand y."

So we turned around and walked down the street oward the marshal's office and I was glad Mustang oberts walked beside me.

12

It was a square frame building in front of the stone jail
It had two rooms: the outer office, and an inner room
where the marshal slept.

John Lang was sitting behind the desk with his fee
on it, and there was another man, a bearded man, wh
sat on an iron safe against the wall.

The floor was dirty, a few scattered cigar and ciga
rette butts lying around, and some old papers, flyspecke
and yellow. There was a rack holding several rifles an
shotguns.

Pushing the door open, I stepped in. Lang looked u
at me, then looked again. He saw that badge on m
shirt and his face set and his eyes grew wary.

"Who're you?"

"The new marshal. I'm to tell you you're fired."

The bearded man chuckled. "You git out'n here, kic
whilst you're able. Ain't nobody firin' us. They don
tried. Ain't they, Hal?"

With some people you don't talk, you don't explair
I'd told 'em; now it was up to me to fire 'em.

Before Lang knew what was happening, I grabbed
he boots on the desk and slammed them to the floor.
His boots hit the floor and he came up with a lunge,
but the advantage was mine, and I kept it. As he
clawed for his gun I hit him in the mouth and he sat
back down in the chair so hard it toppled over backward.

It happened so fast the deputy scarcely got his mouth
open, and he had just started to move when I turned
with the punch and hit him in the teeth, slamming his
skull against the wall with a dull thud.

He was stunned when Mustang grabbed him. As I
swung back, Lang's gun was coming free. So I palmed
mine and shot him. He took the first bullet in the
throat and the second in the chest, and he just lay back
on the floor and stayed there.

Then I turned on the deputy, whom Mustang had
disarmed. "You're fired, too. You want to take a chance
and draw, or do you want to get out of town?"

He wanted to draw but he didn't want to die. He
stared hard at me, sweating it out for a full minute, and
then he said, "Soon's the storm's over I'll ride."

"You'll ride now. Storm or no storm. If you're in
town an hour from now, you can die or go to jail."

He swallowed, backing off. "Wait'll you hear from
Billings! You won't get away with this! Why, he'll break
you! He'll break that damn town council, too."

So I hit him again. "Beat it," I said, and he beat it.

Mustang, who had been holding the deputy's gun,
ready to return it if he decided to gamble, put it in a
desk drawer.

He took out the makings and rolled a smoke. "You
know," he said, "when you first joined up back there in
Texas, some of the boys thought you were a sure-
enough tenderfoot. They should have seen what I seen."

I looked around the dirty little office. It was nothing
that would make a man respect the law. I looked over
at Roberts. "You, you're my deputy. We enforce the
law. We enforce it tough. We don't shoot anybody
unless we have to, we don't hit anybody unless we have
to. But we only give an order once.

"No card cheating. No robbery. No burglary. No

robbing drunks. No beating up innocent people. No
gun fights. No women molested."

"Fist fights?"

"As long as they don't bust up property. If the match
looks pretty even, let 'em have it out. If it gets one-
sided, stop it.

"We protect the helpless, the innocent, and the folks
who are doing legitimate business."

"All right." He glanced at Lang's body. "I guess I
better get him out of here."

"No. We'll let Billings do that."

"Who?"

"Billings. From what the deputy said, he figures he's
boss. We'll let him take Lang out and dig the grave.
We'll let him mop up the floor."

Mustang Roberts drew a deep breath. He looked at
me to see if I was serious, but he needn't have. He'd
known me long enough to know I didn't talk idle.

"This will be something to see." He hesitated. "I
ain't told you before, but this here Billings may know
something about your girl."

That stopped me. I felt myself getting sick inside. In
town only a few hours, I'd heard enough to know that
Billings ran the houses where the red-light women
were. I knew he ran two of the toughest saloons. Men
leaving those saloons with money seldom got far.

"Don't get me wrong," Mustang added. "It's nothing
definite. Only he was seen talking to her, and he was
taking a powerful interest in her. That was right after
she got off the stage."

"All right. First things first. We'll let Billings bury
his dead."

Billings was a big man. He was a man with black,
plastered-down hair on a round skull, a wide face, florid
of complexion, and a black walrus mustache, but trimmed
more neatly than most. He stood about three inches
over six feet, and he must have weighed well over two
hundred pounds. He wore a striped silk shirt with
sleeve garters and black pants. He smoked a big black
cigar and he carried his gun in a holster shoved down in
his waistband. It was good for a fast draw.

His place was smaller than some and dirtier than most, but there were a dozen games going when we pushed through the door bringing a blast of cold, fresh air into the stuffy interior. I walked over to him. "Billings?"

He turned to look at me and his eyes dropped to the badge, then lifted. "You show that to John Lang?"

"Yes." I spoke quietly. "It was the last thing he ever saw."

You could have heard a feather drop in that room. You couldn't hear a breath drawn. The idea was beginning to work its way through their heads. That Texas gunman was gone. John Lang was dead.

Mustang Roberts was obviously another Texan. About me, they didn't know. They were going to learn fast.

Billings took the cigar from his teeth. "I see. Let's go into my office and have a talk."

"We haven't time. Lang is lying on the floor in my office and he needs burying. Also, the floor needs mopping."

He looked at me, his hard pale-blue eyes measuring me. He didn't like what he saw.

"So?"

"So you'll do it."

Somebody swore. I saw a man with cards in his hand lay them down. I saw his smile begin to grow, and I saw his eyes wrinkle with humor. All this I saw from the corners of my eyes. I was watching Billings.

He looked at me. Never had I seen a pair of eyes like that. They were careful eyes. Very hard eyes, but careful. This was the most dangerous man I had seen. Yet I doubted if this man would kill. He would see that it was done by someone else. He was too careful to risk it.

That was what I thought then. I was wrong, but it seemed like that.

"Kid, you don't know what you're talking about. John did all right in this town. He could have got rich. You can, too. Together, we can run it."

"I don't need you," I said. "I'm running it now, and I'm running it honest."

He looked at his cigar. He was doing some fast thinking.

"The council wouldn't stand for this," he said. "I know they wouldn't."

"It will be too late for them to object. You're starting now."

His temper exploded then. "Like hell I am! Why you damn fool, I—"

Right then I hit him. My fist cut his words off, and before he could get set, I hit him again. This he had not expected. Gunfighters rarely used their hands, and he was a powerful man who outweighed me by a good fifty pounds.

My second punch knocked him back against the bar, and then I kicked him on the kneecap with a boot heel.

He went down then. He hit right in his dirty sawdust. I reached a hand for him and he grabbed at it with both of his, as I'd expected. And then I hit him on the cheekbone with a short right.

The skin split as if I'd used a knife, and blood started to trickle. Then I stepped back for him to get up. His hand started for his gun but a voice stopped him. "Don't try it, Ben. That's Ryan Tyler."

Something inside him seemed to relax and he sat back down on the floor. It bothered me, because he was a man who could control his emotions. He hated me. He wanted me dead. But he was a careful man.

It was ten to one his games were rigged.

"All right," I said, "you've got a dirty job to do."

Mustang had two guns out and he was looking across them at the room, smiling that tough, reckless smile of his.

"Get used to him, boys. It'll be easier for you. I came up the trail from Texas with him. I seen him kill Leet Bowers. I seen him trim Ollie Burdette down to size and run him out of town. Get used to the idea. He means what he says."

Ben Billings got up slowly and carefully. "Can't we talk this over?"

"No," I said, and motioned him to the door.

"I'll get my coat."

"You won't need it. You'll be warm enough, working the way you will be."

We went, but we weren't alone. Half the place came along to see this. Ben Billings had been boss of the town. He had been the big boss. He had been his own bouncer, often throwing two men out of his saloon at once. He had ordered men killed. He had ordered men beaten. A few he had beaten thoroughly and cruelly with his own hands.

They saw him take the body of John Lang outside. They saw him get water and mop the floor of the marshal's office. And by the time he was through there were three or four hundred people in the street.

This was more than a cleanup job. This was to show the people of Alta that Billings wasn't as big as he had made them believe. It was to show them that a new system had been born. And there were few disapproving looks in the crowd, even from his own followers.

There was an old coat that had belonged to Lang in the office. There were gloves and a hat. "Put these on," I said. "You'll need them digging the grave."

"The ground's frozen!" he protested. "You couldn't dig a grave in a week."

"I hope it doesn't take you that long," I said, "because you'll be mighty tired by that time."

He dug the grave. It was cold and brutal work, with the pick just breaking the ground in tiny flakes. It took him two days and two nights, with time out for meals, and an hour's sleep I allowed him at three intervals. He dug it with Mustang and me spelling each other in two hour tricks.

By the time that grave was dug, the town knew who was marshal. Me, I went back downtown and started checking the gambling joints. We found a controlled wheel in one of Billings' joints, and when Mustang brought in an ax I busted the table right in front of their eyes.

Two more wheels showed evidence of hasty correction. I let them go. "Just keep 'em that way," I said. "You can live on the percentage."

Key Novak was sitting behind his table waiting for

us. He looked up at me out of those cold, almost white eyes. Only the look in them was different now. It is one thing when you look at an unknown stranger who is scarcely more than a boy. It is another when you look into those same eyes and know the man is fast with a gun, perhaps faster than you.

Key Novak looked up at me and waited. He hated me, and he was a gunman. He was also a sure-thing operator.

"You got a horse?" I asked him.

"Yes."

"Use him, then, or sell him and take the stage. Your game is closed as of now."

He looked up at me, and I saw his eyelids tighten, the corners of his mouth grow white. He wanted to draw, and he had killed men.

But John Lang had tried it, and John Lang was dead.

"It'll be different with you." I spoke quietly, but there was no mercy in me for the man who had killed a miner and would have shot into him as he lay on the floor. "I'll take your gun away and make you dig your own grave."

He looked at me, his face whiter than I had believed a man's face could be. And then his hands started to shake and there was a glisten of sweat on his brow and upper lip. He got up shakily, and then he walked quickly from the room.

We were keeping our ears open as we worked the town over, but there was no word of Liza anywhere.

Then one night a man lurched up to me on the street. He was acting drunk, but he was cold sober when he spoke. "Heard you asking about a girl named Liza Hetrick. You take a look at that place of Billings' up the canyon."

I grabbed him. "She out there?"

"Word to the wise," he said hoarsely. "You take a look."

13

Ben Billings' canyon place was six miles out. It was a winding mountain trail, and I took it fast. The gray had been eating his head off and was ready to go, even in that cold. And it was pushing right close to zero.

It was night when I started, the stars so bright they hurt, the night clear and brittle, the snow crunching underfoot and scintillating with a million tiny brilliants. I liked the look of it, liked it fine. Only I wasn't thinking of snow, I was thinking of Liza.

Once I had the gray warmed up a little, I kept him at a fast walk. I didn't want him working up a sweat on a cold night.

Aside from my Smith & Wesson pistols and my rifle, I was carrying a sawed-off shotgun from the marshal's office. It was one of those Colt revolving shotguns that fire four shots. That one I had slung under the buffalo coat that hung to my knees.

One .44 was thrust down into my waistband where I could draw it without pushing the coat back. But I wasn't figuring on it too much.

Leaving the trail when I sighted a light up ahead, I turned off into the trees. When I had walked my horse close, I could see through the top of the window, and there was a woman sitting with her back to me, sitting in a rocker. She was a young woman and the hair was the right color.

It looked mighty peaceful, mighty quiet. But when a man has lived as I'd lived, he begins to mistrust the looks of things. He gets cautious, if you know what I mean. And me, I didn't like the look of that frost on the window. There wasn't enough of it.

A body who was a mite suspicious might believe just enough had been scraped away so a man could see in, so he could see just what he was supposed to see.

Getting down from my horse, I walked away through the snow. There was a window on the north side, too. It was frosted to within an inch of the top. So right then I did some fast thinking.

A man going into a tight corner would first investigate the stable, and be mighty careful about it. A man would approach the door only after he was sure the girl was alone.

So I did investigate the stable. There were two horses in it, which meant nothing, because the rig I'd seen outside was a cutter for a two-horse team. There was some harness there, but there was no dampness on the horses, and no snow anywhere in that stable. There were no recent tracks near the stable or the house. But I was getting an idea.

From the window I could see a door, maybe to the kitchen. But I couldn't see anything that was on this side of the entrance. If a man entered and was suspicious, he would watch that kitchen door.

If this was a trap, it was a good one laid by smart men who knew what they were doing, and who knew the sort of man I was. But I hadn't come out all that way just to ride back. Anyway, I always believed in taking the bull by the horns.

So I opened the door and stepped in without knocking, but I didn't just step over the threshold and stop. I ducked low and jumped four feet into the room, then spun a chair around and faced the corner I couldn't see from the outside.

It was covered with a red blanket that reached to the floor.

The girl had got up and backed off, her face strained and pale. And she was no more Liza than I was.

"Better close the door, ma'am. Liable to get cold in here."

She hesitated, and put out a hand to steady herself. She was dressed like a ranch woman, but her face was painted, and anybody could tell what she was.

Where I stood, anybody behind that blanket could not see me. If I'd stepped through that door and stopped, I'd have been a sitting duck, but now whoever was there would have to move out from behind that blanket. Nor was I in range from the kitchen door, and as soon as I spoke, I moved.

Walking carefully, the girl crossed and closed the door. The fact that my coming was no surprise, or even the manner of my coming, showed me I had been expected.

"Know anything about a girl named Liza Hetrick?"

"No. . . . No, I never heard of her."

"Who owns this house?"

"Why, I rent it from Mr. Billings."

My eyes never left that curtain and she could see them. She was getting more and more nervous.

By now I'd moved until I had that old sheet-iron stove between me and the curtain. It was a hot stove, and it stood on legs more than a foot high, bringing it more than chest-high on me, and it was wider than me. It was good protection.

The way I stood, only my right side was free of that stove. And that was where my gun hung.

"You behind the curtain," I said. "Come out."

There was no move, no sound.

"You're a crazy fool!" The girl's voice was a little too shrill. "Nobody's back there!"

"All right," I said, "pick up that poker."

She hesitated, then picked it up. "Now lift it shoulder-high and take a full swing with both hands," I said, "and hit that blanket."

"No!" She jerked back, frightened. Then she caught herself. "Why should I do that?"

"Do it!"

She touched her lips with her tongue and drew back. "No," she said, "I won't!"

"All right," I said loudly, "I'll shoot into it with a shotgun."

With sudden triumph she cried out, "He hasn't got a shotgun! He's lying!"

She didn't say, "You haven't got a shotgun," as she would have done if she'd been speaking to me, so I knew she spoke for the benefit of whoever was concealed in the house.

And right then that kitchen door slammed open and a man stepped in and said, "Now, Joe!" and he shot.

Only the trouble was, I had my right hand inside my coat. There was a slit inside the pocket of my buffalo coat that enabled me to grasp the gun at my belt or the shotgun, and my coat was unbuttoned.

The shotgun was suspended by a strap inside my coat and that kitchen door grated on a little sand, a scarcely perceptible sound, and I stepped around the stove and shot into the blanket, shot twice, fast as I could pull the trigger. A bullet rang like a bell against the sheet-iron stove, and then I turned and shot past the stove at the man standing in the door to the kitchen.

It was fast, like the wink of an eye. Three shots gone in the fifth part of a second, maybe. And two men dead.

The man in the kitchen door had taken his in the belt. The man behind the blanket had fallen forward, pulling the red blanket down with him. One charge of buckshot had caught him in the face and one in the chest.

There was an acrid smell of gunpowder, and then the sound was gone and the room was empty and I could hear the clock ticking and the sobs of the girl. Something was stinging my arm. Looking down, I was surprised to see blood there.

The girl had drawn back into the corner and was

staring at the dead men with horror on her face. I
didn't feel sorry for her. She helped set that trap, and
she played along with them all the way.

One of them was Lang's deputy, the one I'd ordered
out of town. The other was a loafer I'd seen around
Billings' saloon.

Me, I stood there, looking down at those two men.
"Six," I said. "Six and seven."

"What?" She stared at me.

"Nothing," I said, "only you'd better get into town. I
don't want you."

"You'll let me go?"

"Sure," I said. "I expect you did what you were told
to do."

She seemed dazed. She picked up her coat and a
woolen muffler, her eyes avoiding the bodies. I helped
her on with her coat. "You'll beat him," she said. "He
didn't think you were so smart."

"Hope so," I said.

She wrapped the muffler around her head and tied it
under her chin.

"Who is this Liza Hetrick? Are you in love with her?"

"Me? Ma'am, she was a child when I saw her last,
but pretty. I guess I was only a kid myself. I . . . I liked
her. And her folks were like my own."

"Ben knows something. I know he does. He talks
about her as if he does." She paused. "I hope you find
her."

"If she's here, where would she be?"

"One of the places in town. Any one of them. Ben
owns them all."

She rode back to town with me and I took her to the
stage station when the stage was there and put her on
it. As she got in, two men started for their horses.

"You," I said. "Get back inside."

"What?"

The shotgun came out from under my coat and they
almost tore the door down getting in.

Right there I stayed until that stage was well out of
town and making fast time on the hard-packed snow. I
walked to the marshal's office then, and Mustang threw

down his cigarette as I came in. "You're a trouble to a man," he said dryly. "I been worried."

So I told him what happened.

"Figured it," he said. "Until a few minutes ago they had four men across the street. My guess is they were to come in fast once they knew you were dead."

He had two shotguns lying on the desk and a sawed-off Henry rifle.

They would have needed more than four men to come in that door with Mustang behind those guns. I'd seen some tough men, but Mustang was born with the bark on. And there was no rabbit in him.

And that night, without further delay, we started a shakedown of the houses in Alta. We started at the first one and worked our way down the street. We embarrassed some folks and frightened others, but house by house we shook the places down. We found nobody held against her will. We found nothing that gave us a lead.

But we gave that town a going over it would never forget, and we started a few people traveling. There was a red-haired man who objected, but Mustang kicked him downstairs and knocked him into the street.

Two weeks passed slowly, but they were weeks of comparative peace. We arrested a couple of men for knife fights, and Mustang caught in action a holdup man who in a misguided moment tried to shoot it out. It was a mistake.

After that, things settled down fast. The town took a second look at the situation and women began to do more shopping than they had done before, and the tough boys sang mighty small. The honest people liked it and the crooks didn't have any choice. Billings came and went about his business and avoided us.

"Too quiet," Mustang said, and I agreed with him.

By the end of February the town had had the most peaceful month in its short history. Murdock came down to see us and told us he was pleased, but even he was wondering how long it would last.

Liza was always on my mind, but I was trying to

think it out now. Billings was not a man one could frighten or force into talking. Whatever he might know he did not plan to tell. Yet something had to break.

Meanwhile, we had been checking. The marshal previous to John Lang had been murdered. He had been shot in the back of the head at close range.

John Lang had not then been in town. He had been sent for and promised the job of marshal. We found the letter in the safe, where it had been left through some oversight. The letter was signed "T. J. Farris."

There was nobody in town by that name.

Yet whoever had written that letter had been known to John Lang. John Lang had known him well enough to come all the way from Texas to take the job. Lang had believed him. . . .

Moreover, whoever wrote that letter had been mighty sure he could do what he wanted in town.

Ben Billings was careful. He was never out of our sight. Yet I couldn't forget what that girl had said. Billings knew something about Liza.

We watched him as he went about his business. He did not ride out of town. He was careful, mighty careful. He never stayed anyplace very long.

He was worried, too. He must have known that we knew he was guilty of arranging that plot to kill me, but we had done nothing. And that bothered him.

Business was good. The mines were shipping ore. Everybody seemed happy . . . except me.

Mustang, he was always on the prowl. He would take his horse and ride away, and he would return just in time to take his shift. We had rounded up two more deputies to handle the day shift, which was usually quiet. They were local men, a tough old ex-soldier named Riley and a miner with a bad lung named Schaumberg.

One night I was standing alone on the street and just about to move on when somebody spoke to me from the shadows.

"Don't make a wrong move. Don't try to see who I

am. My life wouldn't be worth a plug penny. But look down Lang's back trail."

"Thanks."

"All right." The man in the darkness chuckled. "Worth it to see Billings moppin' the floor!"

Footsteps retreated down a narrow alleyway, and I stood quiet until they were gone. Me, I was pretty sure it had been the gambler with the smile.

We wrote some letters, Mustang and me. We wrote letters to Denver and Cheyenne, because we knew Lang had been both places. We found out he had been in Cimarron and Tascosa. And in Cimmaron he had been associated with a gambler known as Ben Blake.

Ben Blake . . . Ben Billings. And the descriptions fitted. The trouble was, that was all. We couldn't tie anybody to them. And nobody in Denver, Cimarron, Tascosa, or Cheyenne knew anything about them, or about anybody known as Farris.

Mustang and me, we sat in the office one night. It was coming on for spring and a soft wind was blowing. I had been around town all day and was getting restless, or maybe it was just the wind.

Mustang, he tipped back in his chair, that long narrow face of his looking uncommon thoughtful. He slid his hat back on his head, showing that cowlick of blond hair.

"You sure was on your own mighty young," he said suddenly. "Wonder you got away from them Indians."

"I had a fast horse. Old Blue."

"Gave him to Liza, didn't you?"

"Well, sort of. She was to ride him."

Mustang rolled him a smoke and when it was lit he said thoughtfully, "You set store by that kid. Maybe she set some by you, too. You're a good-lookin' galoot. All the womenfolks in town say you're handsome. I reckon they could be right. Now, such a girl as that, not seein' many men, she might be so dumb as to fall for you."

"Not much chance."

"S'posin' she did. She have anything to remember you by?"

"Not that I know of."

"Except Old Blue."

"He's prob'ly dead. Old, anyway. And most of the horses were stolen."

Mustang drew deep on his cigarette, and looked superior-like. "Not him," he said. "I seen him today."

14

Come daylight, we rode out there, ready for trouble. Really loaded for bear.

If what Mustang figured was true, Liza would take care of that horse. If she cared a mite about me, she would keep Old Blue close to her.

Mustang, he was a shrewd one. He set around with a poker face most of the time, but he used that head of his, and he reasoned mighty well.

He got to thinking about that girl and that ranch. He reasoned she would keep Old Blue up close to the house. In the stable, prob'ly. He reasoned Old Blue wouldn't get stolen for that reason. Besides, he was mighty old, and no horse thief would want a gelding who was getting along in years.

"Something else," Mustang said. "Whoever this T. J. Farris is, he knows who you are."

"I figure."

"I mean he knows plenty about you. He's gone to some trouble to find out. He even knows things I don't know about you."

"How's that?"

"You'll see. He's been huntin' along your back trail.
Maybe to find something to scare you with."

This ranch was a little outfit back in the hills, not far
from town, but out of the way. A nice little ranch with
pole corrals and rail fences and some good meadowland.
There were some stacks of hay put up, and I could see
some berries trimmed and up on a fence, like. She was
a mighty nice place.

We came riding up mighty slow. Mustang, he had
scouted the place, and he had talked to the man who
owned it. Or said he owned it. Only now it might be a
trap.

Sure enough, Old Blue was there. He still had on his
winter coat and looked mighty rough, but it made a
lump come in my throat to see him. Why, he must be
fourteen years old, maybe older.

Right then, outlaws or no outlaws, trap or none, I
wasn't passing up Old Blue. I swung down and went
over to the fence.

"Blue," I said. "Good Old Blue!"

His head came up and his ears pricked. He came
toward the fence, then stopped, looking at me. "Blue,
you old sidewinder! *Blue!*"

Then I reckon I shed some tears. I reckon I did. In
front of Roberts and all. With maybe guns trained on
me. But this was Old Blue, the horse that had come
across the plains with us, the horse my pap rode, the
horse that carried me that lonely crying time after Pap
was killed. The horse that carried me right up to the
ranch where I'd met Liza.

And he knew me. Don't you ever tell me a horse
can't remember! He remembered, all right. He came
up and I went over that rail fence and put my arms
around his neck. And he nuzzled me with his nose.

"Where is she, Blue? Where's Liza?"

And if he could have talked, he would have told me.
I believe that. If he could have talked. Only he couldn't.
Or . . . could he?

A man was coming down the lane toward us, a tall
old man with gray hair, just such a man as Hetrick

himself had been. Gave me a start for a minute, only when he came nearer I saw it wasn't him. Nor even much like him.

"Knows you, doesn't he?"

"He should. We went through it together."

"So I was told."

"Told? By Liza? Where is she?"

He drew on his pipe. "No idea. I told him." He gestured at Mustang Roberts. "I'd no idea. Only the horse was left here.

"A man came up one day with the horse. I knew the horse because I'd seen him with the girl. She had brought him with her behind the stage. All she had left, she said, and she was going to keep him.

"This man who was with her, he said to keep the horse. He said to take good care of him. He said one day you'd come along to claim him."

"That I would?"

"What he said. That you would. Named you to me. He said Rye Tyler would be along. That if you wanted him, he was yours. Otherwise I was to give him a home here until he died. With the best of care."

Now, that was funny. That was most odd. What would anybody care about my old horse? Unless . . . maybe he was doing it to please Liza. Right then I felt sort of sick. Maybe he was in love with her, and her with him. Why else would a man care about another man's horse?

But this was getting mixed up. Maybe this gent had no connection with T. J. Farris at all. Maybe he was just somebody who met Liza and fell in love with her. Maybe Liza was happily married now. Maybe she was in a good home and I was wasting my time, and Mustang's too. Why else would a man think so of a horse?

"This man. What did he look like?"

"Quiet-looking man. A cowhand, but no kid. He said his boss wanted the horse left here."

"His *boss*?"

"Uh-huh, that's it."

So it was another blind trail. Who might the boss be? "This cowhand. Where was he from? Who was he?"

"Gave no name. Never saw him before. He gave me a hundred dollars and told me to take care of the horse. I'm a man who likes horses, and he knew it. And any man would like Old Blue."

None of this made sense. In one way, I wasn't so much worried. A man who would think that much of another man's horse wasn't the sort to be mean with a woman. Yet in another way, I was worried. That sort of man might be the kind she could love. And that bothered me. I guess Mustang was right. I was in love with Liza.

And this was another dead end. Or mighty near it.

The thing that had me wondering was why Billings would not talk about his connection with the girl. Especially when he must have known I'd get out of his wool if I took out after Liza.

Yet two months later I was no nearer finding her, and on the day when I again heard of her, I killed my eighth man.

We had occasional trouble with drunken miners, but we usually put them in jail to cool off and sober up. Otherwise it was almighty tame. Then one day a man tried to hold up, of all places, Billings' saloon.

Shouldn't say he tried. He did it. Me, I was back of the office saddling the gray when I heard a shot. I stepped around the horse and was looking along the back doors of the buildings when I saw this door burst open and a man lunge out with a sack in his hand.

He had a gun gripped in the other hand, and I could see a horse waiting. He was headed for that horse when I yelled at him. I told him to hold up there, and be quick.

At that, he might have got away. There was a couple of wagons and a wagon yard betwixt us, and he would have been behind them in two more jumps. But when I yelled he skidded to a stop and came up with his gun.

My bullet nailed him just as he fired. His shot went whining off overhead, seeming closer than it was. Always that way with a bullet when a man is shot at. Always seems close.

When I got to him he was in bad shape. The bullet had hit him in the side and gone through both his lungs and he was breathing blood in bubbles. All the fight was knocked out of him. His gun had fallen where he could have reached it, but he didn't try.

When I leaned over him he spoke mighty bitter. "*You!* That . . . that stopped me! I . . . I had to make my try!"

The holdup man was Ollie Burdette. He looked older, grayer. Yet it had been only a few months since I'd run him out of Mason Crossing.

Yet there was a glint in his eyes, a kind of fading triumph. "I seen her!" I could barely hear the words. "Seen her! You'll never get her now! You'll . . . better man!"

"What?" I grabbed his shoulder. "You saw who?"

He was going fast, and folks were coming, but he was having the last laugh. "I . . . seen Liza!" He spoke with that ugly bubbling sound from bleeding lungs. "Better man than you . . . got her!"

And he died.

Ben Billings scooped up the spilled money. He looked at Burdette, then curiously at me. "You know him?"

How much had Billings heard? What was he thinking?

"Ollie Burdette," I told him, "from over at the Crossing."

Billings looked at the dead man, a curious, thoughtful look on his face. "Strange. . . . A man would think he was fated to die by your gun. You didn't kill him there, so unexpectedly you kill him here." He looked around at me. "Makes a man wonder."

It did, at that.

And was there some other meaning behind the words of Ben Billings? Was he, too, fated to die by my gun?

And that night, back at the office, I thought about it. Who could have guessed such a thing would happen? That from the day Burdette saw me on the street, I was marked by some fate to cut him down? Did he know it

in some queer way? Me, I don't set much store by that
sort of thing, but it does beat all.

Billings could have killed him, or a dozen men. Yet it
was me. And he was my eighth man, and I had never
wanted to kill even one.

Sometimes when I got up in the morning I hated to
belt on my gun. Sometimes I just looked at it and
wished I could be shut of the whole thing, that I could
get clean away from it all, and go someplace where men
did not pack guns or shoot to kill.

Maybe you think I could have left my guns off, but I
wouldn't have lived an hour. Not one. Too many of that
Billings crowd around, or others who wanted my hide.

When Mustang and me took over there had been
robberies and murders every night. It was the law of
the gun that we brought to Alta, but it was law. Ours
was a time of violence, of men fiercely independent, of
men who resented every slight and whose only re-
course was to the Colt.

It is all very well for those who live in the East to talk
of more peaceful means, or for those who live in the
later, gentler years, but we were men with the bark on,
and we were opening up raw, new country, mustang
country, bronco country, uncurried, unbroken, and
fierce. Because of the guns I wore, women walked
along our streets now, children were going to a small
school nearby, and people went to church on Sunday. I
wore my guns and the thieves and murderers sat in the
shadows and waited for me to fall or to have a moment
of carelessness.

I thought of Liza. A better man, he had said. A
better man had won her. But better in what sense?
What sort of man could be friendly to Billings and be a
good man?

One thing I had in that town, I had a friend. No man
was ever more understanding or a stronger right hand
than Mustang Roberts. He had only three short years of
schooling. He read, but slowly. He could write, though
not well. But there was in him a purpose and endur-
ance such as I have seen in few men, and a kind of
rocklike strength that let me go ahead knowing he

would always be at my back, ready to back me up with his guns.

He came in that night after the killing of Burdette and I told him about the last words of the man from Mason Crossing. Then we started talking, as we often did, about the gun fighters who were making names for themselves, about Hickok, Allison, Ben Thompson, and King Fisher.

"You ever run into Ash Milo, the Mogollon gunman?"

"Never did. He wasn't one of the Market Square crowd in Kansas City. That was where I saw Hickok."

Mustang rolled a smoke. "He's a mighty mean man. And pure poison with a gun. I never did see him, either, and never heard tell of him until about two years ago. In those two years he's made a name."

He tipped back in his chair. "He killed six men last year. Hunted down two of them, two big names. Deliberately hunted them. He's mean, he's reckless, doesn't seem to care . . . or didn't at first. This past year he's tapered off a little. Maybe he found something worth living for."

"Don't know much about him. Outlaw, isn't he?"

Seemed to me as I spoke that I'd seen his name on some of the circulars we got in the mail.

"Uh-huh. Stuck up a payroll in Nevada. Then a train, some stages. Killed the marshal at Greener."

"Hope he doesn't come this way," I said. "I want no truck with him. I don't want to kill anybody, not ever."

We talked and loafed through the night and finally when daylight began to show we called the day watch and turned in. After I got into bed I got to thinking about Mustang asking me if I'd known Milo. Maybe the question had been more pointed than I'd believed. . . . No, I was getting too suspicious. Finding double meanings everywhere.

By then I had saved eight thousand dollars. Not so much, maybe, but a sight for a kid with no education who was just twenty-one years old.

Folks in town seemed to like me. And I was getting to know them. The toughs passed me by, glad to be unnoticed, but the businessmen often stopped to talk and their wives would bow to me on the street.

I'd always kept the office looking clean and dusted, but lately I'd taken to dressing up a little myself. I'd discarded the old buckskins, and had taken to wearing tailored black or gray trousers.

Also, I'd started a move to clean up the back yards and junk heaps. Not that I needed any help. All I had to do was drop a word here and there.

But always in the back of my mind was Liza, and I knew I would never feel free until I knew she was all right, and until I was sure she was happy. Sometimes I got to studying about it and trying to put it all together: the fact that Billings knew something about her, that Old Blue had been left at a nearby ranch, that Ollie Burdette had known something.

We had tried to find out where Ollie Burdette had been hiding out before he came to Alta, but we got nowhere. His trail vanished utterly. For two months there was a complete blank space in his life.

Mustang never stopped digging around. Sometimes he would come up with odd comments that started me thinking. Mustang was a patient man, and when I said he would make a good Pinkerton, I was right. If I was a crook I'd not want him on my trail.

One day he came into the office just after I got up. It was right after lunchtime. We had stood the night watch, as usual.

"This here Ash Milo," he said; "he killed another man. Killed an outlaw named Ruskin."

"Heard of Ruskin."

"Uh-huh. Bad man. Woman trouble. Ruskin never could leave them alone."

"Where'd this happen?" I was just making conversation. I didn't care where it happened. Or anything about either of them.

"Thieves' hideout. Place back on the plateau called Robbers' Roost."

Of course, I knew about the place. There was an area out there several hundred miles square that was a known hideout for thieves and killers. We had no big crime in

Alta, so it didn't affect us, but every time a bank, train, or payroll was taken, the bandits took off for the Roost. And no posse dared to go after them. Only one ever tried. The two men who survived had been shot to doll rags.

"This Ash Milo is the boss back in there."

"Yeah?"

"You never knew him?"

"Not me."

Mustang, he let his chair legs down to the floor. "That's funny, Rye, because he knows you."

15

That took a few minutes to make itself felt. Then I said, "By reputation, you mean."

"No. He knows you."

I scowled, thinking back. There was no Ash Milo anywhere in my memory. Of course, a man meets a lot of folks, time to time, and back on the cattle drive there had been a lot whose names I never knew. The same was true of Wichita, Dodge, Uvalde, and Kansas City.

There had been a lot of gun-packing men at Red River Crossing, too. But no Ash Milo that I could remember.

"What gives you that idea?" I said at last.

"Because the word's out. None of that gang are to start any trouble over here. They stay out of town and they pull nothing crooked in this town. He told them flatly you were bad medicine and to be left alone."

"Good for him. Saves trouble."

Mustang Roberts wasn't happy about it, I could see. Something was biting him, eating at him. He got up and paced the floor and he was studying this thing out. He had a good head and he thought of a lot of things.

"This may be it, Rye. This may be it."

"What?"

"The tie-up. The link between Billings, Liza, and Old Blue."

"No connection that I can see."

"Me, neither. But it's got the feel. I think it's there."

That night I made my rounds about eleven o'clock. That was the best time, because by then the boys would be liquored up enough to think they were mighty big, but knowing my gun was around usually kept them mighty sober. Most times all I had to do was walk around and show myself.

While I was walking, I got to thinking. It might be. Maybe there was something to this idea. It might just be the connection between Liza, Billings, and the fact that Ollie Burdette had seen Liza recently.

Pausing against the side of a building, I thought that over. Ollie Burdette had dropped from sight for several months, and during that period he must have seen Liza. On Robbers' Roost he would be out of sight and so would she. And nobody would do much talking about it.

And Burdette had said a better man had Liza. Had he meant Ash Milo?

Of course, I knew a little about Milo. And since Mustang had mentioned him I'd begun remembering things and hearing more. I expect I'd been hearing them before without paying them no mind.

Many considered him the most dangerous gunman west of the Rockies. And they weren't giving him second place to Hickok, Earp, or any of them.

Returning to the office, I went through the files. The holdup in Nevada seemed to have been the beginning of his Western career.

It had been a job with timing and finish. It had been planned carefully and had come off without a hitch, and must have taken place while I was on that cattle drive.

The killing of the marshal revealed another side to his character. The account in the files told of Milo's literally shooting the marshal to rags. It had been the act of a killer, of a man in the possession of terrible fury or a homicidal mania . . . or of an extremely cold-blooded man who wanted to shock people into absolute fear.

The marshal before John Lang had kept careful files, and reading what I could find on Milo gave me a picture of a sharp, intelligent, thoroughly dangerous man who shot as quick as a striking snake and asked no questions.

The picture was not pretty. At least twice he had killed men because they got in the way at the wrong time. And when they were only too anxious to get out of his way. He was a man utterly ruthless, but also a man who seemed driven by some inner fury.

Ash Milo shaped up like no easy proposition. He was a very dangerous man, but he did not fit the description of any man I knew. So that part could be ruled out.

Nevertheless, the thought that he might have Liza worried me. And where else could she be? Thinking of Liza made me think of Old Blue. When I awakened the next day at noon, after working the night hitch, I saddled up and rode out to see him.

He trotted to the fence to greet me. It was good to see the old fellow. I fed him some sugar, slapped him on the shoulder, ran my fingers up through his mane . . . and stopped.

My fingers had found something. Something tied or tangled there. Slowly, knowing it was by the feel, I parted the long hairs of the mane and looked at a folded square of paper. Untangling the mane, I untied the knots that held it in place.

It opened out, and I knew the handwriting.

Liza!

My heart pounding, I held it a moment before beginning to read. Then, finally, I lowered my eyes.

Dearest Rye:

Please don't try to find me. Go away. To find me will only bring you heartbreak and misery, and possibly death. I am all right, and I am happy to know you are well, and away from here. Go! If you love me, please go!

LIZA

So . . . at last a message. The gap bridged by a few simple words. But she was sending me away.

That I did not think of at first. Only that she had to be close. She was near.

Vaulting the fence, I stepped into the leather and went to the ranch house at a dead run.

The old man had been washing dishes and he came to the door drying his hands on a towel. "Figured to see you," he said. "That girl was here."

"When was it?"

"Two days ago, along about sundown. She come with that puncher and two others. Looked mighty mean, they did. She went down to see the horse and two of them stayed close all the time. She asked if you had been around and seemed pleased when I told her you was some happy about the horse."

"How's she look?"

"Mighty pretty. Beautiful, even. Hair's pretty, and a good figger. Looks well fed, but ain't fat. Just nice-like. But . . . well, kind of worried. Upset, maybe."

"Where'd they go?"

"Like I said, it was sundown when they showed. By the time they left, it was clean dark. I couldn't even see to the gate, but I figure they went south."

No matter how many questions I asked, that was all he could tell me, except that they had not let her out of their sight, and the one puncher he had seen before had this time stayed well away from the house.

"Mighty interested in you," he added. "Asked a sight of questions." He returned to washing dishes. "Seemed to me they picked that time to get here so's they could leave in the dark. I figure it was planned."

Descriptions of the men meant nothing to me, nor could he tell me if any one of the three seemed to have authority. Liza had been treated politely and with

spect, but they had never left her alone with him for
minute.

Mustang was sitting on the walk with his back against
he wall of the building when I returned to the office. I
old him what had happened and showed him the note.
He frowned over it, reading poorly as he did, but then
he looked up and said, "Man asking for you. He's at the
otel." Mustang got up. "It's that gent from Denver.
hat Denison what's-his-name."

"All right. I'll go see him. He say what he wanted?"

"No. Only he asked a lot of questions about you.
sked about Burdette, and about the fight at Billings'
lace."

The hotel was a long two-story building of unpainted
mber, some weathered by wind and rain. It had been
ut together in a hurry to accommodate the sudden
flux of visitors while the town was booming.

Denison Mead sat by the fire alone when I walked
to the lobby. The place was almost empty, usual for
at time of day.

The room was big and there was a homemade settee,
ome huge old leather chairs, and the desk at one end
f the room with the stairway to the rooms opposite it.
he floor was bare and there were only a few crude
aintings on the wall, and one good drawing of a buck-
g horse, traded to the proprietor for a meal two years
efore.

Mead got up to shake my hand, and seemed really
leased to see me. His eyes searched my face curiously,
nd then he waved at a chair and sat down himself.

"Tyler, I'll get right to business. When I first met
ou in Denver I was struck by your resemblance to
omebody I knew. When you answered my questions,
our answers told me without doubt you were the
erson whom I thought you to be."

"I'm afraid I don't quite get you, mister."

"I told you I was a lawyer handling mining property.
My firm also handles the Blair estate. In fact, they are
ne of our oldest clients."

This Mead seemed like a nice fellow, but whatever

he had in mind, I didn't know. And he was taking
long time getting to it.

"Tyler, do you have anything that belonged to you
mother?"

"A picture, that's all. Everything Pap kept was lost i
that Indian raid."

"A picture? Do you have it?"

When I settled in town I began carrying the pictur
in my pocket instead of keeping it in the saddlebags, s
I had it with me. I took it out and handed it to him an
he smiled. "Of course! Virginia Blair! I'd know the fac
anywhere, although I've only seen pictures of her myself.

"Blair?"

"Her maiden name. The family was fairly well of
Tyler. Not wealthy, but substantially fixed. And with
good position socially."

That meant nothing to me until he told me I'd bee
left some money. Rather, Ma had been left it. Som
money and a good-sized farm in Maryland and Virgini;
It was more than a thousand acres.

"There's a nice home on it, some stables. They use
to raise horses in the old days." He sat back and lit
cigar. "It's all yours, of course. The family was upse
when she married your father, but they were sorry fc
their attitude later, when it was too late. We tried t
locate your mother, but had no luck.

"Now, if you'll take my advice, you'll give up all th
and come East. You seem to know stock. You've ha
experience breaking horses. You could probably do ver
well back there."

Nothing like this had ever come into my mind. I'
have to study it well, yet all the time I was explainin
this to him, I was thinking that back East I wouldn
have to carry a gun. And there was small chance any
body would have heard of Ryan Tyler, the gun fighter

It would be a good thing . . . and then I remembere
Liza.

Her note had told me to go away, but I read mor
into it than that. She was afraid of what would happe
to me if I stayed, and if I persisted in trying to find her
But me, I had my own ideas.

So I got up. "Mr. Mead, I'm taking your advice. I'll go back East and make my home there. You go ahead and get it all fixed up so I can take over. But first I've got a job to do."

He got up, too. "Tyler," he warned, "be careful. I know something of the situation here. I've been kept informed. You've made this town peaceful, but only on the surface. There are men here who hate you and fear you. Make one slip and they'll be on you like a pack of wolves."

"Yes, sir. You get those papers fixed up. I'll be back."

So I walked out on the street, knowing as I walked that my decision was right. This was what I should do. It was a good time to go . . . and, after all, why should I look for Liza? She was with somebody else. If she hadn't made her choice, at least she was doing all right. And I had no actual reason to believe she was living as she was through any reason but her own. So that was over. I'd go back East and stay.

Mustang was pacing the floor when I came in. He turned sharply around. "Got news for you! I went out and hunted up the tracks of those folks who visited Old Blue. They headed south, right into the rough country, and they took a trail that only goes one way."

"Where?" I asked the question, knowing the answer.

"They went to the Roost. And one of those riders was a woman."

Liza . . . and Ash Milo.

Everything had been pointing that way and I couldn't see it until now. Sure enough, that had to be where Ollie Burdette had holed up after leaving the Crossing, and where he'd seen Liza with "a better man." It tied everything into one neat package, and it was the explanation for Billings' knowledge, and why he would not talk. It was common gossip around town that Billings had connections at the Roost.

It explained everything . . . or almost everything.

People all over this part of the country had a justified fear of the Roost and its riders. No rancher would talk. Some were friendly to the outlaws, but even honest ranchers refused to risk incurring their anger. Robber's

Roost lay somewhere on a plateau among a network of canyons, a country unknown to any but themselves.

How many outlaws were in there? Some said fifty, but most said it was nearer a thousand. It was the main hideout on the Outlaw's Trail, which stretched from Canada to Mexico through the Rocky Mountain region. And at the Roost, and for miles around, Ash Milo was king.

Unless a man knew the trails, he had no chance of finding his way in. Or so they said. That was the story all right.

The names of the leaders of the Roost gang were notorious. Ash Milo was the boss, but there were others names feared all through the West; Sandoval, Bronco Leslie, Chance Vader, and Smoky Hill Stevens. All of them wanted in a half-dozen states, all men who were handy with guns.

And that was where Liza was, among a lot of outlaws. But she didn't want me to come. All right, I wouldn't.

"This Milo," Mustang Roberts said, "he knows you all right. He knows a lot about you."

"Stories get around."

"Sure. And I thought I'd heard them all, but the grapevine from the Roost has one story I never heard."

"What's that?"

Mustang Roberts took his time. He pushed his hat back on his head and put a boot up on the desk. His spur jingled a mite. He began to build him a smoke.

"One thing I never heard," he said, touching his tongue to the paper. "That you killed a man named McGarry."

16

Mustang Roberts started me thinking again. He got me to wondering, and an hour before daylight I had my mind made up.

Mustang had turned in, as the night was quiet and he was tired from the riding he'd done that day. Me, I put a saddle on the gray, shoved the new Winchester 73 I'd bought into the boot, and then I belted on one gun and shoved the other into my waistband.

First thing, I switched my shirt and left my badge on the table. Where I was going a badge was an invitation to get shot. The shirt I put on had no pin holes left by the badge. Nor did I shave. Right then I was growing a mustache, which was well along, and I trimmed it a little, but let the stubble of beard stay. Then I shrugged into a coat and packed a bait of grub out to the gray.

We took the trail just as the sky was lightening. Nobody needed to tell me what I was riding into. There was no way this trail could miss leading into trouble. Maybe Liza wanted to live with outlaws. Maybe she

was Ash Milo's girl, and maybe she wasn't. But I was
going to know.

Leaving town by the trail, I turned off up a dry
canyon. It was a long ride I had before me, so I let the
gray make his own speed. In later years they said the
Roost was farther south, but the time I rode into that
country the outfit was located in a canyon back of
Desolation, not far off the Green River.

It was very hot. Back in the canyons there was no
breeze. Soon my gray shirt turned dark with sweat and
my eyes had to squint to stand the glare.

There was no sound but the sound of my horse's
hoofs and the creak of the saddle. Once in a while a
stone rolled underfoot. So it was I started into that
rough, wild country, unexplored except by Indians and
outlaws, and most of it unknown even to them.

The way I figured, it would be midafternoon before
Mustang Roberts realized I was gone. Then he would
figure out where I'd headed. Shrewd as he was, he'd
guess right the first time. But I'd be long gone then and
he'd resign himself to sitting out my stay.

Several times I saw antelope, and once I frightened a
mountain lion away from a big-horn sheep.

This was far-off country, wild and lonesome country.
It was big country, and I'd seen city men shrink from
the immensity of it. Some men are built for this kind of
country, and some aren't. I guess my Maker shaped me
for the land that we had to shape. I liked it.

There was small chance any of these outlaws would
know me as the marshal of Alta. They had been denied
the town by Ash Milo, and if I was lucky I'd get well
back into that country, looking like an outlaw on the
drift.

The gray liked it. He was always a good trail horse,
happier when he was going. He was a saddle bum like
me, liking the dust of far trails, the smell of pines and
sweat, and he would prick his ears at every hill we
came over, at every turn we rounded.

Most of the time I rode off to one side of the dim
trail. I rode alongside the pines, or took the far side of a
ridge, or kept under cover. It was smart in two ways: It

would keep me from being seen as long as possible, and if I was seen I'd look like a man on the dodge.

Twice I made short camps and slept a little, then I pushed on. Time enough to take it easy when I began to get close. Then I would have to look careful.

Nobody in Alta knew where the Roost was. Maybe Ben Billings, but he never went there. He was never out of sight long enough. Oh, probably some of the men who came and went around town did know, but nobody who would talk to me or who would have helped me. So I'd never tried to find out, and now I was glad.

I wouldn't want anybody remembering that the marshal of Alta had been inquiring about trails.

Once into the rougher country, I took my time. Skirting Indian Head peak, I crossed the end of the Roan Cliffs and rode into Nine Mile Valley. It was long and empty, unmarked by trails, and pointed southeast, the way I wanted to go. There were cliff dwellings along the canyon walls, and rocks covered with Indian writing. Several times I saw arrowheads and broken pottery.

With a three-day growth of beard on my face and my clothes dusty from travel, I was beginning to look the part. Also, I was getting wary.

Everywhere was rock. Rocky cliffs and crags, great mesas rising abruptly, shelves of rock and plateaus of rock. It was pink and white, with long streaks of rust red or maroon, all carved by wind and rain into weird shapes and giant forms. Huge pinnacles pointed their ghostly fingers at the sky. It was a land shaped like flames, a land riven and torn, upset and turned over and upset again.

I rode down long corridor canyons to the echoing of my horse's hoofs against the sounding boards of the great walls, walls that sometimes pressed close together, and at other times spread wide.

Suddenly the canyon bent northeast, and I followed it. Here was a creek, and I watered the gray, then loosened the girth.

It was late afternoon. It was very hot and I was very

tired. In all this vast desert through which I was ridin
there seemed to be nothing and no one. Lying down o
the grass beneath some willows, I stretched out wit
my hat over my eyes.

Awakening suddenly, I saw that the gray's head wa
up and that his ears were pricked. With one quic
move I was on my feet. When I see a horse like tha
even swelling himself a little as he gets set, I know he
going to whinny. My left hand grabbed his nostrils an
my right his neck just as he started, and I stopped hin
He shied a little, frightened at my sudden move, the
stood still.

Listening, I could hear voices. They were some di
tance off, but seemed to be coming nearer.

My position was behind the willows and out of sigh
if nothing attracted their attention. Gray knew he wa
supposed to keep quiet now, so I released him an
dropped my hand to my holstered gun. It was in plac
So was the one behind my belt.

Then I picked up my hat and moved back beside n
horse, listening and ready.

At first I heard nothing. Whoever it was had stoppe
talking. Then I heard their horses' hoofs, and, peerin
through the willows, I saw them.

Neither was a man I had seen before. One wore
black vest over a dark-red shirt. He was a lean, dar
man. The other was sandy-haired and freckled, an
from his saddle he could have been a Texan. The
drifted on by and were almost past me when I hear
the redhead call the other one "Bronc." This could l
Leslie, the Malheur County badman.

Stepping into the leather, I slow-walked my horse t
a point where I could watch them. The afternoon wa
almost gone, but here was a chance to find my wa
right to the hideout at the Roost.

If I tried getting closer alone, I might manage it, bu
if I rode in with Bronco Leslie, I'd be asked fe
questions. Pushing the gray, I moved out into the ope
until I could see them plainly.

About the same time they heard me and drew up
waiting.

Bronco Leslie had a scar over one eye and his eyes were the blackest I'd ever seen. His face was thin and drawn down, and he had a quick, nervous way about him. That I saw right off.

"Where you goin'?" he asked, mighty rough.

Drawing up the gray with my left hand, I said, "Hunting the Roost. I figured you boys might be heading that way."

"What made y' figure that?" Red demanded.

This was touch and go, and I knew it. Any moment a wrong word could start somebody shooting, but in some ways it was less risky with men like this. They were good men with guns, and a man who knows guns doesn't fool around. He knows they can kill.

I grinned at them. "Where else would a man go in this God-forsaken country?"

Red looked thoughtful. I saw his eyes taking in the build of my horse, obviously no cow pony, and the rig of my saddle.

"Do I know you?" Bronc asked.

"Damned if I know," I said frankly. "But this ain't my country. Had me some trouble over to Leadville and decided to head west."

This was safe enough, because just a few days before three men had broken jail in Leadville. The three had never been identified, and little was known of them. It had been rumored they were members of the James gang.

"Far's that goes," I said, "I don't know you."

Leslie stared at me. I could see he had no liking for me and was suspicious. I could guess he was figuring what would happen if he'd open the ball with a gun.

But Bronc Leslie was a careful man. He looked me over a little and decided matters could wait. Anyway, if I had a chance out here, I would have none at the Roost.

Red made the peace move. "I'm Red Irons," he said. "This here is Bronco Leslie."

"I'm Choc Ryan," I said, "from down in the Nation."

We drifted along, not saying much. Leslie took to dropping back a little, and as I liked nobody behind

me, I'd drop back with him. He didn't like it much, but
he didn't make an issue of it, either.

"I'm mighty hungry," I said. "Will we make it tonight?"

"Late," Red told me.

Can you imagine country like that country was then?
And not much changed, even now. A lost land, a land
quiet under the sun, where only the wolves prowled
and where the buzzards swung on lazy, easy wings. A
land unpeopled and still, where the sun slowly sank,
and from the cliffs the shadows reached out, filling the
canyons to the brim with darkness.

Ghostly footfalls echoed against the walls, saddles
creaked, and Red lifted a lonesome voice in song, singing "Zebra Dun," and then "Spanish Is a Lovin' Tongue."

It was mighty pleasant riding, mighty pleasant. Only,
up there ahead of me waited a bunch of men who, if
they guessed who I was, would kill me quick. Up ahead
waited death, and I rode alone into a lonely land from
which no officer of the law had ever returned alive, and
where Ash Milo, the man I sought, was king.

Every footfall might be taking me closer and closer to
my death. Yet each took me closer to Liza, and closer
to the solution of my problem. And after this, if I lived,
I would be free.

It was sundown before we made a turn, and by then
the cliffs had turned red and gold with the setting sun.
Tall spires like church steeples loomed ahead. The cliffs,
in those last minutes before darkness filled the canyon,
closed in and grew higher, until we were like ants
walking between those gigantic walls.

In the bottom of the canyon it got dark mighty quick.
"Many in there?" I asked.

Red struck a match and lit a smoke. "Couple dozen at
headquarters."

"Know a gent named Ruskin?"

Bronc looked around at me. This was a feeler I was
putting out, wanting to get a line on Ash Milo without
bringing up his name. Ruskin was safe, because if rumors were right he was the man Milo had trouble with.
Also, according to the handbills, Ruskin was from the
Nation.

"Friend o' yours?"

"Not him. . . . Well, we had trouble. Come near a shoot-out. I was just figurin' I'd best watch myself if he was around."

"He was," Red said. "But he ain't."

Leslie spoke up, real satisfied-like. "He's dead. He made a play for a girl Ash Milo likes, an' Milo up and killed him."

"Ruskin was s'posed to be bad."

"Hell!" Leslie spat. "None of them are bad compared to the boss. I never seen a man in the world could sling a gun with him!"

From another gunman, this was high praise, and me, I figured I'd best start looking at my hole card. Only it might already be too late. If this Milo was as good as they said, I might not stand a chance. But I didn't believe that. Not many gun fighters will believe they don't stand a chance.

For the next hour of riding I heard a lot about Ash Milo. Bronc Leslie, who had few enthusiasms, had one. It was Milo.

"He's too touchy for my taste," Red said. "A man has to walk on his toes around him. I never seen a man grab iron so quick, over nothin'."

This Leslie did not deny. "He's touchy, all right," he admitted. "And maybe he shoots too quick. Someday he'll kill the wrong man."

I'd heard that before. That was what Logan Pollard advised me against. He used to talk to me of that, even while telling me I was good. "You're fast, kid," he'd say, "one of the fastest I ever saw, but watch it. You'll shoot too quick and get the wrong man someday.

"Gunmen," he said, "get worse as they get older. They get to figuring everybody is after them. A man has to quit before he gets to that point. That's why I quit. That's why I'm lucky to have Mary."

Neither of them said anything more about Ash Milo's girl, and I didn't want to ask questions. Only, if I was to find out, now was the time. Turning into the narrow canyon back of a plateau, I took a chance and commented,

"Hell of a place for a woman! How'd he ever get one to come back here?"

"Him?" Red chuckled. "He's a mighty handsome man, and he's got a slick tongue with the ladies. She come willin', I guess, only he watches her mighty close, so I reckon she'd leave if she had her chance."

Leslie spat. "Too slim for my taste," he said. "I never could figure that in Ash. Nothin' between 'em either. He's tryin' to win her honest. Don't know why he fools around like that."

Red was just a black figure in darkness. "She's all right," he said quietly. "A mighty fine girl. She sure fixed me up that time after I got shot. Mighty gentle an' mighty sweet."

The high black wall of the canyon was split by a towering cleft, a narrow opening down which the wind gushed like a strong flow of water. When I looked ahead, all was darkness, with only the narrow strip of gray sky above us. This crack was mighty narrow, and, as I was to discover, mighty long.

When we had been riding maybe a hundred steps, Leslie drew up.

"Three safe men," he said aloud.

"Who?" The voice sounded as if from a cavern.

"This here's Leslie, Jim. Red's with me, an' a new man, name of Choc Ryan."

"Ride ahead, then." After a minute the voice added, "If that new man ain't all right, he'll never ride back out of here."

Me, I had a kind of queasy feeling in my stomach about that time. Riding down that narrow crack to get out of here was going to be rugged, mighty rugged.

"Right back there," Leslie said, "one o' the boys got hisself killed. A man don't speak at the right time, the guard start shootin'. This feller was drunk. It was a bad time to be drinkin'."

For maybe a quarter of a mile it was like that, and then we dipped down into a canyon and ahead of us on a sort of flat we could see lights in some cabins.

"There's the Roost, Choc," Red said. "She ain't much, but she's home, and she's safe. No marshal or sheriff ever seen it."

17

Right then I was tired, and I'd no right to be, because I was going to have to be on my toes. Just when I would see Ash Milo I had no idea, but I was hoping it would not be tonight.

Worst of all, I kept racking my brain over what Mustang Roberts had told me: that I was known to Ash Milo. I couldn't remember him or anybody he might be. But if he knew me, I wouldn't be Choc Ryan much longer. I'd be Rye Tyler, and dead.

With the weariness of the long ride behind me, all my spirits drained into my boots. How was I to see Liza? Suppose she wasn't even here? If I did see her, what could I accomplish? What fool's errand was this, anyway? I was crazy. . . .

Only I was here.

We got down at the stables and put our horses in stalls. There were some of the finest horses in that barn that I ever did see, and I know horses. They were horses built for speed and bottom. Nobody was going to run these boys down on ordinary horses. Yet I wasn't worried about the gray. He was one of the runningest horses I ever did see. And he could walk the legs off a coon hound.

Leslie took off and we followed him. There was a long building with lighted windows, and we went to that. A boardinghouse, sort of.

Inside, two, three men sat around drinking coffee. One was just eating. He looked tired and some beat, and he had a bloody bandage on his arm. He looked up as we came in. They all looked at me, but nobody spoke.

Leslie, he done the honors. "Choc Ryan," he said, "from the Nation."

None of them said anything, and then a big Negro came out of the kitchen with a platter of meat and potatoes and put it down beside the tin plate and eating tools. That big black boy's picture was on a poster in my office in Alta. He was wanted for murder. He'd strangled a guard and broke jail.

There was a pot of coffee on the table and I filled cups for Leslie, Red, and myself.

The man with the wounded arm glanced at me. "What d'you know? A gent!"

I grinned at him. "Ain't that," I said, "on'y these fellers are tougher than me. I figure I better butter 'em up a little."

He chuckled and we all settled down to eat. But my comment seemed to set right, and they sort of settled down.

There was a big man across the table with his shirt open almost to his navel. He had a hairy chest and hair climbed up his neck.

"I'm from the Nation," he said.

Here it comes, I thought. Now they ask me questions. Only he just said, "Where'd you live?"

"On the Cimarron," I said. The trail drive had come through that country and I knew that Leet Bowers had him a hangout on the Cimarron. This fellow might know of that.

He made a few comments on that Oklahoma country,

and I added a few of my own, enough for him to know
I'd been there, all right.

We turned in, bunking on the grass under the trees
near the long bunkhouse. None of us wanted to sleep
inside, and especially me. By this time I was feeling
trapped enough, and I was worried a great deal. This
was a tighter fix than I'd reckoned on, and I could see
they didn't trust me none at all.

Not that anything about me failed to ring true. I
knew I measured up. But men on the dodge can't afford
to be anything but cautious, and I was a stranger.

The next day we puttered around. I curried my horse
and found some corn for him. They had plenty of corn,
growing their own, and the men took turns hoeing it.
Corn-fed horses will outrun any hay-fed horse, and lazy
as some of these men might be, they knew they had to
have fast horses with plenty of strength.

Second day I picked up a hoe and walked out there.
Nobody said nothing, but when I returned after a couple of hours, I saw it set well with them.

Besides it gave me a chance to look around without
being too obvious about it. Any man who uses a hoe
leans on it some, and while leaning, I looked the place
over.

There were maybe ten buildings. Three or four were
houses. Behind one of them I could see a woman's
clothes on a line. Unless there was more than one
woman, that was where Liza would be. It gave me a lift
just to be that close.

But right next door there was another house and two
men sat on the stoop. I noticed that at least one of them
was there all the time. Nobody was going to get close to
her without trouble, that was sure.

There wasn't much talk around, and none about her.
I did hear a man say the boss was mighty touchy, and
he didn't sound very happy about it.

One thing I could see, plain enough: Whatever else
Ash Milo might be, he had this tough bunch buffaloed
to a fare-thee-well. Nobody wanted any part of him,
and that included Leslie and Sandoval.

There was one man there who was a little on the pushy side. It was Chance Vader.

Second day there, I saw him. He was slick. Smooth-shaved and wearing sideburns, he had pressed pants all the time, and he kept his boots shined up. He wore two guns and he wore them low. Me, I am a looking-around man. I saw he had another gun inside his shirt. That was something to remember.

Chance Vader duded up a good bit and he played cards a lot, and watching him, I saw his eyes straying toward that little gray stone house where Liza was. He looked toward it a lot, and sometimes he strayed toward it, but not often.

Once one of the men in front of the house next door got up and walked over to him. This was a big, burly man called Smoky Hill.

I heard raised voices and finally Chance turned and walked back. Red was sitting with me, and he said, low-voiced, "Trouble there. Chance is too proud of hisself."

Talk around was that Chance had killed six men, four of them sure-enough bad men.

He was salty, that was for true. Anybody tangling with him would have to go all the way.

There was a saloon, but I stayed away from it. I hung around the stables, took care of my horse, cleaned my guns, and listened to talk. Sometimes we pitched horseshoes.

All this time I saw nothing of Ash Milo. But I learned that he didn't come around very much. He stayed up on the hill in a house he had. "Reads a lot," Red said. "Always after papers and magazines. But he knows what's going on, for all of that."

It was Red told me that Milo scattered crumpled newspapers all over the floor before he got into bed. He wasn't taking any chances on somebody sneaking up on him in the dark.

No way I could see for me to get close to Liza. Not even to let her know I was there. And that had to be done.

Oddly enough, it was Chance Vader who brought it

out. Right off, he didn't like me much. He would be
oking at me with a cynical smile, and even Leslie
oticed it. Leslie didn't like me, either. He didn't trust
e. Maybe he didn't trust anybody. But he liked me
etter than Chance.

One day he said to me, "You watch that slick-ear.
e'll start on the prod. He's mean. He likes to kill, and
's building a reputation."

"Thanks," I said.

One day I was hoeing corn and had just put down the
oe when I heard a call. "Hey, Choc!"

It was Smoky Hill, and he was standing in front of
hat I called the guardhouse.

Brushing off my hands, I walked up there. My mouth
as dry and my stomach felt funny, and here I was,
ght close to Liza. If it was sure enough her.

"Look," Smoky Hill said, "I got to leave here for a
tle while an' that damn Vader's around. You take my
lace, will you?"

"If Vader comes up here, what do I do?"

He looked at me real cold. "Nobody talks to that girl
ut Milo. You hear that? That means you. But I know
u're all right. You don't drink, an' you're steady. You
ind your own affairs. I been watchin' you." He hitched
is gun belt. "If that Vader comes up here, you stop
im. If he gives you an argument, I'll be hearing about
, and I'll be along."

So he walked off down the hill and I sat down on the
ep, my heart pounding.

Liza was in that house next door, and we were in full
ght of the camp, and I had to get word to her I was
ere. But *how?*

And then all of a sudden it was easy. Out of the
orner of my eye I saw her standing at the window, just
ehind the curtain. So I took off my hat and put it down
n the stoop. I hoped she'd know me.

Stooping forward to pick up a stone, I glanced at the
indow. She was standing there with the curtain drawn
ack, slim and straight and lovely, not fifteen feet away,
nd she knew me. I could see it by the white set of her
ce. Then she gestured. She meant for me to go.

Picking up the stone and a few others, I started casually tossing them at a can, like a man killing time. When I stooped for more stones I shook my head and showed her two fingers, meaning that the two of us would go. She gestured at me again.

And then I heard feet walking.

Chance Vader was standing there sneering at me. "So? You got your eye on the girl, too? She seems ready enough to play."

This was real trouble, and I got up. Worse, there was an odd, puzzled look in Vader's eye.

"Mighty funny," he said, staring at me. "She never looks at me, but you she signals to. Now I wonder. . . ."

"You do your wondering down the hill," I said. "My orders are to keep men away."

He looked at me and I could see in his eyes that he wanted to kill me, but that wasn't as much on his mind right now as something else.

"You got me puzzled," he said. "I seen you before." He turned his head a mite, the way some folks do studying me. "And it wasn't in the Nation. I never been in the Nation."

"You go back down the hill," I said.

Surprisingly enough, he turned and started to walk off. Then he turned around. "Got it!" he said. His voice was hoarse with surprise. "Denver! You're Ryan Tyler!"

Smoky Hill was coming. He was almost loping. He was still some distance off.

"Rye Tyler," Vader said, "from Alta!"

There was no choice now. Not if we were to get out of here alive. I had wanted never to kill another man, even one several times a killer, such as this one. Yet this man told his story, I was a dead man, and worse, Liza would never have her chance. I knew now she was not here willingly.

Chance Vader's eyes were shining. There was a cruel triumph in the man. I saw his eyes suddenly sharpen and his hand moved. Whether he intended to shoot, I'll never know. My hand dropped to my gun and he was a split second slower.

My gun cleared leather and exploded. The bullet hit

im right over the belt buckle just as his gun muzzle
arted to tip upward. Stepping one step to the side to
ause him to shift aim, I fired again, spotting this one
arefully over his shirt pocket. It should have killed
im, but it didn't.

His lips were parted in a wide grin and he had even
hite teeth, mighty nice teeth. A bullet whipped past
ıy skull and then my left-hand gun bucked. It was the
rst time I'd ever used two guns, and I was surprised
hen the bullet broke his elbow. But Smoky Hill was
ınning up the slope, and there was no time to be lost.
stepped in closer, both guns hammering.

For the first time I desperately wanted to kill a man.
had to kill him. Liza's future was at stake, and my life.
hen I stopped shooting I was standing over him.

Smoky Hill caught my arm as I was reloading. "Take
easy, Choc! He's finished!"

"Rye!" Vader got it out, his eyes glittering in triumph
t me, straining with effort. How he managed it I'll
ever know. How a man shot up like that could even
raw a breath I don't know. But he said it again. *"Rye!"*

"Hell!" Somebody spoke wonderingly. "Dyin', an' he
ants a drink!"

Standing back, thumbing shells into my guns, I knew
wasn't a drink he wanted, and I was hoping he
ouldn't say the other name. If he said it I would die
ere, only with my guns loaded I wouldn't go out by
ıyself. I'd take a few along for company.

Chance Vader had been fast, all right. He had been
ıst and dangerous and he had sand. Lying there on his
ack with his lifeblood staining the gravel under him,
e still wanted me dead.

But then it was too late. His eyes glazed over and I
tepped back, slipping one gun into my waistband.

They stood around, a dozen of them, staring at me. I
ad no idea what to expect, but I had my gun in my
and. It might make the difference.

"You saved me a job," Smoky Hill said. "You sure
id."

Somebody said, looking at the nine bullets I'd put
ıto Vader, "Figured Vader was fast, but—"

"He was fast," Smoky Hill said grimly. "I know h
was fast. Only Choc here was faster." He pointed at th
body. "And shot straighter. Look. One over the be
buckle, one through the face, and not one of the othe
missed the heart by over three inches!"

They all looked at me again, sizing me up, getting
straight in their minds. I had outshot Chance Vader.

"He was fast, all right. I had to kill him."

Red Irons shrugged. "Don't let it bother you, Choc
There's a dozen men in this camp wanted to kill hi
. . . and not over two or three who stood a chance wit
him."

So we walked away down the hill. Suddenly, fro
being just a drifting outlaw, I had become known as
dangerous gunman, a man to reckon with.

Inside, the reaction was hitting me. I was sick, wante
to get off alone, but I had to stand the drinks. Ther
had been no way out for me. I'd had to kill him, bu
this was the first time I ever needed to kill a man. Th
first time I ever wanted to kill a man. It scared me.

What would Liza think of me now?

When I put down my glass and turned toward th
door, Smoky Hill was there. He looked sort of strange
and right then I knew I was in for it.

"Choc," he said, "Ash Milo wants to see you up o
the hill."

18

When I walked out on that porch I knew I was in trouble. If Mustang Roberts had guessed right and Ash Milo knew me, I was going to have to kill another man. And I would have the problem of getting out with Liza—if she would still go with me after what she had seen.

Standing there on the porch in front of the saloon, I rolled a smoke. Inside I felt empty. I could feel the slow, heavy beating of my heart, and I had a hard time moistening my cigarette, my mouth was that dry.

That walk up the hill, only a hundred and fifty yards or so, was the longest walk I'll ever take.

I felt the sun on my back. I could smell the grass, and off over a distant ridge there was a fluff of white cloud that left a shadow on the salmon cliffs. It might be the last time I'd see that sky or the cliffs.

Gray was down there in the stable. I suddenly wished he was saddled. I was going to need a horse if I came out of this alive.

In my thoughts were the things I had heard. Milo

was said to be utterly ruthless, without compassion. He had killed suddenly and without warning. He could be dangerous as a striking rattler, with no need to rattle before he struck.

Liza opened the door. But it was a taller, more lovely Liza.

She would be eighteen now, but there was a quiet maturity in her face that made her look older. There was a great sadness, too.

For a long moment our eyes held, and she searched mine as if she expected to find something there, feared to find it.

"Rye," she said, "I wanted to spare you this. I wanted to." And then she stepped aside and I stepped into the door and I was looking at Ash Milo.

Only I knew him . . . I knew him well. He was the man I had admired most in the world. He was the man I had looked up to and respected. The man who had been my friend when I had no other. He was Logan Pollard.

He was slimmer, older. His hair was mixed with gray, his face was drawn tighter and harder, and his lips had thinned down. Above all, there was in him a tension I did not recall. Always, he had seemed so thoroughly calm, so relaxed, so much in command of himself and all around him.

As though it were yesterday, I remembered the day he interceded for me and stopped McGarry from giving me a whipping. I remembered the day he saved me from the horse thieves when I had walked into a gun battle with them. I remembered the advice he had given me.

He walked toward me, smiling that tight smile, and he held out his hand.

"Rye!" he said. "Rye, it's really you! After all this time!"

There was no hesitation in me. I grabbed his hand and held it hard, and he looked into my eyes and smiled.

"You've made a name for yourself, Rye. And you've stayed on the right side of the law. I'm glad."

"So that's why you kept your outfit away from my town," I said. "You were protecting me."

He smiled, still that tight, quick smile. Only this time there was a hint of cynicism in it, and a little mockery. "No, Rye. I've always known you. I knew if we ever crossed you, we were in real trouble.

"You see, Rye," his voice was almost gentle, "a boy who will fight back when his father is killed is a natural boy. He does what anyone would do, given a chance.

"But you were different. You followed those Indians, and you killed at least one. Moreover, I saw you face McGarry. You weren't afraid. There was iron in you. . . ."

He turned and walked across the room. Liza was looking at me strangely, watching me for something. Me, I was confused, but now I was settling down. I was beginning to think.

"What became of Mary?" I asked.

His back was toward me and for a long time he did not reply, nor did he move. Then he said quietly, "She died in childbirth, Rye. If she'd lived I would probably have stayed right there.

"Remember old Sheriff Balcher? He tried to get me to stay, but I wouldn't listen. I couldn't stay there with those memories, so I left."

Logan Pollard came back to the center of the room. "Sit down, Rye. Please sit down."

It wasn't in me to quibble or to beat around the brush. "Logan," I said, "you know why I'm here?"

The smile left his eyes. He looked at me, taut and watchful. I knew then that all they said of the gunman known as Ash Milo was true. He was a dangerous man . . . and a not entirely sane man.

I'd looked many times into the eyes of dangerous men, and I knew how they looked. But in his eyes there was something else . . . something extra.

"Of course. You've come for Liza. On that score I must disappoint you."

So here it was. Here was the line we drew, the line along which neither of us would yield. Yet I had to try.

"It isn't like you, Logan. You're holding her against her will. That's not your sort of man."

He shrugged, a little irritable frown gathering around his eyes. "Don't be a fool, Rye! She may not wish to stay now, but she'll change. I'm not forcing her into anything, just giving her time to change."

"If she were to change at all, Logan, it wouldn't be in this place. No decent woman could live in such a place."

He stood with his feet a little apart, facing me. He was wearing gray-striped trousers and a white shirt with a black string tie. He looked good. He was, I expect, a mighty handsome man. He also wore a gun.

"Rye, you're the man I've needed here. Stay with me. Together we can live like feudal barons. We can have all this!" He waved a hand at the hills. "We can have it to ourselves!"

All this . . . an empire of rock and sand. Someday it would be more, but that was a long way off, and no bunch of outlaws would make it more. Yet this man had helped me. He had been my best friend, and for a long time my only friend. But now I knew I was going to have to leave, and that our friendship was at an end. And I was going to take Liza with me. And it wasn't going to be easy.

"No." I said it flatly. "No, Logan, I'm leaving. And I'm taking Liza with me if she wants to go."

Then I told him about the place back in Maryland. Only I was telling Liza, too. "I'm going to do what you advised, Logan. I'm going to get away from the need for killing before I kill the wrong man, or before I lose all sense of balance and kill too many."

He was very quiet. He rolled a smoke, and then he looked up at me. This was Logan, but it was also the man who had called himself T. J. Farris—the man who had sent for John Lang. The man behind Ben Billings. It was hard to believe how a man could change.

"You can go. Liza stays with me."

"You had Mary," I said quietly. "She was your tie, the person who stood by you, helped you. Liza is the same for me. Liza can be everything to me. We've both known it since we were kids."

"No." He said it as if he didn't want to believe. "No. She stays."

I glanced at Liza. "Will you go with me?"

"Yes, Rye. I will go with you."

"See?" My eyes swung back. "I—"

Logan Pollard was smiling at me. That tight, strange smile, so unlike the warm smile he used to have. He was smiling at me over a gun.

"Rye, I thought I taught you better. Never take your eyes off a man."

"But you're my friend," I said.

His face did not change. He looked a little bored, I thought. Only I'm not always a good judge.

"There are no friends. In this life you take what you want or it's taken from you. You can go now, Rye. You can ride out of the badlands and stay out. I've told the boys to let you go. I told Smoky Hill you were to go after I'd talked with you."

So there it was. He looked at me across a gun the way he had once looked at McGarry, only with that odd difference. He looked at me down the barrel of a gun and I knew he was, with that gun, one of the most dangerous men in the West.

He had taught me other things. Never to draw unless to shoot, never to shoot unless to kill.

The man standing behind that gun was a man who had never drawn but to kill. Rarely in the old days, but now I could see that with the death of Mary, something had happened. The old Logan Pollard was gone.

And here before me in this tight, icy man with the thin-drawn mouth was what I might become. This man who killed wantonly now, who could take a decent girl and hold her until she was finally broken by his will.

And suddenly I knew. I knew that when I turned to go he would kill me.

He would kill me because if I left I would return with armed men to wipe out the Roost. He had admitted I'd been left alone because he'd known how I would react.

"All right," I said. "I'll go. But I wish you'd think it over. We've been friends, and—"

"Stop it!" His tension was mounting. He would have to kill. I knew. "Consider yourself lucky. You did me a

favor by killing Chance Vader. Now get out of here. I'
returning the favor by letting you go."

Liza's eyes were wide and frightened. She was tryin
to warn me, trying to tell me.

I turned, needing the one trick, the thing that woul
throw him off the one instant I needed, for there is
thing called reaction time, the space of delay betwee
the will and the action.

I started to turn, then suddenly looked back. "Logan,
I said, "I've only read Plutarch four times."

"Plutarch?"

He had been set to kill, and the remark threw hi
off. It took an instant for his mind to react and in tha
instant I threw myself aside and drew.

It was an action I had practiced when alone, drop
ping aside and to one knee, the other leg outstretched
And I made the fastest draw of my life. I made
because I had to.

The Smith & Wesson .44 kicked hard against m
palm. In the instant I fired I saw his eyes white an
ugly and his gun blossom with fire. I was smashed bac
to the floor, heard the hammer of another bullet driv
into the wall back of me, and I fired twice.

Yet even as I fired, I saw the red on his shirt front
and I saw him knocked back and twisted by my shots
so that his third shot went into the ceiling.

Rolling over, I came up fast. He swung his gun an
we both shot. He hit me. I felt the numbing shock o
the bullet. And then I fired and he fell, tumbling fac
down, the gun slipping from his hand.

For an instant I stared down at him, holding my gu
ready. He turned over and stared up at me, smilin
faintly.

"Rye," he said. "Good old Rye. You learned, didn'
you?"

His body tightened and twisted, held hard agains
pain, and then his muscles relaxed.

"Liza," I said, "get a rifle. Stand by the window
We're still in trouble."

He was lying there looking at me. "Think I alway

knew it, Rye. Think I always knew it would be you. Fate . . . somehow."

He was dying, and he knew it, yet there was still danger in the man, and I could not trust him. He saw it in me, and smiled. "Good boy," he said. "Good boy."

We could hear them coming up the hill. We could hear them all coming. Thirty or more of them, armed and dangerous men.

"I'm going East, Logan. You're the last. I'm going to put my guns away."

My guns were loaded again. He had taught me that. Reload as soon as you stop shooting.

They had stopped outside. I stepped to the door. "Smoky Hill," I said. "You and Bronc. Come on in."

With Liza holding a rifle on the others, they entered one by one.

Logan Pollard looked up at them. He stared at them for a minute, and then looked back at me. "Told you Plutarch would be good reading," he said. "I—"

And he died, just like that. He died there on the floor, and inside I felt sick and empty and lost.

Across his body I looked at them. "His real name was Logan Pollard," I said. "He was my best friend."

Nobody said anything. "I'm going out of here," I said. "She's going with me. I came after her."

Smoky Hill rubbed his hands down his pants. Bronc rolled his quid in his jaws.

"Any argument?" I asked.

"Not any," Bronc said. "You go ahead."

They turned and walked outside and I took Liza by the arm. She held back, just a minute. "You're wounded, Rye!"

"Get what we'll need," I said. "We can't give them time to change their minds."

My side was stiff and sore. I could feel the wetness of blood inside my shirt. But I felt all right. I could make out. I'd have to.

"Rye . . . he was all right to me. He really was."

"I knew him," I said. "He was a good man."

Nobody said anything as we walked out and went down to the stables. Nobody made any argument. Maybe they didn't want to face my guns. Maybe they were too stunned to think about doing anything. Maybe there wasn't anything they wanted to do.

At a seep a dozen miles down the back trail, Liza looked me over. One bullet had cut through the muscle at the top of my shoulder. The second had hit a rib, breaking it and cutting through the flesh and out the back. I'd lost blood.

We met Mustang Roberts and a posse of twenty men coming down Nine Mile Valley, trying to work out the trail. We were riding along together when they saw us, and they just turned around and fell in behind.

And that was the way it was in the old days before the country grew up and men put their guns away.

Someday, and I hope it never comes, there may be a time when the Western hills are empty again and the land will go back to wilderness and the old, hard ways.

Enemies may come into our country and times will have changed, but then the boys will come down from the old high hills and belt on their guns again.

They can do it if they have to. The guns are hung up, the cows roam fat and lazy, but the old spirit is still there, just as it was when the longhorns came up the trail from Texas, and the boys washed the creeks for gold.

ABOUT THE AUTHOR

LOUIS L'AMOUR, born Louis Dearborn L'Amour, is of French-Irish descent. Although Mr. L'Amour claims his writing began as a "spur-of-the-moment thing," prompted by friends who relished his verbal tales of the West, he comes by his talent honestly. A frontiersman by heritage (his grandfather was scalped by the Sioux), and a universal man by experience, Louis L'Amour lives the life of his fictional heroes. Since leaving his native Jamestown, North Dakota, at the age of fifteen, he's been a longshoreman, lumberjack, elephant handler, hay shocker, flume builder, fruit picker, and an officer on tank destroyers during World War II. And he's written four hundred short stories and over eighty books (including a volume of poetry).

Mr. L'Amour has lectured widely, traveled the West thoroughly, studied archaeology, compiled biographies of over one thousand Western gunfighters, and read prodigiously (his library holds more than twenty thousand volumes). And he's watched thirty-one of his westerns as movies. He's circled the world on a freighter, mined in the West, sailed a dhow on the Red Sea, been shipwrecked in the West Indies, and has been stranded in the Mojave Desert. He's won fifty-one of fifty-nine fights as a professional boxer and pinch-hit for Dorothy Kilgallen when she was on vacation from her column. Since 1816, thirty-three members of his family have been writers. And, he says, "I could sit in the middle of Sunset Boulevard and write with my typewriter on my knees; temperamental I am not."

Mr. L'Amour is re-creating an 1865 Western town, christened Shalako, where the borders of Utah, Arizona, New Mexico, and Colorado meet. Historically authentic from whistle to well, when it is constructed, it will be a live, operating town, as well as a movie location and tourist attraction.

Mr. L'Amour now lives in Los Angeles with his wife, Kathy, and their two children, Beau and Angelique.

BANTAM'S #1
ALL-TIME BESTSELLING AUTHOR
AMERICA'S FAVORITE WESTERN WRITER

Praise for Ruth Ware's instant *New York Times*, *USA Today*, and *Los Angeles Times* bestseller

THE LYING GAME

*A Reese Witherspoon Book Club Pick * Starred review from *Kirkus Reviews* * Starred *Booklist* Review * An *Entertainment Weekly* "Must List" Pick * Named by Today.com as one of "17 Summer Beach Reads You Won't Want to Put Down" * Named by *Elite Daily* as one of "7 Books You Need to Take on Your Vacation This Year" * Included in summer book guides from *The New York Post*, *Time*, *People*, *Parchment Girl*, *BookPage*, *Novel Gossip*, *Shelf Awareness*, *Bustle*, and *Cheat Sheet**

"So many questions . . . until the very last page! Needless to say, I could not put this book down!"

–Reese Witherspoon

"Once again the author of *The Woman in Cabin 10* delivers mega-chills."

–*People*

"Missing *Big Little Lies*? Dig in to this psychological thriller about whether you can really trust your nearest and dearest."

–*Cosmopolitan*

"*New York Times* bestselling author Ruth Ware and her new thriller *The Lying Game* will have you full of anticipation."

–*Library Journal*

"A riveting, atmospheric thriller."

–*Entertainment Weekly*

"Ware masterfully harnesses the millhouse's decrepit menace to create a slow-rising sense of foreboding, darkening Isa's recollections of the weeks leading to Ambrose's disappearance . . . with arguably her most complex, fully realized characters yet, this one may become her biggest hit yet."

—*Booklist*, starred review

"One of 'summer's most intriguing mysteries'!"

—*Time*

"[A] page-turning psychological thriller with intriguing female characters."

—*The Hollywood Reporter*

"I suggest you read Scout Press's *The Lying Game* by Ruth Ware, bestselling author of *The Woman in Cabin 10*. I read this grabber in two days."

—*The New York Post*

"[An] engrossing psychological thriller . . . Ware builds up a rock-solid cast of intriguing characters and spins a mystery that will keep readers turning pages to the end."

—*Publishers Weekly*

"Ware has become a household name in psychological suspense, and her third release is highly anticipated. . . . [*The Lying Game* is] sure to be her next summer hit."

—*Elite Daily*

"Readers who've devoured Ware's bestsellers *The Woman in Cabin 10* and *In a Dark, Dark Wood* won't need much encouragement to pick up a copy of her latest thriller. This story . . . is as gripping and atmospheric as Ware's previous books, with unexpected twists around every corner."

—*BookPage*

"Perhaps one of the most twisty and suspenseful titles of 2017."

—Mystery Tribune

"*The Lying Game* is tense, addictive, and not to be missed."

—Crime by the Book

"You're going to sit down and read this in one sitting."
—Weekend Today in New York

"Ware writes with sharp dialogue and rich psychological drama. If you liked her earlier works, you just may love *The Lying Game*."

—Minneapolis Star Tribune

"This psychological complexity makes the novel more satisfying than the usual thriller, without slowing down its gripping plot."

—The Columbus Dispatch

"*The Lying Game* is definitely more character-driven than Ware's previous novels, it's oozing with human conflict and characterization . . . it was gripping, immersive, and had wonderfully fleshed-out characters."

—The Emporia Gazette

"Ware is a master of setting. . . . [Her] talents for twisting a tale, and for creating flawed, unlikable, and yet wholly realistic and familiar characters are on full display. . . . Readers looking for atmosphere, suspense, and complex relationships will find plenty to enjoy here."

—RT Book Reviews

"Like Paula Hawkins (*The Girl on the Train, Into the Water*), British writer Ruth Ware is finding fans on this side of the pond with her psychological thrillers."

—USA Today

THE
LYING
GAME

RUTH WARE

POCKET BOOKS

New York   London   Toronto   Sydney   New Delhi

Pocket Books
An Imprint of Simon & Schuster, Inc.
1230 Avenue of the Americas
New York, NY 10020

This book is a work of fiction. Any references to historical events, real people, or real places are used fictitiously. Other names, characters, places, and events are products of the author's imagination, and any resemblance to actual events or places or persons, living or dead, is entirely coincidental.

This Pocket Books paperback edition November 2019

POCKET and colophon are registered trademarks of Simon & Schuster, Inc.

For information about special discounts for bulk purchases, please contact Simon & Schuster Special Sales at 1-866-506-1949 or business@simonandschuster.com

The Simon & Schuster Speakers Bureau can bring authors to your live event. For more information or to book an event, contact the Simon & Schuster Speakers Bureau at 1-866-248-3049 or visit our website at www.simonspeakers.com.

Manufactured in the United States of America

10 9 8 7 6 5 4 3 2 1

ISBN 978-1-9821-2342-0
ISBN 978-1-5011-5619-9 (ebook)

To dear Hel, with (seventy?) lots of love

*T*he Reach is wide and quiet this morning, t
   blue sky streaked with pink mackerel-belly
the shallow sea barely rippling in the slight breez
so the sound of the dog barking breaks into the ca
gunshots, setting flocks of gulls crying and wheel
the air.

Plovers and terns explode up as the dog bound
ously down the river bank, scampering down the
nelled side, where the earth turns from spiky gr
dunes to reed-specked mud, where the water wa
between salt and fresh.

In the distance the Tide Mill stands sentinel, bl
and battered against the cool calm of the morning s
the only man-made structure in a landscape slow
crumbling back into the sea.

"Bob!" The woman's voice rings out above the volley
of barks as she pants to catch up. "Bob, you rascal. Drop
it. Drop it, I say. What've you found?"

As she draws closer, the dog tugs again at the obj
protruding from the mud, trying to pull it free.

"Bob, you filthy brute, you're covered. Let it go
God, it's not another dead sheep, is it?"

It's the last heroic yank that sends the dog stag
back along the shore, something in its jaw. Trium
he scrambles up the bank to lay the object at the
his owner.

And as she stands, looking dumbstruck, the d
ing at her feet, the silence returns to the bay l
coming in.

RULE ONE

TELL A LIE

The sound is just an ordinary text alert, a quiet *beep beep* in the night that does not wake Owen, and would not have woken me except that I was already awake, lying there, staring into the darkness, the baby at my breast snuffling, not quite feeding, not quite unlatching.

I lie there for a moment thinking about the text, wondering who it could be. Who'd be texting at this hour? None of my friends would be awake . . . unless it's Milly gone into labor already . . . God, it can't be Milly, can it? I'd promised to take Noah if Milly's parents couldn't get up from Devon in time to look after him, but I never really thought . . .

I can't quite reach the phone from where I'm lying, and at last I unlatch Freya with a finger in the corner of her mouth, and rock her gently onto her back, milk-sated, her eyes rolling back in her head like someone stoned. I watch her for a moment, my palm resting lightly on her firm little body, feeling the thrum of her heart in the birdcage of her chest as she settles, and then I turn to check my phone, my own heart quickening slightly like a faint echo of my daughter's.

As I tap in my PIN, squinting slightly at the brightness of the screen, I tell myself to stop being silly—it's four weeks until Milly's due, it's probably just a spam text, *Have you considered claiming a refund for your payment protection insurance?*

But, when I get the phone unlocked, it's not Milly. And the text is only three words.

I need you.

IT IS 3:30 A.M., AND I am very, very awake, pacing the cold kitchen floor, biting at my fingernails to try to quell the longing for a cigarette. I haven't touched one for nearly ten years, but the need for one ambushes me at odd moments of stress and fear.

I need you.

I don't need to ask what it means—because I know, just as I know who sent it, even though it's from a number I don't recognize.

Kate.

Kate Atagon.

Just the sound of her name brings her back to me, like a vivid rush—the smell of her soap, the freckles across the bridge of her nose, cinnamon against olive. Kate. Fatima. Thea. And me.

I close my eyes and picture them all, the phone still warm in my pocket, waiting for the texts to come through.

Fatima will be lying asleep beside Ali, curled into his spine. Her reply will come around 6:00 a.m., when she gets up to make breakfast for Nadia and Samir and get them ready for school.

Thea—Thea is harder to picture. If she's working nights she'll be in the casino, where phones are forbidden to staff and shut up in lockers until their shifts are finished. She'll roll off shift at eight in the morning, perhaps? Then she'll have a drink with the other girls, and then she'll reply, wired up with a successful night dealing with punters, collating chips, watching for card-sharps and professional gamblers.

And Kate. Kate must be awake—she sent the text, after all. She'll be sitting at her dad's worktable—hers now, I suppose—in the window overlooking the Reach, with the waters turning pale gray in the predawn light, reflecting the clouds and the dark hulk of the Tide Mill. She will be smoking, as she always did. Her eyes will be on the tides, the endlessly shifting, eddying tides, on the view that never changes and yet is never the same from one moment to the next—just like Kate herself.

Her long hair will be drawn back from her face, showing her fine bones, and the lines that thirty-two years of wind and sea have etched at the corners of her eyes. Her fingers will be stained with oil paint, ground into the cuticles, deep beneath the nails, and her eyes will be at their darkest slate blue, deep and unfathomable. She will be waiting for our replies. But she knows what we'll say—what we've always said, whenever we got that text, those three words.

I'm coming.

I'm coming.

I'm coming.

'm coming!" I shout it up the stairs, as Owen calls something down above Freya's sleepy squawking cries.

When I get up to the bedroom he's holding her, pacing back and forth, his face still pink and crumpled from the pillow.

"Sorry," he says, stifling a yawn. "I tried to calm her down but she wasn't having any of it. You know what she's like when she's hungry."

I crawl onto the bed and scoot backwards into the pillows until I'm sitting against the headboard, and Owen hands me a red-faced, indignant Freya who takes one affronted look up at me and then lunges for my breast with a little grunt of satisfaction.

All is quiet, except for her greedy suckling. Owen yawns again, ruffles his hair, and looks at the clock, and then begins pulling on his underwear.

"Are you getting up?" I ask in surprise. He nods.

"I might as well. No point in going back to sleep when I've got to get up at seven anyway. Bloody Mondays."

I look at the clock. Six a.m. It's later than I thought. I must have been pacing the kitchen for longer than I realized.

"What were you doing up, anyway?" he asks. "Did the bin lorry wake you?"

I shake my head.

"No, I just couldn't sleep."

A lie. I'd almost forgotten how they feel on my tongue,

slick and sickening. I feel the hard, warm bump of my phone in my dressing gown pocket. I'm waiting for it to vibrate.

"Fair enough." He suppresses another yawn and buttons up his shirt. "Want a coffee, if I put one on?"

"Yeah, sure," I say. Then, just as he's leaving the room, "Owen—"

But he's already gone and he doesn't hear me.

Ten minutes later he comes back with the coffee, and this time I've had time to practice my lines, work out what I'm going to say, and the semi-casual way I'm going to say it. Still I swallow and lick my lips, dry-mouthed with nerves.

"Owen, I got a text from Kate yesterday."

"Kate from work?" He puts the coffee down with a little bump, it slops slightly, and I use the sleeve of my dressing gown to mop the puddle, protecting my book, giving me time to reply.

"No, Kate Atagon. You know, I went to school with her?"

"Oh, *that* Kate. The one who brought her dog to that wedding we went to?"

"That's right. Shadow."

I think of him. Shadow—a white German shepherd with a black muzzle and soot-speckled back. I think of the way he stands in the doorway, growls at strangers, rolls his snowy belly up to those he loves.

"So . . . ?" Owen prods, and I realize I've stopped talking, lost my thread.

"Oh, right. So she's invited me to come and stay, and I thought I might go."

"Sounds like a nice idea. When would you go?"

"Like . . . now. She's invited me now."

"And Freya?"

"I'd take her."

Of course, I nearly add, but I don't. Freya has never taken a bottle, in spite of a lot of trying on my part, and Owen's. The one night I went out for a party, she screamed solidly from 7:30 p.m. to 11:58, when I burst through the doors of the flat to snatch her out of Owen's limp, exhausted arms.

There's another silence. Freya leans her head back, watching me with a small frown, and then gives a quiet belch and returns to the serious business of getting fed. I can see thoughts flitting across Owen's face . . . That he'll miss us . . . That he'll have the bed all to himself . . . Lie-ins . . .

"I could get on with decorating the nursery," he says at last. I nod, although this is the continuation of a long discussion between the two of us—Owen would like the bedroom, and me, back to himself and thinks that Freya will be going into her own room imminently, when she turns six months. I . . . don't. Which is partly why I've not found the time to clear the guest room of all our clutter and repaint it in baby-friendly colors.

"Sure," I say.

"Well, go for it, I reckon," Owen says at last. He turns away and begins sorting through his ties. "Do you want the car?" he asks over his shoulder.

"No, it's fine. I'll take the train. Kate will pick me up from the station."

"Are you sure? You won't want to be lugging all Freya's stuff on the train, will you? Is this straight?"

"What?" For a minute I'm not sure what he's on about, and then I realize—the tie. "Oh, yes, it's straight. No, honestly, I'm happy to take the train. It'll be easier; I can feed Freya if she wakes up. I'll just put all her stuff in the bottom of the pram." He doesn't respond, and I realize he's already running through the day ahead, ticking things off a mental checklist just as I used to

do a few months ago—only it feels like a different life.
"Okay, well, look, I might leave today if that's all right
with you."

"Today?" He scoops his change off the chest of
drawers and puts it in his pocket, and then comes over
to kiss me good-bye on the top of my head. "What's
the hurry?"

"No hurry," I lie. I feel my cheeks flush. I hate lying.
It used to be fun—until I didn't have a choice. I don't
think about it much now, perhaps because I've been
doing it for so long, but it's always there, in the background, like a tooth that always aches and suddenly
twinges with pain.

Most of all, though, I hate lying to Owen. Somehow
I always managed to keep him out of the web, and now
he's being drawn in. I think of Kate's text, sitting there
on my phone, and it feels as if poison is leaching out
of it, into the room—threatening to spoil everything.

"It's just Kate's between projects, so it's a good time
for her and . . . well, I'll be back at work in a few months,
so it just feels like now's as good a time as any."

"Okay," he says, bemused but not suspicious. "Well,
I guess I'd better give you a proper good-bye kiss, then."

He kisses me, properly, deeply, making me remember why I love him, why I hate deceiving him. Then he
pulls away and kisses Freya. She swivels her eyes sideways to regard him suspiciously, pausing in her feed
for a moment, and then she resumes sucking with the
single-minded determination that I love about her.

"Love you, too, little vampire," Owen says affection-
ately. Then, to me, "How long is the journey?"

"Four hours, maybe? Depends how the connections go."

"Okay, well, have a great time, and text me when
you get there. How long do you think you'll stay?"

"A few days?" I hazard. "I'll be back before the weekend." Another lie. I don't know. I have no idea. As long as Kate needs me. "I'll see when I get there."

"Okay," he says again. "Love you."

"I love you, too." And at last, that's something I can tell the truth about.

I can remember to the day, almost to the hour and minute, the first time I met Kate. It was September. I was catching the train to Salten, an early one, so that I could arrive at the school in time for lunch.

"Excuse me!" I called nervously up the station platform, my voice reedy with anxiety. The girl ahead of me turned around. She was very tall and extremely beautiful, with a long, slightly haughty face like a Modigliani painting. Her waist-length black hair had been bleached gold at the tips, fading into the black, and her jeans were ripped across the thighs.

"Yes?"

"Excuse me, is this the train for Salten?" I panted.

She looked me up and down, and I could feel her appraising me, taking in my Salten House uniform, the navy-blue skirt, stiff with newness, and the pristine blazer I had taken off its hanger for the first time that morning.

"I don't know," she said at last, turning to a girl behind her. "Kate, is this the Salten train?"

"Don't be a dick, Thee," the girl said. Her husky voice sounded too old for her—I didn't think she could be more than sixteen or seventeen. She had light brown hair cut very short, framing her face, and when she smiled at me, the nutmeg freckles across her nose crinkled. "Yes, this is the Salten train. Make sure you get into the right half, though; it divides at Hampton's Lee."

Then they turned, and were halfway up the platform before it occurred to me, I hadn't asked which was the right half.

I looked up at the announcement board.

"Use front seven carriages for stations to Salten," read the display, but what did *front* mean? Front as in the closest to the ticket barrier, or front as in the direction of travel when the train left the station?

There were no officials around to ask, but the clock above my head showed only moments to spare, and in the end I got onto the farther end, where the two other girls had headed, and dragged my heavy trunk after me into the carriage.

It was a compartment, just six seats, and all were empty. Almost as soon as I had slammed the door the guard's whistle sounded, and, with a horrible feeling that I might be in the wrong part of the train completely, I sat down, feeling the scratchy wool of the train seat harsh against my legs.

With a clank and a screech of metal on metal, the train drew out of the dark cavern of the station, the sun flooding the compartment with a suddenness that blinded me. I put my head back on the seat, closing my eyes against the glare, and as we picked up speed I found myself imagining what would happen if I didn't turn up in Salten, where the housemistress would be awaiting me. What if I were swept off to Brighton or Canterbury or somewhere else completely, or worse— what if I ended up split down the middle when the train divided, living two lives, each diverging from the other all the time, growing further and further apart from the me I should have become?

"Hello," said a voice, and my eyes snapped open. "I see you made the train."

It was the tall girl from the platform, the one the other had called Thee. She was standing in the doorway to my compartment, leaning against the wooden frame, twirling an unlit cigarette between her fingers.

"Yes," I said, a little resentful that she and her friend had not waited to explain which end to get. "At least, I hope so. This is the right end for Salten, isn't it?"

"It is," the girl said laconically. She looked me up and down again, tapped her unlit cigarette against the doorframe, and then said, with an air of someone about to confer a favor, "Look, don't think I'm being a bitch, but I just wanted to let you know, people don't wear their uniforms on the train."

"What?"

"They change into them at Hampton's Lee. It's . . . I don't know. It's just a thing. I thought I'd tell you. Only first-years and new girls wear them for the whole journey. It kind of makes you stand out."

"So . . . you're at Salten House, too?"

"Yup. For my sins."

"Thea got expelled," a voice said from behind her, and I saw that the other girl, the short-haired one, was standing in the corridor, balancing two cups of tea. "From three other schools. Salten's her last-chance saloon. Nowhere else would take her."

"At least I'm not a charity case," Thea said, but I could tell from the way she said it that the two were friends, and this goading banter was part of their act. "Kate's father is the art master," she told me. "So a free place for his daughter is all part of the deal."

"No chance of Thea qualifying for charity," Kate said. *Silver spoon*, she mouthed over the top of her teas, and winked. I tried not to smile.

She and Thea shared a look and I felt some wordless question and answer pass between them, and then Thea spoke.

"What's your name?"

"Isa," I said.

"Well, Isa. Why don't you come and join me and Kate?" She raised one eyebrow. "We've got a compartment of our own just up the corridor."

I took a deep breath and, with the feeling that I was about to step off a very high diving board, I gave a short nod. As I picked up my case and followed Thea's retreating back, I had no idea that that one simple action had changed my life forever.

It's strange being back at Victoria. The Salten train is new, with open-plan carriages and automatic doors, not the old-fashioned slam-door thing we used to take to school, but the platform has hardly changed, and I realize that I have spent seventeen years unconsciously avoiding this place—avoiding everything associated with that time.

Balancing my takeaway coffee precariously in one hand, I heave Freya's pram onto the train, dump my coffee on an empty table, and then there's the same long, struggling moment there always is, as I attempt to unclip the cot attachment—wrestling with clasps that won't undo and catches that won't let go. Thank God the train is quiet and the carriage almost empty, so I don't have the usual hot embarrassment of people queuing in front or behind, or pushing past in the inadequate space. At last—just as the guard's whistle sounds again, and the train rocks and sighs and begins to heave out of the station—the final clip gives, and Freya's cot jerks up, light in my hands. I stow her safely, still sleeping, opposite the table where I left my coffee.

I take my cup with me when I go back to sort out my bags. There are sharp images in my head—the train jerking, the hot coffee drenching Freya. I know it's irrational—she's on the other side of the aisle. But this is the person I've become since having her. All my fears—the ones that used to flit between dividing trains, and lift doors, and strange taxi drivers, and talking to people I didn't know—all those anxieties have settled to roost on Freya.

At last we're both comfortable, me with my book and my coffee, Freya asleep, with her blankie clutched to her cheek. Her face, in the bright June sunshine, is cherubic—her skin impossibly fine and clear—and I am flooded with a scalding drench of love for her, as painful and shocking as if that coffee had spilled across my heart. I sit, and for a moment I am nothing but her mother, and there is no one in the world except the two of us in this pool of sunshine and love.

And then I realize that my phone is buzzing.

Fatima Chaudhry, reads the screen. And my heart does a little jump.

I open it up, my fingers shaking.

I'm coming, it reads. *Driving down tonight when the kids are in bed. Will be with you 9/10ish.*

So it's begun. Nothing from Thea yet, but I know it will come. The spell has broken—the illusion that it's just me and Freya, off on a seaside holiday for two. I remember why I am really here. I remember what we did.

I'm on the 12:05 from Victoria, I text back to the others. *Pick me up from Salten, Kate?*

No reply, but I know she won't let me down.

I shut my eyes. I put my hand on Freya's chest so I know she is there. And then I try to sleep.

I WAKE WITH A SHOCK and a belting heart to the sound of crashing and shunting, and my first instinct is to reach out for Freya. For a minute I am not sure what has woken me but then I realize: the train is dividing; we are at Hampton's Lee. Freya is squirming grumpily in her cot, she looks like she may settle if I'm lucky—but then there's another shunt, more violent than the first set, and her eyes fly open in offended shock, her face crumpling in a sudden wail of annoyance and hunger.

"Shh . . ." I croon, scooping her up, warm and struggling from the cocoon of blankets and toys. "Shh . . . it's okay, sweetie pie. It's all right, my poppet. Nothing to worry about."

She is dark-eyed and angry, bashing her cross little face against my chest as I get my top undone and feel the by now routine, yet always alien, rush of the milk letting down.

As she feeds, there is another bang and a crunch, and then a whistle blows, and we begin to move slowly out of the station, the platforms giving way to sidings, and then to houses, and then at last to fields and telegraph poles.

It is heart-stoppingly familiar. London, in all the years I've lived there, has been constantly changing. It's like Freya, never the same from one day to the next. A shop opens here; a pub closes there. Buildings spring up—the Gherkin, the Shard—a supermarket sprawls across a piece of wasteland and apartment blocks seem to seed themselves like mushrooms, thrusting up from damp earth and broken concrete overnight.

But this line, this journey—it hasn't changed at all.

There's the burned-out elm.

There's the crumbling World War II pillbox.

There's the rickety bridge, the train's wheels sounding hollow above the void.

I shut my eyes, and I am back there in the compartment with Kate and Thea, laughing as they pull school skirts on over their jeans, button-up shirts and ties over their summery tops. Thea was wearing stockings; I remember her rolling them up her impossibly long, slender legs, and then reaching up beneath the regulation school skirt to fasten her suspenders. I remember the hot flush that stained my cheeks at the flash of her thigh, and looking away, out across the fields of autumn wheat, with my heart pounding as she laughed at my prudery.

"You'd better hurry," Kate said lazily to Thea. She was dressed, and had packed her jeans and boots away in the case resting on the luggage rack. "We'll be at Westridge soon. There's always piles of beachgoers there; you don't want to give a tourist a heart attack."

Thea only stuck out her tongue, but she finished hooking her suspenders and smoothed down her skirt just as we pulled into Westridge station.

Sure enough, just as Kate had predicted, there was a scattering of tourists on the platform, and Thea let out a groan as the train drew to a halt. Our compartment door was level with a family of three beach-trippers: a mother, a father, and a little boy of about six with his bucket and spade in one hand and a dripping choc ice in the other.

"Room for three more?" the father said jovially as he opened the door and they clambered in, slamming the door behind them. The little compartment felt suddenly very crowded.

"I'm so sorry," Thea said, and she did sound sorry. "We'd love to have you, but my friend here"—she indicated me—"she's out on day release, and part of the terms of her probation is no contact with minors. The court judgment was very specific about that."

The man blinked, and his wife gave a nervous giggle. The boy wasn't listening; he was busy picking bits of chocolate off his T-shirt.

"It's your child I'm thinking of," Thea said seriously. "Plus, of course, Ariadne really *doesn't* want to go back to the young offenders institute."

"There's an empty compartment next door," Kate

said, and I could see she was trying to keep her face straight. She stood and opened the door out onto the corridor. "I'm so sorry. We don't want to inconvenience you, but I think it's for the best, for everyone's safety."

The man shot us all a suspicious look and then ushered his wife and little boy out into the corridor.

Thea burst into snorts of laughter as they left, barely waiting even until the compartment door had slid shut, but Kate was shaking her head.

"You do not get a point for that," she said. Her face was twisted with suppressed laughter. "They didn't believe you."

"Oh, come on!" Thea took a cigarette out of a packet in her blazer pocket and lit it, taking a deep drag in defiance of the NO SMOKING sign on the window. "They left, didn't they?"

"Yes, but only because they thought you were a fucking weirdo. That doesn't count!"

"Is . . . is this a game?" I said uncertainly.

There was a long pause.

Thea and Kate looked at each other, and I saw that wordless communication pass between them again, like an electric charge flowing from one to another, as if they were deciding how to answer. And then Kate smiled, a small, almost secretive smile, and leaned forwards across the gap between the bench seats, so close that I could see the dark streaks in her gray-blue eyes.

"It's not *a* game," she said. "It's *the* game. It's the Lying Game."

THE LYING GAME.

It comes back to me now as sharp and vivid as the smell of the sea, and the scream of gulls over the Reach, and I can't believe that I had almost forgotten it—forgotten the tally sheet Kate kept above her bed, covered with cryptic marks for her elaborate scoring system. This much for a new victim. That much for complete belief. The extras awarded for elaborate detail, or managing to rehook someone who had almost called your bluff. I haven't thought of it for so many years, but in a way, I've been playing it all this time.

I sigh and look down at Freya's peaceful face as she suckles, her complete absorption in the moment of it all. And I don't know if I can do it. I don't know if I can go back.

What has happened, to make Kate call us so suddenly and so urgently in the middle of the night?

I can only think of one thing . . . and I can't bear to believe it.

It is just as the train is drawing into Salten that my phone beeps for the last time, and I draw it out, thinking it will be Kate confirming my lift. But it's not. It's Thea.

I'm coming.

The platform at Salten is almost empty. As the sound of the train dies away, the peace of the countryside rolls back in, and I can hear the noises of Salten in summer—crickets chirping, the sound of birds, the faraway noise of a combine harvester across the fields. Always, before, when I arrived here there would be the Salten House minivan waiting, with its navy and ice-blue livery. Now the car park is hot dust and emptiness, and there is no one here, not even Kate.

I wheel Freya down the platform towards the exit, my heavy bag weighing down one shoulder, wondering what to do. Phone Kate? I should have confirmed the time with her. I'd been assuming she got my message, but what if her phone was out of charge? There's no landline at the Mill anyway, no other number I can try.

I put the brake on the pram and then pull out my phone to check for text messages and find out the time. I'm just tapping in my code when I hear the roar of an engine, funneled by the sunken lanes, and I turn to see a car pulling into the station car park. I was expecting it to be the huge disreputable Land Rover Kate drove down to Fatima's wedding seven years ago, with its bench seats and Shadow sticking his head out the window, tongue flapping. But it's not. It's a taxi. For a minute I'm not sure if it's her, and then I see her, struggling with the rear passenger door, and my heart does a little flip-flop, and I'm no longer a civil service lawyer and a mother, I'm just a girl, running down the platform towards my friend.

"Kate!"

She's exactly the same. Same slim, bony wrists; same nut-brown hair and honey-colored skin; her nose still tip-tilted and sprinkled with freckles. Her hair is longer now, held back in a rubber band, and there are lines in the fine skin around her eyes and mouth, but otherwise she is Kate, my Kate, and as we hug, I inhale, and her own particular scent of cigarettes and turpentine and soap is just as I remember. I hold her at arm's length and find myself grinning, stupidly, in spite of everything.

"Kate," I repeat foolishly, and she pulls me into another hug, her face in my hair, squeezing me so I can feel her bones.

And then I hear a squawk and I remember who I am, the person I've become—and all that's passed since Kate and I last met.

"Kate," I say again, the sound of her name on my tongue so perfect, "Kate, come and meet my daughter."

I pull back the sunshade and pick up the wriggling, cross little bundle, and hold her out.

Kate takes her, her expression full of trepidation, and then her thin, mobile face breaks into a smile.

"You're beautiful," she says to Freya, and her voice is soft and husky just as I remember. "Just like your mum. She's lovely, Isa."

"Isn't she?" I look at Freya, staring up, bemused, into Kate's face, blue eyes fixed on blue eyes. She reaches out a chubby hand towards Kate's hair but then stops, mesmerized by some quality of the light. "She's got Owen's eyes," I say. I always longed for blue eyes as a child.

"Come on," Kate says at last, speaking to Freya, not

me. She takes Freya's hand, her fingers stroking the silken baby pudge, the dimpled knuckles. "Let's get going."

"WHAT HAPPENED TO YOUR CAR?" I say as we walk towards the taxi, Kate holding Freya, me pushing the pram, with the bag inside it.

"Oh, it's broken down again. I'll get it fixed but I've got no money, as usual."

"Oh, Kate."

Oh, Kate, when are you going to get a proper job? I could ask. When are you going to sell the Mill, go somewhere people appreciate your work instead of relying on the dwindling supply of tourists who want to holiday in Salten? But I know the answer. Never. Kate will never leave the Tide Mill. Never leave Salten.

"Back to the Mill, ladies?" the taxi driver calls out his window, and Kate nods.

"Thanks, Rick."

"I'll sling the pram in the back for you," he says, getting out. "Folds, does it?"

"Yes." I'm struggling with the clips again, and then I realize. "Damn, I forgot the car seat. I brought the cot attachment instead, I was thinking she could sleep in it."

"Ah, we won't see no police down here," Rick says comfortably, pushing the boot shut on the folded pram. "'Cept Mary's boy, and he's not going to arrest one of my passengers."

It wasn't the police I was worried about, but the name snags at me, distracting me.

"Mary's boy?" I look at Kate. "Not Mark Wren?"

"The very same," Kate says, with a dry smile, so that her mouth creases at one side. "Sergeant Wren, now."

"I can't believe he's old enough!"

"He's only a couple of years younger than us," Kate points out, and I realize she's right. Thirty is plenty old enough to be a policeman. But I can't think of Mark Wren as a thirty-year-old man—I think of him as a fourteen-year-old kid with acne and a fluffy upper lip, stooping to try to hide his six-foot-two frame. I wonder if he still remembers us. If he remembers the Game.

"Sorry," Kate says as we buckle in. "Hold her on your lap—I know it's not ideal."

"I'll drive careful," Rick says, as we bounce off, out of the rutted car park and into the sunken lane. "And besides, it's only a few miles."

"Less across the marsh," Kate says. She squeezes my hand and I know she's thinking of all the times she and I made that trip, picking our way across the salt marsh to school and back. "But we couldn't do that with the buggy."

"Hot for June, in't it?" Rick says conversationally as we round the corner, and the trees break into a flash of bright dappled sunlight, hot on my face. I blink, wondering if I packed my sunglasses.

"Scorching," I say. "It wasn't nearly so warm in London."

"So what brings you back then?" Rick's eyes meet mine in the mirror. "You was at school with Kate, that right?"

"That's right," I say. And then I stop. What did bring me back? A text? Three words? I meet Kate's eyes and I know there's nothing she can say now, not in front of Rick.

"Isa's come down for the reunion," Kate says unexpectedly. "At Salten House."

I blink, and she gives my hand a warning squeeze, but then we bump across the level crossing, the car shaking and bouncing over the rails, and I have to let go to hold Freya with both hands.

"Very posh, them Salten House dinners are, so I hear," Rick says comfortably. "My youngest does a bit of waitressing up there for pocket money, and I hear all sorts. Canapés, champagne, the works."

"So I hear," Kate says. "I've never been to one before, but it's fifteen years since our class graduated, and I thought this year might be the one to go to."

Fifteen? For a minute I think she's got the maths wrong, but then I realize. It's seventeen years since we left, after GCSEs, but if we'd stayed on for sixth form, she'd be right. For the rest of our class it will be their fifteen-year anniversary.

We swing round the corner of the lane and I hold Freya tighter, my heart in my mouth, wishing I'd brought the car seat. It was *stupid* of me not to think of it.

"You come down here much?" Rick says to me in the mirror.

"No," I say. "I—I haven't been back for a while. You know what it's like." I shift awkwardly in the seat, knowing I am gripping Freya too tight but unable to loosen my hold. "It's hard to find the time."

"Beautiful bit of the world," Rick throws back. "I can't imagine living anywhere else, meself, but I suppose it's different if you wasn't born and bred here. Where are your parents from?"

"They are—were—" I stumble, and I feel Kate's supportive presence at my side and take a breath. "My father lives in Scotland now, but I grew up in London."

We rattle over a cattle grid, and then the trees open up and we are out on the marsh.

And suddenly it's there. The Reach. Wide and gray and speckled with reeds, the wind-rippled waters reflecting the lazy streaks of sun-bleached cloud above, and the whole thing is so bright and clear and wide that I feel a lump in my throat.

Kate is watching my face, and I see her smile.

"Had you forgotten?" she asks softly. I shake my head.

"Never." But it's not true—I had forgotten. I had forgotten what it was *like*. There is nothing, nowhere, like the Reach. I have seen many rivers, crossed other estuaries. But none as beautiful as this, where the land and the sky and the sea bleed into one another, soaking each other, mingling and mixing until it's hard to know which is which, and where the clouds end and the water starts.

The road is dwindling down to a single lane, and then to a pebbled track, with grass between the tire marks.

And then I see it—the Tide Mill: a black silhouette against the cloud-streaked water, even shabbier and more drunken than I remember. It's not a building so much as a collection of driftwood thrown together by the winds, and looking as if it might be torn apart by them at any point. My heart lurches in my chest, and the memories come unbidden, beating at the inside of my head with feathered wings.

Thea, swimming naked in the Reach in the sunset, her skin turned gold in the evening light, the long black shadows of the stunted trees cutting across the flame-colored water and turning the Reach to tiger-striped glory.

Kate, hanging out the mill window on a winter's morning, when the frost was thick on the inside of the glass and furring the reeds and bulrushes, throwing open her arms and roaring her white breath to the sky.

Fatima, lying out on the wooden jetty in her tiny bathing suit, her skin turned mahogany with the summer sun and a pair of giant sunglasses reflecting the flickering light off the waves as she basked in the heat.

And Luc—Luc—but here my heart contracts and I can't go on.

We have come to a barred gate across the track.

"Better stop here," Kate says to Rick. "We had a high tide last night and the ground up ahead is still soft."

"You sure?" He turns to look over his shoulder. "I don't mind giving it a whirl."

"No, we'll walk." She reaches for the door handle and holds out a tenner, but he waves it away.

"Your money's no good here, duck."

"But, Rick—"

"Rick, nothing. Your dad was a good man, no matter what others in this place say, and you done well to stick it out here with the gossips. Pay me another day."

Kate swallows, and I can see she is trying to speak but can't, and so I speak for her.

"Thank you, Rick," I say. "But *I* want to pay. Please."

And I hold out ten pounds of my own.

Rick hesitates, and I put it in the ashtray and get out of the car, holding Freya in my arms while Kate retrieves my bag and the buggy from the boot. At last, when Freya is safely strapped in, he nods.

"All right. But listen, you ladies need a lift anywhere, you call me, understand? Day or night. I don't like to think of you out here with no transport. That place"— he jerks his head at the Mill—"is going to fall down one of these days, and if you need a ride somewhere, you don't hesitate to call me, tenner or no tenner. Got it?"

"Got it," I say, and I nod.

There is something comforting in the thought.

After Rick drives away, we look at each other, each unaccountably tongue-tied, feeling the hot sun beating down on the top of our heads. I want to ask Kate about the message, but something is stopping me.

Before I have made up my mind to speak, Kate turns and opens the gate, closing it behind us, as I make my way down towards the short wooden walkway that joins the Tide Mill to the shore.

The mill itself sits on a little spit of sand, barely bigger than the building itself, which I suppose was once joined to the bank. At some point, when the mill was being constructed, a narrow channel was dug away, severing the mill from the land and funneling the rising and falling tide past the water wheel that used to sit in the channel. The wheel is long gone, only a stump of blackened wood sticking out at right angles from the wall shows where it once stood, and in its place is a wooden walkway, bridging the ten feet of water that separates the mill from the shore. Seventeen years ago I remember running across it, all four of us at a time sometimes, but now I can't quite believe we trusted our weight to it.

It is narrower than I remember, the slats salt-bleached and rotten in places, and no handrail has been installed in the years since I last saw it, but Kate starts across it fearlessly, carrying my bag. I take a deep breath, trying to ignore the images in my head (slats giving way, the pram falling into the salt water), and I follow, my heart in my throat as I bounce the wheels across the treacherous gaps, only exhaling when we reach the comparative safety of the other side.

The door is unlocked, as it always is, always was. Kate turns the handle and stands back, letting me pass— and I wheel Freya up the wooden step and inside.

It's seven years since I last saw Kate, but I have not been back to Salten for more than twice that. For a moment it is like I have stepped back in time, and I am fifteen, the ramshackle beauty of the place washing over me for the first time. I see again the long, asymmetrical windows with their cracked panes, overlooking the estuary, the vaulted roof that goes up and up to the blackened beams above, the staircase drunkenly twisting around the space, hopping from landing to rickety landing until it reaches the three bedrooms lodged high in the rafters. I see the smoke-blacked stove with its snaking pipe, and the long low sofa with its broken springs, and most of all the paintings, paintings everywhere. Some I don't recognize, they must be Kate's, but intermingled are a hundred that are like old friends or half-remembered names.

There, above the rust-stained sink in a gilt frame, is Kate as a baby, her face round with chub, her concentration fierce as she reaches for something just out of view.

There, hanging between the two long windows, is the unfinished canvas of the Reach on a winter's morning, crackling with frost, and a single heron swooping low above the water.

Beside the door that leads to the outside toilet is a watercolor of Thea, her features dissolving at the edges of the rough paper.

And over the desk I catch sight of a pencil sketch of me and Fatima, arms entwined in a makeshift hammock, laughing, laughing, like there is nothing to fear in all the world.

It's like a thousand memories assault me all at once, each of them with clutching fingers pulling me back into the past—and then I hear a loud bark, and I look down to see Shadow, bounding up to me, a flurry of white and gray. I fend him off, patting his head as he butts it against my leg, but he is not part of the past, and the spell is broken.

"It hasn't changed!" I say, knowing I sound foolish. Kate shrugs and begins to unbuckle Freya from her pram.

"It has a bit. I had to replace the fridge." She nods at one in the corner that looks, if anything, older and more disreputable than its predecessor. "And I had to sell a lot of Dad's best paintings, of course. I filled the gaps with mine, but they're not the same. I had to sell some of my favorites—the plover's skeleton, and the one of the greyhound on the sands . . . but the rest, I couldn't bear to let these go."

She looks over the top of Freya's head at the pictures that remain, and her gaze caresses each one.

I take Freya from her arms and bounce her over my shoulder, not saying what I am thinking, which is that the place feels like a museum, like those rooms in the houses of famous men, frozen at the moment they left it. Marcel Proust's bedroom, faithfully reconstructed in the Musée Carnavalet. Kipling's study preserved in aspic at Bateman's.

Only here there are no ropes to hold the viewer back, only Kate, living on, in this memorial to her father.

To hide my thoughts I walk to the window, patting Freya's warm, firm back, more to soothe myself than her, and I stare out over the Reach. The tide is low, but the wooden jetty overlooking the bay is only a few feet above the lapping waves, and I turn back to Kate, surprised.

"Has the jetty sunk?"

"Not just the jetty," Kate says ruefully. "That's the problem. The whole place is sinking. I had a surveyor come and look at it, he said there's no proper foundations, and that if I were applying for a mortgage today I'd never get one."

"But—Wait, hang on, what do you mean? Sinking? Can't you repin it—underpin, that's what I mean. Can't you do that?"

"Not really. The problem is it's just sand underneath us. There's nothing for the underpinning to rest on. You could postpone the inevitable, but eventually it's just going to wash away."

"Isn't that dangerous?"

"Not really. I mean, yes, it's causing some movement in the upper stories, which is making the floor a bit uneven, but it's not going to disappear tonight if that's what you're worried about. It's more stuff like the electrics."

"*What?*" I stare at the light switch on the wall, as if expecting sparks to start flying at any moment. Kate laughs.

"Don't worry, I had a massive fuck-off circuit breaker installed when things started getting dicey. If anything starts to fizz it just trips. But it does mean that the lights have a tendency to go off at high tide."

"This place can't possibly be insured."

"Insured?" She looks at me like I've said something quaint and eccentric. "What the hell would I do with insurance?"

I shake my head, wondering.

"What are you *doing* here? Kate, this is mad. You can't live like this."

"Isa," she says patiently, "I can't leave. How could I? It's completely unsellable."

"So don't sell it—walk away. Give the keys to the bank. Declare yourself bankrupt if that's what it takes."

"I can't leave," she says stubbornly, and goes across to the stove to turn the handle on the gas bottle and light the little burner. The kettle on top starts to hiss quietly as she gets out two mugs, and a battered canister of tea. "You know why."

And I can't answer that because I do. I know exactly why. And it's the very reason I've come back here myself.

"Kate," I say, feeling my insides tighten queasily. "Kate—that message . . ."

"Not now," she says. Her back is towards me, and I can't see her face. "I'm sorry, Isa, I just—it wouldn't be fair. We need to wait, until the others are here."

"Okay," I say quietly. But suddenly, I'm not. Not really.

F atima is the next to arrive.

It's nine thirty and almost dusk, a warm sluggish breeze filtering through the open windows as I turn the pages of a novel, trying to distract myself from my imaginings. Part of me wants to shake Kate, force the truth out of her. But another part of me—and it's equally big—is afraid to face what's coming.

For the moment, this moment, everything is peaceful, me with my book, Freya snoozing in her buggy, Kate at the stove, salt-savory smells rising up from the frying pan balanced on top of the burner. There's a part of me that wants to hold on to that for as long as possible. Perhaps, if we don't talk about it, we can pretend that this is just what I told Owen—old friends, meeting up.

There is a hiss from the pan, making me jump, and at the same time Shadow gives a staccato series of barks. Turning my head, I hear the sound of tires turning off the main road, onto the track that leads down by the Reach.

I get up from my window seat and open the door to the landward side of the Mill, and there, lights streaming out across the marsh, is a big black 4x4 bumping down the track, music blaring, sending marsh birds flapping and wheeling in alarm. It gets closer, and closer, and then comes to a halt with a crunch of stones and a creak of the hand brake. The engine turns off, and the silence abruptly returns.

"Fatima?" I call, and the driver's door opens, and

then I am running across the jetty to meet her. On the shore, she throws her arms around me in a hug so hard I almost forget to breathe.

"Isa!" Her bright eyes are as black as a robin's. "How long has it been?"

"I can't remember!" I kiss her cheek, half hidden with a silky head scarf and cool from the car's air-conditioning, and then pull back to look at her properly. "I think it was after you had Nadia, I came round to see you, so that must be . . . blimey, six years?"

She nods and puts her hands up to the pins that hold the head scarf in place, and for a moment I'm expecting her to take it off, assuming it's an Audrey Hepburn–type thing. But she doesn't, she only pins it more securely, and suddenly I realize. It's not just a scarf—it's a hijab. This is new. New-since-I-last-saw-her new, not just new since school.

Fatima sees me looking, joining up the dots, and she smiles as she pushes the last pin back into place.

"I know, bit of a change, right? I was thinking about it for ages, and then when Sam was born, I don't know. It just felt right."

"Is it—Did Ali—" I start, and then instantly want to kick myself when Fatima gives me the side eye.

"Isa, honey, when have you ever known me to listen to a bloke when it wasn't something I wanted to do myself?" Then she sighs. I think it's a sigh at me, although maybe it's about all the times she's been asked this question. "I don't know," she says. "Maybe having the kids made me reassess stuff. Or maybe it's something I've been working my way back to all my life, I don't know. All I know is I'm happier now than I ever was."

"Well, I'm . . ." I pause, trying to work out how I feel. I am looking at her high-buttoned top, and the sleekly folded scarf, and I can't help remembering her beautiful hair, the way it fell like a river over her shoulders, draping over her bikini top until it looked like she was swathed in nothing else. *Lady Godiva*, Ambrose had called her once, though I didn't understand the reference until later. And now . . . now it's gone. Hidden. But I understand why she might want to leave that part of her past behind. "I'm impressed, I guess. And Ali? Is he—I mean does he do the whole nine yards, too? Ramadan and stuff?"

"Yup. I guess it's something we've kind of come to together."

"Your parents must be pleased."

"I don't know. It's a bit hard to tell—I mean, yeah"— she shoulders her bag and we start to walk across the jetty, picking our way carefully in the last shafts of sunset—"I think they are, although Mum was always very clear that she was okay with me not wearing a scarf, I think she's secretly quite chuffed I've come round. Ali's parents . . . funnily enough, not so much. His mother is hilarious, she's always like, 'But, Fatima, people don't like hijabis in this country. You'll hurt your chances at work; the other mothers at school will think you're a radical.' I've tried to tell her my practice is pathetically grateful to get a female GP who can speak Urdu and is prepared to work full-time, and that half the kids' friends are from Muslim homes anyway, but she just doesn't believe it."

"And how's Ali?"

"He's great! He just got made a consultant. I mean, he's working too hard—aren't we all."

"Not me." I give a slightly guilty laugh. "I'm swanning around on maternity leave."

"Yeah, right." She grins sideways at me. "I remember that kind of swanning. It involves sleep deprivation and cracked nipples. I'll take the podiatry clinic at work, thanks." Then she looks around. "Where's Freya? I want to meet her."

"She's asleep—completely knackered by all the travel, I think. But she'll wake up soon."

We have reached the door of the Mill, and Fatima pauses with her hand on the knob.

"Isa—" she says slowly, and I know, without having to spell it out, what she's thinking, and what she's going to ask. I shake my head.

"I don't know. I asked Kate, but she wants to wait until we're all here. She said it wouldn't be fair."

Her shoulders sag, and suddenly it all seems hollow—the meaningless social questions dry as dust on my lips. I know that Fatima is as nervous as me, and that we are both thinking of that message from Kate and trying not to think about what it might mean. What it *must* mean.

"Ready?" I ask. She blows out a long breath of air from between pursed lips, and then nods.

"As I'll ever be. Fuck, this is going to be weird."

Then she opens the door, and I watch the past envelop her just as it did me.

When I got off the train at Salten that first day, there was no one else on the platform apart from Thea and Kate and a slight, dark-haired girl about eleven or twelve years of age, far up the other end of the train. She looked uncertainly up and down the platform and then began to walk towards us. As she got closer I saw that she was wearing a Salten uniform, and as she got closer still that she was much older than I'd taken her for—fifteen at least—just very petite.

"Hi," she said as she got closer. "Are you for Salten?"

"No, we're a gang of pedophiles wearing these uniforms as a lure," Thea said automatically, and then shook her head. "Sorry, that was dumb. Yes, we're going to Salten, too. Are you new?"

"Yes." She fell in beside us, walking to the car park. "My name's Fatima." She had a London accent that made me feel instantly at home, and an impressive mane of shining dark hair. She shook it back over her shoulders as she looked up and down the platform. "Where are all the others? I thought the train would have lots of Salten girls on it."

Kate shook her head.

"Most people drive their kids, especially after the summer vac. And the day girls and weekly boarders don't start until Monday."

"Are there lots of day girls?"

"About a third of the school. I'm usually just a weekly boarder myself. I'm only here because I've been staying with Thea in London for a few days, and we thought we'd go back together."

"Where's home?" Fatima asked.

"Over there." Kate pointed across the salt marsh towards a glimmering tract of water, far in the distance. I blinked. I couldn't see a house at all, but there might have been something, tucked behind one of the dunes, or the stunted trees that lined the railway.

"How about you?" Fatima turned to me. She had a round, friendly face and eyes the color of chestnuts. "Have you been here long? What year are you in?"

"I'm fifteen; I'm going into the fifth. I—I'm new, like you. I'll be boarding, too." I didn't want to get into the whole story—my mother's illness, the long hospital stays that left me and my thirteen-year-old brother, Will, alone while my father worked late at the bank . . . the sucker-punch suddenness of the decision to send us both away, coming as it did out of a clear blue sky. I had never been any trouble, had I? I hadn't rebelled, or taken drugs, or acted out. I had responded to my mother's illness by being, if anything, even more diligent. By working harder and picking up more loose ends at home. By cooking and shopping and remembering to pay the cleaner when my father forgot.

And then, the talk . . . *Better for you both . . . More fun than being on your own . . . Continuity . . . School work mustn't suffer . . . GCSE's an important year . . .*

I hadn't known what to say. In truth I was still dazed. Will had just nodded, his stiff upper lip firmly in place, but I heard him crying in the night. My father was driving him down to Charterhouse today, which was why I had traveled alone.

"My father's busy today," I heard myself say. The words sounded relaxed, almost rehearsed. "Otherwise I suppose he would have driven me down, too."

"My parents are abroad," Fatima said. "They're doctors. They're doing this, like, charity thing for VSO? Giving a year of work for free."

"Fucking hell," Thea said. She looked impressed. "I can't imagine my dad giving a weekend up, let alone a whole year. Are they getting paid anything at all?"

"Not really. I mean they get a stipend, I think that's the word. Like an allowance. But it's pegged to local wages, so I don't think it's much. That's not the point for them, though—it's like a religious thing for them, their version of sadqa."

As she spoke we rounded the little station house, where a blue minivan was waiting, a woman in a skirt and jacket standing by the door with a clipboard.

"Hello, girls," she said to Thea and Kate. "Had a good summer?"

"Yes, thanks, Miss Rourke," Kate said. "This is Fatima and Isa. We met them on the train."

"Fatima . . . ?" Miss Rourke's pen traveled down the list.

"Qureshy," Fatima said. "That's Q-U-R—"

"Got it," Miss Rourke said briskly, ticking off a name. "And you must be Isa Wilde, is that right?"

She pronounced it "Izza" but I only nodded meekly. "That's right."

"Am I saying it right?"

"Actually, it's to rhyme with nicer."

Miss Rourke made no comment, but noted something on her page, and then took our cases and slung them in the boot of the minivan, and then we climbed in, one after the other.

"Swing the door shut," Miss Rourke said over her shoulder, and Fatima seized the door handle and rattled it closed. Then we were off, bumping out of the rutted car park and down a deep-carved lane towards the sea.

Thea and Kate chatted quietly at the back of the van, while Fatima and I sat nervously in silence, side by side, trying to look like this was something we did every day.

"Have you boarded before?" I said quietly to Fatima. She shook her head.

"No. I wasn't sure if I wanted to come here, to be honest. I was well up for going to Pakistan with my parents, but Mum wouldn't have it. How about you?"

"First time, too," I said. "Have you visited Salten?"

"Yeah, I came down at the end of last year when Mum and Dad were looking at places. What did you think of it?"

"I—I've not been. There wasn't time."

It was a fait accompli by the time Dad told me, too late for open days and visits. If Fatima thought this was strange, she didn't betray her feelings.

"It's all right," she said. "It looks—Okay, now don't get me wrong, 'cause this is going to sound awful, but it looks a bit like a very classy prison."

I smothered a smile and nodded. I knew what she meant—I'd seen the pictures in the brochure and there *was* something slightly prisonlike about the photos—the big rectangular white frontage facing the sea, the miles of iron railings. The photograph on the front of the prospectus showed an exterior that was almost painfully austere, the mathematically precise proportions accentuated, rather than relieved, by four slightly absurd little turrets, one at each corner, as though the architect had had last-minute doubts about his vision and had stuck them on as an afterthought, in some attempt to lessen the severity of the facade. Ivy, or even just some lichen, might have softened the corners of the place, but I guessed that nothing much would survive such a windswept location.

"Do you think we'll get a choice who we're with?

The bedrooms, I mean?" I said. It was a question that had been preoccupying me since London. Fatima shrugged.

"I don't know. I doubt it. I mean, can you imagine the mayhem if everyone was milling around picking mates? I think we'll just get assigned someone."

I nodded again. I'd read the prospectus carefully on this point, as I was used to privacy at home and had been dismayed that Salten didn't offer girls their own room until the sixth form. Fourth- and fifth-years shared with one other girl. At least it wasn't dormitories, like the years below.

We fell into silence after that, Fatima reading a Stephen King novel and me looking out the window at the salt marshes flashing past, the wide expanses of water, the heaped dikes and snaking ditches, and then the sand dunes that flanked the coast road, feeling the minivan buffeted by the wind off the sea.

We slowed as we approached a bend in the coast road, and I saw Miss Rourke indicate left, and then we turned sharply onto the long white-pebbled drive that led up to the school.

IT'S FUNNY, NOW THAT SALTEN House is so graven on my memory, to remember there was a time when it was strange to me, but that day I sat, quite silent in the minivan, as we snaked up the long curving drive in the wake of a Mercedes and a Bentley up ahead, just taking it all in.

There was the wide white facade, eye-hurtingly bright against the blue of the sky—just as I had seen on the front of the brochure—its severity only underlined by the regimented gleaming squares of windows that dotted the building at precisely regular intervals, and the snaking black shapes of fire escapes crawling up the sides and twining the towers like industrial ivy. There were the lacrosse pitches and tennis courts, stretching away into the distance, and the miles of paddock, petering away into the salt marshes behind the school.

As we drew closer, I saw that the black front doors were open wide, and my overwhelming impression was of a bevy of girls of all shapes and sizes running hither and thither, screaming at one another, hugging parents, high-fiving friends, greeting teachers.

The minivan stopped and Miss Rourke handed Fatima and me over to another teacher she introduced as Miss Farquharson-Jim (or possibly, Miss Farquharson, Gym). Thea and Kate melted into the crowd, and Fatima and I found ourselves subsumed into the shrieking mass of girls checking lists on the noticeboard and exclaiming over placements and teams, depositing trunks, comparing the contents of tuck boxes and new haircuts.

"It's quite unusual for us to have two new girls in the fifth," Miss Farquharson was saying, her voice rising effortlessly over the clamor as she led the way into a tall, paneled hallway with a curving staircase leading upwards. "Normally we try to mix and match new girls with old hands, but for various reasons we've ended up putting you both together." She consulted her list. "You're in . . . Tower Two B. Connie"—she grabbed a younger girl bashing another over the head with a badminton racket—"Connie, could you show Fatima and Isa to Tower Two B? Take them past the buttery so they know where to come for lunch afterwards. Girls, lunch is at one p.m. sharp. There will be a bell, but it only gives you five minutes' warning, so I suggest you start off as soon as you hear it as it's quite a walk from the towers. Connie will show you where to go."

Fatima and I both nodded, a little dazed by the

sheer volume of the echoing voices, and lugged our cases after the departing Connie, who was already disappearing into the throng.

"You can't normally use the main entrance," she said over her shoulder as we followed her, weaving and threading through groups of girls and ducking down a long passageway at the back of the hall. "Only on the first day of each term, and if you're an hon."

"An hon?" I echoed.

"On the honor roll. It means heads of house . . . heads of teams . . . prefects . . . that sort of thing. You'll know if you get there. If in doubt, don't use that door. It's annoying because it's the quickest way back from the beach and the lacrosse pitches, but it's not worth the telling-off." She ducked without warning through another doorway and pointed up a long stone-flagged corridor. "That's the buttery, up the end there. They don't open the doors until one, but don't be late; it's a scrum to get a place. Are you really in Tower Two?"

There seemed no answer to this, but Fatima spoke for me.

"That's what the woman said."

"Lucky you," Connie said enviously. "The towers are the best rooms, everyone knows that." She didn't elaborate on why, just pushed on a door in the paneling and began power walking up a flight of narrow dark stairs hidden behind. I was panting, trying to keep up, and Fatima's case was banging with every step. "Come on," Connie said impatiently. "I promised Letitia I'd meet her before lunch, and I won't have time at this rate."

I nodded again, rather grimly this time, and pulled my trunk up another flight and along a landing.

At last we were at a door that read TOWER 2 and Connie stopped.

"Do you mind if I leave you here? You can't go

wrong, just head up and there's only two rooms, A and B. You're B."

"No probs," Fatima said, rather faintly, and Connie disappeared without further discussion, like a rabbit going to ground, leaving Fatima and me rather breathless and nonplussed.

"Well, that was confusing," Fatima said, after she'd gone. "Fuck knows how we'll find our way back to the butlery."

"Buttery, I think it was," I said automatically, and then bit my lip, but Fatima didn't seem to have noticed, or at any rate, she hadn't taken offense at the correction.

"Shall we?" she said, opening the door to the tower. I nodded, and she stood back and made a mock bow. "After you . . ."

I looked inside. Another staircase, this time a spiral one, disappeared upwards, and I sighed and grasped the handle of my trunk more firmly. I was going to be very fit, if breakfast entailed the reverse of this every day.

The first door we passed turned out to be a bathroom—sinks, two toilet stalls, and what looked like a bath cubicle—and we pushed on upwards. At the second landing there was another door. This one simply had *B* on it. I looked down at Fatima, on the spiral stairs below me, and raised an eyebrow.

"What do you think?"

"Go for it," Fatima said cheerfully, and I knocked. No sound came from within, and I pushed cautiously at the door and entered.

Inside was a surprisingly nice room, fitted into the curving wall of the tower. Two windows looked out— north to the marshes, and west over the miles of playing fields and the coastal road—and I realized we must be in the rear, left-hand corner of the building. Below us, smaller outbuildings stretched away into the distance, some of which I recognized from the prospectus—the science wing, the physical education block. Under each window was a narrow metal-framed bed, made up with plain white sheets and a red blanket over each foot. There was a wooden bedside locker, and between the two windows, two longer lockers, not quite wide enough to be described as wardrobes. I. WILDE, read a printed label on one of the lockers. F. QURESHY, said the other.

"At least we can't fight over beds," Fatima said. She heaved her case up onto the one next to the locker marked with her name. "Very organized."

I was just studying the pack on the desk by the door, prominent on which was the "Student, School contract—to be signed by all girls and handed in to Miss Weatherby," when an impossibly jarring, jangling sound rang out, echoing horribly loudly in the corridor outside.

Fatima jumped, visibly as shocked as I was, and turned to me.

"What the fuck was that? Don't tell me we're going to get that every time there's a meal?"

"I guess so." I found my heart was beating with the shock of the noise. "Bloody hell. Do you think we'll get used to it?"

"I doubt it, but I guess we'd better start back, hadn't we? I highly doubt we're going to find that butter place in five minutes."

I nodded and opened the door to the corridor to try to retrace our steps, when I heard footsteps from above and looked up, hoping we might be able to follow these strangers to the dinner hall.

But the legs that I saw descending the stone spiral

stairs were long, very long, and unmistakably familiar. In fact I had watched those legs being swathed in distinctly nonregulation stockings just a few hours earlier.

"Well, well, well," said a voice, and I saw Thea, followed closely by Kate, round the bottom of the spiral. "Look who's in Tower B. It looks like we might be having some fun this year, doesn't it?"

So you really don't drink anymore?" Kate says to Fatima, as she refills my glass and then her own. Her face in the lamplight as she looks up at Fatima is quizzical, her eyebrows quirked in something not quite a frown, and faintly interrogative. "Like . . . at all?"

Fatima nods and pushes her plate away.

"Like, at all. It's part of the deal, innit." She rolls her eyes at her own phrasing.

"Do you miss it?" I ask. "Drinking, I mean."

Fatima takes a sip from the lemonade she brought with her in the car and then shrugs.

"Honestly? Not really. I mean, yes, I remember how fun it was sometimes, and the taste of a gin and tonic and all that. But it's not like . . ."

She stops. I think I know what she was about to say. It wasn't like alcohol had been an unmixed blessing. Maybe without it, we wouldn't have made some of the mistakes we had.

"I'm happy like this," she says at last. "I'm in a good place. And it makes things easier in some ways. You know . . . driving . . . being pregnant. It's not such a big deal, stopping."

I take a sip of the red wine, watching the way it glints in the low lights strung from the ceiling, thinking of Freya sleeping just above our heads, and the alcohol filtering through my blood into my milk.

"I try to keep a lid on it," I say. "For Freya. I mean, I'll have a glass or two, but that's it, while I'm still feeding her. But I'm not going to lie: it was bloody tough not drinking at all for nine months. The only thing that got me through it was thinking of the bottle of Pouilly-Fumé in the fridge for afterwards."

"Nine months." Kate swirls the wine thoughtfully in her glass. "It's years since I've gone even nine *days* without a drink. But you don't smoke anymore, do you, Isa? That's quite an achievement."

I smile.

"Yeah, I gave up when I met Owen, and I've been pretty good on that. But that's it—I can't cope with cutting out more than one vice at a time. You were lucky you never started," I add to Fatima. She laughs.

"It's a good thing, really, makes it easier to lecture my patients on the evils of tobacco. Last thing you want is your GP telling you to quit while stinking of fags. Ali still has the odd one, though. He thinks I don't know, but of course I do."

"Do you say anything?" I ask, thinking of Owen. Fatima shrugs.

"It's his conscience. I'd go mental if he did it in front of the kids, but aside from that, it's between him and Allah what he does with his body."

"It's so . . ." Kate says, and then she laughs. "Sorry, I don't mean to be weird about this. I just can't get over it. You're the same old Fatima, and yet . . ." She waves a hand at the hijab. Fatima has taken it off her head, but it's lying draped around her shoulders, like a reminder of how things have changed. "I mean, don't get me wrong, it's great. It's just going to take me a while to . . . to match things up. Same with Isa and Freya, I guess." She smiles at me, and I see the fine lines at the corner of her mouth. "It was so weird when you turned up at the station, with this little person. And seeing you toting her around, wiping her face, changing a nappy like you've been doing it all your life . . . It's hard to remember you're a mum when you're sitting there, in the same chair as always. You look exactly the same; it's like nothing's changed, and yet . . ."

And yet everything has changed.

IT IS GONE ELEVEN WHEN Fatima looks at her watch and pushes her chair back from the table. We have talked and talked, about everything—from Fatima's patients to the village gossip to Owen's work—but always skirting around the unspoken question: Why has Kate summoned us back so urgently?

"I'm going to have to head up," Fatima says. "Can I use the bathroom?"

"Yes, of course," Kate says, without looking up. She is rolling a cigarette, her slim brown fingers prodding and shaping the tobacco with practiced deftness. She raises it to her lips, licks the paper, and then puts the finished roll-up on the table.

"And am I out the back or . . . ?"

"Oh, sorry, I should have told you." Kate shakes her head, admonishing herself. "No, Thea's got the downstairs bedroom. I've put you in my old room. I'm on the top floor now."

Fatima nods and heads up to the bathroom, leaving me and Kate alone. I watch as Kate picks up the cigarette and taps one end on the table.

"Don't mind me," I say, knowing she is holding back on my account, but she shakes her head.

"No, it's not fair. I'll go out on the jetty."

"I'll come," I say, and she opens the gappy wooden door that leads out onto the jetty on the river side of the mill, and we go out together into the warm night air.

It is quite dark, and a beautiful moon is rising above the Reach. Kate walks to the left-hand edge of the jetty, the end that faces upriver, towards Salten village, and for a minute I don't understand, but then I see why. The other end of the jetty, the unfenced end where we used to sit, our feet dangling in the water at high tide, is completely submerged. Kate sees my gaze and shrugs resignedly.

"It's what happens at high tide now." She looks at her watch. "That's as high as it'll get, though—it'll start to ebb soon."

"But—but, Kate, I had no idea. Is this what you meant when you said the place is sinking?"

She nods, lights up with a flare of her Bic lighter, and inhales deeply.

"But, this is serious. I mean this is *really* sinking."

"I know," Kate says. Her voice is flat as she blows a long plume of smoke into the night. I feel desire twist in my gut. I can almost *taste* the smoke. "But what can you do?" she asks rhetorically, around the roll-up lodged in the corner of her mouth.

Suddenly I can't bear it any longer. The waiting.

"Give me a drag."

"What?" Kate turns to look at me, her face shadowed in the moonlight. "Isa, no. Come on, you've given up!"

"You know full well, you're never an ex-addict, you're just an addict who hasn't had a fix in a while," I say without thinking, and then with a lurch I realize suddenly what I've said, and who I'm quoting, and it's like a knife in my heart. I still think of him, even after all these years—how much worse must it be for Kate?

"Oh God," I say, putting out my hand. "I'm sorry, I—"

"It's okay," she says, though she has stopped smiling, and the lines around her mouth are suddenly graven deeper than before. She takes another long drag and then puts the roll-up between my outstretched fingers. "I think about him all the time. One more reminder doesn't hurt me any more or less."

I hold the roll-up, light as a match between my fingers, and then with a feeling like slipping into a long, hot bath, I put the tip between my lips and I draw the smoke deep, deep into my lungs. Oh God, it's so good . . .

And then two things happen. Far up the Reach, up near the bridge, twin beams of light swing across the waves. A car is stopping at the end of Kate's rutted lane.

And from the baby monitor in my pocket there comes a thin, squawking cry that tugs at my heart, and my head goes up, jerked by the invisible line that connects me to Freya.

"Here." Kate holds out her hand, and I hastily give the cigarette back. I can't believe what I just did. A glass of wine is one thing, but am I really going to go and hold my daughter stinking of cigarette smoke? What would Owen say? "You go to Freya," she says. "I'll see who . . ."

But as I run inside and up the stairs to the bedroom where I've left Freya, I know who. I know exactly who.

It's Thea, coming, just as she promised. We are all here at last.

Upstairs I almost bump into Fatima on the landing, coming out of her room, Kate's old room.

"Sorry," I say breathlessly. "Freya's . . ."

She stands back, letting me pass, and I sprint into the room at the end of the corridor, where Kate has set up the bent wood cradle that once held her as a baby.

It's a beautiful room—the best, perhaps, except maybe the one Kate herself now occupies, a bedroom and studio combined, which is the entire top floor of the Mill and used to be her father's.

When I pick Freya up she is hot and sticky, and I peel her out of her sleeping bag, realizing how warm it is here. As I'm shushing her over my shoulder I hear a noise behind me, and turn to see Fatima in the doorway, looking wonderingly around, and I realize what I failed to notice as I hurried past her on the landing; she's still fully dressed.

"I thought you were going to bed?"

She shakes her head.

"I was praying." Her voice is low and hushed, trying not to spook Freya. "It's *so* weird, Isa. Seeing you here, in *his* room."

"I know," I say. I settle myself on the wicker chair while Fatima steps over the threshold and takes in our surroundings: the low slanting windows; the polished dark wood floor; the leaf skeletons strung from the beams, shivering in the warm breeze from the open window. Kate has taken away most of Luc's possessions, his music posters, the pile of unwashed clothes behind the door, the acoustic guitar propped up against the windowsill, the ancient seventies turntable that used to rest on the floor by the bed. But it is still haunted by his presence, and I can't think of it as anything but Luc's room, even though Kate called it the back bedroom when she took me up.

"Did you keep in touch?" Fatima asks.

I shake my head.

"No, you?"

"No." She sits on the edge of the bed. "But you must have thought about him, right?"

I don't answer for a minute. I take a moment; rearrange the blanket next to Freya's cheek.

"A bit," I say at last. "Now and then."

But that's a lie, and worse, it's a lie to Fatima. That was the most important rule of the Lying Game. Lie to everyone else—yes. But to each other—never.

I think of all the lies I have repeated and repeated over the years, until they became so ingrained they felt like the truth: I left because I wanted a change. I don't know what happened to him; he just disappeared. I did nothing wrong.

Fatima is silent, but her bird-bright eyes are steady on me, and I let my hand drop from where I have been fiddling with my hair. When you watch people lying as often as we have, you get to know each other's tells. Thea bites her nails. Fatima avoids eye contact. Kate goes still and remote and unreachable. And I . . . I fret at my hair, twining it into knots around my fingers, weaving a web as tangled as our falsehoods, without even noticing what I'm doing.

I worked so hard to overcome it, back then. And now I can see from Fatima's sympathetic smile that my old quirk has betrayed me again.

"That's not true," I admit. "I did think about him . . . a lot. Did you?"

She nods.

"Of course."

There is silence, and I know we are both thinking about him . . . about his hands, long and narrow, with strong fingers that ran across the strings of the guitar, first slow as a lover, then faster than you could see. About his eyes, changeable like a tiger's, and the way they flickered from copper-colored in the sunshine to golden brown in the shadows. His face is etched into my memory, and now, I see him, so clearly that it's almost as if he's standing in front of me—the jutting Roman nose that made his profile so distinctive; the broad, expressive mouth; the sweep of his long, low brows and the way they winged upwards slightly at the edges, giving him the look of someone always just about to frown.

I sigh, and Freya stirs in her light slumber.

"Do you want me to go?" Fatima says quietly. "If I'm disturbing her . . ."

"No, stay," I say. Freya's eyes are drifting shut and then snapping open, and her limbs are becoming loose and heavy, and I know she is nearly back to sleep.

Freya is lolling now, and I lay her gently into the cradle.

Just in time, for below I hear the sound of footsteps, and a crash as a door is flung open, and Thea's voice, ringing through the house above Shadow's barking.

"Honeys, I'm home!"

Freya startles, flinging out her arms, starfishwise, but I put a hand on her chest, and her eyes drift shut, and then I follow Fatima out of Luc's room and down the stairs to where Thea is waiting.

Looking back at Salten House, the thing that I remember most is the contrasts. The searing brightness that came off the sea on a sunny winter's day, and the midnight black of a country night—deeper than any London dark. The quiet concentration of the art rooms, and the shrieking cacophony of the buttery, with three hundred hungry girls waiting to be fed. And, most of all, the intensity of the friendships that sprang up after only a few weeks in that hothouse atmosphere . . . and the enmities that went with that.

It was the noise that struck me most, that first night. Fatima and I were unpacking when the bell went for supper, moving around the room in a silence that was already companionable and easy. When the bell shrieked out and we tumbled hastily into the corridor, the wall of sound that met us was like nothing I had heard at my day school—and it only intensified when we walked into the buttery. Lunch had been busy enough, but girls had been arriving all day, and now the hall was rammed, the din of three hundred high-pitched voices enough to make your eardrums bleed.

Fatima and I were standing uncertainly, looking for a space to sit, as girls pushed purposefully past us on all sides, heading for their own particular friends, when I saw Thea and Kate at the end of one of the long polished wood tables. They were facing each other, and there was a spare place beside each of them. I nodded at Fatima, and we began to make our way over—but then another girl cut in front of us, and I realized she was aiming there, too. There would not be enough space for all of us.

"You take it," I said to Fatima resignedly. "I don't mind going to another table."

"Don't be silly." Fatima gave me a friendly shove. "I'm not abandoning you! There's got to be two seats together somewhere."

But she didn't move. There was something about the way the other girl was walking towards Kate and Thea that didn't seem quite right—there was a purpose to it, a hostility that I couldn't quite pin down.

"Looking for a seat?" Thea said sweetly as the girl reached her. I'd later come to know her as Helen Fitzpatrick, and she was cheerful and gossipy, but now she laughed, disbelieving and bitter.

"Thanks, but I'd rather sit by the toilets. Why the hell did you tell me Miss Weatherby was pregnant? I sent her a congratulations card, and she went completely mental. I've been gated for six weeks."

Thea said nothing, but I could see she was trying not to laugh, and Kate, who was sitting with her back to Helen, mouthed *Ten points* and held up her fingers to Thea, grinning.

"Well?" Helen demanded.

"My mistake. I must have misheard."

"Don't bullshit me! You're a filthy liar."

"It was a joke," Thea said. "I never told you it was definite—I said I'd heard through the grapevine. Next time, check your facts."

"I'll give you *facts*. I heard some *facts* about your last school, Thea. I met a girl from there at tennis camp. She said you're not right in the head and they had to expel you. Well, they had the right idea, if you ask me. The sooner they chuck you out of here, the better, as far as I'm concerned."

Kate stood up at that and swung round to face Helen. Her face was quite changed from the mischievous, friendly expression I'd seen on the train. It was full of a cold, hard anger that scared me a little.

"You know what your problem is?" She leaned forward so that Helen took a step back, almost involuntarily. "You spend far too much time listening to rumors. If you stopped believing every nasty bit of gossip floating around, you wouldn't have got a detention."

"Fuck you," Helen spat, and then all the girls jumped as a voice came from behind the little group. It was Miss Farquharson, Gym.

"Everything quite all right here?"

Helen shot a look at Thea and seemed to bite her tongue.

"Yes, Miss Farquharson," she said, her voice sulky.

"Thea? Kate?"

"Yes, Miss Farquharson," Kate said.

"Good. Look, there are two new girls hovering behind you looking for a space, and no one's asked them to sit down. Fatima, Isa, make room for yourselves on the benches. Helen, do you need a seat?"

"No, Miss Farquharson. Jess is saving me one."

"Then I suggest you go and take it." Miss Farquharson turned and was about to go, when she stopped and her expression changed. She bent and sniffed the air above Thea's head. "Thea, what's this I smell? Please don't tell me you have been smoking on school property. Miss Weatherby made it very clear last term that if there were any further instances of this we'd be calling your father and discussing suspension."

There was a long pause. I saw Thea's fingers were gripping the table edge. She exchanged a look with Kate and then opened her mouth—but to my own surprise, I found myself speaking first.

"We were stuck in a smoking carriage, Miss Farqu-harson. On the train. There was a man there with a cigar—poor Thea was sitting next to him."

"It was disgusting," Fatima put in. "Like, really stinky. I felt sick even though I was by the window."

Miss Farquharson turned to look at us, and I could see her appraising us both—me with my clear, girlish face and smile, and Fatima, her dark eyes innocent and guileless. I felt my fingers go nervously to my hair and stopped myself, linking my fingers together behind my back, like a kind of restraint hold. Slowly, Miss Farqu-harson nodded.

"How very unpleasant. Well, we'll say nothing more, Thea. *This* time. Now sit down, girls. The prefects will start serving out in a moment."

We sat down, and Miss Farquharson moved away.

"Bloody hell," Thea whispered. She reached across the table to where I was sitting and squeezed my hand, her fingers cold against mine and still shaking with spent nerves. "And . . . God, I don't know what to say. Thank you!"

"Seriously," Kate said. She shook her head, her expression a mix of relief and rueful admiration. The steely fury I'd seen in her expression as she faced up to Helen was gone, as if it had never existed. "Both of you pulled that off like pros."

"Welcome to the Lying Game," Thea said. She glanced at Kate. "Right?"

And Kate nodded.

"Welcome to the Lying Game. Oh"—her face broke into a grin—"and ten points."

It didn't take Fatima and me long to find out why the tower was considered to have the best rooms; in fact, we worked it out that very first evening. I had returned to our room after watching a film in the common room. Fatima was already there, lying on her bed, writing what looked like a letter on thin airmail paper, her mahogany hair hanging like dark curtains of silk on either side of her face.

She looked up as I came in, and yawned, and I saw she was already in her pajamas—a skimpy vest top and pink flannel shorts. The top rode up as she stretched, showing a strip of flat stomach.

"Ready for bed?" she asked.

"Definitely." I sat down on the mattress with a squeak of springs and pulled off my shoes. "God, I'm shattered. So many new faces . . ."

"I know." Fatima shook back her hair and folded the letter into her bedside table. "I couldn't face meeting more people after supper, so I came back here. Was that awful of me?"

"Don't be silly. It's probably what I should have done. I didn't talk to anyone, really, anyway—it seemed to be mostly younger girls."

"What was the film?"

"*Clueless*," I said, stifling a yawn of my own, and then I turned my back to start unbuttoning my shirt. I had imagined a cubicle, like in boarding school stories, with curtains you could pull around, but it turned out that was only for the dormitories. Girls in bedrooms were expected just to give each other privacy when necessary.

I was in my pajamas, and rummaging in my locker for my sponge bag, when a noise made me stop and look back, over my shoulder. It had sounded like a knock, but it hadn't come from the door side of the room.

"Was that you?" I asked Fatima. She shook her head.

"I was about to ask the same thing. It sounded like it came from the window."

The curtains were closed, and we both stood, listening, feeling oddly tense and foolish. I was just about to shrug it off with a laugh and a comment about Rapunzel, when the sound came again, louder this time, making us both squeak and then giggle nervously.

It had come, quite definitely this time, from the window closest to my bed, and I strode across to it and pulled back the curtain.

I don't know what I was expecting—but whatever it was, it was not what I saw: a pale face peering through the glass, surrounded by the darkness. For a minute, I just gaped, and then I remembered what I had seen from the minivan as it made its way up the drive: the black wiry tendrils of the fire escapes, twining up the sides of the building and round the towers, and I looked closer. It was Kate.

She grinned and made a twisting motion with her wrist, and I realized that she wanted me to open the window.

The clasp was rusty and stiff, and I struggled for a long moment before it gave with a screech.

"Well," Kate said. She waved a hand at a rickety black metal structure below her, silhouetted against the paler background of the sea. "What are you waiting for?"

I looked back over my shoulder at Fatima, who

shrugged and nodded, and then, pulling the blanket off the foot of my bed, I clambered up onto the windowsill and out into the cool autumn darkness.

OUTSIDE, THE NIGHT AIR WAS still and calm, and as Fatima and I followed Kate quietly up the shivering metal steps of the fire escape, I could hear the far-off crash of the waves against the shingle shore, and the screech of the gulls wheeling and calling out to sea.

Thea was waiting at the top of the fire escape as we rounded the last curve of the tower. She had on a T-shirt, and it barely skimmed her long, slim thighs.

"Spread out that blanket," she said to me, and I flung it out across the wire mesh and sat down beside her.

"So now you know," Kate said, with a conspiratorial smile. "You have our secret in your hands."

"And all we can offer in return for your silence," Thea drawled, "is this." She held up a glass bottle of Jack Daniel's. "And these." And she held up a packet of Silk Cut. "Do you smoke?" She tapped the packet and held it out towards us, a single cigarette poking from the top.

Fatima shook her head.

"No. But I'll have some of that." She nodded at the bourbon, and Kate passed her the bottle. Fatima took a long swig, shuddered, and then wiped her mouth with a grin.

"Isa?" Thea said, still holding out the cigarette.

I didn't smoke. I had tried it once or twice at my school in London and hadn't enjoyed it. And more than that, I knew that my parents would hate me smoking, particularly my father, who had smoked himself as a younger man and had periodic relapses into self-hatred and cigars.

But here … here I was someone else … someone new.

There was no one here to smell the smoke on my hair, no one to ask questions, or find a lighter in my pocket.

Here I was not the conscientious schoolgirl who always got her homework in on time, and did the vacuuming before she went out with her friends.

Here I could be anyone I wanted. Here I could be someone completely different.

"Thanks," I said. I took the cigarette from Thea's outstretched packet and when Kate flicked her Bic lighter, I leaned in towards the flame-filled cup made by her hands, my hair falling across her honey-brown arm like a caress, and I took a cautious puff, blinking against the sting in my eyes, and hoping I wouldn't choke.

"Thanks for earlier," Thea said. "The smoking, I mean. You . . . you really saved my bacon. I don't know what would happen if I got expelled again. I seriously think Dad might get me locked up."

"It was nothing." I breathed out, watching the thread of smoke float up, past the rooftops of the school, towards a glorious white moon, just a shade off full. "But listen, what did you mean, that thing you said at dinner? About the points?"

"It's how we keep track," Kate said. "Ten points for suckering someone completely. Five for a really inspired story or for making another player break. Fifteen points for taking down someone really snooty. But the points don't count for anything, really, it's just . . . I don't know. To make it more fun."

"It's a version of a game they used to play at one of my old schools," Thea said. She took a long, languid puff of her cigarette. "They did it to new girls. The idea was to get them to do something stupid—you know, tell them that it was tradition for all students to take their bath towel to evening prep to make it faster for evening showers, or persuade them first-years could only walk clockwise round the quad. Pathetic stuff. Anyway, when I came here I was the new girl all over again, and I thought, fuck them. I'll be the one who lies this time. And this time I'll make it count. I won't pick on the new girls, the ones who can't defend them-selves. I'll do it to the ones in charge—the teachers, the popular girls. The ones who think they're above it all." She blew out a plume of smoke. "Only, the first time I lied to Kate, she didn't hit the roof and threaten to have me ostracized, she just laughed. And that's when I knew. She wasn't one of them."

"And neither are you," Kate said conspiratorially. "Right?"

"Right," Fatima said. She took a swig from the bottle and grinned.

I only nodded. I brought the cigarette up to my lips and puffed again, inhaling deeply this time, feeling the smoke going down into my lungs and filtering through my blood. My head swam, and the hand holding the cigarette shook as I put it down to rest on the meshed wire of the fire escape platform, but I said nothing, hoping only that the others hadn't noticed the sudden head rush.

I felt Thea watching me, and I had the strangest conviction that in spite of my composure, she was not deceived and knew exactly what was passing through my mind, and the struggle I was having to pretend that I was used to this, but she didn't tease me about it, she just held out the bottle.

"Drink up," she said, her vowels sharp as glass, and then, as if recognizing her own imperiousness, she grinned, softening the haughtiness of the command. "You need something to take the edge off the first day."

I thought of my mother, asleep under a sheet in the hospital, poison trickling into her veins; my brother, alone in his new room at Charterhouse; my father, driving back through the night to our empty house in London . . . my nerves sang, tight as violin strings, and I nodded and reached out with my free hand.

When the whiskey hit my mouth it burned like fire, and I had to fight the urge to choke and cough, but I swallowed it down, feeling it scald my gullet all the way to my stomach, feeling the tight fibers of my core relax, just a little. Then I held the bottle out, towards Kate this time.

Kate took it and put it to her lips, and when she drank, it wasn't a cautious swig like the ones Fatima and I had taken, but two, three full-on gulps, without pausing, or even flinching; she might have been drinking milk.

When she had finished, she wiped her mouth, her eyes glinting in the darkness.

"Here's to us," she said, holding the bottle high, the moonlight striking off the glass. "May we never grow old."

Thea, out of all of them, is the person I have not seen for longest, and so the image in my mind's eye as I descend the stairs is the girl of seventeen years ago, with her long beautiful face and her hair like a storm front coming across a sunlit sky.

As I round the corner of the rickety stairs, it's not Thea that I see first, but the watercolor that Ambrose did, in the corner of the staircase, Thea, swimming in the Reach. Ambrose has caught the sunlight on her skin and the prismed light filtering through the water, and her head is flung back, her long hair slicked to her skull, making her even more arresting.

It is with that picture in my head that I turn the final curve, wondering what to expect—and Thea is waiting.

She is more beautiful than ever—I would not have thought that were possible, but it's true. Her face is thinner, her bones more defined, and her dark hair is cropped close to her skull. It's as if her beauty has been pared back to its bones, shorn of the two-tone waterfall of silky hair, of makeup and jewelry.

She is older, more striking, even thinner—*too* thin. And yet she is exactly the same.

I think of Kate's toast, that night, long ago when we barely knew one another. *May we never grow old . . .*

"Thee," I breathe.

And then I am holding her and feeling her bones, and Fatima is hugging her and laughing, and Thee is saying, "For Christ's sake, you two, you're crushing me! And watch out for my boots; the fucker chucked me out of the cab halfway up the Reach. I practically had to wade here."

She smells of cigarettes . . . and alcohol, its sweetness like overripe fruit heavy on her breath as she laughs into my hair, before letting us both go and walking to the table in the window.

"I can't believe you two are mums." Her smile is just as it always was, curved, a little wry, concealing secrets. She pulls out the chair that was always hers when we sat and smoked and drank into the small hours, and sits down, putting a Sobranie cigarette, black with a gold tip, between her lips. "How did they let reprobates like you reproduce?"

"I know, right?" Fatima pulls out her own chair and sits opposite, her back to the stove. "That's pretty much what I said to Ali when they gave me Nadia to take home from the hospital. 'What the hell do I do now?'"

Kate picks up a plate and holds it out to Thea, one eyebrow raised.

"Yes? No? Have you eaten? There's plenty of cous-cous left."

Thea shakes her head and lights her cigarette before she answers, blowing out a stream of smoke.

"I'm fine. I just want a drink. And to find out why the hell we're all here."

"We have wine . . . and wine . . ." Kate says. She looks through the lopsided dresser. "And . . . wine. That's it."

"Christ, you've gone soft on me. No spirits? Go on, then, I guess I'll have wine."

Kate pours into one of the cracked green-blue glasses on the side—a huge glass—a third of a bottle at least, and hands it to Thea, who holds it up, watching the candle in the center of the table through the ruby depths.

"To us," she says at last. "May we never grow old."

But I don't want to drink to that now. I *do* want to grow old. I want to grow old, see Freya grow up, feel the wrinkles on my face.

I am saved from commenting when Thea pauses, her glass halfway to her lips, and points with one finger at Fatima's glass of lemonade.

"Hang on, hang on, what's this shit? Lemonade? You can't drink a toast with lemonade. You're not knocked up again, are you?"

Fatima shakes her head with a smile and then points to the scarf lying loosely around her shoulders.

"Times have changed, Thea. This isn't just a fashion accessory."

"Oh, darling, come *on*. Wearing a hijab doesn't mean you have to be a nun! We get Muslims in the casino all the time. One of them told me for a fact that if you drink gin and tonic it doesn't count as alcohol—it's classified as medicine because of the quinine."

"A, that advice is what's technically termed in theological circles as 'bullshit,'" Fatima says. She's still smiling, but there's a little hint of steel under her light voice. "And B, you have to wonder about the dissociative powers of anyone wearing a hijab in a *casino*, considering the Koranic teachings on gambling."

There is silence in the room. I exchange a glance with Kate and draw a breath to speak, but I can't think of what to say, other than to tell Thea to shut the fuck up.

"You weren't always such a prude," Thea says at last, sipping her wine, and beside me I feel Kate stiffen with anxiety, but Thea is smiling, the corner of her mouth just quirked with that little, wry tilt. "In fact I might be wrong, but I distinctly remember a certain game of strip poker . . . ? Or am I thinking of a different Miss Qureshy?"

"You weren't always such a dick," Fatima replies, but

there's no rancor in her voice, and she is smiling, too. She reaches across the table and punches Thea lightly on the arm, and Thea laughs, and her real, true smile—the one that is wide and generous and full of self-mockery—flashes out in spite of herself.

"Liar," she says, still grinning, and the tension leaches out of the air, like static electricity discharging into the ground with a harmless crackle.

I DON'T KNOW WHAT TIME it is when I get up from the table to go to the bathroom. It must be long past midnight. I look in at Freya on my way back, and she is sleeping peacefully, her arms and legs sprawled in complete relaxation.

As I make my way back down the curving stairs to where my old friends sit, I am overwhelmed by a sharp pang of déjà vu. Fatima, Thea, Kate, they are seated in their old accustomed places, and for a moment, their heads bent around the flickering light of the candle, they could be fifteen again. I have the strangest impression of a gramophone record that has skipped, retracing over the echoes of our former selves, and I feel the ghosts of the past crowd in: Ambrose . . . Luc . . . My heart clutches in my chest, an almost physical pain, and for a moment—a brief, stabbing moment—a picture flashes before my eyes, a scene I have tried so hard to forget.

I shut my eyes, put my hands to my face, trying to scrub the image away—and when I open them again it's just Thea, Fatima, and Kate there. But the memory remains—a body, stretched out on the rug, four shocked white faces, stained with tears . . .

There is a chilly touch on my hand, and I jump, swinging round, my heart thumping as I survey the stairs, winding up into darkness.

I'm not sure who I was expecting—there is no one here but us, after all—but whoever it was, they are not there—just the shadows of the room, and the faces of our former selves looking out from the walls.

Then I hear Kate's low laugh, and I realize, before my eyes refocus a foot down from where I was expecting to see a person. It's not a ghost but a shadow—Kate's dog, Shadow, his cold nose against my hand, looking plaintive and confused.

"He thinks it's bedtime," Kate says. "He's hoping someone will take him out for a walk."

"A walk?" Thea says. She takes out another Sobranie and puts the gold tip between her lips. "Screw that. I say a *swim*."

"I didn't bring my swimsuit," I say automatically, before I realize what her raised eyebrow and wickedly provocative expression means, and I start to laugh, half reluctantly. "No way, and anyway, Freya's asleep upstairs. I can't leave her."

"So don't swim far!" Thea says. "Kate. Towels!"

Kate stands up, takes a gulp from the glass of wine on the table in front of us, and goes to a cupboard near the stove. Inside there are threadbare towels, faded to shades of pastel gray. She throws one at Thea, one at me. Fatima holds up her hands.

"Thanks, but . . ."

"Come on . . ." Thea drawls. "We're all women, right?"

"That's what they all say, until some drunk comes along on the way back from the pub. I'll sit it out, cheers."

"Suit yourself," Thea says. "Come on, Isa, Kate, don't let me down, you losers."

She stands, too, and begins to unbutton her shirt. Underneath I can see already that she is not wearing a bra.

I don't want to undress. I know Thea would laugh at my self-consciousness, but I can't help thinking of my post-pregnancy body and the stretch marks on my still-soft belly. It would be different if Fatima were swimming, too, but she's not—it will be me and Thea and Kate, both of them as slim and lithe as seventeen years ago. But I know I won't get out of it, not without a ribbing from Thea. And besides, there's part of me that *wants* to. It's not just the stickiness of the hair against my neck, and the way my dress is clinging to the perspiration on my back. It's more than that. We are here, all of us. There's part of me that *wants* to relive that.

I take a towel and walk outside into the darkness. I never had the courage to go in first when we were teenagers. I don't know why not—some strange superstition, a fear of what might be lurking in the waters. If the others were there, I would be safe. It was always Kate or Thea who led the charge, usually running off the jetty with a shriek to dive-bomb into the center of the Reach, where the current ran fast. Now, I am too cowardly *not* to go first.

My dress is soft, stretchy cotton and I peel it off in a single movement and drop it to one side, unhook my bra, and step out of my knickers. Then I draw a breath and lower myself into the water—quickly, before the others have time to come out and see my soft nakedness.

"Whoa, Isa's gone in!" I hear from inside, as I surface, spluttering with the cold. The night is warm, sweaty even, but the tide is high and the Reach is salt seawater, straight from the Channel.

Thea strolls out onto the jetty as I tread water, gasping as my skin acclimates. She is naked, and I see for the first time that her body has changed, too, as drastically as mine in some ways. She was always thin, but now she must be close to anorexia, her stomach hollow, her breasts shallow saucers against visible ribs. One thing has not changed, though—her complete unself-consciousness as she saunters to the very edge of the platform, the lamplight casting a long slim shadow over the waters. Thea has never been ashamed of nakedness.

"Out of my way, bitches," she says, and then she dives, a perfect dive, long and shallow. It's also suicidally stupid. The Reach is not that deep and is full of obstructions—pikes in the riverbed, the vestiges of old jetties and mooring posts, lobster pots, junk washed downstream by the current, sandbanks that shift and change with the tides and the passing years. She could easily have broken her neck, and on the jetty I see Kate wince with horror and put her hands to her mouth—but then Thea surfaces, shaking the water off her hair like a dog.

"What are you waiting for?" she calls to Kate, who lets out a long, slow breath of relief.

"You *idiot*," she says, something close to anger in her voice. "There's a sandbank in the middle there; you could have killed yourself."

"But I didn't," Thea says. She is panting with the cold, her eyes bright. Her arm, as she raises it from the water to beckon to Kate, is rough with goose bumps. "Come on, get in the sea, woman."

Kate hesitates . . . and for a minute, I think perhaps I know what she is thinking. There is a picture in my mind's eye . . . a shallow pit, filling up with water, the sandy sides crumbling away . . . Then she straightens her spine, an unconscious defiance in every bone.

"All right." She peels off her vest top, steps out of her jeans, and turns to unhook her bra, and then, last, before she enters the water, she picks up the bottle of wine she has brought out onto the jetty and takes a long, gulping draught. There is something about the tilt of her head and the movement of her throat that is unbearably young and vulnerable, and just for a moment the years slip away and she is the same Kate, sitting out on the fire escape at Salten House, throwing back her head to drain the whiskey bottle.

Then she lets the bottle drop on top of her pile of clothes, squares herself for the plunge, and I feel the ripples as she hits the water, feet away from me, and plunges beneath the moon-dappled surface.

I wait, expecting her to come up somewhere close . . . but she doesn't. There are no bubbles, and it's impossible to see where she is, the moonlight reflecting off the water makes it hard to see anything beneath.

"Kate?" I say, treading water, feeling my anxiety rise as the seconds tick past and there is still no sign of her. And then, "Thea, where the hell's Kate?"

And then I feel something catch on my ankle, a cold, strong grip that jerks me down, deep, deep into the Reach. I catch a breath before I go under, but I am deep below before I can scream, grappling the thing that is pulling me down.

Just as suddenly, it lets go, and I surface, gasping and raking salt water out of my eyes, to find Kate's grinning face next to mine, her arms holding me up.

"You bitch!" I gasp, not sure if I want to hug her or drown her. "You could have warned me!"

"That would have spoiled the point of it," Kate says, panting. Her eyes are bright, and laughing.

Thea is far out in the center of the Reach, where the current is strongest and the water is deep, floating on her back in the sweep of the turning tide, swimming to keep herself in one place.

"Come out," she calls. "It's so beautiful."

With Fatima watching from the jetty, Kate and I swim out to where Thea floats, suspended in reflected starlight, and we turn on our backs, and I feel their hands link with mine, and float, a constellation of bodies, pale in the moonlight, limbs tangled, fingers clutching and bumping and losing hold, and then clutching again.

"Come on, Fati," Thea calls. "It's gorgeous out here."

And it is. Now the shock of the cold has worn off, it's surprisingly warm, and the moon above is almost full. When I dive beneath the surface I can see it, glinting above, refracted into a thousand shards that pierce the milky, muddy waters of the Reach.

When I surface, I see that Fatima has moved closer to the side of the jetty and is sitting right at the edge, trailing her fingers in the sea, almost wistfully.

"It's not the same without you," Kate pleads. "Come on . . . you know you want to . . ."

Fatima shakes her head and stands, I assume to go inside. But I'm wrong. As I watch, treading water, she takes a breath and then she leaps—clothes and all, her scarf fluttering like a bird's wing in the night air, and she hits the surface with a smack.

"No way!" Thea crows. "She did it!"

And we are scything our way through the water towards her, laughing and shivering with a kind of hysteria, and Fatima is laughing, too, wringing out her scarf, and hugging us to keep afloat as the water drags on her clothes.

We are together again.

And for that brief instant in time, that is all that matters.

It is late. We have dragged ourselves from the water, laughing and cursing, scraping our shins on the splintered rotten wood, and we have toweled our hair and dried our goose-bumped skin. Fatima has changed out of her wet clothes, shaking her head at her own stupidity, and now we are lying sleepily on Kate's threadbare sofa in our pajamas and dressing gowns, a tangle of weary limbs and soft worn throws, gossiping, reminiscing, telling the old stories: *Do you remember . . . ?*

Fatima's hair is loose and damp, and with it tangling round her face she looks younger, so much closer to the girl she used to be. It's hard to believe that she has a husband and two children of her own. As I watch her, laughing at something Kate has said, the grandfather clock standing against the far wall gives two faint chimes, and she turns to look.

"Oh blimey. I can't believe it's two a.m.! I've *got* to get some sleep."

"You lightweight," Thea says. She doesn't look in the least tired, in fact she looks as if she could go on for hours—her eyes are sparkling as she knocks back the dregs of a glass of wine. "I didn't even *start* my shift until midnight last night!"

"Well, exactly. It's all very well for you," Fatima says defensively. "Some of us have spent years conditioning ourselves to the rigid timetable of a nine-to-five job and a couple of kids. It's hard to snap out of it. Look, Isa's yawning, too!"

They all turn to look at me, and I try, unsuccessfully,

to stifle the yawn that's already halfway in motion, and then shrug and smile.

"Sorry, what can I say? I lost my stamina along with my waist. But Fatima's right . . . Freya wakes up at seven. I have to get a few hours in before then."

"Come on," Fatima says, standing up and stretching. "Bed."

"Wait," Kate says, her voice low, and I realize that out of all of us, she has been the quietest for this last part of the night. Fatima, Thea, and I, we have all been telling our favorite stories, anecdotes at the expense of one another, dredged up memories . . . but Kate has kept silent, guarding her thoughts to herself. Now, her voice is a surprise, and we all turn to look. She is curled in the armchair, her hair loose and shadowing her face, and there is something in her expression that makes us all stop. My stomach flutters.

"What?" Fatima says, and there is uneasiness in her voice. She sits again, but on the edge of the sofa this time, her fingers twining around the edge of the scarf she has draped to dry on the fireguard around the stove. "What is it?"

"I . . ." Kate says, and then she stops. She drops her eyes. "Oh God," she says, almost to herself. "I didn't know it would be this difficult."

And suddenly I know what she is about to say, and I am not sure that I want to hear it.

"Spit it out," Thea says, her voice hard. "Say it, Kate. We've skirted round it long enough; it's time to tell us why."

Why what? Kate could retort. But she doesn't need to ask. We all know. Why are we here? What did that text mean, those three little words: *I need you*?

Kate draws a long breath, and she looks up, her face shadowed in the lamplight.

But to my surprise, she doesn't speak. Instead, she gets up and goes to the pile of newspapers in the scuttle by the stove, left there for lighting the logs. There is one on the top, the *Salten Observer*, and she holds it out, wordless, her face showing all the fear she has been hiding this long, drunken evening.

It is dated yesterday, and the headline on the front page is very simple.

Human Bone Found in Reach

RULE TWO

STICK TO YOUR STORY

Shit." The voice that breaks the silence is Fatima's, surprising me with her vehemence. *"Shit."*

Kate lets the paper fall and I snatch it up, my eyes darting across the page. *Following last week's reports that police had been called to identify remains found on the north bank of the Reach at Salten . . .*

My hand is shaking so hard that I can hardly read, and disjointed phrases jumble together as I scan the page. *Police spokesperson confirmed . . . human skeletal remains . . . unnamed witness . . . poor state of preservation . . . forensic examination . . . locals shocked . . . area closed to the public . . .*

"Have they . . ." Thea falters uncharacteristically and starts again. "Do they know . . ."

She stops.

"Do they know who it is?" I finish for her, my voice hard and brittle, looking at Kate, who sits with her head bowed beneath the weight of our questions. The paper in my hand trembles, making a sound like leaves falling. "The body?"

Kate shakes her head, but she doesn't need to say the words I know we are all thinking: *Not yet . . .*

"It's just a bone. It might be completely unconnected, right?" Thea says, but then her face twists. "Fuck, who am I kidding? *Shit!*" She slams her fist, the one holding the glass, down onto the table and the glass breaks, shards skittering everywhere.

"Oh, Thee," Kate says, her voice very low.

"Stop being a bloody drama queen, Thee," Fatima says angrily. She goes to the sink to get a cloth and a brush. "Did you cut yourself?" she throws back over her shoulder.

Thea shakes her head, her face white, but she lets Fatima examine her hand, wiping away the dregs of wine with a tea towel. As Fatima pushes back Thea's sleeve, I see what the moonlight outside hid—the trace of white scars on her inner arm, long healed but still visible, and I can't stop myself from flinching and looking away, remembering when those cuts were fresh and raw.

"You idiot," Fatima says, but her touch, as she brushes the shards of glass from Thea's palm, is gentle, and there is a tremor in her voice.

"I can't do this," Thea says, shaking her head, and I realize for the first time how drunk she is, just holding it together well. "Not again, not now. Even rumors— casinos are fucking strict, do you guys realize that? And if the police get involved . . ." There is a crack in her voice, the tremor of a sob trying to rise to the surface. "Shit, I could lose my gaming license. I might never work again."

"Look, we're *all* in the same boat," Fatima says. "You think people want a GP with questions like that hanging over their head? Or a lawyer?" She jerks her head at me. "Isa and I have got just as much to lose as you."

She doesn't mention Kate. She doesn't have to.

"So what do we do?" Thea asks at last. She looks from me to Kate to Fatima. "Shit. Why the hell did you bring us down here?"

"Because you had a right to know," Kate says. Her voice shakes. "And because I couldn't think of a safer way to tell you."

"We need to do what we should have done years ago," Fatima says vehemently. "Get our story straight *before* they question us."

"The story is what it always has been," Kate says. She pulls the newspaper away from me and folds it so she can't see the headline, scoring the page with her nails. Her hands are trembling. "The story is, we know nothing. We saw nothing. There's nothing we *can* do except stick to that—we can't change our account."

"I mean what do we do *now*?" Thea's voice rises. "Do we stay? Go? Fatima has the car, after all. There's nothing keeping us here."

"You stay," Kate says, and her voice has that quality that I remember so well—an absolute finality that was impossible to argue with. "You stay, because as far as everyone's concerned, you came down for the dinner tomorrow night."

"What?" Thea frowns, and I remember for the first time that the others don't know about this. "What dinner?"

"The alumnae dinner."

"But we're not invited," Fatima says. "Surely they wouldn't let us back? Not after what happened?"

Kate shrugs, and for an answer she goes to the corkboard beside the sink and pulls out a pin securing four stiff white invitations, returning with the cards in her hand.

"Apparently they would," she says, holding them out.

The Salten House Old Girls' Association invites

_____

to the Alumnae Summer Ball.

In the space on each card is scrawled our names, handwritten in navy-blue fountain pen.

Kate Atagon
Fatima Chaudhry (née Qureshy)
Thea West
Isa Wilde

Kate holds them, fanned like playing cards, as though inviting us to take one, make a bet.

But I am not looking at the names, or the embossed gilt lettering of the text itself. I am looking at the hole, stabbed through each card by the pin holding them to the corkboard. And I am thinking about how, however much we struggled to be free, this is how it always ends, the four of us, skewered together by the past.

Art was an extra for most of us at Salten House, an "enrichment" the school called it, unless you were studying it for an exam, which I was not, so it was some weeks into the term, when the days at Salten had become almost routine, by the time I encountered the art studios, and Ambrose Atagon.

Like most boarding schools, Salten groups pupils in school houses—in this case each named for a Greek goddess. Fatima and I had been put in the same house, Artemis, goddess of the hunt, so our enrichment came round at the same time, and we both found ourselves searching for the studios one frosted October morning after breakfast, walking back and forth across the quad, looking for anyone more knowledgeable than ourselves to ask.

"Where the bloody hell is it?" Fatima said again, for the tenth time, and for perhaps the eighth time I answered, "I don't know, but we'll find it. Stop panicking."

As the words left my mouth, a second-year clutching a huge pad of watercolor paper shot past in the direction of the maths rooms and I called out, "Hey, you! Are you heading to art?"

She turned around, her face pink with haste.

"Yes, but I'm late. What is it?"

"We've got art, too. We're lost; can we follow you?"

"Yes, but hurry." She turned and bolted through an archway covered with white snowberries and through a wooden door we'd never seen before, hidden in the shadows of the snowberry bush.

Inside there was the inevitable flight of steps—I have never been so fit, since leaving Salten—and we followed her up, and up, two or three flights at least, until I began to wonder where on earth we were heading.

At last, the stairs opened out onto a small landing with a wire-hatched glass door, which the girl flung open.

Inside was a long vaulted gallery, the walls low but the roof arching to a triangular point. The space above our heads was crisscrossed with supporting beams and braces, all hung with drying sketches and balanced with strange items, presumably to be used for still-life compositions—an empty birdcage; a broken lute; a stuffed marmoset, its eyes sad and wise.

There were no windows, for the walls were too low, just skylights in the vaulted roof, and I realized that we must be in the attics above the maths classrooms. The space was flooded with winter sunlight and filled with objects and pictures, entirely unlike any of the other classrooms I had seen so far—white-painted, sterile, and painfully clean—and I stood in the doorway, blinking at the dazzling impression.

"Sorry, Ambrose," the second-year gasped, and I blinked again. Ambrose? That was another strangeness. The other teachers at Salten were routinely female and referred to as Miss whatever their surname was, regardless of their marital status.

No one, but no one, used first names.

I turned, to see the person she had addressed so informally.

And I caught my first sight of Ambrose Atagon.

I ONCE TRIED TO DESCRIBE Ambrose to an old boyfriend, before I met Owen, but I found it almost impossible. I have photographs, but they only show a man of middle height, with wiry dark hair, and shoulders curved from hunching perpetually over a sketch. He had Kate's thin mobile face, and years of sketching in the sun and squinting against the bright light of the bay had worn his skin into lines that made him look somehow paradoxically younger than his forty-five years, not older. And he shared Kate's slate-blue eyes, the only remarkable feature he possessed, but even they don't come alive in a photograph the way they do in my memory—for Ambrose was *so* alive—always working, laughing, loving . . . his hands never still, always rolling a cigarette, or sketching a drawing, or throwing back a glass of the harsh red wine he kept in two-liter bottles under the sink at the Mill—too rough for anyone else to drink.

Only an artist of the caliber of Ambrose himself could have captured all that life, the contradictions of his still concentration and restless energy, and the mysterious magnetic attraction of a man of very ordinary appearance.

But he never made a self-portrait. Or not that I know of. Ironic, really, when he drew anything and everything around him—the birds on the river, the girls at Salten House, the fragile marsh flowers that shivered and blew in the summer breeze, the ripple of wind on the Reach . . .

He drew Kate obsessively, littering the house with sketches of her eating, swimming, sleeping, playing . . . and later he drew me, and Thea, and Fatima, though he always asked our permission. I remember it still, his halting, slight gravelly voice, so like Kate's: "Do you, um, mind if I draw you?"

And we never minded. Though maybe we should have.

One long summer afternoon he drew me, sitting

at the kitchen table with the strap of my dress falling from one shoulder, my chin in my hands, and my eyes fixed on him. And I can still remember the feel of the sun on my cheek, and the heat of my gaze upon him, and the little electric shock that happened every single time he glanced up at my face from his sketch and our eyes met.

He gave me the drawing, but I don't know what happened to it. I gave it to Kate, because there was nowhere to hide it at school, and it didn't feel right to show my parents, or the girls at Salten House. They would not have understood. No one would have understood.

AFTER HIS DISAPPEARANCE THERE WERE whispers—his past, his drug convictions, the fact that he didn't have a single teaching qualification to his name. That first day, though, I knew none of this. I had no idea the part that Ambrose would play in our lives, and we in his, or how the ripples of our meeting would go on reverberating down the years. I just stood, holding the strap of my bag and panting, as he straightened from his position, hunched over a pupil's easel. He looked across at me with those blue, blue eyes, and he smiled, a smile that crinkled the skin above his beard and at the corners of his eyes.

"Hello," he said kindly, putting down the borrowed brush and wiping his hands on his painter's apron. "I don't believe we've met. I'm Ambrose."

I opened my mouth, but no words came out. It was something about the intensity of his gaze. The way you could believe, in the moment that he looked at you, that he cared, utterly and completely. That there was no one else in the universe who mattered to him as much as you did. That you were alone, in a crowded room.

"I'm . . . I'm Isa," I said at last. "Isa Wilde."

"I'm Fatima," Fatima said. She dropped her bag to the floor with a little thump, and I saw her looking around, as full of wonder as I was at this Aladdin's cave of treasures, so different from the plainness of the rest of the school.

"Well, Fatima," Ambrose said, "Isa, I am very pleased to meet you."

He took my hand in his, but he didn't shake it, as I'd expected. Instead, he pressed my fingers between his, a kind of clasp, as if we were promising each other something. His hands were warm and strong, and there was paint so deeply ingrained into the lines of his knuckles and the grooves around his nails that I could see no amount of scrubbing could ever remove it.

"Now," he said, waving a hand to the room behind him. "Come in. Pick an easel. And most important, make yourselves at home."

And we did.

mbrose's classes were different; we learned that straightaway. At first it was the obvious things that I noticed—that Ambrose answered to his first name, that none of the girls were wearing ties or blazers, for example.

"Nothing worse than a tie dragging across your watercolor," he said that first day, as he invited us to take them off. But it was more than that—something other than straight practicality. A loosening of formality. A space, a much needed space, to breathe, in among all the sterile conformity of Salten House.

In class he was a professional—in spite of all the girls who "pashed" on him, unbuttoning their shirts to the point where you could see their bras, as they reached across the canvas. He kept his distance—physically, as well as metaphorically. That first day, when he saw me struggling with my sketch, he came and stood behind me, and I had a sharp memory of my old art mistress, Miss Driver, who used to lean over her students' shoulders to make alterations, so that you could feel the heat of her pressed against your spine and smell her sweat.

Ambrose, by contrast, stood his distance, a foot behind me, silent and contemplative, looking from my page up to the mirror I had propped on the table in front of my easel. We were doing self-portraits.

"It's crap, isn't it?" I said hopelessly. And then I bit my tongue, expecting a reprimand for the bad language. But Ambrose didn't even seem to notice. He just stood, his eyes narrowed, seeming hardly to notice me at all, his whole attention fixed on the paper. I held out the pencil, expecting him to draw in corrections like Miss Driver. He took it, almost absently, but he didn't make a mark on the page. Instead, he turned to look at me. His gaze gave me a jolt like electricity when his eyes met mine.

"It's not crap," he said seriously. "But you're not looking, you're drawing what you think is there. Look. Really look at yourself in the mirror."

I turned to look, trying hard to look at myself and not at Ambrose's lined, weathered face standing over my shoulder. All I saw were flaws—the spots on my chin, the hint of baby fat around the jaw, the way my unruly flyaway hair wisped out from the elastic band.

"Look," he said. "The reason it's not coming together is because you're drawing the features, not the person. You're more than a collection of frown lines and doubts. The person I see when I look at you . . ." He stopped, and I waited, feeling his eyes on me, trying not to squirm beneath the intensity of his gaze. "I see someone brave," he said at last. "I see someone who's trying very hard. I see someone who's nervous, but stronger than she knows. I see someone who's worried, but doesn't need to be."

I felt my cheeks flame, but the words, which would have been unbearably corny coming from anyone else, somehow sounded matter-of-fact, when delivered in Ambrose's graveled voice.

"Draw that," he said. He handed the pencil back to me, and his face broke into a smile, crinkling his cheeks and drawing lines at the corners of his eyes as if someone had sketched them in there and then. "Draw the person I see."

I could find nothing to say. I only nodded.

I can hear his voice in my head now, clipped and husky, so like Kate's. *Draw the person I see.*

I still have that drawing somewhere, and it shows a girl whose face is open to the world, a girl with nothing to hide but her own insecurities. But that person, the person Ambrose saw and believed in, she doesn't exist anymore.

Perhaps she never did.

Freya wakes as I tiptoe quietly into Luc's room (I can't think of it as anything else), and though I try to lull her back to sleep, she's having none of it, and in the end I take her into my bed—Luc's bed—and feed her lying down, bracing myself with an arm arched over her compact little body, so I don't let my weight fall on top of her when I fall asleep.

I lie there, watching her, and waiting for sleep to claim me, and I think about Ambrose . . . and Luc . . . and Kate, all alone now, in this slowly crumbling house, this beautiful millstone around her neck. It is slipping away from her, into the shifting sands of the Reach, and unless she can let go, it will drag her down, too.

The house shifts and creaks in the wind, and I sigh and turn my pillow to the cool side.

I should be thinking of Owen and home, but I'm not. I'm thinking of the old days, the long, lazy summer days we spent here, drinking and swimming and laughing, while Ambrose sketched and Luc watched us all with his lazy almond-shaped eyes.

Perhaps it's the room, but Luc feels very present to me in a way he hasn't for seventeen years, and as I lie there, my eyes closed, the ghosts of his old possessions around me and the cool of his sheets against my skin, I have the strangest sensation that he is lying next to me—a warm, slender stranger with sun-dark limbs and tangled hair.

The impression is so real that I force myself to turn over and open my eyes to try to dispel the illusion, and of course it's only Freya and me in the bed, and I shake my head.

What am I coming to? I am as bad as Kate, haunted by the ghosts of the past.

But I remember lying here, one night, long ago, and I have that feeling again of the record skipped in its groove, tracing and retracing the same voices and tracks.

They are here: Luc, Ambrose, and not just them, but ourselves, the ghosts of our past, the slim laughing girls we used to be before that summer ended with a cataclysmic crash, leaving us all scarred in our own ways, trying to move on, lying not for fun but to survive.

Here, in this house, the ghosts of our former selves are real—as real as the women sleeping around me. And I feel their presence, and I understand why Kate can't leave.

I am almost asleep now, my eyes heavy, and I pick up my phone one last time, checking the clock before I surrender to sleep. It is as I am putting it down that the light from the screen slants across the gapped, uneven floorboards, and something catches my eye. It is the corner of a piece of paper, sticking up between the boards, with something written on it. Is it a letter? Something written by Luc and lost, or hidden there?

My heart beats as though I am intruding on his privacy, which I am in a way, but I tug gently at the corner and the dusty, cobwebbed piece of paper slides out.

The page is covered with lines and seems to be a drawing, but in the dim light from my phone's screen, I can't quite make it out. I don't want to turn on the light and wake Freya, so I take it to the open window, where the curtains flutter in the breeze from the sea, and I hold it up, angling it so the moonlight falls on the page.

It's a watercolor sketch of a girl, of Kate, I think, and it looks like one of Ambrose's, though I can't be sure. The reason I cannot tell for certain is this: the drawing is crossed and slashed again and again with thick black lines, scoring out the face of the girl with lines so thick and vicious that they have torn the paper in places. Pencil holes have been stabbed through where her eyes would have been, if they weren't obscured by the thicket of scribbles. She has been erased, scratched out, utterly destroyed.

For a minute I just stand there, the piece of paper shivering in the sea breeze, trying to understand what this means. Was it Luc? But I can't believe that he would do such a thing, he *loved* Kate. Was it Kate herself? Impossible though it seems, I can believe that more easily.

I am still standing there, trying to work out the mystery of this hate-filled little thing, when there is a gust of wind, and the curtain flaps, and the piece of paper falls from my fingers. I snatch for it, but the wind has caught it, and all I can do is watch as it flutters towards the Reach and sinks into the milky, muddy water.

Whatever it was, whatever it meant, it's gone. And as I turn for bed, shivering a little in spite of the warm night, I can't help thinking—perhaps it's for the best.

I should be tired enough to sleep well, but I don't. I fall asleep with the scratched-out face in my mind, but when I dream, it's of Salten House, of the long corridors and winding stairs, and the endless search for rooms I couldn't find, places that didn't exist. In my dreams I'm following the others down corridor after corridor, and I hear Kate's voice up ahead: *It's this way . . . nearly there!* And Fatima's plaintive cry after her: *You're lying again . . .*

At some point Shadow wakes and barks, and I hear a shushing voice, footsteps, the sound of a door—Kate is putting the dog out.

And then, silence. Or as near to silence as this old, ghost-ridden house ever gets, with its restless creaking resistance against the forces of winds and tides.

When I wake again, it's to the sound of voices outside, sharp whispers of concern, and I sit up, bleary and confused. It's morning, the sun filtering through the thin curtains, and Freya is stirring sleepily in a pool of sunshine next to me. When she squawks I pick her up and feed her, but the voices outside are distracting both of us. She keeps raising her head to look around, wondering at the strange room and the strange quality of light—so different from the dusty yellow sunshine that streams into our London flat on summer afternoons. This is a clear, bright light—painful on the eyes and full of movement from the river, and it dances on the ceiling and walls in little pools and patches.

And all the time the voices . . . quiet, worried voices,

with Shadow whining unhappily beneath like a musical counterpoint.

At last I give up, and I wrap Freya in her blankie, and me in my dressing gown, and head downstairs, my bare feet gripping the worn wooden slats of the stairs. The door to the shoreside of the Mill is open, and sunlight streams in, but I know before I have even turned the corner of the stairs that something is wrong. There is blood on the stone floor.

I stop at the curve of the stairs, holding Freya hard against my thumping heart, as if she can still the painful banging. I don't realize how hard I am holding her, until she gives a squeak of protest, and I realize that my fingers are digging into her soft, chubby thighs. I force my fingers to relax and my feet to follow the staircase to the flagged ground floor, where the bloodstains are.

As I get closer I can see they aren't random droplets, as I'd thought from the top of the stairs, but paw prints. Shadow's paw prints. They lead inside the front door, circle, and then swiftly out again as if someone had shooed the dog back outside.

The voices are coming from the land side of the Mill, and I shove my feet into my sandals and walk, blinking into the sunshine.

Outside, Kate and Fatima are standing with their backs to me, Shadow sitting at Kate's side, still whimpering unhappily. He is on a lead, for the first time since I got here, a very short lead, held tightly in Kate's lean hand.

"What's happened?" I say, nervously, and they turn to look at me, and then Kate stands back, and I see what their bodies have sheltered from my gaze until now.

I inhale sharply, and I clap my free hand over my mouth. When I do manage to speak, my voice shakes a little.

"Oh my God. Is it . . . dead?"

It's not just the sight—I've seen death before—it's the shock, the unexpectedness, the contrast of the bloody mess before us with the blue-and-gold glory of the summer morning. The wool is wet, the high tide must have soaked the body, and now the blood drips slowly through the black slats of the walkway into the muddy shallows. The tide is out, and only puddles of water remain, and the blood is enough to stain them rust red.

Fatima nods grimly. She has put her head scarf on again to go outside, and she looks like the thirtysome-thing doctor she is, not the schoolgirl of last night.

"Very dead."

"Is it—Was it . . ." I trail off, not sure how to put it, but my eyes go to Shadow, sitting unhappily at Kate's side. There is blood on his muzzle, and he whines again as a fly settles on it, and he shivers it off and then licks at the stickiness with his long pink tongue.

Kate shrugs. Her face is grim.

"I don't know. I can't believe it—he's never harmed a fly, but he is . . . well, capable. He's strong enough."

"But how?" But even as the words leave my mouth, my gaze travels across the wooden walkway to the fenced-off section of shore that marks the entrance to the mill. The gate is open. "Shit."

"Quite. I'd never have let him out if I'd realized."

"Oh God, Kate, I'm so sorry. Thea must have . . ."

"Thea must have what?" There's a sleepy voice from behind us, and I turn to see Thea squinting in the bright sunlight, her hair tousled, an unlit Sobranie in her fingers.

Oh God.

"Thea, I didn't mean . . ." I stop, shift uncomfort-ably, but it's *true*, however my words sounded, I wasn't trying to *blame* her, just work out how it happened. Then she sees the bloody mess of torn flesh and wool in front of us.

"Fuck. What happened? What's it got to do with me?"

"Someone left the gate open," I say unhappily, "but I didn't mean—"

"It doesn't matter who left the gate open," Kate breaks in, sharply. "It was my fault for not checking it was closed before I put Shadow out."

"Your dog did *that*?" Thea's face is pale, and she takes an involuntary step back, away from Shadow and his bloodied muzzle. "Oh my God."

"We don't know that," Kate says, very terse. But Fatima's face is worried, and I know she is thinking the same thing I am: if not Shadow, then who?

"Come on," Kate says at last, and she turns, a cloud of flies rising up from the dead sheep's guts, splattered across the wooden jetty, and then settling back to their feast once more. "Let's get inside, I'll phone round the farmers, find out who's lost a ewe. *Fuck*. This is the last thing we need."

And I know what she means. It's not just the sheep, coming as it does on top of our hangovers and too little sleep; it's everything. It's the smell in the air. The water lapping at our feet, that is no longer a friend but polluted with blood. The feeling of death closing in on the Mill.

IT TAKES FOUR OR FIVE calls for Kate to find the farmer who owns the sheep, and then we wait, sipping coffee and trying to ignore the buzzing of the flies outside the closed shore door. Thea has gone back to bed, and Fatima and I distract ourselves with Freya, cutting up toast for her to play with, although she doesn't really eat, just gums it.

Kate paces the room, restlessly, like a caged tiger, walking from the windows overlooking the Reach to the foot of the stairs, and then back, again and again. She is smoking, the rippling smoke from the roll-up the only sign of fingers that are shaking a little.

Suddenly her head goes up, for all the world like a dog herself, and a moment later I hear what she already did: the sound of tires in the lane. Kate turns abruptly and goes outside, shutting the door of the Mill behind her. Through the wood I hear voices, one deep and full of frustration, the other Kate's, low and apologetic.

"I'm sorry," I hear, and then, ". . . the police?"

"Do you think we should go out?" Fatima asks uneasily.

"I don't know." I find I am twisting my fingers in the hem of my dressing gown. "He doesn't sound exactly angry. . . . Do you think we should let Kate handle it?"

Fatima is holding Freya, so I get up and move to the shore window. I can see Kate and the farmer standing close together, their heads bent over the dead sheep. He seems to be more sad than angry, and Kate puts her arm around his shoulder for a brief moment, clasping him in a gesture of comfort that's not quite a hug but near it.

The farmer says something I don't catch, and Kate nods, then together they reach down and pick the ewe up by the fore and hind legs, carrying the poor thing over the rickety bridge, and swinging the body unceremoniously into the back of the farmer's pickup.

"Let me get my wallet," I hear Kate say, as the farmer latches up the tailgate, and when she turns back towards the house, I see something small and bloody in her fingers, something that she shoves into the pocket of her jacket before she reaches the house.

I step hastily back from the window as the door

opens, and Kate comes into the room, shaking her head like someone trying to rid themselves of an unpleasant memory.

"Is it okay?" I ask.

"I don't know," Kate says. "I think so." She rinses her bloody hands under the tap, and then looks on the dresser for her wallet, but when she looks inside at the notes section, her face falls. "Fuck."

"Do you need cash?" Fatima says quickly. She gets up, hands Freya to me. "I've got my purse upstairs."

"I have cash, too," I say, eager to finally do something that could help. "How much do you need?"

"Two hundred, I think," Kate says soberly. "It's more than the sheep's worth, but he'd be within his rights to get the police involved, and I really don't want that."

I nod, and then turn to see Fatima coming back down the stairs with her handbag.

"I've got a hundred and fifty," she says. "I remembered Salten never had a cash machine, so I drew some out at the petrol station on the way through Hampton's Lee."

"Let me go halves." I stand, holding a wriggling Freya over my shoulder, and dig into the handbag I left hanging on the stair post. Inside is my wallet, fat with notes. "I've definitely got enough, hang on. . . ." I count it out, five crisp twenties, hampered by Freya joyfully snatching at each as they go past. Fatima adds a hundred of her own on top. Kate gives a quick, rueful smile.

"Thanks, guys, I'll pay you back as soon as we get into Salten, they've got an ATM in the post office now."

"No need," Fatima says, but Kate has already shut the Mill door behind her, and I hear her voice outside and the farmer's answering rumble as she hands over the cash, and then the crunch of tires as he backs up the lane, the dead sheep in the back of the truck.

When Kate comes back inside, she is pale, but her face is relieved.

"Thank God, I don't think he'll call the police."

"So you don't think it was Shadow?" Fatima asks, but Kate doesn't answer. Instead, she goes over to the sink, to wash her hands again.

"You've got blood on your sleeve," I say, and she looks down at herself.

"Oh God, so I have. Who'd have thought the old sheep to have so much blood in her?" She gives a twisted smile, and I know she's thinking of Miss Winchelsea and the end-of-term Macbeth that she never got to play. She shrugs off the coat and drops it on the floor, and then fills up a bucket at the tap.

"Can I help?" Fatima asks. Kate shakes her head.

"No, it's fine, I'm going to sluice down the jetty, and then I might have a bath. I feel gross."

I know what she means. I feel gross, too—soiled by what I saw, and I didn't even help the farmer sling the corpse into the back of the truck. I shiver, as she shuts the door behind her, and then I hear the slosh of water, and the *scccsh, scccsh* of an outdoor broom. I stand and put Freya in her pram.

"Do you think it was Shadow?" Fatima says in a low voice as I tuck Freya in. I shrug, and we both look down at where Shadow is huddled unhappily on a rug in front of the unlit stove. He looks ashamed, his eyes sad, and feeling our eyes on him, he looks up, puzzled, and then licks his muzzle again, whining a little. He knows something is wrong.

"I don't know," I say. But I know now that I will never leave Shadow and Freya alone together. Kate's jacket is crumpled on the floor by the sink, and I am seized with a need to do something, help in some way, however insignificant. "Does Kate have a washing machine?"

"I don't think so." Fatima looks around. "She always used to put all her clothes through the school laundry. Do you remember Ambrose used to hand-wash all his painting clothes in the sink? Why?"

"I was going to put the jacket in, but I guess I'll just put it in to soak?"

"Cold water's better for blood anyway."

I can't see where a washing machine could be, so I put in the plug, and run cold water into the sink, and then pick up Kate's jacket from the floor. Before I put it in the sink, I feel in each pocket, to make sure I'm not about to submerge anything valuable. It's only when my fingers close on something soft, and unpleasantly squishy, that I remember Kate picking something up from the jetty and shoving it surreptitiously into her pocket.

When it comes out, it's unrecognizable, whatever it is: a matted lump of white and red in my fingers, and I make an involuntary sound of disgust as I swish my fingers in the cold sink water. The thing unfurls like a petal and floats gently to the bottom of the sink, and I fish it out.

I don't know what I thought it would be, but whatever it was, I was not expecting this.

It is a note, the paper soaked crimson with blood and fraying at the edges, the Biro letters blurred but still readable.

Why don't you throw this one in the Reach, too? it reads.

The feeling that washes over me is like nothing I've felt before. It is pure, distilled panic.

For a minute I don't move, don't say anything, don't even breathe. I just stand there, the bloody water running from between my fingers, my heart skittering erratically in my breast, my cheeks hot and flushed with a scarlet wave of guilt and fear.

They know. Someone *knows*.

I look up at Fatima, who isn't watching, who has no idea what has just happened. Her head is bowed over her phone, texting Ali, or something. For a second I open my mouth—and then a kind of instinct takes over, and I shut it again.

I feel my fingers close over the ball of mushy paper, grinding it, grinding it into pulp, feeling my nails in my palm as I rip and shred and mash the paper into flecks of white and crimson until it's gone, quite gone, and nothing remains.

With my free hand, I pull the plug, letting the blood-stained water drain away, out of the jacket, and I dip my fingers in as it disappears down the plug hole, letting the shredded mush float free into the spiraling water. Then I turn on the cold tap and I sluice away every trace of the note, every fiber, every fleck of accusation until it's as if it never existed.

I have to get out.

It's ten o'clock, and Kate is in the bath, Thea has gone back to sleep, and Fatima is working, her laptop open on the table in front of the window, her head bent as she plows intently through her e-mails.

Freya is sitting plump-bottomed on the floor, and I am trying to play with her, quietly, so as not to disturb Fatima. I am reading to her from the flap book that she loves, with the little babies playing peekaboo, but I keep forgetting to turn the page, and she bangs the book with her hand and chirrups at me as if to tell me, *Come on! Turn faster!*

"Where's the baby?" I say quietly, but I'm distracted, not properly entering into the game. Shadow is lying unhappily in the corner, still licking at his muzzle, and all I want to do is snatch Freya up and hug her against me and get her out of here.

Outside I can hear the whine of insects, and I think again of the spilled guts of the sheep, spattered across the walkway. I am just opening the flap to show the baby's surprised face peeking out, when I see, right by Freya's chubby, perfect leg, a jagged splinter of wood sticking up out of the floorboard.

This place, where I have spent so many happy hours, is suddenly full of threat.

I stand, picking up Freya, who gives a hiccup of surprise and drops the book.

"I might go for a walk," I say aloud. Fatima barely looks up from the screen.

"Good plan. Where will you go?"

"I don't know. Salten village, probably."

"You sure? It's a good three or four miles."

I suppress a spurt of irritation. I *know* the distance as well as she does. I walked it often enough.

"Yes, I'm sure," I say evenly. "I'll be fine—I've got good shoes, and Freya's buggy's quite sturdy. We can always get a taxi back if we're tired."

"Okay, well, have fun."

"Thanks, Mum," I say, letting my annoyance break through, and she looks up and grins.

"Oops, was I doing that thing? Sorry, I promise I won't tell you to wear a coat and make sure you've done a wee."

I crack a smile as I strap Freya into her buggy. Fatima could always make me laugh, and it's hard to be pissed off while you're grinning.

"The wee might not be bad advice," I say, pulling on my walking sandals. "Pelvic floor ain't what it used to be."

"Tell me about it," Fatima says absently, tapping out a reply. "Remember those Kegels. And squeeeze!"

I laugh again, and glance out the window. The sun is beating down on the glassy, glinting waters of the Reach, and the dunes shimmer with heat. I must remember Freya's sunscreen. Where did I pack it?

"I saw it in your wash bag," Fatima says, speaking around the pencil gripped between her teeth. My head jerks up.

"What did you say?"

"Sunscreen, you just muttered it as you were look-ing through Freya's nappy bag. But I saw it upstairs in the bathroom."

God, did I really say it aloud? I must be going mad. Perhaps I've got so used to being alone with Freya on maternity leave I've started talking to myself, voicing my thoughts aloud to her at home in the silent flat?

The thought is a creepy one. What else might I have said?

"Thanks," I say briefly to Fatima. "Keep an eye on Freya for a sec?"

She nods, and I run upstairs to the bathroom, my walking shoes clomping on the wooden stairs.

When I try the door, it's locked, and I can hear sloshing from within, and belatedly I remember that Kate is in there.

"Who is it?" Her voice is muffled by the door, and echoey.

"Sorry," I call back. "I forgot you were in here. I've left Freya's sunscreen inside, can you pass it out?"

"Hang on." I hear a rush of water, and then the lock clicks, and a slosh as Kate gets back into the tub. "Come in."

I open the door cautiously, but she's fully submerged beneath icebergs of foam, her hair drawn up into a straggly topknot showing her long slim neck.

"Sorry," I say again. "I'll be quick."

"No worries." Kate sticks a leg out of the tub and begins to shave it. "I don't know why I locked it anyway. It's not like it's anything you lot haven't seen before. Are you going out?"

"Yes, I'm going for a walk. Maybe to Salten, I'm not sure."

"Oh, listen, if I give you my card, could you get out two hundred pounds so I can pay you and Fatima back?"

I have found the sunscreen now, and I stand, twisting the cap in my hands.

"Kate, I—Look, Fatima and I . . . we don't . . ."

God, this is hard, how to say it? Kate has always

been proud. I don't want to offend her. How can I say what I'm really thinking, which is that Kate, with her crumbling house and broken-down car, clearly can't afford two hundred pounds, whereas Fatima and I can?

As I'm scrabbling for the right words, an image flashes sharply into my mind, distracting as a jab from a stray pin when you're dredging for your purse in your handbag.

It's the note, slick with blood, *Why don't you throw this one in the Reach, too?*

I feel suddenly sick.

"Kate," I blurt, "what really happened out there? With Shadow?"

Her face goes suddenly blank, unreadable. It's like someone has drawn a shutter down.

"I should have shut the gate," she says flatly. "That's all." And I know, I *know* she is lying. Kate is suddenly as remote as a statue—and I know.

We swore never to lie to one another.

I stare at her, half submerged in the cloudy, soapy water, at the uncompromising set of her mouth: thin, sensitive lips, clamped together, holding back the truth. I think about the note that I destroyed, long gone now. Kate and I both know she is lying, and I am very close to calling her on it—but I don't quite dare. If she's lying, it must be for a reason, and I'm afraid to find out what that reason might be.

"All right," I say at last. I'm conscious of my own cowardice as I turn to go.

"My card's in my wallet," Kate calls as I shut the door behind me. "The PIN's eight-four-three-one."

But, as I clatter down the stairs towards Fatima and the still-sleeping Freya, I don't even try to remember it. I've got no intention of taking her card, or her money.

Outside, pushing Freya's buggy along the long, sandy track that leads up the side of the Reach, away from the Mill, I begin to feel the oppressive mood lift.

The day is calm and quiet, and the gulls are bobbing tranquilly on the rising tide, the waders stalking the mudflats with intent concentration, darting their heads down to pluck up unsuspecting worms and beetles.

The sun is hot on the back of my neck, and I adjust the sunshade on Freya's pram and wipe the residue of the sunscreen I have slathered over her fat little limbs onto the back of my neck.

The smell of blood is still in my nostrils, and I long for a breath of air to blow it away. *Was* it Shadow? I can't tell. I try to think back to the spilled guts and the whining dog; were those cuts from a knife, or tears from a strong jaw? I just don't know.

There is one thing for sure, though—Shadow could not have written that note. So who did? I shiver in the bright sunshine, the malevolence of it suddenly striking through to my bones. All at once, I have a strong urge to snatch up my sleeping baby and press her into my breast, hugging her to me as if I can fold her back inside myself, as if I can protect her from this web of secrets and lies that is closing in around me, dragging me back to a decades-old mistake that I thought we'd escaped. I am starting to realize that we didn't, none of us. We have spent seventeen years running and hiding, in our different ways, but it hasn't worked, I know that now. Perhaps I always knew that.

At the end of the lane, the track opens up to a road that leads left to the station, or right across the bridge, into Salten itself. I pause on the bridge, rocking Freya gently to and fro, surveying the familiar landscape. The countryside round here is fairly flat, and you can see a long way from the shallow vantage point of the bridge. In front of me, black against the bright waters of the Reach, is the Mill, looking small in the distance. To the left, on the other side of the river, I can just see the houses and narrow twittens of Salten village.

And to the right, far off in the distance, is a white shape that glimmers over the tips of the trees, almost invisible against the sun-bleached horizon. Salten House. Standing here, it's impossible to pick out the route we used to walk across the marsh, when we broke out of bounds. Perhaps it's overgrown; now, I marvel at our stupidity, remembering the first time, that chilly October night, dusk already drawn in as we climbed out of the window onto the fire escape, torches between our teeth, boots in our hands so we didn't wake the teachers as we crept down the rattling iron structure.

At the bottom, we shoved our feet into Wellingtons ("*Not* shoes," I remember Kate telling us, "even after the summer we've just had, it'll be muddy."), and then we set off, running lightly across the hockey fields, suppressing our laughter until we were far enough away from the buildings that no one would hear us.

That first part was always the dangerous bit, particularly as the days grew longer and it was light outside long after curfew. After Easter, any teacher looking out her window would have seen the four of us fleeing across the close-cropped grass: Thea's long legs eating up the distance; Kate in the middle; Fatima and me puffing behind.

But that first time, it was almost pitch-black already, and we scampered under cover of darkness until we reached the clutch of stunted bushes and trees that marked the edge of the marsh, and could let out our suppressed giggles, and turn on our torches.

Kate led the way, the rest of us following her through a dark maze of channels and ditches filled with black, brackish water that glinted in the torchlight.

We climbed over fences and stiles, jumped ditches, paying careful heed to Kate's muttered instructions over her shoulder: "For God's sake, keep to the ridge here, the ground to the left is pure bog. . . . Use the stile here, if you open that gate, it's impossible to shut again and the sheep will escape. . . . You can use this tussock of grass to jump the ditch, see, where I'm standing now? It's the firmest part of the bank."

She had run wild on the marsh since she was a little girl, and although she couldn't tell you the name of a single flower, or identify half the birds we disturbed on our walk, she knew every tuft of grass, every treacherous bit of bog, every stream and ditch and hillock, and even in the dark she led us unerringly through the labyrinth of sheep paths, boggy sloughs, and stagnant drainage ditches, until at last we climbed a fence and there it was—the Reach, the waters glinting in the moonlight, and far up the sandy bank in the distance, the Mill, a light burning in the window.

"Is your dad home?" Thea asked. Kate shook her head.

"No, he's out, something in the village, I think. It must be Luc."

Luc? This was the first I'd heard of a Luc. Was he an uncle? A brother? I was almost sure that Kate had told me she was an only child.

Before I had time to do more than exchange a puzzled glance with Fatima, Kate had started off again, striding up the lane this time without looking back to check on the rest of us. Now we were on firm, sandy ground, and I ran to catch up.

At the door of the Mill she paused for a moment, waiting for Fatima, who was bringing up the rear, panting slightly, and then she opened the door.

"Welcome home, everyone."

And I stepped inside the Mill for the first time.

IT HAS HARDLY CHANGED, THAT'S what's remarkable, as I think back to that first time I saw the place—the pictures on the wall were a little different, the whole place slightly less drunken, less tumbledown, but the twisting wooden staircase, the lopsided windows casting their golden light out across the Reach, all that was the same. It was October, and the night was cold, and a fire was burning in the woodstove, and the first thing that struck me when Kate opened the door was a blast of warmth, and firelight, woodsmoke mingling with the smell of turps and oil paint and seawater.

Someone was there, seated in a wooden rocking chair in front of the fire, reading a book, and he looked up in surprise as we entered.

It was a boy, about our age—or, to be exact, five months younger than me, as I found out later. He was actually only a year older than my younger brother—but he was a world away from little pink-and-white Will in every other respect, his lanky limbs tanned nut brown, his dark hair jaggedly hacked, as if he'd cut it himself, and he had the slight stoop of someone tall enough to have to worry about low doorways.

"Kate." His voice was deep and slightly hoarse, and

there was a slight something that I couldn't place, an accent not quite the same as Kate's. "What are you doing here? Dad's out."

"Hi, Luc," Kate said. She stood on tiptoes and kissed him on the cheek, a rough, sisterly kiss. "Sorry I didn't warn you. I had to get out of that place, and well, I couldn't leave the others to rot at school. You know Thea, of course. And this is Fatima Qureshy."

"Hi," Fatima said shyly. She stuck out her hand, and Luc shook it, a little awkwardly.

"And this is Isa Wilde."

"Hi," I said. He turned and smiled at me, and I saw that his eyes were almost golden, like a cat's.

"Guys, this is Luc Rochefort, my . . ." She stopped, and she and Luc exchanged a glance, and a little smile, which crinkled the tanned skin at the corner of his mouth. "My stepbrother, I guess? Well, anyway. Here we all are. Don't just stand there, Luc."

Luc smiled again, then he ducked his head, awk-wardly, and moved backwards into the room, making space for the rest of us.

"Can I get you a drink?" he said as we filtered past, Fatima and I tongue-tied by the unexpected presence of a stranger, and a strange boy at that, when we'd been shut up for so many weeks with only other girls.

"What have you got?" I asked.

"Wine," he said with a shrug, "Côtes du Rhône," and suddenly I knew what that accent was, what I should have realized from his name. Luc was French.

"Wine is good," I said. "Thanks." And I took the glass he gave me and knocked it recklessly back.

IT WAS LATE, AND WE were drunk and limp with alcohol and laughing and dancing to the records Kate had put on the turntable, when there was the sound of the door handle, and all our heads turned, to see Ambrose coming through the door, his hat in his hand.

Fatima and I both froze, but Kate only stumbled across the room, tripping drunkenly over the rug and laughing as her father caught her and kissed her on both cheeks.

"Daddy, you won't tell, will you?"

"Get me a drink," he said, throwing his hat on the table, and ruffling Luc's hair, where he lay sprawled across the sofa, "and I never saw you."

But he did, of course. And it's his own sketch that gives him the lie, the little dashed-off pencil thing that hangs at the crook of the landing, outside Kate's old bedroom. It's a sketch of the sofa, that very first night, with Luc and Thea and me, tangled together like a litter of puppies, arms around one another, limbs entwined until it was hard to tell where my flesh ended and Thea's or Luc's began. Perched on the arm of the sofa is Fatima, her bare legs acting as a chair back for Thea to lean on. And at our feet is Kate, her spine against the battered couch, her knees to her chin, and her eyes on the fire. There is a glass of wine in her hand, and my fingers are laced in her hair.

It was the first night that we lay and drank and laughed, curled in one another's arms, the stove flames warm on our faces, heating us through, along with the wine—but it was not the last. Again and again we would come back, across fields crunchy with hoarfrost, or past meadows full of baby lambs, drawn again and again, like moths to a flame that shone through the darkness of the marshes, drawing us in. And then back through the pale spring dawns, to sit heavy-eyed in French, or wending our slow laughing way through the marshes on a summer morning, salt water dried into our hair.

We didn't always break out. After the first two weeks of each term, the weekends were "open," which meant that we were free to go home, or to friends', provided our parents gave permission. Home wasn't an option for Fatima or me, with my father permanently with my mum at the hospital, and her parents away in Pakistan. And Thea . . . well, I never inquired about Thea, but it was plain that there was something very wrong, something that meant that she either could not, or would not, go back to her parents'.

But there was nothing in the rules to say that we could not accompany Kate, and we did, most often packing up our bags and walking back across the marshes with her on Friday nights after prep, returning Sunday night for registration.

At first it was the odd weekend . . . then it became many . . . and then, at last, most, until Ambrose's studio was littered with sketches of the four of us, until the Mill was as familiar to me as the little room I shared with Fatima, *more* familiar even, until my feet knew the paths of the marsh by heart, almost as well as Kate.

"Mr. Atagon must be a saint," said Miss Weatherby, my housemistress, with a slightly thin smile, as I signed out yet again with Kate on a Friday night. "Teaching you girls all week, and then boarding you for free all weekend. Are you sure your father is all right with this, Kate?"

"He's fine," Kate said firmly. "He's more than happy for me to have friends back."

"And my parents have given permission," I put in. With alacrity, in fact; my father was so relieved that I was happy at Salten, not adding to his worries by clamoring to come home, that he would have signed a pact with the devil himself. A stack of preauthorized exeat forms, by comparison, was nothing.

"It's not that I don't want you to spend time with Kate," the housemistress said to me later, over tea in her office, concern in her gaze. "I'm very glad you've found friends. But remember, part of being a well-rounded young woman is having a wide *variety* of friends. Why not spend the weekend with one of the other girls? Or indeed stay here, it's not as if the school is empty at weekends."

"So"—I sipped my tea—"is there anything in the rules about the number of exeat weekends I can take?"

"Well, nothing in the rules exactly . . ."

I nodded, and smiled, and drank her tea, and then signed out the following Friday to stay at Kate's exactly as before.

And there was nothing the school could do.

Until they did.

By the time I reach the long, straight stretch of road leading into Salten village, I am hot and sweaty, and I pause under the shade of a clump of oaks by the road, feeling the sweat running down the hollow of my spine, pooling in my bra.

Freya is sleeping peacefully, her rosebud mouth just slightly open, and I stoop to kiss her, very gently, not wanting to wake her, before straightening up and pushing on, my feet a little sore now, towards the village.

I don't turn at the sound of the car behind me, but it slows as it passes, the driver peering out, and I see who it is—Jerry Allen, the landlord of the Salten Arms, in the old flatbed truck that used to take him back and forth from the cash-and-carry. Only now it's older and more ramshackle than ever, more rust than truck. Why is Jerry still driving a thirty-year-old rust bucket? The pub was never a gold mine, but it looks as if he has fallen on hard times.

Jerry himself is craning out the window with frank curiosity, wondering, I expect, what kind of tourist is mad enough to be walking along the main road, alone, in the heat of the day.

He's almost past me when his face changes, and he gives a little blast of the horn that makes me jump, and grinds to a halt on the verge, throwing up a cloud of dust that sets me coughing and choking.

"I know you," he says as I draw level with the truck, its engine still running. There is a touch of sly triumph in his voice, as though he has caught me out. I don't say what I'm thinking, which is that I never tried to deny it. "You're one of that crowd used to hang around with Kate Atagon—one of them girls her pa—"

Too late he realizes where this conversation is leading, and he coughs and covers his mouth, trying to hide his confusion in a fit of smoker's hack.

"Yes," I say. I keep my voice even, refusing to let him see me react to his words. "I'm Isa. Isa Wilde. Hello, Jerry."

"All growed up," he says, his eyes watering a little as his gaze travels over my figure. "And a baby, no less."

"Little girl," I say. "Freya."

"Well, well, well," he says meaninglessly, and he gives a gummy smile, which shows his missing teeth and the gold tooth that always gave me a slight shudder for reasons I could never pin down. He regards me silently for a moment, taking me in, from my dusty sandals to the sweat patches staining my sundress, then he jerks his head back towards the Reach. "Terrible news, isn't it? They've fenced off half the bank, Mick White says, though you can't see it from here. Police teams, sniffer dogs, them white tent things . . . though what good they think that'll do now, I don't know. Whatever's buried there, it's been out there in the wind and rain long enough, from what Judy Wallace's old man said. Her it was that found it, and to hear Mick's account, their dog snapped it right in half at the elbow, brittle as a stick. Between that and the salt, I don't suppose there's much left of it now."

I don't know what to say to this. A kind of sickness is rising in my throat, so I just nod, queasily, and something seems to strike him.

"You going to the village? Hop in, and I'll give you a lift."

I look at him, at his red face, at the rickety old truck

swinging in the breeze, and a general air of dilapidation that shocks me. Salten was never smart, the divide between town and school always sharp. But the tourists have disappeared to France and Spain, and I am dismayed to see that the shop on the corner that sold ice cream and was always bright with plastic buckets and spades is gone, its empty window full of dust and cobwebs.

The post office is still there, though the net above its entrance is new: a broad orange swag, with an old repaired tear still visible.

I look up as I push the door open with my back, reversing the pram into the tiny shop. *Don't drop on me*, I'm praying. In my mind's eye the tangling threads are engulfing me and Freya in their suffocating web.

The bell dings loudly as I go in, but there's no one behind the counter, and no one comes as I walk to the ATM in the corner, where the pick-and-mix boxes used to be. I have no intention of taking Kate's money, but the £100 I gave to Fatima nearly cleaned me out, and I want to be sure I have enough in my wallet to . . .

I pause. To what? It's a question I don't quite want to answer. To get groceries? To pay back Kate for the tickets to the alumnae ball? Both of those, certainly, but they are not the real reason. Enough to get away in a hurry, if I have to.

I'm tapping in my PIN when a voice comes from behind me—a deep, raspy voice, almost like a man's, although I know it's not, even before I turn around.

"Well, well, well. Look what the cat dragged in."

I take the money from the machine's mouth and pocket my card before I turn around, and there behind the counter is Mary Wren—village matriarch, perhaps the nearest thing that Salten has to a community leader. She worked in the post office when I was at school, but now, for some reason, her appearance wrong-foots me. I had assumed that in the years since I left Salten she would have retired, or moved on. Apparently not.

"Mary," I say, forcing myself to smile as I shove my purse back in my bag. "You haven't changed!"

It's both true and untrue—her face is still the same broad, weather-beaten slab, still the same small dark penetrating eyes. But her hair, that used to be a long dark river to her waist, is iron gray now. She has plaited it, the thick gray rope dwindling down into a meager, curling end barely thick enough to hold an elastic band.

"Isa Wilde." She comes out from behind the counter and stands, hands on hips, just as massive and immovable as ever, like a standing stone. "As I live and breathe. What brings you back?"

For a minute I hesitate, my eyes going to a pile of local weekly papers, where *Human Bone Found in Reach* still blares forth.

Then I remember Kate's lie to the taxi driver.

"We—I—It's the Summer Ball," I manage. "At Salten House."

"Well." She looks me up and down, taking in my linen sundress, sticky and limp with sweat, Freya slumbering in her Bugaboo. "I must say, I'm surprised. I didn't think you came back here anymore. Plenty of dinners and balls been and gone and no sign of you and your little clique."

She pronounces it *click*, and for a minute I can't work out what she's saying, but then I understand. *Clique*. It's a loaded word, and yet I can't deny it. We *were* cliquey, Kate, Thea, Fatima, and I. We were pleased with ourselves, and we had no need for others, except as targets for our jokes and games. We thought we could take on anything, anyone, as long as we had one another. We were arrogant and unthinking, and that's the truth of it. My behavior back then is not something I'm proud of, and I don't enjoy Mary's pointed reminder, though I can't fault the justice of her choice of words.

"You see Kate, though, right?" I say lightly, trying to change the conversation. Mary nods.

"Oh, of course. We're the only cash machine in the village, so she's in here pretty regular. And she stuck around, when there's plenty wouldn't have. People respect that, in spite of her little ways."

"*Her ways?*" I echo back, unable to stop a slight acerbity entering my voice. Mary laughs, easily, her big frame shaking, but there's something mirthless about the sound.

"You know Kate," she says at last. "She keeps herself to herself, living out there like she does. Ambrose was never a loner like that; he was always in the village, down at the pub, playing his fiddle in the band. He might have lived out on the Reach, but he was one of us, no mistake about it. But Kate . . . she's got a foot in both worlds, as you might say." She looks me up and down, and then repeats, "She keeps herself to herself."

I swallow, and try to think of some way to change the subject.

"I hear Mark's a policeman now, is that right?"

"Yes," Mary says. "And very convenient it is, too, to have someone living local, as you might say. He works out of Hampton's Lee, but this being his home patch, he comes through here more regular than an outsider might."

"Does he still live with you?"

"Oh, yes, you know what it's like round here with the second homeowners pushing up the prices, very hard for young people to save for their own place now, when there's rich people from London coming down, snapping up the cottages."

She eyes me again, and this time I feel her eyes lingering on the expensive change bag, and my big Marni tote, a present from Owen that can't have been less than £500 and was probably much more.

"It must be hard," I say awkwardly. "But I guess at least they bring in money?"

Mary snorts derisively.

"Not them. They bring their food down in the back of their cars from London, you don't see them in the shops round here. Baldocks the Butcher closed, did you see that?"

I nod, mutely, feeling an obscure sense of guilt, and Mary shakes her head.

"And Croft and Sons, the bakers. There's precious little left now, apart from the post office and the pub. And that won't be round for long if the brewery gets its way. It don't make enough money, you see. It'll be converted into flats before this time next year. God knows what Jerry'll do then. No pension, no savings . . ."

She moves closer and tips back the hood of Freya's pram.

"So you've got a daughter now?"

"That's right." I watch as her strong, thick finger traces a line down my sleeping baby's cheek. There are dark red stains under her nails and in the cuticles. It's probably ink from the post office stamp pads, but I can't help thinking of blood. I try not to flinch. "Freya."

"You're not Wilde anymore?"

I shake my head.

"Still Wilde. I'm not married."

"Well, she's a pretty one." Mary straightens. "She'll be driving the boys wild herself, in a few years, I'll be bound."

My lip curls in spite of myself, and my fingers tighten on the spongy handle of the pram. But I force myself to take a breath, swallow down the biting remark I'm longing to make. Mary Wren is a powerful figure in the village—even seventeen years ago, you didn't cross her, and I can't imagine much has changed since, not now that her son is the local policeman.

I'd thought I'd shaken all this off when I left Salten House, this complicated web of local allegiances, the uneasy relationship between the village and the school, which Ambrose negotiated effortlessly, compared to the rest of us. I would like to pull Freya's pram away from Mary, tell her to mind her own business. But I can't afford to antagonize her. It's not just for the sake of Kate, living down here, it's all of us. The school washed its hands of us long ago—and Salten, if you are rejected by both town and gown, can be a very hostile place indeed.

I shiver, in spite of the heat of the day, and Mary looks up.

"Goose on your grave?"

I shake my head and try to smile, and she laughs, showing stained yellow teeth.

"Well, it's good to see you back," she says easily, patting the hood of Freya's pram. "Seems like only yesterday you were in here, all of you, buying sweets and whatnot. Do you remember those tall tales that your friend used to spin? What was her name . . . Cleo?"

"Thea," I say, my voice low. Yes, I remember.

"Told me her father was wanted for murdering her mother and nearly had me believing her." Mary laughs again, her whole body shaking, making Freya's pram tremble in sympathy. "Course, that was before I knew what terrible little liars you was, all of you."

Liars. One word, tossed so casually into the stream of her conversation . . . is it my imagination, or is there suddenly something hostile in Mary's voice?

"Well"—I tug gently on the pram, loosing the folds of the hood from her fingers—"I'd better be going. . . . Freya will be wanting her lunch . . ."

"Don't let me keep you," Mary says lightly. I duck my head in a kind of submissive apology, and she steps back as I begin maneuvering the pram around to leave the shop.

I'm halfway through a laborious three-point turn in the narrow aisle between the shelves, realizing too late that I should have backed out, the way I came in, when the bell at the entrance clangs.

I turn to look over my shoulder, yanking the pram around. For a moment I don't recognize the figure in the doorway, but when I do, my heart leaps suddenly inside my chest like a bird beating hopelessly against a cage.

His clothes are stained and crumpled, as if he's slept in them, and there is a bruise on his cheekbone, cuts on his knuckles. But what strikes me, like a blow to the center of my chest, is how much he has changed—and yet how little. He was always tall, but the lanky slenderness has gone, and the man standing there now fills the narrow entrance with his shoulders, exuding, without even trying, a sense of lean, contained strength.

But his face, the broad cheekbones, the narrow lips, and, oh God, his eyes . . .

I stand, stupid with the shock, trying to catch my breath, and he doesn't see me at first, just nods a greeting to Mary and stands back, waiting politely for me to exit the shop. It's only when I say his name, my voice husky and faltering, that his head jerks up, and he looks, *really* looks, for the first time, and his face changes.

"Isa?" Something falls to the floor, the keys he was holding in one hand. His voice is just as I remember it, deep and slow, with that strange, little offbeat twist, the only trace of his mother tongue. "Isa, is it—is it really you?"

"Yes." I try to swallow, try to smile, but the shock seems to have frozen the muscles in my face. "I—I thought you were—Didn't you go back to France?"

His expression is rigid, impassive, his golden eyes unreadable, and there is something a little stiff in his voice, as if he's holding something in check.

"I came back."

"But why—I don't understand, why didn't Kate say . . . ?"

"You'd have to ask her that."

This time, I'm sure I'm not imagining it: there is definite coldness in his tone.

I don't understand. What has happened? I feel like I'm groping blindly in a room filled with fragile, precious objects, tilting and rocking with every false step I make. Why didn't Kate tell us Luc was back? And why is he so . . . But here I stop, unable to put a name to the emotion that's radiating from Luc's silent presence. What *is* he? It's not shock—or not completely, not now that the surprise of my presence has worn off. It's a coiled, contained sort of emotion that I can tell he is trying to hold back. An emotion closer to . . .

The word comes to me as he takes a step forwards, blocking my exit from the shop.

Hate.

I swallow.

"Are you . . . are you well, Luc?"

"Well?" There is a laugh in his voice, but there's no trace of mirth. *"Well?"*

"I just—"

"How the fuck can you ask that?" he says, his voice rising.

"What?" I try to step back, but there is nowhere to go—Mary Wren is close behind me. Luc is blocking the doorway, with the pram between us, and all I can think of is that if he lashes out, it will be Freya who gets hurt. What has happened to change him so much?

"Calm down, Luc," Mary says warningly from behind me.

"Kate knew," Luc's voice is shaking. "*You* knew what she was sending me back to."

"Luc, I didn't—I couldn't—" My fingers are gripping the handle of Freya's pram, the knuckles white. I want so badly to get out of this shop. There is a buzzing in my head, a bluebottle battering senselessly at the window, and I am reminded suddenly and horribly of the mutilated sheep, the flies around its spilled guts . . .

He says something in French that I don't understand, but it sounds crude and full of disgust.

"Luc," Mary says more loudly. "Step out of the way and get a hold of yourself, unless you want me to call Mark?"

There is a silence, filled with waiting and the noise of the fly, and I feel my nails tightening on the handle of the pram. And then Luc takes a slow, exaggerated step back, and waves a hand towards the doorway.

"*Je vous en prie*," he says sarcastically.

I push the pram roughly forwards, bashing the front against the closed door with a jolt that makes Freya wake with a startled cry, but I don't stop. I shove us both through, the door closing behind us with a jangling in my ears. And I storm up the street, putting as much distance as I can between us and that shop, until the village buildings are just distant shapes, far off through the heat-hazed summer air, before I pick up my crying baby and hold her to my chest.

"It's okay," I hear myself muttering shakily in her ear, holding her to my shoulder with one hand, as I steer the pram jerkily along the dusty road back to the Mill. "It's okay. The nasty man didn't hurt us, did he? What do they say, sticks and stones may break my bones, but words will never hurt me? There, there, sweetheart. Oh, there, there, Freya. Don't cry, honey. Please don't cry."

But she won't be comforted. She cries and cries, the wailing siren of an inconsolable child, woken with a shock from contented sleep. And it's only when the drops fall onto the top of Freya's head that I notice I am crying myself, and I don't even know why. Is it shock? Or anger? Or just relief that we are out of there?

"There, there," I repeat, senselessly, in time with my feet on the pavement, and I no longer know if I'm talking to Freya or myself. "It's going to be okay. I promise. It's all going to be okay."

But even as I'm saying the words, and breathing in the scent of her soft, sweaty hair, the smell of warm, cared-for baby, Mary's words come back to me, ringing in my ears like an accusation.

Little liar.

RULE THREE

DON'T GET CAUGHT

*L*ittle liar.
    Little liar.

The words sound in time with my footsteps on the pavement as I half walk, half jog out of Salten, their pitch rising with Freya's siren cries.

At last, maybe half a mile outside the village, I can't take it anymore—my back is on fire with carrying her, and her cries drill into my head like nails. *Little liar. Little liar.*

I stop by the dusty side of the road, put the brake on the pram, and sit on a log, where I unclip my nursing bra and put Freya to my breast. She gives a glad little shriek and throws up her chubby hands, but before she latches on, she pauses for a moment, looking up at me with her bright blue eyes, and she smiles, and her expression is so very clearly, *Honestly! I knew you'd get the hint eventually*, that I can't help but smile back, though my back is sore, and my throat hurts from swallowing down my rage and fear at Luc.

    Little liar.

The words come floating back through the years to me, and as Freya feeds, I shut my eyes, remembering. Remembering how it started.

It was January, bleak and cold, and I was just back from a miserable holiday with my father and brother—unspoken words over hard, dry turkey, and presents that my mother hadn't chosen, with her name written in my father's handwriting.

Thea and I came down together from London, but

we missed the train we were supposed to catch, and consequently the connection with the school bus at the station. I stood under the waiting room canopy, sheltering from the cold wind, smoking a cigarette while Thea rang the school office to find out what we should do.

"They'll be here at five thirty," Thea reported back, as she hung up, and we both looked up at the big clock hanging over the platform. "It's barely even four. Bollocks."

"We could walk?" I said doubtfully. Thea shook her head, shivering as the wind cut across the platform.

"Not with cases."

As we were waiting, trying to decide what to do, another train came in, this one the local stopping train from Hampton's Lee, carrying all the schoolkids who went to Hampton Grammar. I looked, automatically, for Luc, but he wasn't there. He was either staying late for some extracurricular thing, or skiving. Both were more than possible.

Mark Wren was, though, shambling down the platform in his habitual hunch, his bowed head displaying the painful-looking acne on the back of his neck.

"Hey," Thea said, as he went past. "Hey, you—Mark, isn't it? How are you getting into Salten? Do you get a lift?"

He shook his head.

"Bus. Drops the Salten kids off at the pub and carries onto Riding."

Thea and I looked at each other.

"Does it stop at the bridge?" Thea asked. Mark shook his head.

"Not normal, like. But the driver might do it if you asked."

Thea raised an eyebrow and I nodded. It would save

us a couple of miles, at least, and we could walk the rest of the way.

We piled onto the bus. I stayed with the cases in the luggage rack, but Thea followed Mark Wren down the aisle to where he was sitting, his bag clutched across his lap like a shield, his Adam's apple nervously bobbing in his throat. She winked at me as she passed.

"KATE'S NEXT WEEKEND?" THEA SAID, as she passed my chair in the common room that evening, on her way to prep. I nodded, and she winked, reminding me of the encounter on the bus. Lola Ronaldo switched channels with the remote and rolled her eyes.

"Kate's again? Why on earth do you lot spend so much time over there? Me and Jess Hamilton are going into Hampton's Lee to watch a film. We're going to have supper at the Fat Fryer, but Fatima said she couldn't come 'cause she was going back to Kate's with you. Why are you moldering away in boring old Salten every weekend? Got your eye on someone?"

My cheeks flushed, thinking of Kate's brother, remembering the last time I had been at the Mill. It had been an unseasonably hot autumn day, the evening sun like flames upon the water, reflecting from the windows of the Mill until the whole place seemed ablaze. We had lolled about all afternoon, soaking up the last summer rays, until at last Kate had stripped off on a dare from Thea, and swum naked in the Reach. I don't know where Luc was when Kate jumped in, but he appeared as she was swimming back from the center of the channel.

"Forgotten something?" He held up her bikini, a mocking smile on his lips. Kate let out a screech that sent gulls wheeling and flapping up from the waves, making the red-gold waters dance.

"You bastard! Give that back!"

But Luc only shook his head, and as she swam towards him, he began pelting her with pieces of seaweed from the flotsam washed up against the Mill. Kate retaliated with splashes of water, and then, as she drew close enough, she grabbed for his ankle, hooking his leg out from underneath him, wrestling him into the water so that they both plunged deep, deep into the bay, arms and legs locked, only the rising bubbles showing their path.

A moment later, Kate shot to the surface and struck out for the jetty, and when she scrambled out I saw that she was holding Luc's swimming shorts, crowing with triumph while he trod water farther out, swearing and laughing and threatening every kind of revenge.

I had *tried* not to look, tried to read my book, listen to Fatima gossiping with Thea, concentrate on anything else but Luc's naked body shimmering through the water, but somehow my gaze kept straying back to him, gold and brown and lithe in the fractured blaze of autumn sun, and the picture rose up in front of me now, making me feel a strange emotion, something between shame and longing.

"It's Thea," I said abruptly, feeling my face hot beneath Lola's gaze. "She's pining with love for someone in the village. Keeps hoping we'll bump into him if we spend enough time there."

It was a lie. But it was a self-serving one, a lie against one of us. Even as I said it, I knew I'd crossed a line. But I couldn't take it back now.

Lola looked towards Thea's retreating back, and then at me, her face uncertain. We had developed a reputation, by this time, for piss-taking and insincerity, and I could tell she wasn't sure whether this was true or not, but with Thea, who knew?

"Oh yeah?" she said at last. "I don't believe you."

"It's true," I said, relieved now that she was off the scent. And then, some stupid impulse compelled me to add a fatal detail. "Look, don't tell her I told you but . . . it's Mark Wren. They sat together on the bus back from the station." I lowered my voice, leaned towards her over the top of my book. "He put his hand on her thigh . . . you can imagine the rest."

"*Mark Wren?* That kid who lives above the post office, with the spots?"

"What can I say?" I shrugged. "Thea doesn't care about looks."

Lola snorted and moved away.

I DIDN'T THINK OF THE scene again until the following week. I didn't even remember to tell Kate, so she could mark my points in the book. By this time the game had become less of a competition than an end in itself. The point was not to beat Fatima, Thea, and Kate but to outwit everyone else—"us" against "them."

We spent Saturday night at the Mill, and then all four of us walked down into Salten village to buy snacks from the shop, and a hot chocolate at the pub, which doubled up as the town café out of season, if you were prepared to put up with Jerry's suggestive cracks.

Fatima and Kate were sitting in the window seat while Thea and I were at the bar. She was ordering drinks, and I was waiting to help carry them back to the table.

"Excuse me, I said *no* cream on the last one," I heard her say sharply as the bartender pushed the last foaming cup over the counter. He sighed and began to scrape off the topping, but Thea broke in. "No, thank you. I'll have a fresh cup."

I winced at her autocratic tone, at the way those

cut-glass vowels turned a perfectly ordinary remark into a haughty command.

The bartender swore under his breath as he turned to pour away the carefully prepared drink, and I saw one of the women waiting at the bar roll her eyes and mouth something at her friend. I didn't catch the words, but her gaze flicked back towards me and Thea, and her look was contemptuous. I crossed my arms over my chest, trying to make myself smaller and more invisible, wishing I had not worn my button-up shirt dress. The button at the top had broken off, making it lower cut than normal, and I was painfully conscious of the flash of bra lace that kept creeping out from the neckline, and of the way the women were looking at us both—at my neckline, and at Thea's ripped jeans, which showed scarlet silk knickers through the tears.

As I stood, waiting for Thea to pass the mugs over her shoulder, Jerry came up behind me with a tray of dirty glasses. He held it up at shoulder height as he squeezed through the throng, and I felt a shock of recognition at the pressure of his crotch against me as he passed. The bar was full, but not crowded enough to explain that deliberate grind against my buttocks.

"Excuse me," he said with a wheezy chuckle, and I felt his free hand on my waist. "Don't mind me."

I felt my face flush, and I said to Thea, "I'm going to the loo. Can you manage the drinks?"

"Sure." She barely looked up from counting out change, and I bolted for the door of the ladies' and locked myself in, feeling my breath coming fast.

It was only when I went into the cubicle to get some tissue to blow my nose that I noticed the writing on the toilet door. It was scrawled in eyeliner, smudged and blurred already.

Mark Wren is a dirty perv, it read. I blinked. It

seemed like such an incongruous accusation. Mark Wren? Shy, mild-mannered Mark Wren?

There was another one by the sink, this time in a different color.

Mark Wren fingers Salten House girls on the bus.

And then finally, on the door out to the pub, in Sharpie, *Mark Wren is a sex offender!!!!*

WHEN I GOT OUT OF the loo, my cheeks were burning.

"Can we go?" I said abruptly to Kate, Fatima, and Thea. Thea looked up, confused.

"What the fuck? You've not even touched your drink!"

"There's something I need to tell you," I said. "I don't want to talk about it here."

"Sure," Kate said. She scooped up the last spoonful of marshmallow, and Fatima began looking for her bag. But before we had time to do anything more, the door of the pub banged open, and Mary Wren came in.

I wasn't expecting her to come to our table—she knew Kate, of course, she was a good friend of Ambrose, but she had never taken any notice of Kate's friends.

But she did. She walked straight across and looked from me to Thea to Fatima, her broad lip curling.

"Which of you is Isa Wilde?" she asked, in her deep, hoarse voice.

I swallowed.

"M-me."

"All right." She put her hands to her hips, towering over us where we sat. The hubbub in the pub seemed to die away, and I saw that people were listening, craning to see round Mary's broad, muscular back. "Listen to me, my lass. I don't know how people behave back where you were brought up, but round here, people care what's said about them. If you go spreading lies about my boy again, I will break every bone in your body. Do you understand? I will snap them, one by one."

I opened my mouth, but I couldn't speak. A deep, spreading shame was rising up from my gut, paralyzing me.

Beside me, Kate's face was shocked, and I realized she had no idea what this was all about.

"Mary," she said, "you can't—"

"Keep out of it," Mary snapped at her, wheeling round. "You were in on it, I'll be bound, all of you. I know what you're like." She folded her arms and looked around our little circle, from me to Fatima to Thea and finally to Kate, and I realized that in some perverse way she was enjoying this—enjoying our shock and upset. "You're little liars all of you, and if I had charge of you, you'd be whipped."

Kate gasped at that, and half stood, as if to fight in my corner, but Mary put a heavy hand on her shoulder, physically forcing her back down against the cushions.

"No, you don't. I imagine that fancy school is too modern for that sort of thing, and your dad, he's too nice for his own good, but I'm not, and if you hurt my boy again"—she looked back at me, her sloe-dark eyes meeting mine unflinchingly—"you'll live to regret the day you were born."

And then she straightened, turned on her heel, and went out.

The door slammed behind her, loud in the sudden quiet she left behind, and then there was a gust of laughter and the noises of the bar began to return—the clink of glasses, the deep rumble of the men at the bar. But I felt the eyes of the villagers on us, speculating about what Mary had said, and I wanted to sink into the floor.

"Jesus!" Kate said. Her face was white, with a flush

of anger high on her cheekbones. "What the hell is wrong with her? Dad will be so furious when—"

"No—" I grabbed at her coat, interrupting her. "No, Kate, don't. It was my fault. Don't tell Ambrose."

I couldn't bear it. I couldn't bear for it to come out—the stupid, unworthy lie I had told. The thought of repeating that back to Ambrose's face, seeing his disappointment . . .

"Don't tell him," I said. I felt tears prick at the back of my eyes, but it wasn't sorrow—it was shame. "I deserved it. I deserved what she said."

It was a mistake, that's what I wanted to tell Mary, as I sat there speechless in front of her wrath. *It was a mistake, and I'm sorry.*

But I didn't say it. And the next time I went into the post office, she served me as usual, and nothing more was said about it. But seventeen years later, as I feed my baby and try to smile down at her laughing, chub-cheeked face, Mary Wren's words ring in my ears, and I think, I was right. I did deserve them. We all did.

Little liars.

K ate, Thea, and Fatima are seated around the scrub-top table as I burst back into the Mill, hot and footsore, and my throat dry as dust.

Shadow barks a short sharp warning as the door crashes back against the wall, making the cups on the dresser rattle, and the picture frames bang against the wall in sympathy.

"Isa!" Fatima says, her face surprised as she looks up from her plate. "You look like you've seen a ghost!"

"I have. Why didn't you tell us, Kate?"

The words were a question in my head. Spoken, they sound like an accusation.

"Tell you what?" Kate stands, full of bewildered concern. "Isa, did you just walk all the way to Salten and back in three hours? You must be exhausted. Did you take a bottle of water?"

"Fuck the water," I say angrily, but when she brings me a glass from the tap and sets it gently down on the table beside me, I have to swallow against the pain in my throat before I can drink.

I take a sip, and then a gulp. Fatima is putting salad on a plate for me, cutting the leaves into smaller chunks so I can spear them one-handed with a fork.

"What happened?" She sits down beside me on the sofa, holding the plate, and her face is worried. "Did you say you saw a *ghost*?"

"Yes, I saw a ghost." I look over Fatima's head, straight at Kate. "I saw Luc Rochefort in the village."

Kate's face crumples, before I've even finished the

sentence, and she sits abruptly on the edge of the sofa as if she doesn't completely trust her legs.

"Shit."

"Luc?" Fatima looks from me to Kate. "But I thought he went back to France after . . ." She trails off.

Kate makes an unhappy movement with her head, but it's impossible to tell whether it's a nod or a shake, or a combination of both.

"What's happened to him, Kate?" I hug Freya closer, thinking of his closed, impassive face, the fury I felt radiating out of him in the small post office. "He was . . ."

"Angry," she finishes. Her face is pale, but her hands, as she reaches in her pocket for her tobacco, are steady. "Right?"

"That's an understatement. What happened?"

She begins to roll up, very slowly and deliberately, and I remember this from school, how Kate would always take her time, she would never be hurried into an answer. The more difficult the question, the longer she would pause before replying.

Thea puts down her fork, picks up her wine and cigarette case, and comes over, too.

"Come on, Kate." She sits on the bare boards at our feet, and I have a sudden, painful memory of all the nights we spent like this, curled together on the sofa: watching the river, the flames; smoking, laughing, talking . . .

There is no laughter now, only the rustle of paper as Kate rolls back and forth on her knee, biting her lip. When the cigarette is done, she licks the paper, and then she speaks.

"He did go back to France. But not . . . willingly."

"What do you mean?" Thea demands. She taps her cigarette case against the floorboard and looks at

Freya, and I know she wants to smoke but is waiting until Freya is out of the room.

Kate sighs and puts her bare feet up onto the sofa, beside Fatima's hip, and she pushes the loose strands of hair off her face.

"I don't know how much you knew about Luc's background . . . You know Dad and Luc's mother, Mireille, were together, years back, right? And they lived with us here."

I nod; we knew all this. Luc and Kate were toddlers—almost too small to remember, Kate said, although she had faint recollections of parties by the river, Luc falling in once when he was too little to swim.

"When Dad and Mireille broke up, Mireille took Luc back to France, and we didn't see him for several years, and then Dad got a call from Mireille—she couldn't cope with Luc, he was running wild, social services were involved—could he come and spend the summer holidays here, give her a break? You know Dad, he said yes, of course. Well, when Luc got here, it turned out that there was maybe a bit more to the story than Mireille had said. Luc *was* acting out, but there were . . . reasons. Mireille had her own problems . . . she'd started shooting up again, and well, she maybe hadn't been the best parent to Luc."

"What about Luc's dad?" Fatima asks. "Didn't he have anything to say about his son disappearing off to England with a strange man?"

Kate shrugs.

"I don't know if there was a dad. From what Luc said, Mireille was pretty fucked-up when she had him. I'm not sure if she ever knew . . ."

She trails off and then takes a breath, and starts again.

"Anyway, he came back to live with us when we

were . . . maybe thirteen, fourteen? And the holidays turned into a term . . . and the term turned into a year . . . and then another . . . and then somehow Luc was enrolled at the secondary school in Hampton's Lee and living with us full-time, and you know . . . he was doing well. He was happy, I guess."

We know this, too, but no one interrupts.

"But after Dad . . ." Kate swallows, and I know the bad part is coming, the time none of us can bear to think about. "After Dad . . . disappeared, Luc—he couldn't stay here anymore. He was only fifteen, I'd just turned sixteen that summer, but Luc was still several months off and a minor, and in any case, once social services got involved . . ." She swallows again, and I can see the emotions passing across her face, cloud shadows flitting across a valley.

"He got sent back," she says abruptly. "He wanted to stay here with me, but I had no choice." She spreads her hands out pleadingly. "You realize that, right? I was sixteen, there was no way they were going to let me act as legal guardian to a stray French boy with no parents in the country. I did what I had to do!" she repeats, her voice desperate.

"Kate"—Fatima puts a hand on her arm, her voice gentle—"this is us, you don't have to justify yourself. Of *course* you had no choice. Ambrose wasn't Luc's dad—what could you have done?"

"They sent him back," Kate says, almost as if she hasn't heard. Her face is blank, remembering. "And he wrote and wrote, pleading with me, saying that Dad had promised he'd take care of him, and accusing me of betraying him, accusing me—"

Her eyes well up with tears, and she blinks them away, her expression suddenly bleak and raw. Shadow, sensing her unhappiness without understanding it, comes to lie at her feet, with a little whine, and Kate puts her hand down, ruffling his white fur.

"A few years ago he came back, got a job at Salten House as a gardener. I thought all the years would have given him perspective, that he'd have realized that I had no choice. I could barely keep myself out of a children's home, let alone him. But he hadn't. He hadn't forgiven me at all. He cornered me one night coming back along the river, and oh God!" She buries her face in her hands. "Fatima, the stories! You must hear them all the time as a GP, but I'd never—the beatings, the abuse, God, what he"—her voice cracks—"what he suffered—I couldn't bear to listen. But he kept on and on, telling me, like he wanted to punish me—what his mother's boyfriends had done to him when he was little, and later when he went back to France and got taken into care, the man at the children's home who used to—who used to—"

But she can't finish. Her voice dissolves into tears, and she covers her face.

I look from Fatima's and Thea's shocked faces, and then back to Kate. I want to say something. I want to comfort her, but all I can think is how they used to be, the two of them, their laughing faces as they splashed in the Reach, their companionable silence as they bent their heads over a board game . . . They were so close— closer than my brother and I ever were. And now this.

In the end it's Fatima who sets down the plate of food very carefully and stands. She puts her arms around Kate, rocking her, wordlessly, back and forth, back and forth.

She's saying something, very low, but I think I can make out the words.

"It wasn't your fault," she's saying, over and over. "It wasn't your fault."

I should have known. That's what I think, as I sit by Freya's crib, trying to lull her into sleep, with a pain in my throat from unshed tears.

I should have *known.*

Because it was all there in front of me, for me to see. The scars on Luc's back as he swam in the Reach; the marks on his shoulder that I assumed were botched inoculation scars, but when I asked him about them, his face only twisted and he shook his head.

I am older now, less innocent. I understand those small circular burns for what they really were, and I feel sick at my own blindness.

It explains so much that I never understood—Luc's silence, and his doglike adoration of Ambrose. His unwillingness to talk about France, however much we pestered him, and the way Kate would squeeze his hand and change the subject for him.

It even explained something that I had never understood—the way he would let the village boys tease and mock and swagger at him, and he would just take it and take it and take it . . . and then crack. I remember one evening in the pub, when the village kids had been ribbing him, gently but relentlessly, about hanging out with "snooty" Salten House girls. Luc's position, not quite town, not quite gown, had always been a tough one. Kate was firmly Salten House, and Ambrose somehow effortlessly straddled the two worlds. But Luc had to negotiate an uneasy class divide between the state school in Hampton's Lee that he attended with the majority of the village kids, and his family connection to the private school on the hill.

And yet, he managed. He put up with the teasing, the "our girls not good enough for you, mate?" remarks, and the veiled comments about posh girls liking a "bit of rough." That night, in the pub, he had just smiled and shaken his head. But then, right at the end of the night, as last orders were being rung, one of the village boys bent down and whispered something in Luc's ear in passing.

I don't know what he said. I only saw Kate's face change. But Luc stood, so fast his chair hit the floor behind him, and he punched the kid, hard and straight on the nose, as if something inside him had snapped. The boy fell to the ground, sobbing and groaning. And Luc stood over him as he bled, and watched him cry, his face as expressionless as if nothing had happened at all.

Someone from the pub must have called Ambrose. He was sitting in the rocking chair, waiting for us when we got in, his normally good-humored face without a trace of a smile. He stood up when we entered.

"Dad," Kate said, breaking in before Luc could speak. "It wasn't Luc's—"

But Ambrose was shaking his head before she'd even finished.

"Kate, this is between me and Luc. Luc, can I speak to you in your room, please."

They closed the door to Luc's room, so we couldn't hear the ensuing argument, only the rise and fall of the voices: Ambrose's full of disappointment and reproach; Luc's pleading, and then at last angry. The rest of us huddled below in the living room, in front of a fire that we barely needed, for the night was warm, but Kate was shivering as the voices above us grew louder.

"You don't understand!" I heard from above. It was Luc's voice shaking and cracked with angry disbelief. I could not hear the words of Ambrose's reply, only his tone, even and patient, and then the crash as Luc threw something at the wall.

When Ambrose came down, he was alone, his wiry hair standing up on end as if he'd raked it through and through. His face was weary and upset, and he reached for the unlabeled wine bottle under the sink and poured himself a tumblerful, downing it with a sigh.

Kate stood as Ambrose sank into the armchair opposite, but Ambrose shook his head, knowing where she was heading.

"I wouldn't. He's very upset."

"I'm going up," Kate said defiantly. She stood, but as she passed Ambrose's chair he put out his free hand, catching her wrist, and she stopped, looking down at him, her expression mutinous. "Well? What?"

I waited, my heart in my throat, for Ambrose to explode as my father would have done. I could hear him now, raging at Will for answering him back, *I'd have been thrashed for cheeking my father like that, you little shit*, and *When I give you an order, you listen, got it?*

But Ambrose . . . Ambrose didn't shout. He didn't even speak. He held Kate's wrist, but so gently, his fingers barely circling it, that I could see that was not what was keeping her there.

Kate stood, looking down at her father, searching his face. Neither of them moved, but her expression changed, as if reading something in his eyes that none of the rest of us could understand, and then she sighed and let her hand drop.

"Okay," she said. And I knew that whatever Ambrose had wanted to say, Kate had understood, without needing to be told.

There was another crash from above, breaking the silence, and we all jumped.

"He's trashing his room," Kate said under her breath, but she made no further move towards the stairs, she only sank back down to the sofa. "Oh, Dad, I can't bear it."

"Aren't you—Can't you stop him?" Fatima asked Ambrose, her eyes wide with disbelief. Ambrose winced as the sound of broken glass came from above, and then shook his head.

"I would if I could, but there's some kinds of pain that only stop hurting when you lash out. Maybe this is what he needs to do. I just wish . . ." He rubbed his face, and suddenly he looked every day his age. "I just wish he wasn't breaking up his own stuff. God knows, he's not got much. He's hurting himself more than me. What *happened* in that pub?"

"He took it, Dad," Kate said. Her face was white with upset. "He really did. You know what they're like—it's that kid, Ryan or Roland or whatever his name is. The big one with the dark hair. He's always had it in for him. But Luc was putting up with it really well, he was just laughing it off. But then Ryan, he said something else, and Luc—he just lost it."

"What did he say?" Ambrose asked, leaning forward in his armchair, but for the first time I saw the shutter come down between Kate and her father. Her expression changed, and she went completely still, a kind of wary reserve behind the blank mask of her face.

"I don't know," was all she said, her voice suddenly flat and strange, "I didn't hear."

AMBROSE DIDN'T PUNISH LUC, AND Fatima shook her head over it on the way home because we all knew, relaxed though he was, that he would never have tolerated that kind of behavior from Kate. There would have been recriminations, reproaches, repairs taken out of her allowance.

With Luc, though, Ambrose seemed to be an unfailing well of patience. And now I understand why.

Freya is asleep, her breathing even and featherlight, and I stand, stretching, lost in memories as I stare out across the estuary towards Salten, remembering the Luc I knew, before we went away, and trying to work out why his anger in the post office has shaken me so much.

I knew that that fury was there, after all. I'd seen it, directed at others, sometimes even at himself. And then I realize. It's not his anger that has scared me. It's seeing him angry at *us*.

For back then, no matter how furious he was, he treated the four of us like bone china, like something too precious to be touched, almost. And God knows, I wanted it—I wanted to be touched, *so* very much. I remember lying beside him on the jetty, the heat of the sun on our backs, and turning to look at his face, his eyes closed, and longing with a heat so fierce that I thought it might consume me, longing for him to open his eyes and reach out towards me.

But he did not. And so, with my heart beating in my chest so hard that I thought he could surely hear it, I reached out and put my lips to his.

Whatever I expected to happen, it was not this.

His eyes flew open instantly, and he shoved me away, crying out, "*Ne me touche pas!*" and scrambling up and back so hard he almost fell into the water, his chest rising and falling, his eyes wild, as if I'd ambushed him while sleeping.

I felt my face turn scarlet, as if the sun were burning me alive, and I got up, too, taking an involuntary step back, away from his furious incomprehension.

"I'm sorry," I managed. "Luc?"

He said nothing, just looked around, as if trying to understand where he was and what had happened. In that moment, it was almost as if he didn't recognize me, and he looked at me as if I were a stranger. And then recognition came back into his eyes, and with it a kind of shame. He turned on his heel, and he ran, ignoring my cry of "Luc! Luc, I'm sorry!"

I didn't understand then. I didn't understand what I had done wrong, or how he could react so violently to what was, after all, barely more than the sisterly kiss I'd given him a hundred times.

Now, though . . . now I think I know what kind of experiences were at the back of that terrified reaction, and my heart is breaking for him. But I am wary, too, for that moment gave me a taste of what I felt again in the post office.

I know what it's like to be Luc's enemy. I have seen him lash out.

And I can't help thinking of the dead sheep, of the fury and pain behind that act, of its guts spilling out like festering secrets into the clear blue water.

And now, I am afraid.

What are you going to do?" Fatima says in a low voice, handing me a cracked porcelain cup.

Lunch is over. Fatima and I are washing up—or rather she's washing, I'm drying. Freya is playing on the hearth rug.

Kate and Thea have gone out for a cigarette, and to walk Shadow, and I can see them through the window opposite, walking slowly back along the bank of the Reach, heads bent in conversation, the smoke from their cigarettes dispersing in the summer air. It's odd: they're walking the opposite way of the route I would have gone—north towards the main road to Salten, rather than south to the shore. It's not nearly as nice a walk.

"I don't know." I wipe the cup and set it on the table. "How about you?"

"I—I honestly don't know, either. All my instincts are shouting at me to go home; it's not like we can change anything by being here, and at least in London we're less likely to get a knock on the door from the police."

Her words give me a shiver, and I glance involuntarily at the door, imagining Mark Wren walking across the narrow bridge, knocking on the blackened wood . . . I try to imagine what I would say. I remember Kate's vehement injunction last night—*we know nothing. We saw nothing.* That has been the script for seventeen years. If we all stick to it, there is nothing they can do to prove otherwise, surely?

"I mean, I want to support Kate," Fatima continues. She puts down the sponge and pushes back her scarf, leaving a smudge of white foam on her cheek. "But a school reunion when we've never been to one before? Is that really a good idea?"

"I know." I put another cup on the table. "I don't want to go, either. But it'll look worse if we bail out at the last minute."

"I know. I know all that. Rule two—stick to your story. I mean, I get it, I do. For better or worse, she's bought the bloody tickets and told everyone that's why we're coming down, so I can see it's better to see it through. But that thing with the sheep . . ."

She shakes her head and returns to washing the lunch things. I sneak a quick glance at her face as she scrubs.

"What *was* that about? You saw the body better than I did. Was it really Shadow?"

Fatima shakes her head again, but this time it's an answer.

"I don't know," she says. "I've only seen a couple of dog attacks, and maybe it's different when they attack people, but it didn't look . . ."

My stomach clenches, and I'm not sure if I should come clean. If the police get involved then perhaps it's better if Fatima doesn't know, doesn't have anything to conceal, but we swore never to lie to one another, didn't we? And this is lying of a kind—a lie by omission.

"There was a note," I say at last. "Kate saw it, but she hid it in her pocket. I found it when I went to rinse her coat."

"*What?*" Fatima looks up at that, her face alarmed. She drops the dishcloth and turns to face me. "Why didn't you say?"

"Because I didn't want to worry you. And I didn't want . . ."

I didn't want the police to find out about it. But I don't want to say that. Speaking those fears aloud makes them real, and I can't admit to myself that this is a possibility, that the whole nightmare could be starting up again.

"What did it say?"

"It said . . ." I swallow. The words are almost unbearable to speak, and I have to force myself to make them real. "It said, 'Why don't you throw this one in the Reach, too?'"

There is a crack, as Fatima drops the cup she is holding, and all the color and expression drains from her face, leaving it a pale Noh mask of horror, framed by her dark head scarf.

"What did you say?" Her voice is a croak.

But I can't bring myself to repeat it, and I know full well she heard me; she is just too scared to admit what I already know—that someone knows and is bent on punishing us for what happened.

"No." She is shaking her head. "*No*. It's not possible."

I put down the tea towel and go to the sofa where Freya is playing, and I slump down, my face in my hands.

"This changes everything," Fatima says urgently. "We have to leave, Isa. We have to leave *now*."

There is a sound outside, the scamper of paws, the noise of feet on the jetty, and my head comes up in time to see Kate and Thea open the shore door and come inside, stamping the sand and mud off their feet. Kate is laughing, some of the strain that has been in her face for the last twenty-four hours ebbing away, but her expression turns wary as she looks from Fatima to me and back.

"What's going on?" she asks. "Is everything all right?"

"I'm going." Fatima picks up the shards of broken cup from the floor and dumps them on the drainer, then she wipes her hands on the tea towel and comes to stand beside me. "I need to be back in London. So does Isa."

"No." Kate's voice is firm, urgent. "You can't."

"Come back with me!" Fatima says desperately. She waves a hand around at the Mill. "You're not safe here and you know it. Isa—tell them about the note!"

"What note?" Thea is looking from one of us to the other, her face alarmed. "Will someone explain?"

"Kate got a note," Fatima spits, "saying 'Why don't you throw this one in the Reach, too?' Someone knows, Kate! Is it Luc? Did you tell him? Is that what this is all about?"

Kate doesn't answer. She is shaking her head in a kind of mute misery, but I'm not sure what she's saying no to—the idea that she would tell Luc, or the idea that it's him, or whether she's answering Fatima at all.

"Someone *knows*," Fatima says again, her voice rising in pitch. "You *have* to leave!"

Kate shakes her head again, and she closes her eyes, pressing her fingers against them as if she doesn't know what to say, but when Fatima says again, "Kate, are you *listening* to me?" she looks up.

"I can't leave, Fati. You know why."

"Why not? Why *can't* you just pack up and walk away?"

"Because nothing has changed—whoever wrote that note hasn't gone to the police, which means either they're just speculating, or they've got more to lose than we have. We're still safe. But if I run, people will know I have something to hide."

"Well, you stay if you want"—Fatima turns, begins

picking up her bag, her sunglasses from the table—
"but I'm not. There's no reason for me to stay here."

"There is." Kate's voice is hard now. "At least for one
night. Be reasonable, Fatima. Stay for the alumnae
dinner—if you don't, it punches a hole a mile wide in
the reason you're down here. If you don't go to the dinner, why would you all suddenly be here after so long?"

She doesn't say what that reason is. She doesn't
need to. Not with the headline still blaring from every
copy of the local newspaper.

"Fuck," Fatima says suddenly, loudly and viciously.
She drops her bag on the floor and paces to the window, banging her forehead gently against the rippled
glass pane. *"Fuck."*

When she turns back, her face is accusing.

"Why the hell *did* you bring us down here, Kate? To
make sure we're as implicated as you?"

"What?" Kate's face looks like Fatima has slapped
her, and she takes an involuntary step back. "No! Jesus,
Fatima, of course not. How can you even say that?"

"Then why?" Fatima cries.

"Because I couldn't think how else to tell you!" Kate
shouts back. Her olive cheeks are flushed, though
whether with shame or anger, I can't tell. When she
speaks again, it's to Shadow, as if she can't bear to look
at us. "What was the alternative? E-mail you? Because
I don't know about you, but that's not something I
wanted on my computer records. Phone you up and
spill it out while your husbands listened in the background? I asked you to come down because I thought
you deserved to be told face-to-face, and because it
seemed like the safest option, and yes, if I'm honest,
because I'm a selfish bitch, and I *needed you.*"

Her chest is rising and falling, and for a minute I
think she is going to burst into tears, but she doesn't,

instead it's Fatima who stumbles across the room to pull Kate into a hug.

"I'm sorry," she manages. "I should never—I'm so sorry."

"I'm sorry, too," Kate says, her voice muffled by Fatima's scarf. "This is all my fault—"

"Stop," Thea cuts her off. She goes across to the two of them and puts her arms around them both. "Kate, this is on all of us, not just you. If it hadn't have been for what we did . . ."

She doesn't finish, but she doesn't need to. We all *know* what we did, the way that slow, sunlit summer unraveled beneath our fingers, taking Ambrose with it.

"I'll stay the night," Fatima says at last, "but I still don't want to go to the dinner. After everything that happened—how can you think of going back, Kate? After what they did?"

"We have the invitations . . ." Thea says slowly. "Isn't that enough? Can't we say we decided not to go at the last minute, that Fati's car wouldn't start, or something? Isa? What do you think?"

They turn to me, all three of them—three faces, so physically different, and yet their expressions are identical: worry, fear, expectation.

"We should go," I say at last. I don't want to; I want to stay here in the warmth and quiet of the Mill. Salten House is the last place I want to go back to. But Kate has already bought the tickets in our names, and we can't undo that. If we don't attend, there will be four empty places on the seating plan and four unclaimed name tags at the entrance. People know we came down—in a small town like this there are no secrets. If we don't attend they will ask why. Why we changed our minds. And worst of all, why we came down in the first place, if not for the dinner. And we can't afford questions.

"But what about Freya?" Fatima asks, and I realize she's right. I hadn't even thought about Freya. Our eyes turn to her, playing contentedly on her back on the rug, chewing some garish piece of bright-colored plastic. She feels our eyes on her and looks up and laughs, a gurgling joyous laugh that makes me want to snatch her up and hold her close.

"Could I take her?" I ask doubtfully. Kate's face is blank.

"Shit, I never thought of Freya. Hang on." She gets her phone out, and I peer over her shoulder as she brings up the school website and clicks on the "Alumnae" tab.

"Dinner . . . dinner . . . here we are. FAQs . . . tickets for guests . . . oh crap."

I read aloud over her shoulder, "Partners and older children are welcome, but we regret this formal event is not suitable for babies or children under ten. We can supply a list of local sitters, or bed-and-breakfasts with babysitting facilities upon request."

"Great."

"I'm sorry, Isa. But there's half a dozen girls in the village who'd come out."

I bite back the remark that it's not that simple. Freya has never taken bottles well, and besides, even if she did, I don't have any feeding equipment with me.

I could blame it on the bottles, but it would be a kind of lie, because the bigger truth is that I simply don't *want* to leave her.

"I'll have to try to get her down before they come," I say reluctantly. "There's no way she'll go down for a stranger, she won't sleep for Owen, let alone someone she's never met. What time does it start?"

"Eight," Kate says.

Shit. It will be touch and go. Freya is sometimes asleep

by seven, sometimes she's awake and chirruping at nine. But there's no way around this.

"Give me a number," I say to Kate. "I'll call. It's better if I talk to them direct, make sure they're reasonably savvy about babies."

Kate nods.

"Sorry, Isa."

"She'll be fine," Fatima says sympathetically. She puts a hand on my shoulder, squeezes gently. "The first time is always the hardest."

I feel a wave of irritation. She doesn't mean to pull the "experienced mother" card, but she can't help it, and the worst of it is, I know she's right: she has two children and a vast amount more experience than I have, and she has been here before and knows what it's like. But she doesn't know Freya, and even if she thinks she remembers the edgy nervousness of the first time she left her baby with a stranger, she doesn't *really*, not with the visceral immediacy that I am feeling in this moment.

I've left Freya with Owen a few times. But never like this—never with someone I don't know from Adam.

What if something happens?

"Give me the numbers," I say to Kate again, ignoring Fatima, shrugging her hand off my shoulder, and I pick up Freya and take her upstairs, the list of numbers clutched in my hot fist, trying not to give way to tears.

It is late. The sun is dipping in the sky, the shadows over the Reach are lengthening, and Freya is nodding at my breast, her hand still clutched around the fragile necklace of twisted silver wire that I rarely wear anymore, for fear she'll tug it and snap the links.

I can hear the others conversing downstairs. They've been ready for hours, while I try and fail to get Freya to sleep. But she's picked up on my nerves, wrinkled her face disgustedly at the unaccustomed smell of the perfume I've dabbed behind my ears, batted angry hands at the slippery black silk of a too-tight sheath dress borrowed from Kate. Everything is wrong—the strange room, the strange cot, the light slanting through the too-thin curtains.

Every time I lower her to the mattress of the cot she jumps and flails and snatches at me, her angry wail rising like a siren above the noise of the river and the low voices downstairs.

But now . . . now she seems really and truly asleep, her mouth gaping, a little trickle of milk oozing from the side of her lips.

I catch it with the muslin before it can stain the borrowed dress, and then rise, very stealthily, and edge my way to the cot in the corner.

Lower . . . lower . . . I bend over, feeling my back twinge and complain, and then at last she's on the mattress, my hand firm on her belly, trying to merge the moment of my *being* there into the moment of my *not* being there so smoothly and stealthily that it passes unnoticed.

And then at last I stand, holding my breath.

"*Isa!*" comes a whispered hiss up the stairs, and I grit my teeth, screaming *Shut up!* inside my head, but not daring to say it.

But Freya slumbers on, and I tiptoe as silently as possible towards the corridor and down the rickety stairs, my finger to my lips as the others raise a muted cheer, and then hastily hush at the sight of my face.

They are standing, huddled together at the bottom of the stairs, their eyes upturned to mine. Fatima is dressed in a stunningly beautiful jeweled salwar kameez in ruby silk that she somehow found in a formal-wear shop in Hampton's Lee this afternoon. Thea has refused to bow to the dictates of the black-tie invitation and is wearing her usual skinny jeans and a spaghetti-strap top that starts out gold at the bottom hem and deepens into midnight black at the neck, and it reminds me so much of the hair she used to have as a girl that my breath catches in my throat. Kate is wearing a rose-pink handkerchief dress that looks like it could have cost either pence or hundreds of pounds, and her hair is loose around her shoulders and damp from the shower.

There is a lump in my throat as I come to the foot of the stairs—and I don't even know why. Perhaps it's the sudden, heart-shattering realization of how much I love them, or the way they have grown from girls to women in the space of a heartbeat. Perhaps it's the way their faces in the evening sunlight are overlaid by the memory of the girls they once were—they are polished, a little wary, eyes a little tired, but more beautiful than I ever remember them being as girls, and yet at the same time they are clear-skinned, hopeful, poised like birds to take flight into an unknown future.

I think of Luc, and his anger in the shop, the veiled

threats, and I feel a sudden clenching fury—I cannot *bear* for them to be hurt. Any of them.

"Ready?" Kate says with a smile, but before I can nod, there is a cough in the corner, and I turn to see Liz, the girl from the village who has come to take care of Freya, standing by the dresser.

She is horrifyingly young—she said she was sixteen but I don't know if I believe it now that I've seen her—and she has pale brown hair and a broad, blank face that is hard to read, but looks anxious.

"We need to go." Thea looks at her phone.

"Wait," I say, and I begin again the speech that I've already run through twice already—the cup of expressed milk in the fridge, the blankie she doesn't like but I keep hoping she'll take to, where the nappies are, what to do if she won't settle.

"You've got my number," I say for maybe the twentieth time, as Fatima shifts from one foot to the other and Thea sighs. "Right?"

"Right here," Liz pats the pad on the dresser, next to the pile of tenners that is her fee for the night.

"And the milk in the fridge—I don't know if she'll take it—she's not very used to sippy cups—but it's worth a try if she wakes up."

"Don't worry, miss." Her small eyes are a guileless blue. "My ma always says there's no one to beat me with my little brother. I look after him all the time."

This doesn't really reassure me, but I nod.

"Come on, Isa," Thea says impatiently. She is standing at the door, her hand on the latch. "We've really got to get going."

"Okay," I say. I feel the wrongness of what I'm doing twist at my gut as I walk towards the door, but what choice do I have? The distance between me and Freya stretches, like a cord around my throat tightening as I pull away. "I'm going to try to duck out early, but call me, okay?" I say to Liz, and she nods, and I'm peeling myself away from her, from Freya, every step making a hollow place inside my chest.

And then I'm across the rickety wooden bridge, feeling the evening sunlight on my back, and the feeling lifts a little.

"So I guess I'm driving . . . ?" Fatima says, getting out her keys. Kate looks at her watch.

"I don't know. It's ten miles round by the road and we're very likely to hit a tractor at this time. They're all working late on the fields in this weather, and there's only one route they can take. If we get stuck behind one we could be there for ages."

"So what?" Fatima looks almost comically horrified. "Are you saying we should walk?"

"It'd probably be quicker. It's only a couple of miles if we cut across the marsh."

"But I'm wearing evening shoes!"

"So change into your Birkenstocks." Kate nods at Fatima's shoes, left neatly outside the door. "But it'll be easy walking. It's dry in this weather."

"Come on," Thea says, surprising me. "It'll be like old times. And anyway, you know what parking will be like at the school. We'll get boxed in, and you won't be able to get the car out until all the other rows have left."

It's that suggestion that swings it. I can see in Fatima's eyes that she is as reluctant as the rest of us to be stuck at school, unable to get away. She rolls her eyes but kicks off her shoes and pushes her feet into her Birkenstocks. I switch my heels for the sandals I wore to walk to the village, wincing slightly as they rub the same sore places from the long walk. Kate is already wearing low, sensible flats, and so is Thea—she doesn't need the extra height.

I give one last look at the window where Freya is sleeping, feeling the painful tug. And then I turn my face towards the track, south, towards the coast, and I take a deep breath.

Then we set off.

IT IS LIKE OLD TIMES, that's what I think as we walk down the same track we always used to take back to Salten House. It is a pure, beautiful evening, the sky streaked with pink clouds reflecting the setting sun, the sandy track giving back the day's warmth to our feet.

But we are only halfway along the shore path when Kate stops abruptly and says, "Let's cut through here."

For a minute I can't even see where she means— and then I see it—a gap in the tangled, thorny hedge, a broken-down stile just visible among the nettles and brambles.

"What?" Thea gives a short laugh. "You joking?"

"I—" Kate's face is uncomfortable. "I just thought . . . it'll be quicker."

"No, it won't." Fatima's face, behind her outsize black shades, is puzzled. "You know it won't—it's a less direct route, and anyway, there's no way I can get through there, it'll rip my outfit to shreds. What's wrong with the stile farther down? The one we always used to take back to school?"

Kate takes a deep breath, and for a minute I think she's going to persist, but then she turns and stalks off ahead of us up the path.

"Fine." It's muttered under her breath, so low that I'm not sure if I heard.

"That was weird," I whisper to Fatima, who nods.

"I know. What's going on? But I wasn't being unreasonable, was I? I mean"—she gestures to the flowing, fragile silk, the easily caught jewels—"seriously, right?

There's no way I could have got through those thorn-bushes."

"Of course not." I shake my head as we increase our pace to catch up with Kate's retreating back. "I don't know what she was thinking."

But I do know. As soon as we get to the place where we always used to turn, I know instantly, and I can't believe I had forgotten. And I understand, too, why Kate took Thea north up the Reach for their walk this afternoon, instead of south towards the sea.

For where our route turns right, over a stile onto the marsh, the shore path carries on towards the sea, and in the distance, almost hidden in the lee of a sand dune, I can see a white shape, and the blue-and-white flutter of police tape.

It is a tent. The sort used to shelter a site where forensic samples are being taken.

My heart sinks, a sickness fluttering in my gut. How could we have been so crass?

Thea and Fatima realize it, too, at the same instant. I can see by the way their faces change, and we exchange a single, stricken look behind Kate's back as she walks ahead of us to the stile, her face averted from the stark beauty of the shore, and the sparkling sea stretching far out, as far as the eye can see, and in the midst of it all, that little, unassuming tent that has changed everything.

"I'm sorry," I say, as Kate swings her leg over the fence, the rose-patterned silk fluttering in the wind. "Kate, we didn't think—"

"It's fine," she says again, but her voice is stiff and hard, and it is not fine. How *could* we have forgotten? It's not like we didn't know. It's why we're here, after all.

"Kate . . ." Fatima says pleadingly, but Kate is over the stile and striding onwards, her face turned away from us so we cannot see her expression, and we can only look at one another, wretched, guilty, and then hurry to catch up.

"Kate, I'm sorry," I say again, catching at her arm, but she pulls out of my grip.

"Forget about it," she says, and it's a punch in the gut, an accusation I can't refute. Because I already did.

"Stop," Thea says, and there's a note of command in her voice, a sound that I haven't heard for years. She used to use it so easily, that whipcrack tone that more or less compelled you to listen, even if you didn't obey. *Stop. Drink this. Give me that. Come here.*

Somewhere along the line she stopped—stopped ordering others around, became frightened of her own authority. But it's back, just for a flicker, and Kate turns, halting on the short, sheep-cropped turf with a look of resignation in her eyes.

"What?"

"Kate, look . . ." The note is gone now, Thea's voice is conciliatory, uncertain, reflecting all our feelings as we stand around, unsure what to say, unsure how to make the unbearable okay, when we know we can't. "Kate, we didn't—"

"We're sorry," Fatima says. "We really are, we should have realized. But don't be like this—we're here for *you*, you know that, right?"

"And I should be more grateful?" Kate's face twists, and she tries to smile. "I know, I—"

But Fatima interrupts.

"*No.* That's not what I'm saying—for fuck's sake, Kate, when did *gratitude* ever come between any of us?" She spits out the word like a swearword. "Gratitude? Don't insult me. We're beyond that, aren't we? We certainly used to be. All I meant was, you think you're alone, you think you're the only one who cares—

you're *not*. And you should take this—all of us"—she waves a hand round at our little group, our long black shadows streaming across the marsh in the evening sun—"as proof of that. We *love* you, Kate. Look at us— Isa trekking down with her baby; Thea throwing up work at a moment's notice; me dropping Ali, Nadia, Sam, all of them, for *you*. That's how much you mean to me, to us. That's how much we will never let you down. Do you understand?"

Kate shuts her eyes, and for a minute I think she may be about to cry, or rail at us, but she doesn't, she reaches out, blind, for our hands, and pulls us towards her, her strong, paint-covered fingers hard against my wrist, as if we're keeping her afloat.

"You—" she says, and her voice cracks, and then our arms are around one another, all four of us, huddled together like four trees twisted in the coastal winds into a single living thing, arms tangled, foreheads pressed, warmth against warmth, and I can feel them, the others, their pasts so woven with mine that there's no way to separate us, any of us.

"I love you," Kate croaks, and I am saying it back, or I think I am, the chorus of choked voices must include mine, but I can't tell, I can't tell where I end and the others begin.

"We go in together," Fatima says firmly. "Understand? They broke us once, but they won't do it again."

Kate nods and straightens, wiping her eyes beneath the mascara.

"Right."

"So, we're agreed? United front?"

"United front," Thea says, a little grimly, and I nod.

"United we stand," I say, and then I wish I hadn't, because the unspoken final half of the saying hangs in the air, like a silent echo.

*D*o you remember . . . ?

That's the refrain running through our conversation as we trudge the last mile of the walk across the marshes.

Do you remember the time Thea got caught with vodka in her sports bottle at the away hockey match with Roedean?

Do you remember when Fatima told Miss Rourke that *fukkit* was Urdu for *pen*?

Do you remember when we broke out to go night swimming, and Kate got caught in the riptide and nearly drowned?

Do you remember, do you remember, *do you remember . . . ?*

I thought I remembered everything, but now, as the memories sweep over me like floodwater, I realize that I didn't, not fully. Not like this—not so vividly that I can smell the seawater; see again Kate's shaking limbs, white in the moonlight, as we staggered up the beach with her. I remembered, but I didn't remember the detail, the colors, the feel of the playing field grass beneath my feet and the sea wind against my face.

But it's as we cross the last field and climb the last fence, that Salten House comes into view and it really hits home. We are *back*. We are really and truly back. The realization is unsettling, and I feel my stomach tighten as the others fall silent, knowing that they must be remembering as I am, some of the *other* memories, the ones we have tried to forget. I remember Mark

Wren's face when a group of fifth-years met him on the coast road one day, the tide of red climbing up the back of his neck as the sniggers and whispers started, the way he hung his head and shot a look at Thea that was pure misery. I remember the look of alarm on a first-year's face as she turned away from Fatima and me in the corridor, and I realized that she must have heard rumors about us—about our sharp tongues and capacity for deceit. And I remember the expression on Miss Weatherby's face that final day . . .

I am suddenly glad that Salten House has changed, far more than Salten itself, which gives the air of being set in stone and salt. Unlike the Tide Mill, which has only grown more battered with the years, there is a perceptible air of smartness to the place now that is absent from my memories. Whatever impression it tried to give, Salten House was never a top-tier school in my day. It was, as Kate had said, a "last-chance saloon" in many ways—the kind of place that would have space for a pupil enrolled in a hurry due to trouble at home, and would not ask questions about a girl kicked out of three other schools in a row. I remember noticing, when I arrived that first day so long ago, that the paint-work was peeling and salt-stained, the lawns were yellowing after a hot summer. There were weeds growing up through the gravel of the drive, and in among the Bentleys and Daimlers, many parents drove Fiats and Citroëns and battered Morris Minors.

Now, though, there is an air of . . . money. There's no other way of putting it.

The silhouette of the tall building casting its long shadows across the croquet lawns and tennis pitches is the same, but the stark, cheap white paint has been changed to a deep expensive cream, subtly softening the edges, an effect enhanced by the flowers that have been placed in window boxes, and the creepers that have been planted at the corners of the building and are beginning to twine across the facade.

The lawns are lusher and greener, and as we make our way across them there is an almost inaudible *click* and small spigots rise from the grass and begin spraying a fine mist of water, a luxury unimaginable when we were there. Outbuildings and covered walkways have sprung up so that girls no longer need to scurry from lesson to lesson in the driving rain. And as we pass the all-weather tennis courts, I see they have been updated from their unforgiving knee-skinning tarmac to a kind of rubbery green sponge.

What hasn't changed are the four towers still standing sentinel, one at each corner of the main block, the black skein of the fire escapes still twining up them like postindustrial ivy.

I wonder if the tower windows still open wide enough to admit a slim fifteen-year-old, and whether the girls break out now like they did then . . . Somehow I doubt it.

It is half term, of course, and the place is strangely silent . . . or almost silent. As we walk across the playing fields, cars sweep up the drive, and I hear faint voices coming from the front of the building.

For a minute my ears prick, and I think, *Parents!* with much the same sense of danger as a rabbit might think, *Hawks!* But then I realize—these aren't parents; they're girls. Old girls. *Us*.

Only not us. Because, somehow, it was always us and them, even back then. That's the trouble with having a "click" as Mary Wren might call it. When you define yourself by walls, who's in, who's out. The people on the other side of the wall become, not just them, but *them*. The outsiders. The opposition. The enemy.

It's something that I didn't understand, in those early days at Salten House. I was so grateful to have found friends, so happy to have found my own niche, that I didn't understand that every time I sided with Kate and Thea and Fatima, I was siding *against* the others. And that soon they might side against me.

A wall, after all, isn't just about keeping others out. It can also be for trapping people inside.

"Oh. My. God." The voice floats across the evening air, and we turn, sharply, all four of us as one, towards the sound.

A woman is coming towards us, her heels crunching and teetering on the gravel.

"Thea? Thea West? And—oh my God, you must be Isa Wilde, is that right?"

For a minute I go blank and can't place her name, and then it comes to me. Jess Hamilton. Captain of hockey in the fifth form and widely tipped for head girl in the sixth. *Did she make it?* I wonder. But before I can open my mouth to say hello, she's barreling on.

"Fatima! I nearly didn't recognize you with that scarf! And Kate, too! I can't believe you're here!"

"Well . . ." Thea raises an eyebrow and waves a hand slightly deprecatingly around the group. "Believe it now. Is it that unlikely that we made it this far in life? I know I had a *live fast, die young* poster on the wall of the dorm, but you weren't supposed to take it literally."

"No!" Jess gives a shrill laugh and shoves Thea's shoulder playfully. "You know it's not that. It's just . . ." She falters for a second, and we all know what she's really thinking, but she recovers and continues. "It's just that, well, that you've never shown up to any of these things, any of you, even Kate, and she only lives five minutes down the road. We'd quite given up hope!"

"How nice to know we've been missed," Thea says, with a little twisted smile.

There is a moment's awkward silence, and then Kate begins to walk.

"So, gosh," Jess says. She falls into step with us as we make our way round the corner to the main entrance, and I find myself admiring her determined cheerfulness, her desire to build bridges. "What are you all up to? Kate, I know, of course. No surprise that she's become an artist. What about you, Isa, let me guess—something to do with education?"

"Nope," I say, forcing a smile. "Civil service, actually. Unless you count trying to give ministers a crash course in law. How about you?"

"Oh, I'm *very* lucky. Alex—that's my husband—did awfully well out of the dot-com boom, he got in and out just at the right time. So we're full-time parents to Alexa and Joe."

Thea's eyebrows nearly disappear into her fringe.

"Do you have kids?" Jess asks, and I nearly don't reply, before I realize her question is directed at me, and I nod hastily.

"Oh, yes. One little girl—Freya. She's nearly six months."

"Home with the nanny?"

"Nope." I manage another smile. "We don't have a nanny, in fact. She's at Kate's, with a babysitter."

"And how about you, Fatima?" Jess continues. "I must say, I didn't know you'd become"—she nods at the scarf—"you know. A *Muslim*." She sort of mouths the last word, like someone not wanting to articulate something slightly taboo.

Fatima's smile is even thinner than mine feels, but she doesn't let it slip.

"I was always a Muslim," she says evenly. "I just wasn't very observant at school."

"And so . . . what's . . . you know, what changed your mind?" Jess asks as we round the corner of the building.

Fatima shrugs.

"Kids. Time. Adulthood. Who knows?" I can tell she doesn't want to talk about it, or not to Jess, not now.

"So you're married?" Jess says.

Fatima nods.

"To another doctor. I know, right? What a cliché! Two lovely kids, a boy and a girl. They're at home with Ali. What about yours?"

"Same as you—a girl and a boy—Alexa, she's nearly five—can't believe where the time goes! And Joe, who's two. They're at home with the au pair; Alex and I took a couple of sneaky nights off for a long weekend. Gotta have some couple time, right?"

Fatima and I exchange a fleeting look. I'm not sure what to reply to this—Owen and I have not had any "couple time" since Freya was born—but we're saved by the appearance of a tall blond woman on the path up ahead, who does a mock feint, hand to her heart, and then says, "Not Jess Hamilton? *No!* You *can't* be; you don't look old enough!"

"The very same," Jess says, with a little bow, and then she waves a hand at the four of us. "And you probably remember . . ."

There is a sudden silence as I see the woman registering our faces, recalling names, and her expression changes, the polite society smile falling away. She does remember. She remembers exactly.

"Of course," she says, and there is a kind of cold reserve in her voice that makes my heart sink. Then she turns back to Jess, linking her arm with hers, turning her back on the rest of us. "Jess, darling, you simply *must* meet my husband," she says conspiratorially.

And just like that Jess is swept up, borne away, and it's just the four of us again. Alone. Together.

But not for long. For as we round the corner to the drive, the double doors are open, light streaming out into the evening air and people streaming in.

I feel someone reaching for my hand, and when I look, it's Kate, her fingers twining into mine for support, her grip painfully hard.

"Are you okay?" I whisper, and she gives a single, sharp nod, but I'm not sure if she's trying to convince me, or herself.

"Armor on?" Thea says, nodding at the shoes I am holding in my free hand, and I realize, I'm still wearing my walking sandals, covered with dust. I kick them off, balancing against Kate's shoulders, and slip my feet into the high heels. Fatima is doing the same, supporting herself against Thea's arm. Kate's dress flutters in the wind, like a flag—like a distress signal, I think suddenly, the image popping into my mind uninvited, and I push it away.

We glance at one another, and in one another's eyes we read the same feelings—trepidation, nervous excitement, perhaps even a little fear.

"Ready?" Kate says, and we all nod. And then we walk up the steps into the school that kicked us out so painfully, so many years ago.

Oh God. It's not even an hour into the evening and I'm not sure I can do this anymore.

I am sitting on the toilet, my head in my hands, trying to get a hold of myself. I have been drinking from nerves, letting my glass get topped up by passing waiters, not counting my units. It feels like a dream, one of those where you're back at school, but everything is subtly different, more Technicolor, everything has shifted up a gear. There was a slightly nightmarish quality to the wall of faces and voices that greeted us as we entered the hall, a mix of total strangers, and of half-remembered faces changed by age, the features sharpened as puppy fat fell away, or alternatively thickened and flattened, the skin loosening imperceptibly like a latex mask that has slightly slipped.

And the worst is, *everyone* knows us, even the girls who arrived at the school after we left. I hadn't anticipated that. The way we left, slipping out between one term and the next, our departure unannounced . . . it felt low-key. It was one of the things the headmistress said to my father at the time, "If Isa leaves of her own volition, we can keep this very quiet."

But I had forgotten the echo chamber we left behind, where the space left by our absence must have been filled over and over again by rumor and speculation until an edifice of lies and half-truths had built up, fueled by the meager facts of Ambrose's disappearance. And now—enough old girls live locally to have seen the *Salten Observer*. They have read the headlines. And they're not stupid—they have put two and two together. Sometimes they've made five.

The worst of it is their eyes, which are *avid*. People are pleasant enough to our faces, though their conversation feels a little forced, and I sense, though maybe I'm imagining it, a kind of wariness behind their smiles. But every time we turn away, I hear the whispers behind our back start up. *Is it true? Weren't they expelled? Did you hear . . . ?*

The memories are no longer gentle little *do you remember?* taps on my shoulder; they are slaps, each one an assault. Even away from the crowd they keep coming. I remember sitting, crying in this very stall because a girl, a harmless little first-year, had seen me and Fatima coming back from Kate's one night and I had completely overreacted. I had threatened her, told her that if she told anyone what she'd seen I would ensure she was sent to Coventry for the rest of her days at Salten. I could do that, I told her. I could make her life a misery.

It was a lie, of course. Both parts. I couldn't have isolated her like that even if I'd wanted to. We were too isolated ourselves, by that point. Seats were mysteriously saved in the buttery when we tried to sit in them. If one of us suggested a particular film in the common room for an evening, the vote somehow always went the other way. And besides—I would never really have done it. I only wanted to scare her a little, keep her quiet.

I don't know what she did or said, but Miss Weatherby called me into her office that evening and gave me a long talk about community spirit and my responsibility to the younger girls.

"I'm beginning to wonder," she said, her voice full of disappointment, "whether you truly have it in you to be a Salten girl, Isa. I know that things at home are very hard right now, but that doesn't excuse your snapping at others, particularly those younger than yourself. Please don't make me talk to your father, I am sure he has enough on his plate right now."

My throat had seemed to close up with a combination of shame and fury. Fury at her, at Miss Weatherby, yes. But mostly at myself, for what I'd done, for what I'd allowed myself to become. I thought of Thea, that first night, her account of how the Lying Game had started. *I won't pick on the new girls, the ones who can't defend* themselves, she'd said. *I'll do it to the ones in charge—the teachers, the popular girls. The ones who think they're above it all.*

What had I become, threatening eleven-year-olds?

I thought of what my father would say if Miss Weatherby called him, between trips to the hospital. I thought of how his face, already gray with worry, would tighten more in lines of disappointment.

"I'm sorry," I said, forcing the words out. Not because I didn't want to say them, but because of the constriction in my throat. "I really am. Please—it was a mistake. I'll apologize. And I'll try harder, I promise."

"Do," Miss Weatherby said. There was something worried in her eyes. "And, Isa, I know I've spoken to you about this before, but please do consider mixing more. Tight-knit friendships are all very well and good, but they can close us off from other chances. They can cost us a great deal, in the end."

"ISA." THE KNOCK ON THE cubicle door is low but decisive, and my head comes up. "Isa, are you there?"

"Thea?" I say. My voice is croaky. "Is that you?"

"Yes, it's me. Are you staying in there all night?"

"I'm coming."

I stand, flush, and leave the safety of the toilet cubicle to wash my hands at the row of sinks. Thea is standing by the drier, her arms folded.

"We were worried," she says flatly. I grimace. How long had I been in there? Ten minutes? Twenty?

"I'm sorry, it just . . . it was all too much, you know?"

The water is cool on my hands and wrists, and I suppress an urge to splash it over my face.

"Look, I understand," Thea says. Her face is gaunt, her thinness making her look almost haggard in the unforgiving lights of the school toilets—the guest facilities have been updated, too, and now feature soft towels and scented hand cream, but the lighting is just the same as it was, harsh and fluorescent. "I want to get out, too. But you can't hide all night, they're about to sit down for dinner and you'll be missed. Let's get through the meal and then we can get out."

"Okay," I say. But I can't make myself move. I'm holding on to the basin, feeling my nails against the porcelain. *Shit*. I think about Freya back at Kate's, wonder if she's okay. I am almost overcome by the urge to duck out of here and run back to my soft, warm, home-smelling baby. "Why the hell did Kate think this was a good idea?"

"Look"—Thea glances over her shoulder at the empty cubicles, and lowers her voice—"we discussed this. You were the one who voted to come."

I nod grimly. She's right. And the thing is, I understand Kate's panicked reaction, scrabbling around for a reason to explain all her friends coming down here after so many years' absence, the weekend that a body just *happened* to turn up in the Reach. The reunion must have seemed like a heaven-sent coincidence. But I wish, I *wish* she hadn't done it.

Shit, I think again, and I feel the swearwords bubbling up inside me, a poison I can't contain. I have a sudden vision of myself sitting down at the white-clothed dining table and letting them spew out—*Shut your fucking faces, you rumormongering bitches. You know nothing. Nothing!*

I breathe, slow and quiet, try to steady myself.

"Okay?" Thea says, more gently. I nod.

"I'm okay. I can do this." Then I correct myself. "*We* can do this, right? I mean God knows, if Kate can, I can. Is she holding up?"

"Just," Thea says. She holds open the toilet door and I make my way out into the echoing hallway, empty now except for a few teachers milling about and a large easel at one end, holding the table plans.

"Ooh, be quick!" a teacher says, seeing us emerge. She is young, too young to have been there when we were. "They're sitting down for the speeches. What table are you on?"

"Pankhurst, according to the woman who was here before," Thea says, and the teacher looks at the list, runs her finger down the names. "Thea West," Thea supplements.

"Oh, that's right, you're here. And you are . . . ?" She looks at me. "Sorry, as you can probably tell, I'm a recent arrival, so all you old girls are new faces to me!"

"Isa Wilde," I say quietly, and to my relief her face, as she turns to check the list, registers neither recognition nor shock, just concentration as she scans the tables.

"Oh yes, Pankhurst, too, with a few others from your year by the looks of it. It's a table of ten on the far side of the hallway, by the buttery hatch. Best way round is to slip in this door and edge round underneath the gallery."

I know, I think. I know this place by heart. But Thea and I just nod, and we follow her direction, sliding through the half-opened door under the cover of the sound of clapping. Apparently the speeches are already under way, a woman at the podium smiling and waiting politely for the applause to die down.

I had prepared myself for seeing Miss Armitage, the headmistress in our day, up there, but it's not her on the dais, and I'm not surprised—she must have been in her fifties when I started at the school. She's probably retired by now.

But the reality is, in a way, more shocking.

It's Miss Weatherby, our former housemistress.

"Fuck," Thea whispers under her breath as we make our way around the tables of well-to-do old girls and their husbands, and I can see from her pallor that this is just as much of a shock to her as it is to me.

As we tiptoe around chairs and over handbags, past gilt-lettered plaques listing hockey captains and girls who died in the war, and unflattering oil portraits of former heads, Miss Weatherby's well-bred tones echo around the paneled hall, but the words pass over my head, unheard. All I can hear is her voice that final day, "Isa, this is best for everyone, I'm very sorry your time here at Salten didn't work out, but we all think—your father included—that a fresh start is the best thing."

A fresh start. Another one.

And all of a sudden I became one of *them*, a girl like Thea, with a string of schools behind her that she had been asked to leave, with the threat of expulsion over my head.

I remembered my father's stony face in the car. He asked no questions; I told no lies. But the reproach that hung in the air, as we sped back to a London filled with the smell of hospitals and the beep of monitors, was *How could you? How could you when I have all this to deal with already?*

Fatima's parents were still abroad, but a grim-faced

aunt and uncle came down from London in their Audi and took her away in the middle of the night as I watched from an upstairs window—I never even got to say good-bye.

Thea's father was the worst—loud and brash, laughing as if bravado could make the scandal go away, making suggestive cracks as he slung Thea's case into the back of the car, the smell of brandy on his breath though it was only noon.

Only Kate had no one to take her away. Because Ambrose . . . Ambrose was already gone. "Disappeared before they could sack him," said the whispers in the corridor.

All this is fresh in my mind as we make our way, with whispered apologies, to the table marked PANKHURST, where Fatima and Kate are waiting, their faces full of anxious relief as we slide into our seats, and a final burst of clapping breaks out. Miss Weatherby is finished, and I can't recall a word she said.

I open up my phone and text Liz under the cover of the table. *All okay?*

"Vegetarian or meat, madam?" says a voice behind me, and I jerk round to see a white-coated waiter standing there.

"Sorry?"

"Your meal choice, madam, did you tick the meat option or the vegetarian option?"

"Oh—" I look across at Kate, who is deep in conversation with Fatima, their heads bent over their plate. "Um, meat, I guess?"

The waiter bows and places a plate of something swimming in a thick brown sauce, accompanied by bronzed piped potato shapes and a vegetable that I identify, after some thought, as a roasted artichoke. The effect is fifty shades of beige.

Kate and Fatima both have the vegetarian option, which looks nicer by far—some kind of tartlet with the inevitable goat cheese, by the looks of it.

"Ah," says a man's voice from my right. "This must be a dish in tribute to Picasso's lesser known brown stage."

I look, nervously, to see if he is talking to me, and somewhat to my dismay he is. I manage a smile.

"It is rather that way, isn't it?" I poke at the artichoke with my fork. "What do you think the meat is?"

"I haven't checked, but I would lay you favorable odds that it's chicken—it always is at these things, in my experience. No one objects to chicken."

I slice a piece off the end of the amorphous brown-clad lump and put it cautiously into my mouth, and yes, it is indeed chicken.

"So, what brings you here?" I say, after swallowing. "Clearly you're not an old girl."

It's a thin enough joke, but he has the grace to laugh as if it were not entirely predictable.

"No, indeed. My name's Marc, Marc Hopgood. I'm married to one of your contemporaries, Lucy Etheridge, she was back then."

The name means nothing to me, and for a moment I hesitate, unsure whether to pretend a knowledge that I don't have, but I realize quickly that it will be pointless—one or two questions will reveal my ignorance.

"I'm sorry," I say honestly, "I don't remember her. I wasn't at Salten House for very long."

"No?"

I should stop there, but I can't. I've said too much and too little, both at the same time, and I can't stop myself filling in at least some of the blanks.

"I only came at the start of the fifth, but I left before the sixth form."

He's too polite to ask why, but the question is there in his eyes, unspoken, as he refills my glass, like the nicely brought-up public school boy he almost certainly is.

My phone beeps, and I look down briefly to see *all ok :) :) :)* flash up from Liz, and at the same time a voice from Marc's other side says, "Isa?"

I look up, and Marc edges his chair back a few inches to allow his wife to lean across him, her hand extended.

"Isa Wilde? It is you, isn't it?"

"Yes," I say, thankful that Marc has already mentioned her name. I push the phone hastily into my bag and shake. "Lucy, isn't it?"

"Yes!" Her cheeks are pink and white as a baby's and she looks jolly and delighted to be here, in her husband's company. "Isn't this fun! So many memories . . ."

I nod, but I don't say what I'm thinking—that the memories I have from Salten House are not all fun.

"So," Lucy says after a moment, picking up her knife and fork again. "Tell me *all* about yourself, what have you been up to since you left?"

"Oh . . . you know . . . this and that. I studied history at Oxford, then I went into law, and now I'm at the Civil Service."

"Oh really? So's Marc. What department are you in?"

"Home Office, currently," I say. "But you know what it's like." I shoot Marc a sideways smile. "You tend to rattle around a bit. I've worked across a few departments."

"Don't take this the wrong way," Lucy says, hacking busily at her chicken, "but I always assumed you'd go into something creative. What with your family history."

For a minute I'm puzzled. My mother was a solicitor before she gave up work to have children, and my father has always worked in financial compliance. There is no hint of creativity in either of them. Has she got me mixed up with Kate?

"Family history . . . ?" I say slowly. And then, before Lucy can answer, I remember and I open my mouth, trying to head her off, but it's too late.

"Isa's related to Oscar Wilde," she says proudly to her husband. "Isn't he your great-grandfather or something?"

"Lucy," I manage, my throat tight with shame and my face hot, but Marc is already looking at me quizzically, and I know what he's thinking. Oscar Wilde's children all changed their name after the trial. He had no great-granddaughters—let alone any called Wilde. As I know perfectly well. There is only one thing for it. I have to confess.

"Lucy, I'm so sorry." I put down my fork. "I . . . It was a joke. I'm not related to Oscar Wilde."

I want the ground to swallow me up. Why, *why* were we so vile? Didn't we understand what we were doing, when we pitted ourselves against these nice, credulous, well-brought-up girls?

"I'm sorry," I say again. I can't meet Marc's eyes, and I look past him to Lucy, knowing that my voice is pleading. "It was . . . I don't know why we said those things."

"Oh." Lucy's face has gone pink, and I am not sure if she is cross at her own credulity or at me, for landing her in it. "Of course. I should have realized." She picks up her knife and fork again, pushing at the food on her plate, but she is no longer eating. "How silly of me. Isa and her friends used to have this . . . game," she adds to Marc. "What was it you called it?"

"The Lying Game," I say. My stomach is twisting, and I see Kate shoot a questioning look from across the table. I shake my head very slightly and she turns back to her neighbor.

"I should have known," Lucy says. She is shaking her head, her expression rueful. "You could never believe a word any of them said. What was that one about your father being on the run, Isa, and that was why he never visited? I fell for that one hook, line, and sinker. You must have thought me very stupid."

I try to smile and shake my head, but it feels like a rictus grin, stretched across my cheekbones. And I don't blame her when she turns away from me, quite deliberately, and begins to talk to the guest on her other side.

SOME HOUR AND A HALF later, and the meal is winding to a close. Across the table from me, Kate has been eating grimly and determinedly, as if only by demolishing her meal will she be able to leave. Fatima has picked, and more than once I see her shake her head irritatedly at yet another waiter trying to serve her wine.

Thea has sent away plate after plate untouched, but she's made up for it with drink.

At last, though, it's the final speeches, and I feel a rush of relief as I realize this is it—the final furlong. We drink bad coffee, while we listen to a woman I vaguely remember from two or three years above us, called Mary Hardwick. She, it seems, has written a novel, and this apparently qualifies her to make a long, digressive speech about the narrative of the human life, during which I see Kate rise from her seat. As she passes mine she whispers, "I'm going to the cloakroom to get our bags and shoes before the rush starts."

I nod, and she slips around the edges of the tables, taking the route Thea and I used at the beginning of the evening. She has almost reached the main doors when there is a burst of clapping and I realize the speech is over, everyone is standing up, gathering belongings.

"Good-bye," Marc Hopgood says, as he slings his jacket back on and hands his wife her handbag. "Nice meeting you."

"Nice meeting you, too," I say. "Good-bye, Lucy." But Lucy Hopgood is already walking off, looking away from me determinedly, as if she's seen something very important on the other side of the room.

Marc gives a little shrug and a wave, and then follows. When they are gone I feel in my pocket for my phone, checking for messages, although I didn't feel it buzz.

I'm still staring down at the screen when I feel a tap on my shoulder and I see Jess Hamilton standing behind me, her face flushed with wine and the heat of the room.

"Off so soon?" she asks, and when I nod she says, "Come for a nightcap in the village. We're staying at a B and B on the seafront and I think a few old girls are planning to meet up in the Salten Arms for a quick one before bed."

"No, thanks," I say awkwardly. "It's kind of you, but we're walking back across the marsh to Kate's; the pub would be miles out of our way. And plus, you know, I left Freya there with a sitter, so I don't want to be too late."

I don't say what I am really thinking, which is that I would rather chew off my own foot than spend another minute with these cheerful, laughing women who have such happy memories of their school days and will want to talk and endlessly reminisce about times that are much less happy for Kate, Thea, Fatima, and me.

"Shame," Jess says lightly. "But listen, don't let it be another fifteen years before you come to one of these things, okay? They run a dinner most years, admittedly not as big as this one. But I should think the twentieth will be something pretty special."

"Of course," I say meaninglessly, and I make a move to go, but as I do, she catches my shoulder. When I turn, her eyes are bright, and she is swaying, ever so slightly, and I see that she is very, very drunk. Much drunker than I had realized.

"Oh sod it," she says. "I can't let you go without asking. We've been speculating all night at our table and I *have* to ask this. I hope it's not—Well, I mean, don't take this the wrong way, but when you all left, the four of you—*was* it for the reason everyone said?"

The bottom seems to drop out of my stomach, and I feel hollow, as if the food and drink I have consumed tonight have been nothing but sea mist.

"I don't know," I say, trying to keep my voice light and even. "What reason did everyone give?"

"Oh, you *must* have heard the rumors," Jess says. She lowers her voice, glances behind her, and I realize, she is looking for Kate, making sure she's not in earshot. "That . . . you know . . . Ambrose . . ."

She trails off meaningfully and I swallow against a hard, painful lump that suddenly constricts my throat. I should turn away, pretend to see Fatima or someone calling me, but I can't, I don't want to. I want to make her say it, this vile thing she's circling around, prodding at, poking.

"What about him?" I say, and I even manage a smile. "I haven't a clue what you mean."

That's a lie.

"Oh God," Jess says with a groan, and I don't know whether her sudden compunction is real or feigned—I can't tell anymore; I've spent so long steeped in deceit. "Isa, I didn't . . . You really don't know?"

"Say it," I say, and there's no smile in my voice now. *"Say it."*

"Shit." Jess looks unhappy now, the alcohol wearing

off in the face of my fierce disgust. "Isa, I'm sorry, I didn't mean to stir up—"

"You've been speculating about it all night, apparently. So at least have the guts to say it to our faces. What's the rumor?"

"That Ambrose . . ." Jess gulps, she looks over my shoulder, looking for a way out, but the hall is emptying fast, none of her friends are in sight. "That Ambrose . . . that he . . . he did . . . drawings, of you all. The four of you."

"Oh, but not just drawings, right?" My voice is very cold. "Right, Jess? What sort of drawings, exactly?"

"N-naked drawings," she says, almost whispering now.

"And?"

"And . . . the school found out . . . and that's why Ambrose . . . he . . ."

"He what?"

She is silent, and I grab her wrist, watching her wince as she feels the pressure of my grip on the fine bones.

"*He what?*" I say, loudly this time, and my voice echoes round the almost empty hall so that the heads of the few girls and staff remaining turn to look at us.

"That's why he committed suicide," Jess whispers. "I'm sorry. I shouldn't have brought it up." And she pulls her wrist out of mine, and, hitching her handbag up her shoulder, she half walks, half stumbles across the emptying hall to the exit, leaving me gasping, holding myself as if against an imaginary blow, trying not to cry.

When at last I pull myself together enough to face the thronged hallway, I force my way out into the crowd, looking, desperately, for Fatima, Kate, and Thea.

I scan the hallway, the queue for the cloakroom, the toilets—but they aren't there. Have they left already?

My heart is thumping, and my cheeks are flushed from the encounter with Jess. Where *are* they?

I'm shoving my way to the exit, elbowing aside laughing little knots of old girls and their husbands and partners, when I feel a hand on my arm and turn, relief written all over my face, only to find Miss Weatherby standing there.

My stomach tightens, thinking of our last meeting, the furious disappointment on her face . . .

"Isa," she says. "Always rushing everywhere—I remember that so well. I always said you should have played hockey, put all that nervous energy to good use!"

"I'm sorry," I say, trying to not gasp, trying not to pull away too obviously. "I—I have to get back, the babysitter . . ."

"Oh, you have a baby?" she asks. I know she is only trying to be polite, but I just want to get away. "How old?"

"Nearly six months. A little girl. Listen, I must . . ." I trail off, and Miss Weatherby nods and releases my arm.

"Well, it was lovely to see you here after so many years. And congratulations on your daughter. You must put her name down here!"

She says the words almost lightheartedly, but I feel my features go stiff, even as I smile and nod, and I know from the change in Miss Weatherby's expression that my feelings must be evident, that my smile must be as false as a painted marionette's, for her face crumples.

"Isa, I can't tell you how much I regret all that business surrounding your leaving. There aren't many points of my career that I feel ashamed of, but I can honestly say, that business is one of them. The school handled it—well, there's no point in pretending, we handled it very badly, and I must take my share of responsibility for that. It is not mere lip service to say that things have improved very much in that respect—matters would be treated . . . well, I think everything would be handled very differently these days."

"I—" I swallow, try to speak. "Miss Weatherby, please, don't. It—it's water under the bridge, honestly."

It is not. But I can't bear to talk about this now. Not here, where it all feels so raw still. Where are the others?

Miss Weatherby only nods, once, her face tight as if she is holding back her own memories.

"Well, good-bye," I say awkwardly, and she forces a smile, her stern face seeming almost to crack.

"Come again, Isa," she says as I turn to leave. "I—I did wonder if perhaps you felt you wouldn't be welcome, and quite honestly, nothing would be further from the truth. I hope you won't be a stranger in the future—can I count on your presence at next year's dinner?"

"Of course," I say. My face feels stiff with effort, but I manage a smile as I tuck my hair behind my ear. "Of course, I'll come."

She nods and lets me go, and as I finally make my

escape towards the exit, looking for Kate and the others, I reflect; it's amazing how quickly it comes back, the facility to lie.

IT'S FATIMA I FIND FIRST, standing at the big double doors looking anxiously up and down the drive. She sees me at almost exactly the same time as I see her, and pounces, her fingers like a vise on my arm.

"Where have you *been*? Thea's thoroughly pissed; we need to get her home. Kate's got your shoes, if that's what was holding you up."

"I'm sorry." I hobble across the gravel, my heels turning and grating on the stones. "It wasn't that, I got cornered by Jess Hamilton, and then by Miss Weatherby. I couldn't get away."

"Miss *Weatherby*?" Fatima's face is alarmed. "What did she want to talk to you about?"

"Nothing much," I say. It's half true, after all. "I think she feels . . . well, bad."

"She deserves to," Fatima says stonily, turning away and beginning to walk.

I crunch breathless in her wake as we leave the lighted front of the school. She forges down one of the long gravel paths towards the hockey pitches. In our day it would have been completely dark—now there are dim little solar lights at intervals, but they serve only to drown out the moonlight, making the pools of blackness in between more inky.

When we were fifteen, the marshes felt like home, near enough. I don't recall being frightened on any of the long, dark treks to Kate's house.

Now as I pant to catch up with Fatima, I find myself thinking of rabbit holes in the darkness, of my ankle turning and snapping. A picture comes to me of myself, sinking into one of the bottomless pits of the marsh, water filling my mouth so I can't cry out, the others walking on ahead oblivious, leaving me alone. Except . . . perhaps not alone. There is someone out here after all. Someone who wrote that note, and who dragged a dead and bloodied sheep to Kate's door . . .

Fatima has drawn ahead of me in her eagerness to catch up with the others, her figure just a dim, fluttering silhouette that blends into the dark shapes of the marsh.

"Fatima," I call out, "will you please slow down?"

"Sorry."

She pauses at the stile and waits for me to catch up, and this time she walks more slowly, matching her strides to my more cautious pace as we begin to cross the marsh itself, my narrow heels sinking into the soft ground. We walk in silence, just the sound of our breathing, my occasional stumble as my high heels turn on a stone. Where *are* the others?

"She asked me to send Freya there," I say at last, more as a way to break the eerie quiet of the marsh and get Fatima to slow down than because I think she wants to know—and it works, in fact it stops Fatima in her tracks. She turns to face me with a mixture of horror and incredulity in her expression.

"Miss Weatherby? You are *shitting* me."

"Nope." We start walking again, slower this time. "I did find it quite hard to respond."

"*Over my dead body* is what you should have said."

"I didn't say anything."

There's another silence and then she says, "I'd never let Sami or Nadia board. Would you?"

I think about it. I think about the circumstances at home, what my father went through. And then I think about Freya, about the fact that I can't manage even an evening away from her without feeling that my heart is being put through an industrial shredder.

"I don't know," I say at last. "I can't imagine it, though."

We walk on through the darkness, across a make-shift rotting bridge over a ditch, and at last Fatima says, "Bloody hell, how did they get so far ahead?"

But almost as the words leave her mouth we hear something, see a moving shape in the darkness up ahead. It's not the shape of a person, though, it's a hunched and huddled mass, and a wet, bubbling sound comes through the darkness—a sound of distress.

"What's that?" I whisper to Fatima, and I feel her hand close over mine. We both stop, listening. My heart is beating uncomfortably fast.

"I have no idea," she whispers back. "Is it . . . is it an animal?"

The picture in front of my eyes is as vivid as a flashback—torn guts, bloodied wool, someone crouched, animallike, over the ripped corpse . . .

The sound comes again, a wet splatter followed by what sounds like a sob, and I feel Fatima's fingers digging into my skin.

"Is it . . ." she says, her voice uncertain. "Do you think the others . . . ?"

"Thea?" I call out, into the black. "Kate?"

A voice comes back.

"Over here!"

We hurry forward into the darkness, and as we get closer the hunched shape resolves itself: Thea on her hands and knees over a drainage ditch, Kate holding back her hair.

"Oh bollocks," Fatima says, a mixture of weariness and disgust in her voice. "I knew this would happen. No one can drink two bottles on an empty stomach."

"Shut up," Thea growls over her shoulder, and then

retches again. When she stands up, her makeup is smeared.

"Can you walk?" Kate asks her, and Thea nods.

"I'm fine."

Fatima snorts.

"The one thing you are not, is fine," she says. "And I say that as a doctor."

"Oh shut up," Thea says acidly. "I said I can walk, what more d'you want?"

"I want you to eat a proper meal and get to noon without a drink—at least once."

For a minute I'm not sure if Thea has heard her, or if she's going to reply. She's too busy wiping her mouth and spitting in the grass. But then she says, almost under her breath, "Christ, I miss when you used to be normal."

"*Normal?*" I say, incredulously. Fatima just stands there, speechless—too shocked to find words, or too angry, I'm not sure which.

"I really hope that doesn't mean what I think it means," Kate says.

"I don't know." Thea straightens and begins to walk, more steadily than I would have given her credit for. "What do you think it means? If you think it means that she's using that head scarf as a bandage, then yes, that's what I mean. It's great that Allah's forgiven you," she shoots over her shoulder at Fatima. "But I doubt the police will take that as a plea bargain."

"Will you just fuck *off*?" Fatima says. She is almost incoherent, choking with anger. "What the hell have my choices got to do with you?"

"I could say the same thing to *you*." Thea swings round. "How dare you judge me? I do what I have to do to sleep at night. So do you, apparently. How about you respect my coping mechanisms and I'll respect yours?"

"I *care* about you!" Fatima shouts. "Don't you get that? I don't give a fuck how you cope with your shit. I don't care if you become a Buddhist nun, or take up Transcendental Meditation, or go to work for an orphanage in Romania. All of that is *entirely* your own business. But watching you turn into an alcoholic? No! I will not pretend I'm okay with that just to fit in with some misguided shit about personal choices."

Thea opens her mouth, and I think she is about to reply, but instead she turns to one side and vomits again into the ditch.

"Oh for goodness' sake," Fatima says resignedly, but the shaking anger has gone from her voice, and when Thea straightens, wiping water out of her eyes, she reaches into her bag and pulls out a packet of wet wipes. "Look, take these. Clean yourself up."

"Thanks," Thea mutters. She stands up, shakily, and almost stumbles, and Fatima takes her arm to steady her.

As they make their slow way over the turf, I hear Thea say something to Fatima, almost too low for me and Kate to hear, but I catch Fatima's reply.

"It's okay, Thee, I know you didn't. I just—I care about you, you know that?"

"Sounds like they've made up," I whisper to Kate, and she nods, but her face in the moonlight is troubled.

"This is only the beginning, though," she says, her voice very low. "Isn't it?"

And I realize she's right.

Nearly there," Kate says, as we clamber painfully over yet another stile. The marsh is so strange in the darkness, the route I thought I remembered in daylight retreating into the shadows. I can see lights in the distance that must, I think, be Salten village, but the winding sheep paths and rickety bridges make it hard to plot your course, and I realize, with a shudder, that if it weren't for Kate, we'd be screwed. You could be lost out here for hours, in the darkness, wandering in circles.

Fatima is still holding Thea's arm, guiding her steps as she stumbles with a drunkard's concentration from tussock to ridge, and she's about to say something when I stiffen, put my finger to my lips, shushing her, and we all stop.

"What?" Thea says, her voice slurred and too loud.

"Did you hear that?"

"Hear what?" Kate asks.

It comes again, a cry, from very far away, so like Freya's sobbing wail when she's at almost the peak of her distress that I feel a tightness in my breasts and a spreading warmth inside my bra.

A small part of my mind registers the irritation, and the fact that I forgot to put breast pads in before I left—but below that the much, much larger part of me is frantically trying to make out the sound in the darkness. It *cannot* be Freya, surely?

"That?" Kate says as it comes again. "It's a gull."

"Are you sure?" I say. "It sounds like—"

I stop. I can't say what it sounded like. They will think I'm crazy.

"They sound like children, don't they?" Kate says. "It's quite eerie."

But then the wail comes again, longer, louder, rising to a hysterical bubbling pitch, and I *know* that is not a gull—it can't be.

I set off at a run into the darkness, ignoring Kate's cry of "Isa, *wait!*"

But I can't—I can't wait. Freya's cry is like a hook in my flesh, pulling me inexorably across the darkened marsh. And now I'm not thinking, my feet remember the paths almost automatically. I vault the muddy slough before I've even remembered it was there. I sprint along the raised bank with the mud-filled ditches on either side. And all the time I hear Freya's high, bubbling cry coming from somewhere up ahead—like something out of a fairy tale, the light that lures the children into the marsh, the sound of bells that tricks the unwary traveler.

She is close now—I can hear everything, the siren pitch as she reaches the furious peak of her scream, and then the choking snotty gasps in between as she revs up again for the next wail.

"Freya!" I shout. "Freya, I'm coming!"

"Isa, *wait!*" I hear from behind me, and I hear Kate's footsteps pounding after me.

But I'm almost there. I scramble over the final stile between the marsh and the Reach, hearing the rip of the borrowed dress without caring—and then everything seems to slow down to the pace of a nightmare—my breath roaring in my ears, my pulse pounding in my throat. For there, in front of me, is not Liz, the girl from the village, but a man. He is standing near the water's edge, his silhouette a dark hulk against the moon-silvered waters—and he is holding a baby.

"Hey!" I shout, my voice a roar of primal fury. "Hey, you!"

The man turns, and the moonlight falls upon his face, and my heart seems to stutter in my chest. It's him. It's Luc Rochefort, holding a child—*my child*— like a human shield across him, the deep waters of the Reach shimmering behind him.

"Give her to me," I manage, and the voice that comes out of my mouth is almost alien—a snarling roar of contained fury that makes Luc take an involuntary step back, his fingers tightening on Freya. She has seen me, though, and she reaches out her little chubby arms, her scarlet face sparkling in the moonlight with tears, so furious that she can't even muster a scream now, just a long, continuous series of gasps as she attempts to draw breath for a final, annihilating shriek.

"Give her to me!" I scream, and I bound forwards and snatch her out of Luc's grasp, feeling her cling to me like a little marsupial, her fingers digging into my neck, clutching at my hair. She smells of cigarette smoke and alcohol—bourbon maybe, I'm not sure. It's *him*. It's his smell, all over her skin. "How *dare you* touch my child!"

"Isa," he says. He holds out his hands pleadingly, and I can smell the spirits on his breath. "It wasn't like that—"

"It wasn't like *what*?" I snarl. Freya's small, hot body flails and arches against mine. She won't calm down now until she's had a feed, but there's no way in hell I'm doing that here, in front of Luc.

"What's going on?" I hear from behind me, and Kate comes running up, panting and flushed. Then, incredulously, "*Luc?*"

"He had Freya," I say furiously. "He *took* her."

"I didn't take her!" Luc says. He takes a step forwards, and I fight the urge to turn and run. I will not show this man I'm afraid of him.

"Luc, what the hell were you *thinking*?" Kate says.

"It wasn't like that!" he says, louder, his voice almost a shout. And then again, more levelly, trying to calm himself, and us, "It wasn't like that. I turned up at the Mill to talk to you, to apologize to Isa for being . . ." He stops, takes a breath, turns to me, and his expression is almost pleading. "In the post office. I didn't want you to think— But I turned up and Freya, she was beside herself—she was screaming like this—" He gestures to Freya now, still red-faced and sobbing but calmer now that she can smell me. She is very tired, I can feel her flopping against me between bursts of screeching. "Whatsername— Liz—she was panicking; she said she'd tried to call you but her phone was out of credit, and I said I'd take Freya outside for a walk, try to calm her down a bit."

"You *took* her!" I manage. I am almost incoherent with rage. "How do I know you weren't about to drag her off across the marsh?"

"Why would I do that?" His face is full of angry bewilderment. "I didn't take her anywhere—the Mill's right there." He gestures at the shape behind him, black against the silver shimmers of the Reach. "I was just trying to calm her down. I thought the stars and the night—"

"Jesus Christ, Luc," Kate snaps. "That's not the point, Isa entrusted her baby to Liz—you can't just take matters into your own hands like that."

"Or what?" he says sarcastically. "You'll call the police? I don't think so."

"Luc . . ." Kate's voice is wary.

"God," he spits. "I came to apologize. I was trying to *help*. Just once—just *once*—you'd think I'd learn from my mistakes. But no—you haven't changed, none of you. She whistles, and you come running, all of you, like dogs."

"What's going on?" It's Fatima from behind us, with a staggering Thea on her shoulder. "Is that . . . *Luc*?"

"Yes, it's me," Luc says. He tries for a smile, but his mouth twists, and it comes out halfway between a sneer and the expression someone makes when they're trying not to cry. "Remember me, Fatima?"

"Of course I do," Fatima says in a low voice.

"Thea?"

"Luc, you're drunk," Thea says bluntly. She steadies herself on the stile.

"Takes one to know one," Luc says, taking in her muddied dress and smeared makeup. But Thea only nods, without rancor.

"Yes. Maybe it does. I've been on the edge enough times to know you're pretty fucking close right now. Go home, sober up, and if you've got something to say, say it in the morning."

"*If* I've got something to say?" Luc gives a short, hysterical laugh. His hands, as he runs them through his tangled dark hair, are shaking. "*If?* What a fucking joke! What would you like to talk about, Kate? Maybe we could have a nice chat about Dad?"

"Luc, shut *up*," Kate says urgently. She looks over her shoulder, and I realize, unsettlingly, that it's not impossible that anyone will be out at this time of night. Dog walkers, people from the dinner, night fishermen . . . "Will you *please* be quiet? Look—come back to the Mill, we can talk about this properly."

"What, don't you want the world to know?" Luc says mockingly. He puts his hands to his mouth, making a trumpet, and shouts the words out to the night. "You want to know who's responsible for the body in the Reach? Try right here!"

"He knows?" Fatima gasps. Her face has gone pale as clay. I feel my stomach dropping, and suddenly I feel as sick as Thea looks. Luc *knows*. He has always known. Now suddenly all his anger makes sense.

"*Luc!*" Kate hisses. Her voice is a sort of screaming whisper. She looks beside herself. "Will you please shut up, for *God's* sake? Think about what you're doing! What if someone hears?"

"I don't give a fuck who hears," Luc snarls back.

Kate stands, facing him, her fists clenched, and for a minute I think that she is going to hit him. Then she spits out the words as though they are poison.

"I've had it with your threats. Get away from me and my friends, and don't you dare come back. I never want to see your face again."

I can't see Luc's face in the darkness, only Kate's, hard as stone and full of fear and anger.

He doesn't say anything. For a long time he only stands, facing Kate, and I feel the wordless tension between them—strong as blood but now turned to hate.

At last, though, Luc turns and begins to walk away into the darkness of the marsh, a tall black figure melting into the night.

"You're welcome, Isa," he calls back over his shoulder as he disappears. "In case I didn't say. Looking after your baby—it was nothing. I'd be happy to take her again."

And then the sound of his footsteps fades away into the night. And we are alone.

As we walk the last short stretch back to the Mill, I try not to let Luc's words get inside my head, but I can't help it. Every step is like an echo of that night, seventeen years ago. Sometimes what happened then seems like something done in another place, another time, that has nothing to do with me. But now, stumbling across the marsh, I know that is not true. My feet remember that night, even if I have tried to forget, and my skin crawls with the memory of the hot summer stickiness.

The weather was just the same, the insects still buzzing in the peat, the warm air a strange contrast to the chilly moonlight as we stumbled over stiles and ditches, our phones casting a ghostly glow over our faces as we checked and checked again for another message from Kate, one that would tell us what was going on. But there was nothing—just that first, anguished text: *I need you.*

I had been ready for bed when it came through, brushing my hair in the light of Fatima's reading lamp as she plowed through her trigonometry homework.

The *beep beep!* shattered the quiet of our little room, and Fatima's head came up.

"Was that yours, or mine?"

"I'm not sure," I said. I picked up my phone. "Mine, it's from Kate."

"She's texted me, too," Fatima said, perplexed, and then, as she opened the text, I heard her indrawn breath at the same time as mine.

"What does it mean?" I asked. But we both knew. They were the same words I had texted the day my father phoned and told me that my mother's cancer had metastasized, and that it was now a matter of when, not if.

The same words Thea had texted when she had cut herself too deeply, by accident, and the blood wouldn't stop flowing.

When Fatima's mother's Jeep crashed on a remote country road in a dangerous rural area; when Kate had trodden on a rusty nail, coming back one night from breaking out of bounds . . . each time those three little words, and the others had come, to comfort, to help, to pick up the pieces as best we could. And each time it had been okay, or as okay as it could be—Fatima's mother had turned up, safe and well the next day. Thea had gone to the emergency room, armed with some story or other to cover up what she had done. Kate had limped back, held up between us, and we had bathed the scratch with antiseptic and hoped for the best.

We could solve anything, between us. We felt invincible. Only my mother, dying by slow degrees in a London hospital, remained, like a distant reminder that sometimes, not everything would be okay.

Where are you? I texted back, and as I was waiting for an answer, we both heard the sound of running footsteps on the spiral stairs above, and Thea burst into the room.

"Did you get it?" she panted. I nodded.

"Where is she?" Fatima asked.

"She's at the Mill. Something's happened—I asked what, but she hasn't replied."

I hurried back into my clothes and we climbed out the window and set out, across the marsh.

Kate was waiting for us when we arrived at the Mill,

standing on the little gangway that led across the water, her arms wrapped around herself, and I knew from her face, before she even spoke, that there was something very, very wrong.

She was bone white, her eyes red with crying, and her face was streaked with the drying salt of tears.

Thea began to run as we caught sight of her, Fatima and I jogging after her, and Kate stumbled across the narrow gap of water, her breath hitching in her throat as she tried to say, "It—it—it's Dad."

KATE WAS ALONE WHEN SHE found him. She hadn't invited the rest of us that weekend, making an excuse when Thea suggested coming over, and Luc was out with his friends from Hampton's Lee. When Kate arrived at the Mill, bag in hand, she thought at first Ambrose was out, too, but he was not. He was sitting on the jetty, slumped back in his chair, a wine bottle on his lap and a note in his hand, and at first she couldn't believe that he was really gone. She dragged him back into the Mill, tried mouth-to-mouth, and only after God knows how long, begging and pleading, and trying to get his heart to start again, did she break down and begin to realize the hugeness of what had just happened.

I'm at peace with my decision . . . the note read, and he did look at peace—his expression tranquil, his head flung back for all the world like a man taking an afternoon nap. *I love you . . .*

The letters trailed almost into incoherence at the end.

"But—but, why, and *how*?" Fatima kept asking. Kate didn't answer. She was crouched on the floor, staring at her father's body as if, if she looked at it for long enough, she would begin to understand what happened, while Fatima paced the room behind her and I sat on the sofa, my hand on Kate's back, trying without words to convey everything that I didn't know how to express.

She didn't move—she and Ambrose the still, hunched center of our restless panic, but I had the sense that it was only because she had cried herself into numbness and despair before we arrived.

It was Thea who picked up the object lying on the kitchen table.

"What's this doing here?"

Kate didn't answer, but I looked up, to see Thea holding something that looked like an old biscuit tin, covered with a delicate floral pattern. It was oddly familiar, and after a moment I realized where I'd seen it before—it was usually on the top shelf of the kitchen dresser, tucked away, almost out of sight.

There was a padlock on the lid, but the thin metal clasp had been wrenched open, as if by someone too distraught to bother with a key, and there was no resistance when Thea opened it. Inside was what looked like a jumble of medical equipment wrapped in an old leather strap, and lying on top was a crumpled-up piece of cling film, with traces of powder still clinging to the folds; powder that stuck to Thea's fingers as she touched the plastic wrap.

"Careful!" Fatima yelped. "You don't know what that is—it could be poison. Wash your hands, quick."

But then Kate spoke, from her position on the floor. She didn't turn to face us, but spoke into her hunched knees, almost as if she were talking to her father, stretched out on the rug in front of her.

"It's not poison," she said. "It's heroin."

"Ambrose?" Fatima said incredulously. "He—he was a *heroin* addict?"

I understood her disbelief. Addicts were people lying in alleyways, characters in *Trainspotting*. Not

Ambrose, with his laughter and his red wine and his wild creativity.

But something in her words had struck a chord—a phrase written above his painting desk, in his studio on the top floor, words that I'd seen so often but never tried to understand. *You're never an ex-addict, you're just an addict who hasn't had a fix in a while.*

And they suddenly made sense.

Why hadn't I asked him what they meant? Because I was young? Because I was selfish and self-absorbed, still at an age where only my own problems mattered?

"He was clean," I said huskily. "Right, Kate?"

Kate nodded. She didn't look away from her father as she spoke, her eyes fixed on his gentle, sleeping face, but when I came and sat beside her, she reached for my hand, her voice so low that it was hard to hear her.

"He took it at university, but I think it only got out of control after my mother died. But he got clean when I was still a baby—he's been clean for as long as I can remember."

"Then why . . ." Fatima began uncertainly. She trailed off, but her gaze went to the box on the shelf, and Kate knew what she meant.

"I think . . ." She spoke slowly, like someone trying hard to make themselves understand. "I think it was some kind of test. . . . He tried to explain it to me once. It wasn't enough just to keep it out of the house. He had to wake up every day and make a choice to stay— to stay c-clean for m-me."

Her voice shook, and broke on the last word, and I put my arms around her, turning my face away from the sight of Ambrose lying sprawled peacefully on the rug, his olive skin pale as beeswax.

Why? I wanted to ask. *Why?*

But somehow I couldn't say the words.

"Oh my God," Fatima said. She sank down on the sofa arm, and her face was gray. I knew she was probably thinking, as I was, of the last time we'd seen Ambrose, his long legs stretched out at the table in front of the Mill's long windows, smiling as he sketched us playing in the water. It was only a week ago, and yet there had been nothing wrong. No hint of what was to come. "He's dead," she said slowly, as if she was trying to make herself believe it. "He's really dead."

With those words, the reality of the situation seemed to sink into all of us, and I felt a shiver of cold run from my neck, all the way down my back, prickling at the skin, as if my body was trying to keep me here, now, in the present.

Fatima put her hands to her face and swayed visibly, and for a moment I thought she was about to pass out.

"Why?" she asked again, her voice choked. "Why would he do this?"

I felt Kate flinch beside me, as if Fatima's questions were blows striking home.

"She doesn't know," I said angrily. "None of us do. Stop asking, okay?"

"I think we all need a drink," Thea said abruptly, and she opened the bottle of whiskey Ambrose kept on the kitchen table and poured herself a tumblerful, gulping it down.

"Kate?" Thea asked. Kate hesitated, and then nodded, and Thea poured three more glasses and topped up her own. I wouldn't have chosen to drink—I wanted a cigarette more—but somehow when I raised the glass to my lips, I found myself gulping down the harsh spirits, feeling it burn acidly in my throat, and, somehow, it took the edge off what was happening, blurring the reality of Ambrose lying there on the rug, in front of us—*dead*.

"What are we going to do?" Fatima asked at last

when the glasses were empty. The color had come back into her face a little. She put down the glass, rattling slightly against the table as her hand shook. "Do we phone the police, or the ambulance . . . ?"

"Neither," Kate said, and her voice was hard. There was a shocked silence, and I knew my own face must be showing the same uncomprehending blankness that I saw reflected in the others.

"*What?*" Thea said at last. "What do you mean?"

"I can't tell anyone," Kate said doggedly. She poured another glass and choked it back. "Don't you get it? I've been sitting here since I found him trying to think of a way out of this, but if anyone knows he's dead—" She stopped, and put her hands to her stomach as if she had been stabbed and were trying to stanch a terrible wound, but then she seemed to force herself on. "I can't let anyone find out." Her voice was mechanical, almost as if she had been rehearsing these words, repeating them to herself over and over. "I can't. If they find out he's dead before I'm sixteen, I'll be taken away, taken into care. I *can't* lose my home, not on top of—on top of—"

She broke off, unable to finish, and I had the impression of someone holding themselves together with a great effort, someone who might snap and break down at any moment. But she didn't need to say it; we knew what she meant.

Not on top of losing her only parent, her father.

"It—it's just a house—" Fatima faltered, but Kate shook her head. The truth was it *wasn't* just a house. It was Ambrose, from the paintings in his studio down to the red wine stains on the floorboards. And it was Kate's link to us. If she got sent away to some far-off foster home, she would lose everything. Not just her father, but us, too, and Luc. She would have no one at all.

It seems . . . God, looking back, it seems not just stupid, but *criminal*. What were we thinking? But the answer was . . . we were thinking of Kate.

There was nothing we could do to bring back Ambrose, and even now when I weigh up the alternatives—foster care for Kate, and the Mill seized by the bank . . . even now, it makes a kind of sense. It was so *unfair*. And if we couldn't help him, we could at least help Kate.

"You can't tell anyone he's gone," Kate said again. Her voice was broken. "Please. Swear you won't."

We nodded, one by one, all of us. But Fatima's brow was furrowed with worry.

"So . . . what do we do?" she asked uncertainly. "We can't—we can't just *leave* him here."

"We bury him," Kate said. There was a silence, the shock of her words slowly sinking in. I remember the cold of my hands, in spite of the heat of the night. I remember looking at Kate's white, shuttered face and thinking, *Who* are *you?*

But as she said the words, they seemed somehow to crystalize into the only possible course of action. What alternative did we have?

Now, looking back, I want to shake myself—the drunk, blinkered child that I was, swept along with a plan so stupid that it somehow seemed the only way out. What alternative did we have? Only a hundred different possibilities, all of them better than concealing a death and embarking on a lifetime of deceit and lies.

But none of them seemed like an option on that hot summer night, as Kate spoke those words, and we stood facing one another around Ambrose's body.

"Thea?" Kate asked, and she nodded, uncertainly, and put her hands to her head.

"It—it seems like it's the only way."

"It can't be," Fatima said, but she didn't say it as if she believed it, she said it like someone trying to come to terms with something they know to be true but can't bear to accept. "It *can't* be. There must be another way. Isn't there something we could *do*? Raise some money?"

"It's not just the money, though, is it?" Thea said. She ran her hands through her hair. "Kate's fifteen. They won't let her live alone."

"But this is mad," Fatima said, and there was despair in her voice as she looked around the circle. "Please, Kate, please let me call the police."

"No," Kate said harshly. She turned to face Fatima, and there was a strange mix of pleading desperation and reluctance in her face. "Look, I'm not asking you to help me if you feel you can't, but please, *please* don't tell the police. I'll do it, I swear. I'll report him missing. But not now."

"But he's *dead*!" Fatima sobbed out, and as she said the words something in Kate seemed to snap and she grabbed Fatima by the wrist, almost as if she was about to strike her.

"Do you think I don't know that?" she cried, and the despair in her voice and face—I hope I never witness another human being go through that again. "That's why this is the only—the only—"

For a moment I thought she might be about to lose control completely—and in a way it would have been a relief, to watch her scream and rail against what had happened, and the great hammer blow that had been struck against the security of her existence.

But whatever storm was passing through her, she reined it in with a great effort, and her face, when she let Fatima's wrist drop, was calm.

"Will you help me?" she said.

And one by one, first Fatima, then Thea, and then last of all me, we nodded.

WE WERE RESPECTFUL, OR AS respectful as we could be. We wrapped the body in a groundsheet and carried it as far as we could, to a place where Ambrose had loved to sketch, a little headland a few hundred yards down the Reach, towards the sea, where the views were at their most beautiful, where the track petered out and no cars could drive, and where few people came, except the odd dog walker and the fishermen with their boats and lines.

There, among the reeds, we dug a hole, taking it in turns with the shovel until our arms ached and our backs screamed, and we tipped Ambrose in.

That was the worst part. No dignified lowering— we couldn't. He was too heavy, even with four of us, and the hole was too deep and too narrow. The sound he made as he hit the wet, shaley bottom—it was like a kind of smack. I hear it still, sometimes, in my dreams.

He lay facedown, completely still, and behind me I heard Kate give a kind of retching, choking sob, and she fell to her knees in the sand, burying her face in her hands.

"Cover him up," Thea said, her voice hard. "Give me the shovel."

Slap. The sound of wet sand flung into a shallow grave. *Slap. Slap.*

And over it all, the shushing of the waves on the shore, and Kate's dry terrible sobs behind us, reminding us what we were doing.

At last the hole was full and the tide rose to cover the marks we'd made, smoothing over our muddied, troubled footprints, and the scar we had cut in the bank. And we stumbled back with the torn ground-sheet in our arms, holding Kate between us, to begin the rest of our lives as they would be from now on, in the knowledge of what we had done.

Sometimes, when I wake in the night, the sound of a shovel grating on shale in my dreams, I still cannot believe it. I have spent so long running from the memories, pushing them away, drowning them in drink and routine and everyday life.

How. The word rings in my ears. How did you bring yourself to do it? How did you ever think this was right? How could you think what you did was the solution to Kate's terrible situation?

And most of all, how have you coped, living with this knowledge, living with the memory of that panicked, drunken stupidity?

But back then it was a different word that reverberated in my head all that night as we smoked and drank and cried on Kate's sofa, holding her in our arms as the moon rose and the tide washed away the evidence of what we'd done.

Why.

Why had Ambrose done it?

We found out the next morning.

We had planned to stay the rest of the weekend, to look after Kate, keep her company in her grief, but when the clock that hung between the long windows showed four, she stubbed out her cigarette, and wiped her tears.

"You should go back."

"What?" Fatima looked up from her glass. "Kate, no."

"No, you should go. You've not signed out, and anyway, it's better that you're not . . . that you have . . ."

She stopped. But we knew what she meant, and that she was right, and as dawn began to break over the marshes, we set out, shaking and nauseous with wine and shock, our muscles still aching, but our hearts aching harder at the sight of Kate, huddled white and sleepless in the corner of the sofa as we left.

It was a Saturday, which meant that when we crawled under our blankets, drawing the curtains against the bright morning light, I didn't bother to set my alarm. There was no roll call at Saturday breakfast, no one checked us in and out, and it was quite acceptable to skip it and go straight in for lunch, or make toast in the senior common room, with the toaster that was one of the privileges of being in the fifth.

Today, though, we didn't get a chance to sleep in. The knock came early, quickly followed by the scrape of Miss Weatherby's staff key in our bedroom lock, and Fatima and I were still prone beneath our red felt blankets, blinking and dazed as she strode into the room, pulling back the curtains.

She said nothing, but her shrewd eyes took it all in—the sand-spattered jeans lying on the chair where I'd left them, the sandals clagged with mud from the salt marsh, the red wine stains on our lips, and the unmistakable cherry-ripe scent of alcohol leaching out through the skin of two hungover teenagers . . .

In the bed across from mine, Fatima was struggling upright, raking hair out of her face, blinking in the cruelly bright light. I looked from her to Miss Weatherby, feeling my heart begin to thump in my chest. Something was wrong.

"What's going on?" Fatima asked. Her voice cracked a little on the last syllable, and I could feel her worry rising in pitch with mine. Miss Weatherby shook her head.

"My office, ten minutes," she said shortly. Then she turned on her heel and left Fatima and me staring at each other, terrified but silent as unspoken questions passed between us.

We dressed in record time, though my fingers were shaking with a mix of fear and hangover as I tried to button my top. There was no time for a shower, but both Fatima and I splashed water on our faces and brushed our teeth, me hoping to mask the worst of the cigarettes on my breath, trying not to retch as the brush slipped in my trembling fingers, making me gag.

At last, after what felt like an impossibly long time, we were ready, and we slipped out of our bedroom. My heart was thumping so hard in my chest that for a moment I almost didn't hear—them—footsteps from above. Thea was hurrying down the stairs, her face white, her nails bitten to blood.

"Weatherby?" she asked shortly, and Fatima nodded, her eyes dark pools of fear. "What d'you—" Thea began.

But we were on the landing now, and a passing crowd of first-years looked at us curiously, wondering perhaps what we were doing up so early with our pale faces and trembling hands.

Fatima shook her head, a kind of sickness in her expression, and we hurried on, the clock in the main hallway striking nine just as we reached Miss Weatherby's office door.

We should have got our stories straight, I thought, desperately, but there was no time now. Even though none of us had knocked, it was exactly ten minutes since we'd been summoned, and we could hear noises coming from behind the door—Miss Weatherby gathering up her pens, pushing back her chair . . .

My hands were cold and shaking with adrenaline,

and beside me I could see Fatima looking as if she was about to be sick—or pass out.

Thea had a look of grim determination, like someone going into battle.

"Volunteer nothing," she hissed as the door handle began to turn. "Understand? Yes/no answers. We know nothing about Am—"

And then the door swung open and we were ushered inside.

W ell?"

One word, just that. We sat, ranged opposite Miss Weatherby, and I felt my cheeks burn with something that was not quite shame but close to it. Beside me, to my left, I could see Thea, looking out the window. Her face was pale and bored, for all the world like she'd been called in to discuss name tags and lost hockey sticks, but I could see her fingers moving restlessly beneath the cover of her shirt cuffs, picking, picking relentlessly at the dry skin around her nails.

Fatima, to my right, was making no pretense at coolness. She looked as shocked as I felt, slumped down in her chair as though she could make herself shrink down to nothing. Her hair had fallen across her face as though trying to hide her fear, and she kept her eyes firmly fixed on her lap, refusing to meet Miss Weatherby's gaze.

"Well?" Miss Weatherby said again, something like anger in her tone, and she flicked contemptuously at one of the papers on the desk.

My eyes flickered to the others, waiting for them to speak, but they didn't and I swallowed.

"We've—we've done nothing wrong," I said, but my voice cracked on the last word, because we *had*, it was just not this.

They were pictures—pictures of me, of Thea, of Fatima, of Kate, spread out across the polished wood in a way that made me feel naked and exposed as I never had when Ambrose drew us.

There was Thea, swimming in the Reach, lying on her back, her arms stretched lazily above her head. There was Kate, poised to dive from the jetty, a long slim streak of flesh, pale against the azure splash of watercolor sea. There was Luc, sunbathing naked on the jetty, his eyes closed, a lazy smile on his lips. There were all five of us, skinny-dipping in the moonlight, a tangle of limbs and laughter, all pencil shadows and bright moonlit splashes . . .

My eye went from one to the next, and with each sketch the scenes came back to me, leaping off the paper into my mind's eye as clear and fresh as when we were there—feeling the cool of the water, the heat of the sun on my skin . . .

The last one, the one closest to Miss Weatherby's hand, was me.

I felt my throat close and my cheeks burn.

"*Well?*" Miss Weatherby said again, and her voice shook.

They had been chosen, that much was clear. Out of all the hundreds of drawings Ambrose had done of us curled on the sofa in pajamas, or eating toast in dressing gowns at his table, or stomping in boots and mittens across a frost-flecked field, whoever sent these had picked out the most incriminating examples—the ones where we were naked, or seemed to be.

I looked at the one of myself, bent over, painting my toenails, at the curve of my spine, the ridges drawn with such care that it seemed as if you could reach out and touch them, feel the knots. I had been wearing a halter neck that day, in fact. I remembered it—the heat on my spine, the knot of the top digging into my neck, the acrid smell of the pink polish in my nostrils as I stroked on the lacquer.

But in the drawing I was seated with my back to the

viewer, with the hair on my neck hiding the strings of the top. It had been picked not for what it was but for what it looked like. It had been chosen with care.

Who had done this? Who would want to destroy Ambrose like this, and us along with him?

You don't understand, I wanted to say. I knew what she thought—what anyone would think, seeing those drawings, but she was wrong. So horribly, horribly wrong.

It wasn't like *that*, I wanted to sob.

But we said nothing. We said nothing while Miss Weatherby railed at us about personal responsibility and the conduct of a Salten girl, and asked us again and again and again for a name.

And we said nothing.

She must have known. There was no one who could draw like that, except maybe Kate. But Ambrose rarely signed his rough sketches, and perhaps she thought that if she could just get us to say the words out loud . . .

"Very well, then; where were you last night?" she said at last.

We said nothing.

"You had no permission to leave the school and yet you broke out of bounds. You were seen, you know."

We said nothing. We only sat, ranged together, taking our refuge in muteness. Miss Weatherby folded her arms and as the painful silence stretched, I felt Fatima and Thea exchange a quick glance at my side, and I knew what they were wondering. What did this all mean, and how long could we keep this up?

A knock at the door broke into the hush, making all of us jump, and our heads turned, as the door opened and Miss Rourke came into the room, a box in her hands.

She nodded at Miss Weatherby and then tipped the

contents onto the table in front of us, and it was then that Thea broke her silence, her voice high with fury.

"You searched our rooms! You *bitches*."

"Thea!" Miss Weatherby thundered. But it was too late. All the pathetic contraband—Thea's hip flask, my cigarettes and lighter, and Kate's wrap of weed, the half bottle of whiskey Fatima had kept under her mattress, a packet of condoms, the copy of *Story of O*, and the rest of it—they all lay spilled over the desk, accusing us.

"I have no choice," Miss Weatherby said heavily. "I will be taking this to Miss Armitage. And given a large proportion of this was found in her locker, where is Kate Atagon?"

Silence.

"Where is Kate Atagon?" Miss Weatherby shouted, so that I blinked and felt tears start in my eyes.

"We have no idea," Thea said contemptuously, turning her eyes from the window to rest on Miss Weatherby. "And the fact that you don't, either, says volumes about this school, don't you think?"

There was a long pause.

"Get out," Miss Weatherby said at last, the words hissing between her teeth. "Get out. You will go to your rooms and stay there until I send for you. Lunch will be sent up. You will *not* speak to the other girls, and I will be telephoning your parents."

"But—" Fatima said, her voice quavering.

"That's enough!" Miss Weatherby shouted, and suddenly I could see that she was almost as distraught as we. This had happened on her watch, whatever it was, and it would be her neck on the block as much as ours. "You've had your chance to speak, and since you didn't want to answer my questions, I'm certainly not going to listen to your objections. Go to your rooms, and think about your behavior and what you're planning to say to Miss Armitage, and to your parents when she sends for them, as I have no doubt she will."

She stood at the door, held it wide, and her hand on the door handle trembled ever so slightly as we traipsed out, one after the other, still in silence, and then looked at one another.

What had just happened? How had those drawings got into the hands of the school? And what had we *done*?

We didn't know, but one thing was clear. Whatever it was, our world was about to come crashing down, and it had taken Ambrose with it.

It is late. The curtains, what curtains the Mill possesses, anyway, are drawn. Liz went home hours ago, picked up by her dad, and after she left, Kate bolted the door of the Mill for the first time I could remember, and I told them about the conversation with Jess Hamilton.

"How do they *know*?" Fatima asks desperately. We are huddled together on the sofa, Freya in my arms. Thea is smoking cigarette after cigarette, lighting one from the butt of the other, breathing the smoke out across us all, but I can't bring myself to tell her to stop.

"The usual way, I'd imagine," Thea says shortly. Her feet, curled next to my hip, feel cold as ice.

"But," Fatima persists, "I thought the whole point of us agreeing to leave midterm was so that it wouldn't get out. Wasn't that the point?"

"I don't know," Kate says wearily. "But you know what the school gossip circuit is like—perhaps an old teacher told an old girl . . . or one of the parents found out."

"What happened to the drawings?" Thea asks. Kate shakes her head.

"The ones the school found? I'm pretty sure they were destroyed. I can't imagine Miss Armitage wanted them found any more than we did."

"And the others?" I ask. "The ones Ambrose had here?"

"I burned them." Kate says it with finality, but there's something about her eyes, the way her gaze flickers when she says it—I'm not absolutely certain she's telling the truth.

It was Kate who salvaged the situation—as far as it could be salvaged—back at school. When she turned up on Sunday afternoon, pale but composed, Miss Weatherby was waiting, and Kate was marched straight into the headmistress's study and didn't come out for a long time.

When she emerged, we flocked around her, our questions beating at her like wings, but she only shook her head and nodded towards the tower. *Wait*, her nod said. *Wait until we're alone.*

And then, at last, when we finally *were* alone, she told us, while she packed her trunk for the last time.

She had said that the drawings were hers.

I have no idea, even today, whether Miss Armitage believed her, or whether she decided, in the absence of concrete proof to the contrary, to accept a fiction that would create the least fallout. They *were* Ambrose's sketches, anyone with an eye for art could have told that. Kate's style—her natural style, at any rate—was completely different—loose, fluid, with none of Ambrose's fineness of detail.

But when she wanted, Kate could imitate her father's style to perfection, and perhaps she showed them something that convinced them—made a facsimile of a sketch in the office, maybe. I don't know. I never asked. They believed her, or said they did, and that was enough.

We had to go—there was no question of that. The breaking out of bounds, the alcohol and cigarettes in our room, all of that was explosive enough—grounds for expulsion, certainly. But the pictures, even with Kate's confession, the pictures added a dose of nuclear uncertainty to the whole thing.

At last, the unspoken pact was arrived at. Go silently, without expulsion, was the message, and pretend the whole affair never happened. For all our sakes.

And we did.

We had finished our exams, and it was only a few weeks until the summer vac started, but Miss Armitage wouldn't wait for that. It was all over astonishingly fast—within twenty-four hours, before the end of the weekend, we were gone, all of us, first Kate, packing her belongings into a taxi with white-faced stoicism, then Fatima, pale and tearful in the back of her aunt and uncle's car. Then Thea's father, excruciatingly loud and jovial, and finally mine, sad and drawn beyond all recognition almost.

He said nothing. But his silence, on the long, long drive back to London, was almost the hardest to bear.

We were scattered, like birds—Fatima got her wish, at last, and went out to Pakistan, where her parents were finishing up their placement. Thea was sent to Switzerland, to an establishment halfway between a finishing school and a remand home, a place with high walls and bars on the windows and a policy against "personal technology" of any kind. I was packed off to Scotland, to a boarding school so remote it had once had its own railway station, before Beeching closed it down.

Only Kate stayed in Salten, and now, it seems to me, her home was as much a prison as Thea's finishing school, except that the bars on the windows were of our own making.

We wrote, weekly in my case, but she answered only sporadically, short, weary notes that spoke of an endless struggle to make ends meet, and of her loneliness without us. She sold her father's paintings, and when she ran out she began to forge them. I saw a print in a gallery in London that I know for a fact was not one of Ambrose's.

All I knew of Luc was that he had disappeared—and that Kate lived alone, counting down the weeks until she turned sixteen, fending off the endless questions about where her father had gone, what he had done, and realizing that slowly, slowly his very absence was turning the vague suspicions of wrongdoing into hardened certainty of his guilt.

We wrote, on her sixteenth birthday, each of us, sending our love, and this time at least she wrote back.

I am sixteen, she wrote in her letter to me. *And you know what I thought, when I woke up this morning? It wasn't presents, or cards, because I didn't have any of those. It was that I can finally tell the police he's gone.*

We met up only once more, all of us, and it was at my mother's funeral, a gray spring day in the year I turned eighteen.

I was not expecting them. I hoped—I couldn't deny that. I had e-mailed and told them all what had happened, and the date and time of the funeral, but without any kind of explanation. But when I turned up at the crematorium in the car with my father and brother, they were there, a huddle of black in the rain, by the gate. They lifted their heads as the car made its slow way up the crematorium drive, following the hearse, such sympathy in their eyes that I felt my heart crack a little, and suddenly I found my fingers numbly scrabbling for the door handle, heard the crunch of tires on gravel as the driver stamped hurriedly on the brake, and I stumbled from the car.

"I'm so sorry," I heard the driver saying, "I would have stopped—I had no idea she—"

"Don't worry." My father's voice was weary. "Keep going. She'll make her own way up."

And the engine roared to life again, and the car disappeared up the drive, into the rain.

I can't remember what they said; I only remember the feel of their arms around me, the cool of the rain, dripping down my face, hiding the tears. And the feeling that I was with the only people who could fill the gaping hole that had opened up inside me, that I was home.

It was the last time the four of us would be together for fifteen years.

Does he know?" Thea's voice, croaky with smoke, at last breaks through the silence of the room where we have been sitting and thinking, as the candles burned low in their sockets and the tide outside swelled to its height and then slowly retreated.

Kate's head turns from where she has been staring out at the quiet black waters of the Reach.

"Does who know what?"

"Luc. I mean, he clearly knows something, but how much? Did you tell him what happened that night, what we did?"

Kate gives a sigh and stubs out her cigarette in a saucer. Then she shakes her head.

"No, I didn't tell him. I never told anyone, you know that. What we—what we did—" She stops, unable to finish.

"What we did? Why not say it," Thea says, her voice rising. "We concealed a body."

It's a shock, hearing the words so baldly spoken, and I realize that we have been skirting round the truth of what we did for so long that hearing it aloud is like a kind of reality check.

For that is what we did. We *did* conceal a body, although that's not how the courts would phrase it. *Preventing the lawful and decent burial of a body*, would likely be the offense. I know the wording, and the penalties. I have looked it up enough times under the cover of checking something else, my fingers shaking every time I read and reread the words. Possibly also *disposing of a body with the intent to prevent a coroner's inquest*, although that made me give a little, bitter laugh the first time I came across the phrase in the law journals. God knows, there was no thought in our heads of a coroner's inquest. I'm not sure I even knew what a coroner was.

Was that part of the reason I went into law, this desire to be armed with the knowledge of what I had done, and the penalties for it?

"Does he know?" Thea says again, banging her fist on the table with each word in a way that makes me wince.

"He doesn't know, but he suspects," Kate says heavily. "He's known something was wrong for ages, but with the newspaper reports . . . And on some level he blames me—*us*—for what happened to him in France. Even though it's completely irrational."

Is it? Is it really so irrational? All Luc knows is that his beloved adoptive father disappeared, that a body has surfaced in the Reach, and that we have something to do with it. His anger seems very, very rational to me.

But then I look down at Freya, at the cherubic peacefulness of her expression, and I think again of her red-faced fear and fury as Luc held her out to me. Was that really the act of a rational person, to snatch my child, drag her screaming across the marshes?

Christ, I don't know, I don't *know* anymore. I lost sight a long time ago of what rationality was. Perhaps I lost it that night, in the Mill, with Ambrose's body.

"Will he tell anyone?" I manage. The words stick in my throat. "He threatened . . . he said about calling the police . . . ?"

Kate sighs. Her face in the lamplight looks gaunt and shadowed.

"I don't know," she says. "I don't think so. I think if

he were going to do anything, he would have done it already."

"But the sheep?" I say. "The note? Was that him?"

"I don't know," Kate repeats. Her voice is level, but her tone is brittle, as if she might break beneath the strain one day. "I don't know. I've been getting things like that for—" She swallows. "For a while."

"Are we talking weeks? Months?" Fatima says. Kate's lips tighten, her sensitive mouth betraying her before she answers.

"Months, yes. Even . . . years."

"Jesus Christ." Thea shuts her eyes, passes a hand over her face. "Why didn't you tell us?"

"What would be the point? So you could be as scared as me? You did this for *me*; it's my burden."

"How did you cope, Kate?" Fatima says softly. She picks up Kate's thin, paint-spattered hand, holding it between hers, the jewels on her wedding and engagement rings flashing in the candlelight. "After we left, I mean. You were here, all alone, how did you manage?"

"You know how I managed," Kate says, but I see the muscles of her jaw clench and relax as she swallows. "I sold Dad's paintings, and then when I ran out I painted more under his name. Luc could add forgery to the list of things he thinks I've done, if he really wanted."

"That's not what I meant. I meant how did you not go mad, living alone like this, no one to talk to? Weren't you scared?"

"I wasn't scared . . ." Kate says, her voice very low. "I was never scared, but the rest . . . I don't know. Perhaps I was mad. Perhaps I still am."

"We *were* mad," I say abruptly, and their heads turn. "All of us. What we did—what we did—"

"We had no choice," Thea says. Her face is tight, the skin drawn over her cheekbones.

"Of *course* we had a choice!" I cry. And suddenly the reality of it hits me afresh, and I feel the panic boiling up inside me, the way it does sometimes when I wake in the middle of the night from a dream of wet sand and shovels, or when I come across a headline of someone charged with concealing a death and the shock makes my hands go weak for a moment. "Christ, don't you understand? If this comes out—I'll be struck off. It's an indictable offense; you can't practice law with something like this on your record. So will Fatima—you think people want a doctor who's concealed a death? We are all completely *screwed*. We could go to prison. I could lose"—my throat is closing, choking me, as if someone has their hands around my windpipe—"I could lose F-Fre—"

I can't finish; I can't say it.

I stand up, pace to the window, still holding my baby, as if the strength of my grip could stop the police forcing their way in and snatching her from my arms.

"Isa, calm down," Fatima says. She rises from the sofa to come across to where I'm standing, but her face doesn't comfort me, there is fear in her eyes as she says, "We were minors. That has to make a difference, right? You're the lawyer."

"I don't know." I feel my fingers tightening on Freya. "The age of criminal responsibility is ten. We were well over that."

"What about the statute of limitations, then?"

"It's mainly for civil matters. I don't think it would apply."

"You think? But you don't know?"

"I don't *know*," I say again, desperately. "I work in the civil service, Fatima. There's not much call for this kind of thing." Freya gives a little sleepy wail, and I realize I am hurting her and force myself to loosen my grip.

"Does it matter?" Thea says from across the room. She has been picking at the dead skin around her nails, and they are raw and bleeding, and I watch as she puts one finger in her mouth, sucking the blood. "I mean, if it comes out, we're fucked, right? It doesn't matter about charges. It's the rumors and the publicity that'll screw us. The tabloids would fucking *love* something like this."

"Shit." Fatima puts her hands over her face. Then she looks up at the clock and her face changes. "It's two a.m.? How can it be two? I have to go up."

"Are you going in the morning?" Kate asks. Fatima nods.

"I have to. I have to get back for work."

Work. It seems impossible, and I find myself giving a little, bubbling hysterical laugh. And Owen. I can't even picture his face, somehow. He has no connection to this world, to what we've done. How can I go back and face him? I can't even bring myself to *text* him right now.

"Of course you should go," Kate says. She smiles, or tries to. "It's been lovely having you here, but anyway, regardless of anything else, the dinner's over. It will look more . . . more natural. And yes, we should all get some sleep."

She stands, and as Fatima makes her way up the creaking stairs, Kate begins to blow out the candles, put out the lamps.

I stand in between the windows, watching her gather up glasses, holding Freya.

I can't imagine sleeping, but I will have to, to cope with Freya and the journey back tomorrow.

"Good night," Thea says. She stands, too, and I see her tuck a bottle beneath her arm, quite casually, as if taking a demijohn of wine to bed were the normal thing to do.

"Good night," Kate says. She blows out the last candle, and we are in darkness.

I PUT FREYA, STILL HEAVY with sleep, in the middle of the big double bed—Luc's bed—and then I make my way to the empty bathroom and brush my teeth, wearily, feeling the bitter fur of too much wine coating my tongue.

As I wipe off the mascara and the eyeliner in the mirror, I see the way the fine skin around my eyes stretches beneath the cotton wool pad, its elasticity slowly giving way. Whatever I thought, whatever I felt tonight, walking through the doors of my old school, I am not the girl I once was, and nor are Kate, Fatima, and Thea. We are almost two decades older, all of us, and we have carried the weight of what we did for too long.

When my face is clean and bare, I make my way down the corridor to my room, treading quietly, so as not to wake Freya and the others, who are probably asleep by now. But there is a light showing through the crack in Fatima's bedroom door, and when I pause, I can hear an almost imperceptible murmur of words.

For a moment I think she's talking to Ali on the phone, and I feel a twinge of guilt about Owen, but then I see her rise, roll up a mat on the floor, and with a rush of comprehension, I realize—she was praying.

My gaze suddenly feels like an intrusion, and I begin to walk again, but the movement, or perhaps the sound, catches Fatima's eye and she calls out softly, "Isa, is that you?"

"Yes." I stop, push the door to her room a few inches. "I was just going to bed. I didn't mean . . . I wasn't watching."

"It's fine," Fatima says. She puts the prayer mat carefully on her bed, and there's a kind of peace in her face that was not there before, downstairs. "It's not like I'm doing something I'm ashamed of."

"Do you pray every day?"

"Yes, five times a day, in fact. Well, five times when I'm at home. It's different when you're traveling."

"*Five* times?" I realize suddenly how ignorant I am about her faith, and I feel a wash of shame. "I—I guess I did know that. I mean I know Muslims at work . . ." But I stop, feeling hot prickles at the clumsiness of my words. Fatima is my friend, one of my best and oldest friends, and I am only now realizing how little I know about this central pillar of her life, how much about her I have to relearn.

"I'm late, though," she says regretfully. "I should have prayed the Isha around eleven. I just didn't notice the time."

"Does that matter?" I ask awkwardly.

She shrugs.

"It's not ideal, but we're told that if it's a sincere mistake, Allah forgives."

"Fatima," I say, and then stop. "Never mind."

"No, what?"

I take a breath. I'm not sure if what I'm about to say is very crass, I can't tell anymore. I press my hands to my eyes.

"Nothing," I say. And then, in a rush, "Fatima, do you think—do you think that he forgives us? You, I mean?"

"For what we did, you mean?" Fatima asks, and I nod. She sits on the bed, begins to plait her hair, the rhythm of her fingers comforting in its regularity. "I hope so. The Koran teaches that Allah forgives all sins, if the sinner shows sincere repentance. And God knows, I have plenty to repent, but I've tried to atone for my part in what we did."

"What *did* we do, Fatima?" I ask, and I'm not meaning to be quizzical or rhetorical, I suddenly, honestly don't even know. If you had asked me seventeen years ago, I would have said we did what was necessary to keep a friend safe. If you had asked me ten years ago, I would have said we did something unforgivably stupid that kept me awake at night in fear that a body would surface and I would be asked questions I could not bear to answer.

But now that body *has* surfaced, and the questions ... the questions are waiting for us, little ambushes we can't yet see. And I'm no longer sure.

We committed a crime, I'm sure of that. But did we do something worse, to Luc? Something that twisted him from the boy I remember into this angry man I barely recognize?

Perhaps our real crime was not against Ambrose but against his children.

After we say good night and I walk into Luc's room, to lie in his bed and stare into the darkness over the top of Freya's sleeping head, that is what I keep asking myself. Did *we* do this to Luc?

I close my eyes, and his presence seems to fold around me, as real as the sheets that cling to my hot skin. He is here—just as much as the rest of us, and the thought should make me feel afraid, but it doesn't. Because I can't disentangle the man we met tonight from the boy I knew so many years ago, with his long hands, and golden eyes, and the husky, hesitant laugh that made my heart skip. And that boy is inside Luc somewhere, I saw it in his eyes, beneath the pain and the anger and the drink.

As I lie in bed, my arms around Freya, his words twist and tumble inside my head.

You want to know who's responsible for the body in the Reach?

She whistles, and you come running, like dogs.

But it's the last phrase, the one that comes into my head just as I am falling asleep and sticks there, that makes my arm tighten over her, so that she shifts and squirms in her sleep.

You're welcome, Isa. . . . Looking after your baby—it was nothing. I'd be happy to take her again.

Are you *sure* you don't want a lift?"

Fatima stands by the door, her case in one hand and her sunglasses in the other. I shake my head, swallow the tea I am drinking.

"No, it's fine. I need to change Freya and pack, and I don't want to hold you up."

It's a quarter to seven in the morning. I am curled on the sofa in a patch of morning sun, playing with Freya, pretending to pinch off her nose and then put it back on. She bats at my hands, trying to catch them with her little scratchy-soft nails, her eyes screwed up against the brightness of the morning sun reflecting off the Reach. Now I hold her hands gently, trying to stop her grabbing at my tea as I put it back on the floor.

"You go, honestly."

Thea and Kate are still asleep, but Fatima is itching to get away, back to Ali and the kids; I can see it. At last she nods, reluctantly, pushes the arms of her sunglasses beneath her hijab and feels in her pocket for her car keys.

"How will you get to the station?" she asks.

"Taxi, maybe. I don't know. I'll sort it out with Kate."

"Okay," Fatima says. She weighs the keys in her hand. "Say good-bye to them for me, and listen, please, try to get Kate to come, okay? I talked to her about it yesterday and she didn't—"

"She didn't what?"

The voice comes from the floor above. Shadow gives a glad little whine and heaves himself up from his place in a puddle of sunshine by the window. Fatima and I look up to see Kate coming down the stairs in a sun-bleached cotton robe that was once navy blue but now has only the faintest wash of color in it. She is rubbing her eyes and trying not to yawn.

"Going so soon?"

"I'm afraid so," Fatima says. "I've got to get back—I need to be at the surgery by noon, and Ali can't pick up the kids tonight. But listen, Kate, I was just telling Isa—please, won't you reconsider, come and stay for a few days? We've got the room."

"You know I can't do that," Kate says flatly, but I can tell that her resolve isn't quite as firm as she's making out. She gets out the coffeemaker from underneath the sink, a little tremor in her hands as she fills up the pot at the tap and pours in coffee. "What would I do with Shadow?"

"You could bring him," Fatima says unconvincingly, but Kate is already shaking her head.

"I know how Ali feels about dogs. Anyway, isn't Sam allergic or something?"

"There are dog sitters, aren't there?" Fatima pleads, but without conviction. We both know that Shadow is *a* reason, but not *the* reason. Kate will not leave; it's as simple as that.

There's a silence, broken only by the bubble of the moka on the stovetop, and Kate says nothing.

"It's not safe," Fatima says at last. "Isa—tell her. It's not just the electrics—what about Luc—bloodstained notes and dead sheep, for goodness' sake."

"We don't know it was him," Kate says, her voice very low, but she's not looking at either of us.

"You should be reporting him to the police," Fatima says angrily, but we all know, without Kate having to say it, that's never going to happen.

"I give up," Fatima says at last. "I've said my piece. Kate—my spare room is always open to you, don't forget that." She comes across, kisses us both. "Say goodbye to Thea for me," she says as she bends over me, her cheek warm against mine. Her perfume is heady in my nostrils as she whispers in my ear, "Please, Isa, try to change her mind. Maybe she'll listen to you."

Then she straightens, picks up her bag, and a few minutes later we hear the sound of music and the roar of a car engine, and at last she is bumping away, up the sun-baked track towards Salten, and the silence washes back into the Mill.

"Well," Kate says. She looks at me over the top of her coffee, raises one eyebrow, inviting me to sympathize with her in the face of Fatima's paranoia, but I can't do it. I don't really believe that Luc would hurt Kate, or any of us for that matter, but I don't think that Kate should stay here. Her nerves are stretched too thin, and sometimes I have the impression that she is very close to her breaking point, closer than she realizes, perhaps.

"She's right, Kate," I say. Kate rolls her eyes and takes another sip, but I push her, picking at the issue like Thea picking at the skin around her nails, until it bleeds. "You know that, right? And she's right about the stuff with the sheep, too—that was a pretty sick stunt."

Kate doesn't answer at first, just stares down into her coffee.

"It . . . it *was* Luc, wasn't it?" I say at last.

"I don't know," Kate says heavily. She puts down the cup and pushes her hands through her hair. "I was telling the truth when I said that. Yes, he's angry, but he—he's not the only person around here with a grudge against me."

"What?" This is the first I've heard of this, and I can't hide my shock. "What do you mean?"

"The girls at school aren't the only people who spread rumors, Isa. Dad had a lot of friends. I . . . don't."

"You mean . . . the people in the village?"

"Yes," she says, and Rick's words in the taxi come back to me: *You done well to stick it out here with the gossips.*

"What do they say?" I ask, my throat suddenly dry.

Kate shrugs.

"What do you think? I've heard it all, I can tell you. Pretty ugly stuff, some of it."

"Like what?" I don't want to know, but the question comes out in spite of myself.

"Like what? Well, let me see. The least worst is probably that Dad fell back into his old ways and ran off with a junkie from Paris."

"*That's* the nicest one? Bloody hell—what's the worst?"

It's a rhetorical question, I wasn't expecting Kate to answer, but she gives a bitter little laugh.

"Hard to say . . . but I'd probably go for the version where Dad's sexually abusing me and Luc killed him for it."

"What?" I can't find any more words, and so I just say it again, chokingly. *"What?"*

"Yup," Kate says shortly. She drains the last of her coffee and puts the cup on the draining board. "Plus everything in between. And they wonder why I don't go down to the Salten Arms on a Saturday night, like Dad did. It's amazing what old men will come out and ask, when they've drunk enough."

"You're kidding me, they really asked you if that was true?"

"That one, they didn't ask. They stated. It's well known,

apparently." Her face twists. "Dad was fucking me, and the rest of you, too, sometimes, depending who you ask."

"Jesus, Kate, *no*! Why didn't you *tell* us?"

"Tell you what? That, years on, people round here still use your names as a kind of salacious cautionary tale? That opinion is divided between the idea that I'm a murderer, or that my father is still at large, too ashamed to come back and face what he did to me and my friends? For some reason I didn't fancy mentioning any of that."

"But—but, can't you set them straight? Deny it?"

"Deny what, though? That's the problem." Her face is full of weary despair. "Dad disappeared, and I waited four weeks before reporting that to the police. That part is true, and it's no wonder rumors started. It's the grain of truth that makes them plausible."

"There is *no* truth in those disgusting lies," I say fiercely. "None. None that matters, anyway. Kate, please, *please* come back to London with me. Fatima's right, you can't stay here."

"I have to stay," Kate says. She stands and walks out to the jetty. The tide is low, the muddy banks of the Reach sighing and crackling as they bask in the sun. "Now more than ever. Because if I run now, they'll know I've got something to hide."

On my lap, Freya snatches for the empty cup and crows with delight as I let her catch it, still warm from the dregs of the tea. But I am completely silent as I stare down at her. Because I can't think of an argument against that.

It takes so long to get everything packed and Freya changed, and then fed again, and then changed again, that by the time I'm almost ready to go Thea is awake and stumbling along the corridor from her room on the ground floor, half dressed and rubbing the sleep from her eyes.

"Did I miss Fati?"

"You did," Kate says laconically. She pushes the coffeepot towards Thea. "Help yourself."

"Thanks." Thea drains the dregs of the pot. She is wearing jeans and a skimpy spaghetti-strap top that shows, very clearly, that she's not wearing a bra underneath. It also shows her thinness, and her scars, white and faded, and I find myself looking away.

"I need to get back to London today, too," she says, oblivious to my discomfort as she runs the cup under the tap and plonks it on the draining board. "Can I get a lift to the station with you, Isa?"

"Sure," I say. "But I need to leave soon. Is that okay?"

"Yup, I've hardly got any luggage. I can be packed in ten minutes."

"I'll call a cab," I say. "What's Rick's number, Kate?"

"It's on the dresser." She points to a pile of dog-eared business cards in a dusty butter dish, and I rummage through until I find one that reads, "Rick's Rides," and dial the number.

Rick answers at once, and agrees to meet us at the Mill in twenty minutes, with a borrowed car seat for Freya.

"Twenty minutes," I say to Thea, who is sitting at the table sipping her coffee. "Okay?"

"Yup." She nods. "I'm basically done. I just need to actually shove my stuff in a bag—it won't take a minute."

"I'm going to walk Shadow," Kate says, without warning, and I look up, surprised.

"Now?"

"But you'll miss us going!" Thea says. There is a touch of indignation in her voice. Kate shrugs.

"I was never good with good-byes, you know that." She stands, and so does Thea. I follow suit after a moment's struggle with Freya's weight, and we stand uncertainly around, the motes of sun-dappled dust swirling round us like a kind of small tornado.

"Come here," Kate says at last, and she pulls me into a hug that is so fierce that I lose my breath for a moment and have to pull back to shift Freya to one side, where she won't be crushed.

"Kate, please come," I say, knowing it's hopeless, but she's already shaking her head before I've finished the words.

"No, no, I can't, please stop asking me, Isa."

"I can't bear to go and leave you—"

"So don't," she says laughing, but there's a kind of sadness in her eyes that I can't bear to see. "Don't go. Stay."

"I can't stay," I say. And I smile, even as I feel my heart cracking a little. "You know I can't. I have to get back to Owen."

"Oh God," she says as she hugs me again, pulling Thea in, too, our foreheads pressed together. "God, I've loved having you all here so much. Whatever happens—"

"What?" Thea straightens, her face alarmed. "What kind of talk is that? You sound like you're preparing—"

"I'm not," Kate says. She swipes at her eyes, laughs a little in spite of herself. "I promise. It was just a figure of speech. But I just—I can't believe how long it's been. Doesn't it feel right, when we're all here together? Doesn't it feel like yesterday?"

And it does.

"We'll be back," I say. I touch her cheek, where a tear is gathered in her lashes. "I promise. Right, Thea? We won't leave it so long this time, I swear."

It's a platitude, a phrase I've said a thousand times at a thousand partings, and without always meaning it. This time, I mean it with all my heart, but it's only when I see Thea hesitate that the realization hits home—we may be back here sooner than we want, and under very different circumstances if things go awry, and I feel the smile stiffen on my face.

"Right," Thea says at last.

Before we can say anything else, Shadow gives a series of short barks, and our heads turn to the shore windows to see Rick's taxi bouncing over the stones.

"Oh crap, he's early," Thea says, and she bolts up the corridor to her room, grabbing up belongings as she goes.

"Okay," Kate says. "I'm going to take Shadow and get out of your way while you pack up." She clips on Shadow's lead, opens the shore doorway, and strides out towards the little gangway over the shore. "Be safe, lovelies."

It is only afterwards, when we are in Rick's car, bouncing along the track towards the main road, and Kate and Shadow are just specks against the green of the marsh, that I realize what a sad, strange thing it was for her to say. *Be safe.*

Sad, because it shouldn't be something you have to wish for—it shouldn't be in doubt.

And strange because out of all of us, it should have been us saying that to her.

I look out the window, as the car jolts over the rutted flints, towards the receding shape of her and Shadow, their six feet eating up the miles of marsh, moving fearlessly between the ever-changing ditches and sloughs, and I think, *Be safe, Kate. Please, be safe.*

Rick's taxi has reached the tarmac road, and is indicating left to go to the station, when Thea looks up from her handbag.

"I need to get money out. Is there an ATM at the station?"

Rick turns off the indicator, and I sigh. I left the money I drew out yesterday tucked inside a mug on the dresser, where Kate will find it after I've gone. Payment for the dinner tickets, which she refused to let us refund but which my conscience wouldn't let me ignore. I kept only twenty pounds—just enough to pay Rick, and a bit to spare.

"You know there's not," I say. "Since when was there a bank machine at the station? We'll have to go via the post office. Why do you need money, anyway? I can pay for the cab."

"I just want some cash for the journey," Thea says. "Post office, please, Rick."

Rick indicates right, and I cross my arms, suppressing a sigh.

"We've got plenty of time until the train." Thea closes her bag and shoots a sideways look at me. "No need to be mardy."

"I'm not mardy," I say crossly, but I am, and as Rick begins to turn across the bridge towards Salten, I realize why. I don't want to go back there. Not at all.

"GOING ALREADY?"

The voice comes from behind us, making me jump.

Thea is bent over the cash machine, typing in her PIN, so it falls to me to turn and answer the person behind us in the post office.

It is Mary Wren, come out quite silently from whatever back room she was in when we entered the empty shop.

"Mary!" I put my hand to my chest. "Gosh, you gave me a shock. Yes. We're heading back to London today. We—we only came for the dinner, you know, at the school."

"So you said . . ." she says slowly. She looks me up and down, and for a moment, I have the disquieting impression that she doesn't believe a word of what I've said, that she sees through all of us—through all the lies and deception, and knows exactly what secrets we've been hiding. She was one of Ambrose's closest friends, and it occurs to me to wonder, for the first time, what he told her, all those years ago.

I think of what Kate said, the rumors in the village, and I wonder what part Mary played in all this. I have never been in the Salten Arms when she was not seated by the bar, her loud, deep laugh ringing out across the drinkers. She knows everything that goes on in Salten. She could have quashed those rumors if she wanted to—defended Kate—told the drinkers to wash their mouths out or get out. But she didn't. Not even to protect the daughter of a man she once called a friend.

Why not? Is it because part of her thinks Kate is guilty, too?

"Funny time to come down," Mary Wren says at last. She nods her head towards the stack of weekly papers, still blazoned with the photograph.

"Funny?" I say, my voice cracking a little with nerves. "How do you mean?"

"Awkward time for the dinner to fall, I mean," she says. Her face is unreadable, impassive. "With the rumors and all. Must have been hard for Kate, seeing all those people, wondering . . ."

I swallow. I'm not sure what to say.

"Wondering?"

"Well, it's natural, isn't it? To . . . speculate. And it never made sense to me."

"What didn't make sense?" Thea says. She turns around, shoving the wallet back in her jeans pocket. "What are you trying to say?" Her face is belligerent, and I want to tell her to calm down, this is not the way to handle Mary Wren. She needs deference, a show of respect.

"The notion that Ambrose just . . . disappeared," Mary says. She looks at Thea, at her skintight jeans and her bare breasts just showing through the sheer vest. "Whatever his faults, he loved that girl. He would have walked through hellfire for her. It never made sense that he would just . . . go, like that, leave her to face all this alone."

"Well, we've no proof of anything else," Thea says. She is as tall as Mary, and she stands, her hands on her hips in an unconscious echo of Mary's stance, almost as if they are squaring up. "And in the absence of any proof, I don't think speculation is very healthy, do you?"

Mary's lip curls, and for a minute I can't read her expression. Is it a kind of suppressed anger? Disgust?

"Well," she says at last. "I suppose we won't need to speculate much longer, will we?"

"What do you mean?" I say. My heart is thumping in my chest. I look over my shoulder at the taxi, where Freya is playing peacefully in the borrowed car seat that Rick provided, sucking at her fingers. "What do you mean, not much longer?"

"I probably shouldn't be telling you this, but Mark, he tells me a body's been recovered by the police and, well . . ." She makes a little beckoning motion with her fingers and in spite of myself, I find myself leaning in, her breath hot on my cheek as she whispers, "Let's just say, if it's *proof* you want, I think that body might have a name very soon."

I cannot lose Freya. *I cannot lose Freya.*

These are the words that circle inside my head like a mantra as the train speeds north, back to London.

I cannot lose Freya.

It beats time with the rattle of the wheels on the track.

I cannot *lose Freya.*

Thea sits opposite me, sunglasses on, head lolling against the window, eyes closed. As we round a particularly sharp curve, her head leans away from the glass and then thunks back with an audible sound as the train straightens. She opens her eyes, rubbing the spot on her head.

"Ow. Was I asleep?"

"You were," I say shortly, not trying very hard to disguise the annoyance in my voice. I'm not sure why I'm irritated, except that I am so very tired myself, and somehow I *can't* sleep. We didn't go to bed last night until two or three, and then this morning I was up at six thirty with Freya. I haven't had an unbroken night's sleep in months, and I can't sleep now, because Freya is slumbering in a sling on my chest, and I can't relax in case I slump forward and crush her. But it's not just that—everything feels edgy and heightened, and seeing Thea's face relaxed feels like an insult to my own tense anxiety. How can she snooze so peacefully when everything is balanced on a knife-edge?

"Sorry," she says, pushing her fingers under the sunglasses to rub her eyes. "I didn't sleep last night. Like, at all. I couldn't stop thinking about . . ." She glances over her shoulder at the sparse carriage. "Well, you know."

I feel instantly bad. Somehow, I always misjudge Thea. She's so much harder to read than either Fatima or Kate, she plays her cards close to her chest, but beneath her fuck-you exterior she's just as frightened as the rest of us. More, maybe. Why can't I remember that?

"Oh," I say penitently. "Sorry. I haven't been sleeping properly, either. I keep thinking—"

But I can't say it. I can't voice my fears aloud. What if I get prosecuted? What if I lose my job? *What if they take Freya?*

I don't dare say the words. Just saying them would make the possibility real, and that's too terrifying to even think of.

"Even if they find out—" Thea says. She breaks off, looks over her shoulder again and leans forward, closer to me, her voice barely audible. "Even if they find out that it's *him*, we're still okay, right? He could have fallen into a ditch after he OD'd."

"But so deep?" I whisper back. "How could he have got so deep?"

"Those ditches change all the time. You know that. Especially down by the Reach—that whole section has been eroded right back—the dunes are always shifting and changing. We didn't"—she glances again and changes what she was going to say—"I'm pretty sure *it*, the place, I mean, was a good ten or twenty yards back from the shore, right?"

I think back, trying to remember. Yes . . . I remember the track was farther back then; there were trees and bushes between us and the shore. She's right.

"But that tent, it was right on the shoreline. Everything's moved. They won't be able to find too much out from the exact placement, I'm sure of it."

I don't answer. I feel sick to my stomach.

Because although there's something comforting about her certainty, although I *want* to believe her, I'm not so sure she's right. It's a long time since I've done criminal work, and I know more from watching *Cold Case* than I can remember from the cases we studied at uni, but I'm pretty sure they have forensic specialists who can tell exactly how an object might have moved and shifted through the sands over the years.

"Let's not talk about it here," I mutter, and Thea nods and forces a smile. "Tell me about work," I say at last. She shrugs.

"What's to tell? It's good, I guess."

"You're back in London?"

She nods.

"I had a pretty fun stint last year on one of the big cruise ships. And Monte Carlo was excellent. But I wanted . . ." She stops, looks out of the window. "I don't know, Isa. I've been wandering around for so long; Salten was probably the longest I ever stayed at a school. I felt it was probably time to put down some roots."

I shake my head, think of my own plodding progression through school, uni, bar exams, the civil service, and life in London with Owen. We are the exact opposite, she and I. I am limpet-like in my tenacity. I found my job, and I stuck to it. I found Owen, and I stuck to him, too. Salten House, for me, was this dizzyingly brief interlude. And yet both of us are equally defined by what happened there. We're just coping with it in very different ways. Thea, restlessly running from the shadow of the past. Me, clinging on to the things that anchor me to safety.

I look at her thinness, at the shadows beneath her cheekbones, and then down at myself, Freya clamped to my body like a human shield, and for the first time I wonder—am I really dealing with this any better than her, or have I simply worked harder to forget?

I am still wondering, when there is a croaking cry at my breast, and a wriggling inside the sling, and I realize that Freya is waking up.

"Shhh . . ." Her cries are getting louder and more cranky as I pull her out of the swaths of material, her fat little cheeks flushed and annoyed as she gears up for a full-on tantrum. "Shhh . . ."

I pull open my top and put her to my breast, and for a minute there is silence, beautiful silence. Then, without warning, we go into a tunnel, and the train plunges into blackness. Freya tips her head back in wonder, her eyes dark and wide at the sudden change, exposing a wet flash of nipple to the carriage before I can grab for a muslin.

"Sorry," I say to Thea, as we pass, blinking, into the sunshine and I push Freya's head back into place. "I think at this point half of North London has seen my tits, but you've had more than your fair share this week."

"It doesn't bother me," Thea says, with a shrug. "God knows, I've seen it all before."

I can't help but laugh as I lean back, Freya warm and heavy in my arms, and as the train enters another tunnel and emerges into the searing sunshine I think back, back to that first time we met, to Thea, rolling her stockings up her long, slim legs, the flash of thighs and me blushing. It seems like a lifetime ago. And yet, as Thea stretches out her legs across the gap between the seats, gives me a lazy wink, and closes her eyes, it could be yesterday.

RULE FOUR

NEVER LIE TO EACH OTHER

sa?"

Owen's call as he opens the front door is low, cautious, but I don't reply at first. I'm putting Freya down in her crib in our room, and I don't want to wake her. It's right at the tricky stage where she might sleep . . . or she might go for another hour of crankiness and fussing. She has been hard to get down tonight, unsettled by yet another change of scenery.

"Isa?" he says again, appearing at the door of our bedroom, and when he sees me his face breaks into a huge grin, and he pulls off his shoes and tiptoes across the boards even as I frantically put my finger to my lips, signaling quiet.

He comes to stand beside me, his arm around my waist, and together we look down at this creature we've made.

"Hello, sweetie," he whispers, but not to me, to Freya. "Hello, honeybunch. I've missed you."

"We missed you, too," I whisper back, and he kisses my cheek and draws me out into the hallway, part-shutting the door behind us.

"I wasn't expecting you for ages," he says as we go downstairs to where baked potatoes are cooking in the oven. "You made it sound like you'd be gone for days. It's only Wednesday—what happened? Did things not work out with Kate?"

"Things were fine," I say. I turn my back, ostensibly taking the potatoes out of the oven, but really so I don't have to see his face as I lie to him. "It was lovely, actually. Fatima and Thea were there, too."

"Then why are you back so soon? You didn't have to hurry back for me—you know that. I mean, don't get me wrong, I missed you. But I didn't get around to half the stuff I meant to do. The nursery's still a wreck."

"That doesn't matter," I say, straightening up. My cheeks are flushed with the heat from the oven. Baked potatoes was a silly choice for such a hot day, but it was all we had in the fridge. I put them on a board on the countertop and slice the sides open, watching the steam billow out. "You know that."

"It matters to me." He puts his arms around me, his day-old beard rough against my cheek, his lips questing for my ear, the side of my neck. "I want you back, all to myself."

I let him kiss me, but I don't say what I'm thinking, which is that if that's what he wants, he will never be happy. Because I will never be his alone. I will always be nine-tenths Freya's, and what little there is left over, I need for myself, and for Fatima, Thea, and Kate.

"I missed you," I say instead. "Freya missed you, too."

"I missed you both," he says, his voice muffled in my collarbone. "I wanted to call, but I thought you'd be having such a good time . . ."

I feel a twinge of guilt as he says the words, as I realize that I barely thought about calling him. I texted, to say we'd arrived safely. That was it. Thank God he didn't ring—I try to imagine his phone going—when? During that long, painful dinner? During the fight with Luc? On that first night as we all gathered, full of fear about what we were about to hear?

It's impossible.

"I'm sorry I didn't phone, too," I say at last, disengaging myself and turning off the oven. "I meant to—it's just, you know what it's like with Freya. She's so whiny in the evenings, especially in a strange place."

"So . . . what was the occasion?" Owen asks. He begins to get salad out of the drawer, sniffing the limp lettuce and picking off the floppy outer leaves. "I mean, it's a funny time to get together—midweek, I mean. I can see it doesn't make any difference to you and Kate. But doesn't Fatima work?"

"Yes. There was a dinner—an alumnae dinner at Salten House. They held it on a Tuesday, I don't know why. I suppose because the school's empty then."

"You didn't tell me about that." He starts to chop tomatoes, slice by slice, the pale juice bleeding across the plates. I shrug.

"I didn't know. Kate bought the tickets. It was a surprise."

"Well . . . I've got to say, I'm surprised, too," Owen says at length.

"Why?"

"You always said you'd never go back. To that school, I mean. Why now?"

Why now. Why now. Fuck. *Why now?*

It's a perfectly reasonable question. And I can't think of an answer.

"I don't know," I say at last, testily. I push his plate towards him. "Okay? I don't know. It was Kate's idea and I went along with it. Can we stop with the third degree? I'm tired, and I didn't sleep very well last night."

"Hey." Owen's eyes open wide; he holds up his hands. He's trying not to show it, but there is hurt in his face, and I want to bite my own tongue. "Sure, blimey, sorry. I was just trying to make conversation."

And he picks up his plate and goes out into the living room without another word.

I feel something twist inside me, a pain in my gut

like a real, physical pain. And for a second I want to run after him and blurt it all out, what has happened, what we did, the weight that is hanging around my neck, threatening to drag me down . . .

But I can't. Because it's not only my secret—it's theirs, too. And I have no right to betray them.

I swallow it down, the confession that is rising inside me. I swallow it down, and I follow Owen into the living room to eat our supper side by side, in silence.

WHAT I LEARN, IN THE days that follow, is that time can grind down anything into a kind of new normality. It's a lesson I should have remembered from last time, as I struggled to come to terms with what had happened, with what we'd done.

Back then, I was too busy to feel constantly afraid— and the whole business began to feel like a kind of vague nightmare, something that had happened to someone else, in another time. My mind was taken up by other things—by the effort of establishing myself at a new school, and by my mother, who was getting progressively sicker. I did not have time to check the papers, and the idea of combing the Internet for information never occurred to me back then.

Now, though, I have time on my hands. When Owen leaves for work, the door closing behind him, I am free to obsess. I don't dare search Google for the terms I want—"Body" "Salten Reach" "Identified"— even a private window on a browser doesn't mask your Internet searches completely, I know that.

Instead, I search around the edges, terms carefully designed to be explicable, non-incriminating. "News Salten Reach." "Kate Atagon Salten." Headlines I hope will bring up what I want, but without a digital trail of bloodstained fingerprints.

Even then I wait until Owen is out of the house, use a private window, erase my history. Once, I consider going to the Internet café at the bottom of our road, but I can't bring myself to do it. Freya and I would stick out in there like a sore thumb, among the earnest young foreign students. No. No matter what, I must not draw attention to myself.

The news is released about a week after I return, and in the event, I don't need to search for it. It's there on the *Salten Observer* website as soon as I log on. It makes the *Guardian* and the BBC News, too, albeit a small paragraph under "Local Interest."

> The body of local artist Ambrose Atagon, cel-
> ebrated for his studies of coastal landscapes
> and wildlife, has been discovered, more than
> fifteen years after his unexplained disappear-
> ance, on the banks of Salten Reach, a beauty
> spot close to his home on the south coast. His
> daughter, Kate Atagon, did not return calls,
> but family friend and local resident Mary
> Wren said that closure would be welcome
> after so many years of looking for answers.

It's a shock—as I stand there, reading the paragraph again and again, I feel my skin prickle with it, and I have to steady myself against the table. It has happened. The thing I've spent so long fearing. It's finally happened. And yet, it's not as bad as it could have been. There's nothing about it being treated as a suspicious death, no mention of coroners or inquests. And as the days wear on, and my phone doesn't ring, and there are no knocks at the door, I tell myself I can relax . . . just a little.

And yet, I am still tense and jumpy, too distracted to

read or concentrate on TV in the evenings with Owen. When he asks me a question over dinner, my head jerks up, torn from my own thoughts and unsure what he said. I find myself apologizing more and more.

God, how I wish I could smoke. My fingers itch for a cigarette.

Only once do I crack and have one, and I hate myself afterwards. I buy a packet in a rush of shame as we pass the shop at the corner of the road, telling myself that I am going in for milk, and then—almost as a pretend afterthought—asking for ten Marlboro Lights as I go up to pay, my voice high and falsely casual. I smoke one in the back garden, and then I flush the butt and shower, scrubbing my skin until it is pink and raw, ignoring Freya's increasingly cross screeches from the bouncy chair just inside the bathroom door.

There is no way I am feeding my child stinking of smoke.

When Owen comes home, I feel riven with guilt, jumpy and on edge, and at last, when I drop a wine-glass and burst into tears, he says, "Isa, what's the matter? You've been weird ever since you came back from Salten. Is something going on?"

At first I can only shake my head, hiccuping, but then at last I say, "I'm sorry—I'm so sorry. I—I had a cigarette."

"*What?*" It's not what he was expecting, I can tell that from his expression. "Blimey . . . how, when did that happen?"

"I'm sorry." I'm calmer now, but still gulping. "I—I had a few drags at Kate's and then today, I don't know, I just couldn't resist."

"I see." He takes me in his arms, rests his chin on my head. I can feel him thinking of what to say. "Well . . . I can't say I'm thrilled. You know how I feel about it."

"You couldn't be more pissed off at me than I am at myself. I felt disgusting—I couldn't hold Freya until I'd had a shower."

"What did you do with the rest of the packet?"

"I threw them away," I say after a pause. But the pause is because this is a lie. I didn't throw them away. I have no idea why not. I meant to—but somehow I shoved them into the corner of my handbag instead, before I went for my shower. I'm *not* having another one, so it doesn't matter, does it? It all comes to the same thing. I *will* throw them away, and then what I've said will be true. But for now—for now, as I stand there, stiff and ashamed in Owen's arms . . . for now it's a lie.

"I love you," he says to the top of my head. "You know that's why I don't want you smoking, right?"

"I know," I say, my throat croaky with tears. And then Freya cries out, and I pull away from him to pick her up.

He is puzzled, though. He knows something is wrong . . . he just doesn't know what.

GRADUALLY THE DAYS FORM A kind of semblance of normality, though small touches remind me that it's not, or at least if it is, it's a new normal, not the old one. For one thing, my jaw hurts, and when I mention it in passing, Owen tells me that he heard me last night grinding my teeth in my sleep.

Another is the nightmares. It's not just the sound of the shovel on wet sand anymore, the scrape of a groundsheet across a beach track. Now it's people, officials, snatching Freya from my arms, my mouth frozen in a soundless scream of fear as she is taken away.

I have coffee with my antenatal group as usual. I walk to the library as usual. But Freya can feel my tension and fear. She wakes in the night, crying, so that

I stumble from my bed to her crib to snatch her up before she can wake Owen. In the daytime she is fretful and needy, putting her arms up to be carried all the time, until my back hurts with the weight of her.

"Maybe she's teething," Owen says, but I know it's not that, or not just that. It's me. It's the fear and adrenaline pumping through my body, into my milk, through my skin, communicating themselves to her.

I feel constantly on edge, the muscles in my neck like steel cords, perpetually braced for something, some bolt from the blue to destroy the fragile status quo. But when it comes, it's not in the form that I was expecting.

IT IS OWEN WHO ANSWERS the door. It is Saturday, and I am still in bed, Freya beside me, sprawled out froglegged on the duvet, her wet red mouth wide, her thin violet lids closed over eyes that dart with her dreams.

When I wake, there's a cup of tea beside my bed, and something else. A vase of flowers. Roses.

The sight jolts me awake, and I lie there, trying to think what I could have forgotten. It's not our anniversary—that's in January. My birthday's not until July. Crap. What is it?

At last I give up. I will have to admit ignorance and ask.

"Owen?" I call softly, and he comes in, picks up the stirring Freya, and puts her to his shoulder, patting her back as she stretches and yawns, with catlike delicacy.

"Hello, sleepyhead. Did you see your tea?"

"I did. Thanks. But what's with the flowers? Are we celebrating something?"

"I was going to ask you the same thing."

"You mean they're not from you?" I take a sip of the tea and frown. It's lukewarm, but it's wet, and that's the main thing.

"Nope. Take a look at the card."

It's tucked beneath the vase, a little anonymous florist's card in an unsealed, unmarked white envelope. I pull it out and open it.

Isa, it says, in handwriting I don't recognize, probably the florist's. *Please accept these as an apology for my behavior. Yours always, Luc.*

Oh God.

"So, um . . . who's Luc?" Owen picks up his own cup of tea and takes a sip, eyeing me over the top of the cup. "Should I be worried?"

He makes the comment sound like a joke, but it's not, or not completely. He's not the jealous type, but there is something curious, a little speculative, in his gaze, and I can't blame him. If he got red roses from a strange woman, I would probably be wondering, too.

"You read the card?" I ask, and then realize, instantly, as his expression closes that that was the wrong thing to say. "I mean, I didn't mean—"

"There was no name on the envelope." His voice is flat, offended. "I read it to see who they were for. I wasn't spying on you, if that's what you meant."

"No," I say hurriedly, "of course that's not what I meant. I was just—" I stop, take a breath. This is all going wrong. I should never have started down this track. I try—too late—to turn back. "Luc is Kate's brother."

"Her brother?" Owen raises an eyebrow. "I thought she was an only child?"

"Stepbrother." I twist the card between my fingers. How did he get my address? Owen must be wondering what he's apologizing for, but what can I say? I can't tell him what Luc really did. "He—there was a misunderstanding while I was at Kate's. It was silly, really."

"Blimey," Owen says lightly. "If I sent roses every time there was a misunderstanding I'd be broke."

"It was about Freya," I say reluctantly. I have to somehow tell him this but without making Luc sound like a psycho. If I say—bluntly—that Luc took my child, *our* child, away from the person looking after her without permission, Owen will probably want me to call the police, and that's the one thing I can't do. I have to tell the truth, but not the whole truth. "I—oh, it's complicated, but we went out one night and I got a babysitter, but she was a bit young and she couldn't handle things when Freya kicked off. It was stupid—I shouldn't have left Freya with a stranger, but Kate said the girl was experienced . . . Anyway, Luc happened to be there, so he offered to take Freya out for a walk to calm her down. But I was cross he hadn't asked me before he took her out of the house."

Both of Owen's eyebrows are up now.

"The guy helped you out and you chewed him out, and now he's sending roses? Bit over the top, no?"

Oh God. I am making this worse.

"Look, it was a bit more complicated at the time," I say, a trace of defensiveness coming into my tone. "It's a long story. Can we talk about it after I've had a shower?"

"Sure." Owen holds up his hands. "Don't mind me."

But as I grab a towel from the radiator and swathe my dressing gown around me, I catch him looking at the vase of roses on the bedside table, and his expression is the look of a man putting two and two together . . . and not really liking the answer.

LATER THAT DAY, WHEN OWEN has taken Freya out to Sainsbury's to buy bread and milk, I take the flowers out of the vase and I shove them deep into the outside bin, not caring how the thorns prick and rip my skin.

On top of them I shove the week's rubbish in a plastic

sack, pressing it down as though the accumulated garbage can cancel out the presence of the flowers, and then I slam the lid down and go back inside.

My hands, as I rinse them under the tap, washing away the blood from the thorns, are shaking, and I itch to call up Kate or Fatima or Thea and tell them what Luc has done, unpack his motives. Was he really trying to apologize? Or was it something else, more subtle, more damaging?

I even go as far as picking up the phone and bringing up Kate's number—but I don't call. She has enough to worry about—they all do—without me adding to their fears over what could be nothing but a simple apology.

One thing that bothers me is how he got my address. Kate? The school? But I am in the phone book, I realize with a sinking sensation. Isa Wilde. There are probably not that many of us in North London. It wouldn't be that hard to track me down.

I pace the flat, thinking, thinking, and in the end I realize I have to distract myself from my thoughts or I will go mad. I go up to the bedroom and empty out Freya's clothes drawer, sorting out the too-small onesies and rompers from a few months ago. The task is absorbing, and as the piles grow I find I'm humming something between my teeth, a silly pop song that was on the radio at Kate's, and my heart rate has slowed, and my hands are steady again.

I will iron the outgrown clothes and put them in the loft in plastic boxes for when—if—Freya has a baby brother or sister.

But it's only when I come to pick up the pile and take it downstairs to where I keep the iron that I notice. They are stained, with minute pricks of blood from the roses.

I could wash them, of course. But I'm not sure if the bloodstains would come out of the fragile, snowy fabric, and anyway, I realize as I gaze at the spreading crimson spots, turning to rust, I can't bring myself to do it. The things, the perfect, innocent little things, are ruined and soiled, and I will never feel the same way about them again.

I lie in bed that night, listening to Freya snuffling in her crib and Owen snoring lightly beside me, and I can't sleep.

I'm tired. I'm always tired these days. I haven't had an unbroken night's sleep since Freya was born, but it's more than that—I can't seem to turn off anymore. I remember the mantra of visitors when she was a newborn—*sleep when the baby sleeps!* And I wanted to laugh. I wanted to say, *Don't you get it?* I can't ever sleep again, not completely. Not into that complete, solid unconsciousness I used to have before she came along, the state Owen seems to slip back into so easily.

Because now I have *her*. Freya. And she is mine and my responsibility. Anything could happen—she could choke in her sleep, the house could burn down, a fox could slink into the open bathroom window and maul her. And so I sleep with one ear cocked, ready to leap up, heart pounding, at the least sign that something is wrong.

And now, everything is wrong. And so I can't sleep.

I keep thinking about Luc, about the tall angry man in the post office, and the boy I used to know so many years ago. And I am trying to join them up.

He was *so* beautiful, that's what I keep remembering. Luc, lying out on the jetty in the starlight, his fingers trailing in the salt water and his eyes closed. And I remember lying beside him, looking at his profile in the moonlight and feeling my stomach twist with the sickness of desire.

He was my first . . . well, crush, I suppose, although that word doesn't do justice to the way the feeling hit me. I had met boys before, friends of Will's, brothers of my school friends. But I had never lain in the darkness within touching distance of a boy beautiful enough to break your heart.

I remember lying there and putting out my hand towards his shoulder—my fingertips so close that I could feel the heat from his bare, tanned skin, silver in the starlight.

Now, as I lie in bed beside my baby and the father of my child, I wonder. I imagine putting out my hand and Luc turning in the quiet moonlight and opening those extraordinary eyes. I imagine him putting out a hand to my cheek, and I imagine kissing him, as I did once, all those years ago. But this time he would not flinch away—he would kiss me back. And I feel it again, welling up inside me, the kind of desire you could drown yourself in.

I shut my eyes, pushing down the thought, feeling the heat in my cheeks. How can I be lying in bed beside my partner, fantasizing about a boy I knew nearly two decades ago? I am not a girl anymore. I am an adult, a grown-up woman with a child.

And Luc . . . Luc is not that boy anymore. He is a man, and an angry one. And I am one of the people he is angry with.

Before the Salten reunion I went months, years even, without speaking to the others. But now the urge to talk to them is like a constant itch on my skin, a craving beneath the surface like the cigarettes I suddenly want again.

Every morning I wake up and I think of the packet that is still shoved down in the bottom of my handbag, and I think, too, of my mobile phone with their numbers stored in it. Would it hurt so much, to meet up?

It feels like tempting fate, but as the days tick past, and the urge grows stronger, I start to justify the idea to myself. It's not just Luc's unwelcome gift of flowers—although talking that through with them would be a relief, it's true. But I feel the need to make sure they are okay, bearing up under the pressure. As long as we stick to our story—that we know nothing, that we saw nothing—there is precious little evidence against us. And if we all stick to that account, they will have a hard time proving otherwise. But I am worried. Worried about Thea in particular, about her drinking. If one of us cracks, we all break. And now that Ambrose's body has been discovered, it is surely just a matter of time before we get a call.

It plays on my mind, the idea of that call. Every time the phone goes I jump and look at the caller display before answering. The one time it was a withheld number, I let it go to answerphone, but there was no message. Probably just a cold caller, I told myself, dread churning in my stomach as I waited to see if they would ring back.

They didn't. But I still can't stop myself playing and replaying the call in my head. I imagine the police asking about the timings, picking apart our accounts. And there is one thing that I keep coming back to, imagining their questions gnawing at the issue like a rat at a knot, and I don't have an answer.

Ambrose committed suicide because he was being sacked for gross misconduct. Because they'd found the drawings in his sketchbook or in his studio or something of that kind. That's what we have always thought, all of us.

But the question I keep coming back to is this—if that's the case, why were we only called into the meeting with Miss Weatherby on Saturday?

It's a timeline I have spelled out again and again in the middle of the night, as Owen snores beside me, and I cannot make sense of it. Ambrose died on the Friday night, and that day at school was completely normal— we went about our lessons as usual, I even saw Miss Weatherby at evening prep, and she was completely calm.

When did they find the drawings, and where? There is an answer stirring in the back of my mind, and it's not one that I want to face up to alone.

AT LAST, ABOUT FIVE OR six days after the piece in the *Guardian*, I crack and I send Fatima and Thea a text.

> Are either of you around to meet up? Would be great to see you.

Fatima texts back first.

**Could do coffee this Sat? Can't do anything before
then. 3pm somewhere central?**

Great, I text back. *That works for me. Thea?*
Thea takes twenty-four hours before she replies, and
when she does, it's with her usual brevity.

P Quot in S Ken?

It takes me a good ten minutes of puzzling before
the penny drops, and when it does, Fatima's reply
comes before I can type out my acceptance.

**Okay, 3pm Sat at Pain Quotidien in South Ken. See
you there.**

"CAN YOU TAKE FREYA THIS Saturday?" I ask Owen casually
that night, while we're eating supper.

"Sure." He forks pasta into his mouth and nods
through a mouthful of Bolognese. "You know that. I
wish you'd go out more. What's the occasion?"

"Oh, seeing friends," I say vaguely. It's true, but
I don't want him to know the whole truth—that I'm
meeting Fatima and Thea. He would wonder why, so
soon after I saw them at Kate's.

"Anyone I'd know?" Owen says, and I feel a prickle
of irritation. It's not just that I don't want to answer, it's
that I don't think even a week ago he would have asked
the question. It's those flowers of Luc's. Owen said
nothing when he came home and found them gone,
but he is still thinking about them. I can tell.

"Just friends," I say. And then I add stupidly, "It's a
birthing class reunion thing."

"Oh, nice, who's going to be there?"

I feel my heart sink, realizing the lie I have backed myself into. Owen and I went to those classes together. He knows all of them. I'm going to have to be specific, and as Kate always said, it's the specifics that catch you out.

"Um . . . Rachel," I say at last. "And Jo, I think. I'm not sure who else."

"Will you express?" Owen asks as he reaches for the pepper. I shake my head.

"No, I'll only be gone a couple of hours. It's just coffee."

"No probs," he says. "It'll be fun. I'll take her to the pub and feed her pork scratchings."

I know he's joking—about the pork scratchings, at least—but I also know he's said it for the rise it will get from me, so I go along with it, mock frowning and cuffing him across the table, grinning as we play out our little marital pantomime. Do all relationships have this back-and-forth, I wonder, as I clear the plates. These little rituals of call and response?

When we fall into bed that night, I'm expecting Owen to fall asleep as he always does—disappearing into unconsciousness with a speed and ease I've grown increasingly to envy, but to my surprise he reaches for me in the darkness, his hand straying down over my still slack stomach, between my legs, and I turn to him, feeling for his face, his arms, the streak of sparse, dark hair where his ribs meet.

"I love you," he says afterwards, as we lie back, hearts still thrumming. "We should do it more often."

"We should," I say. And then, almost as an afterthought, "I love you, too."

And it's true: I do, with my whole heart in that moment.

I am falling asleep when he speaks again, his voice soft.

"Isa, is everything okay?"

I open my eyes in the dark, my heart suddenly quickening.

"Yes," I say, trying to keep my voice sleepy and level. "Of course. Why d'you ask?"

He sighs.

"I don't know. I just . . . I feel like you've been kind of weird, tense, ever since that trip to Kate's."

Please. I shut my eyes, clench my fists. *Please don't do this, don't make me start lying to you again.*

"I'm fine," I say, and I don't try to keep the weariness out of my tone. "I'm just . . . I'm tired, I guess. Can we talk about this tomorrow?"

"Sure," he says, but there's something in his voice, disappointment, maybe. He knows I am keeping something from him. "I'm sorry you're so tired. You should let me get up more at night."

"No point, is there?" I say with a yawn. "While she's still on the boob. You'd only have to wake me up."

"Look, I keep saying we should try a bottle," Owen begins, but I feel frustration boil up inside me, and I let myself snap, just a little bit.

"Owen, can we please, *please* not have this conversation now? I told you, I'm tired, I want to go to sleep."

"Sure," he says again, and his voice this time is flat and quelled. "Sorry. Good night."

I want to cry. I want to hit him. I cannot cope with this, on top of everything else. Owen is my one constant, the one thing in my life right now that is not about paranoia and deceit.

"Please, Owen," I say, and my voice cracks a little in spite of myself. "Please, don't be like that."

But he doesn't answer. He just lies there, hunched and silent beneath the sheets, and I sigh and turn to face the wall.

G ood-bye!" I shout from the downstairs hall. "Call me if—you know . . ."

"We'll be fine," Owen calls down the stairs. I can almost hear him rolling his eyes. I look up, and he's there in the doorway, holding Freya. "Go. Have fun. *Stop worrying.* I can look after my own child, you know."

I know.

I know, I know and yet as the front door to our flat slams upstairs, leaving me alone in the entrance hall, I feel that familiar tightness in my chest, the tugging pull of the bond between me and Freya stretching, stretching . . .

I check my handbag for my phone . . . yup. Keys . . . yup. Wallet . . . where is my wallet? I'm hunting for it when my eye alights on a letter in the rack, addressed to me.

I pick it up, intending to take it upstairs when I go back to look for my wallet, but then two things happen at the same time.

The first is that I feel the bump of my wallet in my jeans pocket and realize where it is. The second . . . the second is that I notice that the letter has a Salten postmark.

My heart begins to beat a little faster, but I tell myself, there's no reason to panic. If it were something from the police it would be franked, not stamped, surely, and would look like business correspondence— typewritten, in one of those envelopes with a plastic window.

This is something else—a brown A5 envelope, through which I can feel several sheets.

The writing isn't Kate's. It's neat, anonymous block capitals, quite unlike Kate's generous looping scrawl.

Could it be something from the school? Photos from the dinner, perhaps?

I hesitate for a moment, wondering whether to tuck it back into the rack and deal with it when I get back. But then curiosity gets the better of me and I hook a finger in the flap and rip it open.

Inside there's a sheaf of papers, three or four sheets, perhaps, but they seem to be photocopies—drawings, rather than letters. I shake them out, looking for a top sheet to tell me what this is about, and as the pieces of paper flutter to the floor, it feels like a hand wraps round my heart and squeezes, so hard that I can feel a pain in my chest. The blood drains from my face, and my fingertips are cold and numb, and I wonder for a moment if I am having a heart attack—if this is what it feels like.

My heart is thumping erratically in my breast, and I can feel my breath coming sharp and shallow.

And then there's a sound from above and an instinct of raw self-preservation takes over and I fall to my hands and knees, scrabbling for the pictures with a desperation I cannot even try to hide.

Only when they are back inside the envelope can I try to process what has happened, what I have seen, and I put my hands to my face, feeling the hot flush on my cheeks and a pulse beating hard in the pit of my stomach. Who has sent these? How did they know?

Suddenly it is more urgent than ever that I get out, talk to Fatima and Thea, and with hands that shake I shove the envelope deep, deep into my handbag and yank open the front door.

When I step into the street I hear a noise from above, and I look up, to see Owen and Freya standing by the open window upstairs. Owen is holding Freya's pudgy little hand, and as he sees me turn, he waves it in a solemn good-bye.

"Thank God!" he says. He is laughing, trying to stop Freya from diving out of his arms. "I was starting to think you were planning to spend the whole afternoon in the hallway!"

"S-sorry," I stammer, knowing that my cheeks are burning, and my hands are shaking. "I was checking the train times."

"Bye-bye, Mummy," Owen says, but Freya jerks against him, kicking her fat little legs, wanting to be put down, and he bends and lets her go. "'Bye, love," he says as he straightens.

"'Bye," I manage, though my throat is tight and sore, as if there is something huge and choking there, stopping me from speaking or swallowing. "See you later."

And then I flee, unable to face him any longer.

Fatima is sitting at a table at Le Pain Quotidien when I arrive, and as soon as I see her, tense and upright, her fingers drumming the table, I know.

"You got one, too?" I say as I slide into the seat. She nods, her face pale as stone.

"Did you know?"

"Did I know what?"

"Did you know that they were coming?" she hisses.

"What? No! Of course not. How can you ask that?"

"The timing—this meeting. It seemed a little . . . planned?"

"Fatima, *no*." Oh God, this is worse than I had thought. If Fatima suspects that I was involved in this . . . "No!" I am almost crying at the idea that I could have had something to do with this, and not have warned her, protected her. "Of course I didn't know anything—how can you think that? It was a total coincidence. I got one, too."

I pull the corner of my own envelope out of my bag and she stares at me for a long minute, and then seems to realize fully what she's suggesting, and covers her face.

"Isa, I'm sorry—I don't know what I was thinking. I just—"

A waiter comes over and she breaks off, staring at him as he asks, "Can I get you ladies anything? Coffee? Cake?"

Fatima rubs a hand over her face, and I can see she is trying to order her thoughts and is as shaken as I am.

"Do you have mint tea?" she asks at last, and the waiter nods and turns to me with a smile. I feel my face is fixed, false, a mask of cheerfulness over an abyss of fear. But somehow I manage to swallow against the constriction in my throat.

"I'll have . . . I'll have a cappuccino, please."

"Anything to eat?"

"No, thank you," Fatima says, and I find myself shaking my head in vehement agreement. I feel like food would choke me now, if I tried to swallow it.

The waiter has disappeared to get our drinks when the entrance door flings back, the bell jangling, and Fatima and I both look up to see Thea, wearing dark glasses and a slash of red lipstick, looking wildly around her. Her gaze fixes on us and she gives a kind of start and comes across.

"How did you know?" She shoves the envelope under my nose, standing over me so that I have to rise out of my seat, my hands held out pleadingly. "How the fuck did you know?" She almost shouts the words, the envelope in her fingers trembling as she holds it out.

"Thee—I—" But my throat is closing against the words, and I can't force them out.

"Thee, calm down." Fatima rises out of her seat— palms outstretched. "I asked the same thing. But it's just a coincidence."

"A coincidence? Pretty fucking big coincidence!" Thea spits, and then she does a double take. "Wait, you got one, too?"

"Yes, and Isa, too." Fatima points to the envelope sticking out of my bag. "She didn't know they were coming any more than we did."

Thee looks from Fatima to me and puts the envelope back in her own bag and sits slowly down in the free seat.

"So . . . we have no idea who sent these?"

Fatima shakes her head, slowly, but then says, "But we have a pretty good idea where they came from, right?"

"What do you mean?" Thea demands.

"Well, what do you think I mean? Kate said she destroyed all of . . . of these kinds of pictures. Either she lied, or these came from the school."

"*Fuck*," Thea says vehemently, so that the waiter who has come to hover, waiting for her order, does a double take and slides unobtrusively away to wait for a better time. "Fucking cunting twatting wank-badgers." She puts her head in her hands, and I see that her nails are bitten to the quick, blood speckling the torn skin around the edges of her fingers. "Do we ask her?" she says at last. "Kate, I mean?"

"I think not, don't you?" Fatima says grimly. "If this is a kind of blackmail on her part, she's gone to the trouble of disguising her handwriting and sending them anonymously, so I hardly think she's going to fess up the moment we ask her if she sent them."

"It *can't* be Kate," I burst out, just as the waiter comes back with our drinks, and we sit, scarlet-cheeked and silent, while he sets them down and takes Thea's order for a black double espresso. After he has melted away, I say, more quietly, "It can't. It just can't—what possible motive could she have for sending these?"

"I don't like the idea any more than you do," Fatima snaps back. "Shit. *Shit*, this is all such a mess. But if Kate didn't send them, who did? The school? What possible motive could *they* have? Times have changed, Isa. Judges don't condemn schoolgirls as *no angels* anymore—this would be an abuse scandal, plain and simple, and Salten House would be right at the center of it. The way they handled the whole business was shocking—they've got almost as much to lose as we have."

"We weren't abused," Thea says. She takes off her sunglasses and I can see there are deep shadows around her eyes. "Ambrose was a lot of things, but he wasn't an abuser."

"That's not the point," Fatima says. "Whatever his motives were, he abused his *position*, there's no two ways about it, and you know that as well as I do. He was an irresponsible fool."

"He was an artist," Thea retorts. "And he never laid a finger on any of us, unless you want to say different?"

"But that's not how the press will see it!" Fatima hisses. "Wake up, Thee. This is a *motive*, don't you get that?"

"A motive for—for his suicide?" Thea's face is puzzled for a moment, but then I speak, spelling it out for her.

"A motive for us to . . . kill him, right, Fatima? That's what you're saying."

She nods, her face pale beneath the dark wine-colored hijab, and I feel the constriction in my throat again, choking me. The images rise up in front of my mind's eye—Ambrose's delicate pencil sweeps, a curve here, a line there, a brush of hair . . . the body in the images has changed, but my face, my face is still horrifyingly, unmistakably mine, even after all these years, staring out from the paper, so unself-conscious and so very, very vulnerable . . .

"What?" Thea gives a shaky laugh, shakes her head. "No. No! That's ridiculous! Who'd believe it? I just don't buy the logic!"

"Look," Fatima says wearily. "Back then, we were only seeing the discovery of the drawings from one perspective—Ambrose's. They were a disaster for him, plain and simple. But look at it from the viewpoint of an adult. What would you think if you saw this in the press? You've got a group of girls at a residential school being groomed by a teacher, one of them his own daughter. You heard Kate—people in the village are already speculating about whether Ambrose was abusing her. These pictures, surfacing *now* after all Kate's attempts to erase them? This changes our relationship to Ambrose pretty radically, Thee. We go from being his students to his victims. And sometimes victims fight back."

She is whispering, her words barely audible beneath the coffee shop hubbub, but suddenly I want to put my hand over her mouth, tell her to hush, for God's sake be quiet. Because she's right. We buried the body. We have no alibi for the night he died. Even if it didn't get to court, people would talk.

Thea's coffee arrives in the silence that follows and we drink, each of us lost in our own world, thinking about the possible consequences of this scandal to our careers, our relationships, our kids . . .

"So who, then?" Thea says at last. "Luc? Someone from the village?"

"I don't know," Fatima groans. "Whatever I said before, I *don't* think Kate sent these, I just don't. But the fact remains, whether she sent them or not, she lied about destroying the pictures. These aren't the ones that the school showed us, are they?"

"Funnily enough," Thea says, almost snappishly, "admiring my pose wasn't the first thing on my mind that day. Isa? Do you remember?"

"I don't know," I say slowly. I am trying to remember back to the spread of images on the desk. There were only half a dozen bits of paper, only one was of me alone, at least I think so . . . Christ, it is so hard to remember. But I am sure of one thing—the envelope I received today contained at least three or four sheets, many more images than were scattered on Miss Weatherby's desk. "I think you're right," I say at last. "I don't think these are the ones the school had. At least, not unless they kept some back. The ones they showed us . . . there weren't enough to cover this. But I think Fatima's right—there's no motive for the school to send them, surely? They have as much to lose as we do."

"Who then—Luc?" Thea demands. I shrug helplessly. "Mary Wren? And what, is it a warning, or is someone trying to stop us from getting hurt? Could it be Kate giving us back the images so we can't get ambushed by them in the future?"

"I doubt it," I say. I would love to believe that version—the version that doesn't involve us looking over our shoulders for the demand that is coming next. "But they're copies, not originals. Why post us copies?" Though even as I say it, I can imagine Kate being unable to part with the drawings. God knows, after all, she has hung on to every other part of her father.

"Could she be giving us a heads-up about their existence?" Thea says, but her voice is uncertain. I shake my head.

"She would have told us at the Mill. Posting them now . . . it doesn't make sense."

"You're right," Fatima says. "The timing's all wrong."

Her words trigger an uncomfortable echo inside me, and suddenly I remember my middle-of-the-night doubts, almost submerged by the arrival of the pictures and my fear over what they might mean.

I swallow my cappuccino, and when I put the cup down, it rattles a little on the saucer, betraying my nervousness about what I am about to say. I so want to be wrong. I so want Fatima and Thea to explain away my doubts—and I am not sure if they can.

"Well, that's another thing," I say, reluctantly, and Fatima and Thea both turn to look at me. I swallow again, my throat suddenly dry and bitter with caffeine. "It—it's something I've been thinking about, the timings of the pictures—not these ones," I add, seeing their puzzlement. "The ones the school found."

"What do you mean"—Fatima frowns—"timings?"

"The day before Ambrose died was completely normal, right?" They both nod. "But I don't understand how it could have been. If the school knew about the pictures, if they'd spoken to Ambrose about them, then why did they wait twenty-four hours before confronting us? And why did they talk to us as if they didn't know for sure who drew the pictures?"

"B-because . . ." Thea says, and then stops, trying to order her thoughts. "Well, I mean, I always thought that they spoke to us before they spoke to Ambrose. They must have done, surely? Otherwise they would have known they were his—he wouldn't have denied it, would he?"

But Fatima has already got there before me. Her face is very pale, her dark eyes fixed on mine, and there's a kind of fear in them that makes me even more frightened.

"I see what you're saying. If they hadn't spoken to Ambrose, how did he know it was all about to come out?"

I nod, silent. I have been hoping against hope that Fatima—cool, deductive Fatima, with her clear mind and logical thinking—would see a hole in my reasoning. Now I know there isn't one.

"My guess," I say slowly, "in fact it's not a guess, I think it's pretty damn near certain, the school didn't see those drawings until *after* Ambrose was dead."

There is silence. A long, dread-filled silence.

"So what you're saying . . ." Thea says at last, and I can see her trying to figure it out, trying to make it mean something else, other than the obvious conclusion we are all trying to skirt around. "What you're saying is . . ."

She stops.

Silence fills the air, the hubbub of the café suddenly seeming very far away, and almost muted in comparison to the words that are screaming inside my head.

I can't believe I am about to voice this aloud, but someone has to. I draw a breath and force myself to come out with it.

"What I'm saying is, either someone was blackmailing him . . . and he knew those images were about to be sent and acted before the shit could hit the fan . . . or . . ."

But then I stop, too, because I can't say the last thing, it's too horrific, it changes everything—what happened, what we did, and most of all the possible consequences . . .

It's Fatima who spells it out. Fatima, who is used to giving out life-or-death information—life-changing diagnoses, stomach-punching test results. She swallows the last of her mint tea, and finishes my sentence for me, her voice flat.

"Or someone murdered him," she says.

On the tube on the way home the facts seem to jostle and tumble inside my head, ordering and reordering, as if I could make sense of all this if only I shuffle the deck in a different way.

Accessory to murder. Maybe even a suspect myself if Fatima is right.

This changes everything, and I feel hot and cold at the realization of what we may have blundered into. I feel angry—more than angry. Furious. Furious with Fatima and Thea for not being able to reassure me. Furious with myself for not working this out sooner. For seventeen years I have been pushing away thoughts of what we did that night. For seventeen years I have been *not* thinking of what happened, trying to bury the memories under a hundredweight of mundane, everyday worries and plans.

I should have thought about it.

I should have thought about it every day, questioned every angle. Because now that I have unpicked that one thread, the whole tapestry of the past is beginning to unravel.

The more I think back, the more certain I am that the drawings had surfaced only that morning, the morning *after* Ambrose's death. I had spoken to Miss Weatherby the night before at supper, she had asked after my mother and my weekend plans. There was absolutely no hint of what was to come, no hint of the naked shock and fury we saw in her face the following day. She could have been a truly extraordinary dissembler—but *why*? There was no reason for the

school to wait before confronting us. If Miss Weatherby had seen those pictures on Friday, she would have
hauled us into her office that same day.

No, the conclusion was inescapable: the drawings
turned up after Ambrose died.

But *who*? And almost as important, *why*?

Someone blackmailing him, who had finally followed through with their threat?

Or someone who had murdered him, trying to provide a motive for his suicide?

Or . . . was it possible . . . could Ambrose himself
have possibly sent them, in a fit of remorse, before taking his fatal dose?

But I shake that idea off almost straightaway. What
Ambrose did in drawing us might have been wrong,
legally and ethically, an abuse of his position as Fatima
had said. He might even have come to feel that himself,
with time.

But I am absolutely and utterly convinced that however guilty he felt himself, Ambrose would never have
posted those drawings to the school. Not to save his own
shame, but because he would never have put us through
the kind of public humiliation that ensued, would never
have put *Kate* through it. His affection, his *love* for us,
was too great, and one thing I know, as the tube train
rattles through the tunnel, the dusty wind warm in my
face, he did love us, for Kate's sake, and for our own.

So who then?

A blackmailer from the village, who came to the
Mill one day and caught sight of something he thought
he could use?

I want it to be true. Because the alternative . . . the
alternative is almost unthinkable. Murder.

And then there are far fewer people with a motive.

Not Luc. He is the one person who lost most from

Ambrose's death. He lost his home, and his sister, and his adoptive father. He lost any security he had.

Not any of the villagers, at least not that I can see. They might have blackmailed him. But they have no reason to kill a man who was one of their own.

So who then? Who had access to the drawings, and access to Ambrose's stash, and was in the house before he died?

I press my hands to my temples, trying not to think about that, and trying not to think about the last conversation we had—Fatima, Thea, and I—as we walked to South Kensington tube, sunglasses on against the fierce bleaching summer sun.

"Listen, there's just one more thing . . ." Thea said, and then she stopped, in the archway to the tube station, putting her fingers to her mouth.

"Stop biting your fingers," Fatima said, but with concern, not censure. "What. What is it?"

"It—it's about Kate. And Ambrose. Shit." She ran her fingers through her short hair, and her face was stiff with apprehension. "No. No, it doesn't matter."

"You can't say something like that and not tell us." I put out my hand to her arm. "Besides, it's obviously eating you up. Spit it out, whatever it is. You'll feel better. What do they say—a problem shared?"

"Fuck that," Thea said brutally. "Much good it's ever done us." Her face twisted and then she said, "Look, what I'm about to tell you—it's not that I think—I don't want *you* to think . . ."

She faltered, pinching the bridge of her nose beneath the sunglasses, but Fatima and I kept silent, sensing that only waiting would bring this confession out.

And at last she told us.

Ambrose had been planning to send Kate away. Right away. To a different boarding school.

He had told Thea just the weekend before, when he was very drunk. Kate, Fatima, and I were swimming in the Reach, but Thea wasn't swimming that weekend, I can't remember why, and she had stayed up in the Mill with Ambrose, as he drank red wine, and stared up at the vaulted ceiling, and tried to come to terms with a decision he did not want to make.

"He was asking me about schools," Thea said. "What Salten was like, in comparison to the other places I'd been. Whether I thought changing so often had screwed me up. He was drunk, very drunk, and not making complete sense, but then he said something about the parent-child bond, and I had this horrible cold lurch in my stomach. He was talking about Kate."

She takes a deep breath, as if even now the realization shocks her.

"I said, 'Ambrose, don't do this. You'll break Kate's heart.' He didn't answer straightaway, but at last he said, 'I know. But I just . . . I can't let it go on like this. It's all wrong.'"

What can't go on? Thea had questioned him, or tried to, but we others were coming back, and Ambrose had shaken his head, and taken his bottle of red wine and gone up the stairs to his studio, shutting the door, before the rest of us had come in from the Reach, wringing water out of our hair and laughing.

And all that night, and the rest of the week, Thea had looked at Kate wondering, does she know what he's planning? Does she *know*?

And then Ambrose had died. And everything fell apart.

I CAN'T LET IT GO ON. Thea's voice, echoing Ambrose, rings in my head as I walk back from the tube station, hardly feeling the hot afternoon sun on the back of my head, I'm so preoccupied with my own thoughts.

It's all wrong. What did he mean? I try to imagine what Kate could have done that would be bad enough for him to consider sending her away—but my imagination fails. He had watched Kate, all of us, stumble through that year making mistakes and questionable decisions, exploring drink and drugs and our sexuality. And he had said nothing. In a way it was no wonder, with his own past he had few stones left to cast. He only watched with love and tried to tell Kate and the rest of us when we were putting ourselves in danger, without judgment. The only time I can remember him getting really angry was over the pill Kate took at the disco.

Are you mad? he shouted, his hands in his wiry hair, making it stand up on end like a rat's nest. *Do you know what those things do to your body? What's wrong with some nice healthy weed, for crying out loud!*

But even then, he never grounded her; there was no punishment—just his disappointment and concern. He cared for her, for us. He wanted us to be okay. He shook his head when we smoked, looked on with sadness when Thea turned up with plasters and bandages over strange cuts and burns. When we asked him, he counseled, offered advice. But that was it. There was no condemnation, no moral outrage. He never made us feel wrong, or ashamed.

He loved us all. But most of all, above all else, he loved Kate—loved her with an affection so fierce that it took my breath away sometimes. Perhaps it was the fact that it had been just the two of them for so long, after Kate's mother died—but sometimes, there was something about the way he looked at her, the way he tucked her hair behind her ear, even the way he evoked her in sketches, as though he were trying . . . not to trap her exactly, but to pinpoint that quintessence that would enable him to preserve something of her forever on a page where it could never be taken away from him. It sang of an adoration that I glimpsed sometimes in my own parents, but dimly, as if through misted glass or far away. In Ambrose, though, it was a flame that burned fierce and bright.

He loved us, but Kate *was* him. It was impossible to think of him sending her away.

So what could be so bad that he felt he had no choice but to part with her?

"Are you sure?" I asked Thea, with a feeling like my whole life had been shaken like a snow globe and left to resettle. "Is that really what he said?"

And she only nodded, and when I pressed said, "Do you think I'd get something like that wrong?"

I can't let it go on . . .

What happened, Ambrose? Was it something Kate did? Or . . . the thought twists in my stomach . . . was it something else? Something Ambrose was protecting Kate from? Or something he himself had done?

I don't know. I can't answer the questions, but my head is spinning with them as my feet eat up the distance between the tube station and home.

Our road is coming closer, and soon I will have to push these thoughts aside and become Owen's partner and Freya's mother.

But the questions beat at me, things with wings and claws, battering against me so that I flinch as I walk, turning my face as if I can avoid them, but I can't.

What did she do? What did she do, to deserve being sent away? And what might she have done to stop it?

Accessory to murder.

Accessory to murder.

No matter how many times the phrase repeats inside my head, I can't seem to understand it. Accessory to murder. An offense that carries a prison sentence. In the darkness of my bedroom, the blackout blinds drawn against the evening sun, Freya in my arms, the repeated phrase washes over me in a wave of cold terror. Accessory to *murder*.

And then it comes to me like a chink in the darkness. The suicide note. That's what I have to hold on to.

I am feeding Freya down to sleep, and she is almost unconscious, but when I try to take her off she grips me, monkey-like, with her strong little fingers, and begins sucking again with renewed determination, burrowing her face into my breast as if she can return to the safety of my body.

After a minute of this, I realize she is not going to let go without a struggle, and I sigh and let my weight fall back in the nursing chair, and my thoughts return to their round-and-round, their back-and-forth.

Ambrose's note. A *suicide* note. How could he have written a note, if he was murdered?

I read it, though all I can remember now are short phrases and snatches and the way the writing seemed to disintegrate into straggling letters at the end. *I am at peace with my decision . . . Please know, darling Kate, that I do this with love—the last thing I can do to protect you . . . I love you, so please go on: live, love, be happy. And above all, don't let this all be in vain.*

Love. Protection. Sacrifice. Those were the words that had stayed with me over the years. And it made sense, in the context of what I'd always believed. If Ambrose lived, the whole scandal with the drawings would have come out—he would have been sacked, and his name, along with Kate's, would have been dragged through the mud.

Back then, when we got that call into Miss Weatherby's office, I had had a sense of pieces falling into place. Ambrose had seen the storm coming, and had done the only thing he could do to protect Kate—taken his own life.

But now . . . now I am not so sure.

I look down at the baby in my arms and I cannot imagine ever leaving her willingly. It's not that I can't imagine a parent killing themselves—I know that they do. Being a parent doesn't grant you immunity from unbearable depression or stress, quite the opposite.

But Ambrose was not depressed. I am as certain of that as I can be. And more than that, he was the last person I could imagine giving a shit about his reputation. He had means. He had friends abroad, many friends. And above all, he loved his children, both of them. I cannot imagine him leaving them to face music he was too frightened to face himself. The Ambrose I knew, he would have scooped his children up and taken them to Prague, to Thailand, to Kenya—and he would not have given the smallest of shits about the scandal left behind, because he would have had his art, and his family, with him, and that was all that mattered to him.

I always knew that, I think. It's just that it took having a child of my own to realize it.

At last Freya is properly asleep, her mouth slack, her head lolling back, and I lower her gently to the white sheet and tiptoe out of the room, downstairs to where Owen is sitting, watching something soothingly mind-numbing on Netflix.

He looks up as I come into the room.

"Is she down?"

"Yes, she was knackered. I don't think she was very happy about me being out today."

"You've gotta cut those apron strings sometime . . ." Owen says teasingly. He's only trying to wind me up, I know it, but I'm tired and stressed and knocked off-balance by everything that happened today, still trying to make sense of the envelope of drawings and Thea's revelations, and I snap back, without meaning to.

"For Christ's sake, Owen, she's six months."

"I know that," he says, nettled, taking a sip of the beer that's sitting at his elbow. "I know her age as well as you do. She's my kid, too, you know. Or so I'm led to believe."

" 'So you're led to believe'?" I feel the blood rising up in my cheeks, and my voice when I repeat his words is high and cracked with anger. " '*So you're led to believe*'? What the fuck does that mean?"

"Hey!" Owen puts down his glass of beer with an audible thud. "Don't swear at me! Jesus, Isa. What's got into you lately?"

"What's got into *me*?" I am almost speechless with fury. "You make a crack about Freya not being your baby and you ask what's got into *me*?"

"Freya not being—What the hell?" His face is genu-inely confused, and I can see him replaying the con-versation of the last few minutes, and then realizing. "No! Are you out of your mind? Why would I mean that? I was just trying to say that you need to chill out sometimes; I *am* Freya's dad, but you wouldn't know it by the amount of childcare I get to do. How the hell could you think I'd imply that she's—"

He stops, lost for words, and I feel my cheeks flaming as I realize what he meant, but my anger doesn't abate, if anything, it rises. There's nothing like being in the wrong to make you fight back.

"Oh, well, that's okay, then," I spit. "You were just implying I'm some kind of controlling obsessive lunatic who won't let her husband change a nappy. That changes everything. Of course I'm not cross *now*."

"Oh Jesus, will you stop putting words into my mouth?" Owen groans.

"Well, it's hard not to, when you make these cracks without ever coming out with your point." My voice is shaking. "I'm fed up with these constant little jibes about stuff—if it's not childcare it's bottles, and if it's not that, it's getting Freya out of our bedroom and into her own. It feels like I—"

"They weren't jibes, they were suggestions," Owen interrupts, his voice plaintive. "Yes, look, I put my hands up: it *is* something I've been starting to get frustrated about, especially now that she's six months. She's on solids, isn't it a bit weird breastfeeding her when she's getting teeth?"

"What's that got to do with anything? She's a *baby*, Owen. So give her solids! What's stopping you?"

"You are! Every night it's the same thing, of course she won't go down for me, why would she when you won't stop breastfeeding?"

I'm shaking with anger, so furious I can't speak for a minute.

"Good night, Owen."

"Hang on." He stands up as I begin to walk out of the room. "Don't come all high-and-mighty. I didn't want to have this bloody argument in the first place. *You* were the one who dragged it all out in the open!"

I don't answer. I begin to climb the stairs.

"Isa," he calls, urgently but softly, trying not to wake Freya. "*Isa!* Why the hell are you being like this?"

But I don't answer. I can't answer. Because if I do, I will say something that might damage my relationship beyond recovery.

The truth.

I wake with Freya beside me, but the rest of the double bed is empty, and for a moment I can't work out why I feel so wretched and ashamed, and then I remember.

Shit. Did he sleep downstairs, or come up late and get up early?

I get up very carefully, pile the duvets on the floor in case Freya wakes and rolls off the bed, and, pulling my dressing gown on, I tiptoe downstairs.

Owen is sitting in the kitchen, drinking coffee and staring out the window, but he looks up as I come in.

"I'm sorry," I say, straight off, and his face crumples with something between relief and unhappiness.

"I'm sorry, too," he says. "I was a right dick. What I said—"

"Look, you have a right to feel that way. And you're right—I mean, not about the breastfeeding, that was horseshit, but I *will* try and involve you more. It's going to happen anyway. Freya's getting older, she won't need me as much, and I'll be going back to work soon, anyway."

He stands up and hugs me, and I feel his chin resting on the top of my head, and the warm muscles of his chest beneath my cheek, and I draw a long, tremulous breath and let it out.

"This is nice," I manage at last, and he nods.

We stand like that for a long time, I don't know how long. But at last there's a noise from above, a kind of chirrup, and I straighten.

"Crap, I left Freya in the bed. She'll roll off."

I'm about to pull away, but Owen pats my shoulder.

"Hey, new resolution, remember? *I'll* go."

I smile and nod, and he sprints up the stairs. As I put the kettle on for my morning cup of tea, I can hear him, cooing at Freya as he picks her up, her squeaking giggles as he plays peekaboo with her blankie.

While I drink my tea, I listen to Owen padding about in the room upstairs. I can hear him pulling out wipes and nappies to change Freya, and then the sound of our chest of drawers as he gets out a fresh vest for her.

They take a long time, longer than I would over a nappy change, but I resist the urge to go up, and at last there are footsteps on the stairs and they appear together in the doorway, Freya in Owen's arms, their expressions heart-meltingly similar. Freya has a comical case of bedhead almost as good as Owen's, and they are both grinning at me, pleased with themselves, with each other, with the sunny morning. She reaches out a hand towards me, wanting me to pick her up, but, mindful of Owen's words, I just smile at her and stay where I am.

"Hello, Mummy," Owen says solemnly, looking at Freya and then back at me. "Me and Freya have been discussing, and we've decided that you should have a day off today."

"A day off?" I feel a little spurt of alarm. "What kind of day off?"

"A day of complete pampering. You've been looking absolutely knackered, you deserve a day not worrying about us."

It is not Freya that I'm worrying about. In fact, in many ways she's the only thing keeping me sane right now. But I can't say that.

"I don't want to hear any protests," Owen says. "I've

booked you an appointment at a day spa already, and I've paid in full, so unless you want me to lose my money, you've got to be down in town by eleven. Me and Freya are going to manage all by ourselves from"—he glances at the kitchen clock—"from ten until four, and we don't want to see you."

"What about her nap?"

"I'll give her one of those cartons of follow-on milk. And maybe"—he chucks her under the chin—"*maybe* we'll go wild and have some mashed broccoli, won't we, funny face? What do you say?"

I don't want to. The idea of spending the day at a spa with all this in my head—it's . . . it's obscene somehow. I need to be moving, doing, pushing away the what-ifs and the fears. The thought of a day alone with my thoughts, with nothing to think about except this . . .

I open my mouth . . . but I can't find anything to say. Except . . .

"Okay."

AS I WAVE GOOD-BYE, THERE is a sickness in my stomach at the prospect of being left with nothing to think about but Salten and what happened there. And yet, some-how, it doesn't work out like that. For the tube journey I am tense, gritting my teeth, feeling the tension head-ache building at the base of my skull and in my temples. But when I arrive at the salon, I give myself over to the practiced hands of the spa therapist, and somehow all the obsessive thoughts are pummeled out of me, and for the next two hours I think of nothing but the ache in my muscles, the tightness at the back of my neck and between my shoulders that she is pressing away.

"You're very tense," she murmurs in a low voice. "There's a lot of knots at the top of your spine. Are you carrying a lot of stress at work?"

I shake my head blearily, but I don't speak. My mouth is open. I feel the cool slack wetness of drool against the spa towel, but I am so tired, I can't find it in myself to care.

Part of me never wants to leave here. But I must go back. To Kate, Fatima, and Thea. To Owen. To Freya.

I emerge from the spa blinking and dazed some four or five hours later with my hair light around my neck where it has been cut, and my muscles loose and warm, and I feel a little drunk—drunk with possession of my own body again. I am *me*. Nothing is weighing me down. Even my handbag feels light, for I left at home the Marni tote I've used since having Freya—a big capable thing with space for nappies and wipes and a change of top—and decanted my purse and keys into the bag I used before she was born. It's a tiny thing, not much bigger than a large envelope, and covered with impractical decorative zips that would be a magnet to an inquisitive baby. It feels like the old me, even though it's only big enough for my purse, phone, keys, and lip balm.

As I walk home from the tube, I feel overwhelmed with a rush of love for Owen and Freya. I feel like I've been away for a hundred years, over an impossible distance.

It will be okay. I am suddenly sure of that. It will be okay. What we did was stupid and irresponsible, but it wasn't murder or anything close to it, and the police will realize that, if it ever gets that far.

As I climb the stairs to the flat I cock my head, listening for Freya's cry . . . but everything is silent. Are they out?

I slip my keys into the door, quietly, in case Freya is asleep—and call out their names, softly. No answer. The kitchen is empty, filled with summer sunshine, and I put on a coffee and then take it upstairs to drink it.

Except . . . I don't.

Instead, I stop dead in the doorway, as if something has hit me, and I cannot breathe.

Owen is sitting on the sofa, his head in his hands, and in front of him, sitting on the coffee table, are two objects, laid out like exhibits at a trial. The first is the packet of cigarettes from my bag—my tote—the one I left behind.

And the second is the envelope—postmarked Salten.

I stand there, my heart hammering, unable to speak, as he holds up the drawing in his hand—the drawing of me.

"Do you want to explain this?"

I swallow. My mouth is dry, and my throat feels again as if there is something lodged in it, something painful I cannot swallow away.

"I could say the same thing," I manage. "What were you doing spying on me? Going through my bag?"

"How dare you." He says it softly, so as not to wake Freya, but his voice is shaking with anger. "How *dare* you. You left your fucking bag here, and Freya went through it. She was chewing on these"—he throws the packet of cigarettes down at my feet, spilling the contents—"when I found her. How could you lie to me?"

"I—" I begin, and then stop. What can I say? My throat hurts with the effort of not speaking the truth.

"As for this . . ." He holds out the drawing of me, his hands trembling. "I can't even . . . Isa, are you having an affair?"

"What? No!" It's jerked out of me before I have time to think. "Of course not! That drawing, it's not—it's not *me*!"

I know as soon as it's out of my mouth that that was a stupid thing to say. It is me—it's self-evidently me. Ambrose is too good an artist for me to be able to deny that. But it's not me *now*, is what I meant. It's not my body—my soft, post-pregnancy body. It's me as I *was*, as I used to be.

But the look on Owen's face tells me what I've done.

"I mean—" I struggle. "It is me, it *was* me, but it's not—"

"Don't lie to me," he breaks in, his voice anguished, and then he turns away from me as though he can't bear to look at me, walks to the window. "I rang Jo, Isa. She said there *was* no bloody meet-up yesterday. It's that man, isn't it, Kate's brother, the one who sent you roses?"

"*Luc?* No, how can you ask that?"

"Then who? It's from Salten; I saw the postmark. Is that what you were doing down there with Kate, meeting him?"

"He didn't draw these!" I shout back.

"Then who?" Owen cries, turning back to me. His face is contorted with anger and distress, his skin blotchy, his mouth square like a child trying not to cry. "Who did?"

I hesitate—just long enough for him to make a noise of disgust, and then he rips the drawing in half with one shocking gesture, tearing through my face, my body, ripping apart my breasts, my legs, and he throws the two halves at my feet and turns as if to go.

"Owen, don't," I manage. "It wasn't Luc. It was—"

But there I stop. I can't tell him the truth. I can't say it was Ambrose without everything unraveling. What can I tell him? There is only one thing I can say.

"It was—it was Kate," I say at last. "Kate drew them. A long time ago."

He comes up to me, very close, and takes my chin, staring into my eyes, holding my gaze as if he's trying to look inside me, into my soul. I try to brazen it out, to stare back at him, hold his gaze fearlessly—but I can't. My eyes shift and falter and I have to look away from that naked pain and anger.

His face twists as he drops his hand.

"Liar," he says, and then he turns to go.

"Owen, no—" I move between him and the door.

"Get off me." He pushes roughly past, heads for the stairs.

"Where are you going?"

"None of your business. Pub. Michael's. I don't know. Just—" But he can't speak now, he's close to crying, I think, his face twisted with the effort of keeping his despair reined in.

"Owen!" I cry after him as he reaches the front door, and for a moment he stops, his hand on the lock, waiting for me to speak, but then there's a sound from above, a rising wail. We've woken Freya.

"I—" I say, but I can't concentrate, Freya's cry, high and bubbling, drills into my brain, driving everything else out. "Owen, please, I—"

"Go to her," he says, almost gently, and then he lets the door slam shut, and he is gone, and I can only crouch on the stairs, while Freya screams from above, and try to muffle my sobs.

HE DOESN'T COME BACK AT all that night. It's the first night he's ever done this—gone out, stepped out, without telling me where he was going and when he would be back.

I eat a lonely supper with Freya, put her to bed, and then I pace the flat in the growing darkness, trying to work out what to do.

The worst of it is, I can't blame him. He knows I am lying to him, it's not just the stupid, stupid slip I made over Jo, he has felt it ever since I left for Kate's. And he's right. I am lying to him. And I don't know how to stop.

I send him a text, just one, I don't want to beg. It says, *Please come home. Or at least let me know you're okay?*

He doesn't answer. I don't know what to think.

Sometime around midnight I get a text from Ella, Michael's girlfriend. It reads, *I have no idea what happened, but Owen is here. He's spending the night. Please don't tell him I sent this, it's not my business to get involved, but I couldn't bear to think of you worrying.*

I feel relief flood me, as real and physical a sensation as stepping under a hot shower.

Thank you so much!!!! I text back. And then, as an afterthought, *I won't tell him, but thank you.*

It is half past two before I go upstairs, and even later before I finally cry myself to sleep.

WHEN THE MORNING COMES, MY mood has changed. I am no longer full of despair. I am angry. Angry at myself, at my past, at my own stupidity.

But I am angry at Owen as well.

I try to imagine the situation reversed—him getting roses from an old friend, an anonymous drawing through the post, and I can imagine myself seeing red. I can even imagine myself throwing accusations. But I cannot imagine myself walking out on my partner and child without telling them where I was going, without even trying to believe their side of the story.

It's Monday, so I'm not expecting him to come home until after work. He keeps a spare suit at his office for emergencies, so there's no need, except perhaps for him to shave, but the times are over when the Civil Service expected baby-smooth skin on their male employees, and in any case, Michael could lend him a razor if he needed one.

I go to the park with Freya. I push her on the swings. I pretend nothing is wrong, and I refuse to think about all the what-ifs crowding my head.

Seven o'clock comes . . . and goes. I eat supper, feeling the pain in my throat again, choking me.

I put Freya to bed.

And then, just as I am lying on the sofa, pulling a rug over me in spite of the summer heat, I hear it—the sound of a key in the door—and my heart jumps into my throat.

I sit up, pulling the rug around me as if it can shield me from what's coming . . . and I turn to face the door.

Owen is standing in the doorway, his suit rumpled, and he looks as if he has been drinking.

Neither of us says anything. I'm not sure what we are waiting for—for a clue, perhaps. For the other person to apologize.

"There's risotto on the stove," I say at last, my throat sore with the effort of speaking. "If you're hungry."

"I'm not," he says shortly, but he turns and goes down into the kitchen, and I hear him rattling plates and cutlery. He is drunk, I can hear it in the way he cracks the plate down harder than he means to onto the work surface, in the way he drops the knife and fork, picks them up, and then somehow drops them again.

Shit, I have to go down. He will scald himself at this rate—or set his tie on fire.

When I get to the kitchen he is sitting at the kitchen table, his head in his hands, and a plate of cold risotto in front of him, and he is not eating. He is just sitting there, staring down at the plate, and there is a kind of drunken despair in his eyes.

"Let me," I say at last, and I take the plate, and put it in the microwave for a few seconds. When I put it back in front of him it is steaming, but he begins to eat, mechanically, not seeming to notice how hot the food is.

"Owen," I say at last. "About last night—"

He turns his face towards me, and there's a sort of painful, naked pleading in his expression, and I see, suddenly, that he doesn't want this any more than I do. He wants to believe me. If I offer him an explanation now, he will accept it, because he wants so much for this to all be over, for those accusations he hurled last night to be untrue.

I take a deep breath. If I can only find the right words . . .

But just as I'm about to speak, my phone rings, making us both jump.

It's Kate, and I almost don't answer it. But something— habit, or worry, I'm not sure which—makes me tap it to pick up.

"Hello?"

"Isa?" Her voice is panicked, and immediately I know something is wrong. "Isa, it's me."

"What's the matter? What's happened?"

"It's about Dad." She is trying not to cry. "About his body. They've asked . . . They told me—"

She stops, her breathing coming fast, and I can tell she's struggling against sobs.

"Kate, Kate, slow down. Take a deep breath. What have they told you?"

"They're treating it as a suspicious death. They want me to come in. For questioning."

I go completely cold. My legs go weak and I grope my way to the kitchen table and sit down opposite Owen, suddenly unable to support my own weight.

"Oh my God."

"Can you come down? We—I need to talk."

I know what she is saying. She is trying to make it sound innocuous, in case Owen is listening, but we need to speak, urgently, before the police interview her, and perhaps us. We need to straighten out our stories.

"Of course," I manage. "I'll come tonight. The last train to Salten isn't until nine thirty. I can make it if I can get a cab to the station."

"Are you sure?" There's a sob in her voice. "I know I'm asking a lot but Fatima can't come, she's on duty at the surgery, and I can't get hold of Thea. She's not answering her phone."

"Don't be stupid. I'm coming."

"Thank you, *thank* you, Isa. I—This means a lot. I'll call Rick now, tell him to pick you up."

"I'll see you soon. Hang on. I love you."

It's only when I hang up that I see Owen's face, his eyes red with tiredness and drink, and I realize how this will seem to him. My heart sinks.

"You're going back to Salten?" He spits the words out. *"Again?"*

"Kate needs me."

"Fuck Kate!" He shouts the words so that I flinch, and then he stands and picks up the bowl of risotto, food he's barely eaten, and throws it into the sink so that the contents splatter across the tiles. Then he speaks again, more softly, a crack in his voice. "What about *us*, Isa? What about me?"

"This is not about you," I say. My hands are shaking as I pick the bowl out of the mess of risotto, run the tap. "This is about Kate. She needs me."

"*I* need you!"

"Her father's body has been found. She's in pieces. What do you want me to do?"

"Her father's—*what*? What the hell is this about?"

I put my head in my hands. I can't face this. I can't face explaining it all—negotiating between the truths and the lies. And Owen won't believe me anyway, not in the mood he's in. He is spoiling for a fight, looking for a way to feel slighted.

"Look, it's complicated—but she needs me, that's the bottom line. I have to go."

"This is bullshit! It's all bullshit. She's managed without you for seventeen *years*, Isa. What's got into you? I don't understand it—you haven't seen her for years, and suddenly she clicks her fingers and you come running?"

The words—they're so close to Luc's that for a minute I can't say anything in response, I just stand, gasping, like he's slapped me. And then I curl my fingers into fists, trying to control myself, and I turn to leave.

"Good-bye, Owen."

"Good-bye?" He steps towards me, through the slick of risotto still on the floor. "What the fuck does that mean?"

"Whatever you want."

"What I want," he says, his voice trembling, "is for our relationship to be a priority for you. Ever since Freya, I feel like I've been last on the fucking list—we never *talk* anymore—and now this!" And I'm not sure if he means Salten and Luc, or Fatima, Thea, and Kate . . . or even Freya. "I'm sick of it, do you hear me? I'm sick of coming last!"

And suddenly, with those words, I am no longer sad and afraid, I am angry. Very, very angry.

"*That's* what this is really about, isn't it? It's not about Luc, or Kate, or some stupid packet of fags. It's about *you*. It's about the fact that you can't bear the fact that you don't come an automatic first anymore."

"How *dare* you say that?" He is almost incoherent. "You lied to me, and you're trying to make it my fault? I'm trying to *talk* to you, Isa. Don't you give a shit about *us*?"

I do. Of course I do. But right now I am at the limit of what I can deal with. And I cannot deal with this. If Owen pushes me, I am very, very scared that I will tell him the truth.

I shove past him and go upstairs where Freya is sleeping, and I begin stuffing things into bags with trembling hands. I'm not sure what I'm packing. Nappies. A clutch of underwear and baby vests. Some tops. God knows if I will have anything to wear. Right now I don't care, I just want to get out.

I pick up Freya, feeling her stir and grumble against me, and slide her into a woolen cardigan, protection against the summer night air. Then I pick up the shoulder bag.

"Isa!" Owen is waiting in the hall, his face red with suppressed anguish and fury. "Isa, don't do this!"

"Owen, I—" Freya is squirming against my shoulder. The phone in my bag beeps. Thea? Fatima? I can't think. I can't *think*.

"You're going to him," he bursts out. "Kate's brother. Aren't you? Is that message from him?"

It's the last straw.

"Fuck you," I snarl. And I push past him and slam the flat door behind me, making Freya startle and wail. In the hallway I tuck her kicking legs into the pram with shaking hands, ignoring her increasingly siren shrieks, and then I open the communal front door and bump the pram furiously out of the house and down the steps.

I am barely out of the front garden when I hear the door open and Owen comes out, his face anguished.

"Isa!" he cries. But I keep going. "*Isa!* You can't walk away from this!"

But I can. And I do.

Even though the tears are coursing down my face, and my heart is close to breaking.

I keep walking.

The weather breaks as the train pulls out of Victoria, and by the time we leave the London sprawl behind and the train enters the countryside, it is lashing with rain, and the temperature has dropped from a sultry pre-storm humidity to something closer to autumn.

I sit there, numb and cold, holding Freya to my breast like a living, breathing hot-water bottle, and I'm unable to process what I have done. Have I *left* Owen?

This is not the first argument we've had, not by a long shot. We've had our quarrels and squabbles like any other couple. But this is by far the most serious, and more than that—it's the first we've had since having Freya. When I gave birth to her, something shifted in our relationship—the stakes became higher, we consciously spread our roots, stopped sweating the small stuff, as if realizing that we could no longer afford to rock the boat so often, for her sake, if not for our own.

And now . . . now the boat is tipping so perilously, I'm not sure if I can save us both.

It's the unjustness of his accusations that burns in my throat like acid. An affair. An *affair*? I've barely been out of the house alone since Freya was born. My body is not my own anymore—she is glued to me like Velcro, sucking out my energy and my libido along with my milk. I am so exhausted and touched out that just summoning up the desire to fuck Owen is almost more than I can cope with—he knows that, he *knows* how tired I am, how I feel about my slack, postnatal body. Does he honestly think I tucked Freya under my arm and hauled myself off for a passionate, illicit affair? It's so ridiculous I could laugh, if it wasn't so outrageously unfair.

And yet, furious as I am, I'm forced to admit that on some level . . . he's right. Not about the affair. But as the train forges south and my anger cools, a kernel of guilt begins to form inside of me. Because the core of what he is saying is this: I have not been true to him. And he's right. Not in the way that he means—but in other ways, just as important. Ever since the day we met I have been keeping secrets, but now, for the first time in our relationship, I am doing more than that; I am outright lying. And he knows it. He knows that something is wrong, and that I am covering it up. He just doesn't know what it is.

I wish I could tell him. I wish it like a hunger in the pit of my stomach. And yet . . . and yet a part of me is relieved that I can't. It is not my secret, so it's not my decision to make. But if it were? If it were only me involved? Then . . . I don't know.

Because although I don't want to have to lie to him, I also don't want him to know the truth. I don't want him to look at me, and see the person who did this—a person who lied, not just once, but repeatedly. A person who concealed a body, who colluded in a fraud. A person who, perhaps, has helped cover up a murder.

If it comes out, will he still love me?

I am not sure. And it makes me feel sick to my stomach.

If it were only Owen's love I was risking, I would take the chance. At least, that's what I tell myself. But it's his career, too. The disclosure forms you sign when you join the civil service are long and detailed. They ask about gambling habits and finance, about drug use and yes . . . about criminal behavior. They are looking for levers—things that could be used against you, to blackmail you into releasing information you shouldn't, or to force you to commit fraud.

They ask you about your partner. They ask about your family and friends—and the higher up you get in the organization, the more questions they ask, the more sensitive the information becomes.

The final question is, basically, is there anything in your life that could be used to bring pressure to bear on you? If so, declare it now.

We have both filled these forms out multiple times—me, every time I changed departments, Owen each time his security clearance in the Home Office got higher. And I have lied on them. Repeatedly. The fact that I lied at all is grounds for dismissal. But if I tell Owen the truth, I make him party to the lie. I put his neck on the line as well as mine.

It was bad enough when what we did was only conceal a body. But if I'm an accessory to murder . . .

I shut my eyes, shutting out the darkness and the rain that beats on the carriage windows. And I have the sudden feeling that I am out on the salt marsh, picking my way over an unfamiliar track. But the ground isn't firm beneath me—it's soft and wet, and every false step I take, I am straying farther from the path, and sinking deeper into the salt-soaked mud. Soon I may not be able to find my way back.

"DID YOU SAY SALTEN, DEARIE?" says a cracked, elderly voice, and I jerk awake, Freya startling convulsively against my heart and yelping crossly.

"What?" There is drool at the corner of my mouth and I swipe it away with Freya's muslin and blink at the old lady sitting opposite me. "What did you say?"

"We're just coming into Salten, and I heard you tell the ticket inspector that's where you're getting off. Is that right?"

"Oh God, yes!"

It's so dark, I have to cup my hands around my eyes as I peer through the rain-spattered window, squinting at the dimly lit platform sign to be sure I'm at the right stop.

It *is* Salten, and I stagger upright, grabbing for bags and coats. Freya wriggles sleepily against me, as I wrestle the door open one-handed.

"Let me hold the door," says the old lady, seeing me struggling to get Freya into her pram and the rain cover buttoned down.

The guard's whistle is blowing peremptorily as I bump the pram onto the wet platform, the rain lashing at my coat. Freya's eyes open wide in affronted horror, and she lets out a squawking yell of indignation as I sprint down the platform, coat flapping, hoping to hell that Kate is waiting.

She is, thank God, along with Rick, the engine running, the windows of the taxi steamed up with their breath. And this time I remembered to pack the car seat, rather than the pram adaptor, so that I can strap Freya in as he starts up the rutted track towards the village.

There is no room for conversation, over Freya's increasingly inconsolable howls of wrath at being woken from a warm, dry sleep by this chilly rainy assault, and although her wails pluck at my skin like claws, part of me is glad that I don't have to make small talk with Rick. All I can think of is the drawings, Ambrose's letter, the roses, the blood on my hands.

Back at the Mill, there is water on the floor, puddles beneath the doorjambs. Rain has forced its way in through the rickety windows and is pooling on the uneven boards, and around the window frames.

"Kate," I try, over the top of Freya's wails and the sound of the waves against the jetty, but she shakes her head, points at the clock, which shows half past midnight.

"Go to bed," she says. "We'll talk in the morning."

And I can only nod and take my sobbing child up the stairs, into the bedroom where we stayed, where our sheets are still on the bed, Luc's bed, and I lie there on my side, listening to her frantic snorting and gulping slowly calm themselves . . . and I drift into sleep.

I wake early, lying quiet while my eyes adjust to the light in the room. The room is bright, in spite of the early hour, but it's a cold light, chilly and diffuse, and looking out over the Reach I see that a sea mist has drifted in up the estuary to wrap the Mill and its surroundings in a fine gray gauze. There is a cobweb across part of the window, jeweled with microscopic droplets, and I watch it for a while, reminded unsettlingly of the clinging nets in Salten village.

The air is cold on my arms, and I pull up the blankets and roll over to check on Freya, uncharacteristically quiet in the cradle beside me.

What I see makes my heart seem to stop in my chest, and then restart, thumping at a hundred miles an hour.

Freya is not there.

Freya is not there.

Before I can think I have stumbled out of bed, shaking as if I've been given an electric shock. I'm searching in the covers of the bed—stupidly, for I know I put her down in the wooden cradle last night and she's not even crawling yet, let alone able to climb the side of the cot and crawl into bed.

Freya. Oh Jesus.

I am making little whimpering noises in my throat, unable to believe she's not here, and then I burst out of the room and down the corridor.

"Kate!" It's meant to be a shout, but panic makes the

words stick and choke in my throat, and it sounds like a strangled cry of fear. "Kate!"

"Down here!" she calls, and I stumble down the wooden stairs, barking my heels, missing the last step and staggering into the kitchen so that Kate looks up from where she's standing at the sink, her surprise turning to concern as she sees me standing there, wild-eyed and empty-armed.

"Kate," I manage. "Freya—she—she's gone!"

Kate puts down the coffeemaker she has been rinsing and I see, as I say the words, her expression turning to a look of . . . can it be guilt?

"I'm so sorry," she says, and she points to the rug behind me. I whirl round—and she's there. Freya is there. Sitting on the rug with a piece of bread in her fist, and she looks up at me and gives a shriek of happiness, throwing the mushed-up toast onto the rug and holding out her arms to be picked up.

I snatch her up, my heart thrumming in my chest as I press her to me. I can't speak. I don't know what to say.

"I'm sorry," Kate repeats guiltily. "I—It didn't occur to me you'd worry. I must have woken her up when I used the bathroom, because I heard her when I came out—you were still asleep and I just thought—" She twists her fingers. "You always look so tired. I thought you'd like a lie-in."

I say nothing, letting my racing heartbeat subside, feeling Freya's small pink fingers tangle in my hair, smelling the baby smell of her head and feeling her weight in my arms . . . oh God. It's okay. Everything is okay.

My legs are suddenly weak with relief and I sit on the sofa.

"I'm sorry," Kate says again. She rubs the sleep out

of her eyes. "I should have realized you'd wonder where she was."

"It's okay," I manage at last. Freya pats my cheek, trying to make me look at her. She knows something is wrong, she just can't tell what. I force a smile as I look down at her, wondering what's happened to me, what kind of person I am becoming, if my first reaction on finding my child gone is to imagine she's been snatched. "I'm sorry," I say to Kate. My voice trembles a little, and I take a deep breath, trying to calm my breathing. "I don't know why I panicked so much. I'm just . . . I'm kind of on edge at the moment."

Her eyes meet mine in rueful acknowledgment.

"Me too."

She turns back to the sink.

"Want a coffee?"

"Sure."

Kate puts the machine on the stove, and as we both sit there, listening to the silence before it begins to wheeze and hiss, she says, "Thanks."

I look up, surprised.

"Thanks for what? Shouldn't I be saying that?"

"For coming down at such short notice. I know it's a lot to ask."

"It's nothing," I say, although that's not true. Choosing Kate may have been the last straw between Owen and me, and that's frightening. "Tell me . . . tell me about the police," I say instead, trying not to think about what I may have done.

Kate doesn't answer straightaway, instead she turns back to where the moka pot is hissing and takes it off the heat, pours out two small cups, and brings one across to me. I put Freya back down on the rug, as I take it, careful not to put it anywhere her soft chubby hands can reach.

"That fucking Mark Wren," Kate says at last, as she curls onto the armchair opposite. "He came to see me. Full of '*This must be a difficult time for you*,' but he knows. I don't know what Mary's told him, but he knows something's not right."

"So the body . . . it's definitely been identified?" I ask, even though I know it has, I've seen the newspaper reports. But somehow I need to hear from Kate's lips, see her reaction as she tells me.

There is nothing I can glean from her expression, though, as she nods in weary confirmation.

"Yes, it's definite, I think. They took a DNA swab from me, but I think they know it's pretty much a certainty. They said something about dental records, and they showed me his ring."

"Did they ask you to identify it?"

"Yes, I said it was his. It seemed . . . well. It seemed foolish not to."

I nod. Kate's right, of course. Part of the Lying Game was always to know when the game was up, when to bail out. Rule five—know when to stop lying. *Throw in your hand before the shit hits the fan*, as Thee used to put it. The trick was to know when you'd got to that point. But I'm not sure if we've succeeded this time. It feels like the trouble is coming no matter what we do.

"So what next?"

"They've asked me to come in and make a statement, about the night he disappeared. But that's the thing, we need to decide—do I tell them you were all here?" She rubs her hands over her face, the shadows beneath her eyes brown against her olive skin. "I don't know what to say for the best. I could tell them I called you, when I found Dad was missing—asked you to come over. We could back up each other's stories—just say we were all here, but there was no sign of Dad and you left early. But then they'll ask you all for statements, too. It all comes down to what the school knows."

"What the school knows?" I echo stupidly.

"About that night. Did anyone see you leave? If I say you weren't here and people find out you were, it could all backfire."

I understand. I try to think back. We were in our rooms when she came to find us, but Miss Weatherby, she saw our clothes, the mud on my sandals. And she said something, in her office, something about us breaking out of bounds, about a witness . . .

"I think we were seen," I say reluctantly. "Or at least, Miss Weatherby said we were. She didn't say who. We didn't admit anything—well, I didn't; I don't know about Fatima and Thea."

"Fuck. So I'll have to tell them I was here that night, and you were, too. And that means you'll all be dragged in for questioning, probably." Her face is white, and I know what she is thinking—it's not just the worry about the distress this will cause to the rest of us, there's a more practical, more selfish element to it, too. Whether four sets of stories can hold together under questioning. Whether someone might crack . . .

I think about Thea, about her drinking, about the marks on her arms, about the toll that this is taking on her. And I think about Fatima, and her newfound faith. Sincere repentance, she said. What if that includes confession, as part of making things right? Surely Allah can't forgive someone who continues to lie and cover up?

And I think, too, about the pictures. Those bloody pictures in the mail. About the fact that there is someone else out there who knows something.

"Kate," I say, and I swallow, and then stop. She turns

to look at me, and I force myself on. "There's something I have to tell you. Fatima and Thea and I, we got . . . we got some pictures. In the mail. Copies. Of drawings."

Kate's face changes, and I realize she knows already what I am going to say. I am not sure whether that makes it easier, or harder, but I force myself onwards, bringing the words out in a rush so I can't lose my nerve.

"Did you *really* destroy all the pictures your dad did of us?"

"Yes," Kate says. Her face is wretched. "I swear it. But not . . ." She stops, and suddenly I don't want to hear what she's about to say, but it's too late. She presses her lips together in a white, bloodless line. "But not straightaway."

"What do you mean?"

"I couldn't bring myself to burn them right after he died, I meant to, but I just—I don't know, I could never find the right time. But one day I went up to his studio and someone had been there."

"What?" I don't try to hide my shock. "When was this?"

"Years ago. Not long after it all happened. There were paintings missing, and drawings, and I knew someone had been in there looking. I burned them all after that, I swear it, but then the letters started."

I feel coldness drip through me like poison.

"Letters?"

"It was just one at first." Kate's voice is low. "I sold a painting of Dad's. The auction was reported in the local press along with what it sold for, and a few weeks later I got a letter asking for money. It didn't make any threats, just asked for a hundred pounds to be left in an envelope behind a loose panel in the Salten Arms. I did nothing, and a few weeks later the letter came again, only this time it was asking for two hundred and there was a drawing enclosed."

"A drawing of us." My voice is flat, sick. Kate nods.

"I paid up. The letters came again, every now and again, maybe one every six months, and I paid and paid, but at last I wrote a letter saying that was it, I couldn't pay anymore—that the Mill was sinking and Dad's paintings were gone, and they could ask all they wanted but the money just wasn't there. And the letters stopped."

"When was that?"

"About two or three years ago. I didn't hear anything after that, and I thought it had stopped, but then a few weeks ago they started again. First it was the sheep and then . . ." She swallows. "Then after you left, I got a letter saying, *Why don't you ask your friends?* But I never dreamed . . ."

"Jesus Christ, Kate!" I stand up, too full of nerves to keep still, but there is nowhere to go and I sit again, picking restlessly at the frayed material of the sofa. I want to say, *Why didn't you tell us?* But I know why. Because Kate has been trying to protect us, all these years. I want to ask, *Why didn't you go to the police?* But I know that, too. I want to say, *They're only pictures.* But we know—we both know—that's not true. The pictures don't matter. It's the note with the sheep that tells the whole story.

"I keep wondering . . ." Kate says in a low voice, and then stops.

"Go on," I prompt her. She twists her fingers together, and then gets up and goes across to the dresser. In one of the drawers is a sheaf of papers, bound together with a piece of red string, and right in the middle of the sheaf is a letter in an envelope, very old and creased. It's a letter that makes my heart stutter in my chest.

"Is that—" I manage, and Kate nods.

"I kept it. I didn't know what else to do."

She holds it out to me, and for a minute I'm reluctant to take it, thinking of forensics and fingerprints, but it's too late. We handled that note seventeen years ago, all of us. I take it, very gently, as though using the tips of my fingers will make it harder to trace back to me, but I don't open it. I don't need to. Now that the letter is in my hands, the phrases float up from the deep water of my memory—*so sorry . . . don't blame yourself, my sweet . . . the only thing I can do to make things right . . .*

"Should I give it to Mark Wren?" Kate asks huskily. "I mean, it might stop this whole thing. It answers so many questions . . ."

But it raises so many more. Like, why didn't Kate go to the police with this note seventeen years ago?

"What would you say?" I say at last. "About where you found it? How would you explain it?"

"I don't know. I could say I found it that night, but I didn't tell anyone—I could say the truth, basically, that Dad was gone, that I was afraid of losing the house. But I don't have to involve the rest of you—the burial, everything else; I could leave that out. Or I could say that I only found it later, months afterwards."

"God, Kate, I don't know." I scrub my fists into my eyes, trying to chase away the remnants of bleary-eyed exhaustion that seem to be stopping me from thinking properly. Behind my lids, lights spark and dark flowers bloom. "All those stories, they seem to be asking more questions than they answer and besides—"

And then I stop.

"Besides what?" Kate says, and there's a note in her voice I can't quite read. Defensiveness? Fear?

Shit. I did not mean to go down this route. But I

can't think what else to say. Rule four of the Lying Game—we don't lie to each other, right?

"Besides . . ." I say slowly. "If you give them that note they'll want to verify it."

"What do you mean?"

"Kate, I have to ask this." I swallow, trying to think of a way to phrase it that doesn't sound like I am thinking what I'm thinking. "Please understand, whatever you say, whatever happened, I won't judge you. I just have to know—you owe us that, right?"

"Isa, you're scaring me," Kate says flatly, but there's something in her eyes I don't like, something worried and evasive.

"That note. It—it doesn't add up. You know it doesn't. Ambrose committed suicide because of the drawings, that's what we always thought, right?"

Kate nods, but slowly, like she's wary of where I am going.

"But the timings are all wrong—the drawings didn't turn up at school until *after* he died." I swallow. I think of Kate's facility for forgery, of the paintings she faked for years after Ambrose's death. I think of the black-mail demands she has been paying for more than fifteen years, rather than go to the police with this note—demands she has concealed from us, though we had a right to know. "Kate, I guess what I'm asking is . . . did Ambrose definitely write that note?"

"He wrote that note," she says, and her face is hard.

"But it doesn't make *sense*. And look, he took a heroin overdose, right? That's what we've always thought. But then why were his works all neatly packed up in the tin? Wouldn't he have just shot up and dropped them beside his chair?"

"He wrote that note," Kate repeats doggedly. "If anyone should know, I should."

"It's just—" I stop. I can't think how to say this, say what I'm thinking. Kate squares her shoulders, pulls her dressing gown around herself.

"What are you asking, Isa? Are you asking if I killed my own father?"

There is silence.

The words are shocking, spoken aloud like that— my vague, amorphous suspicions given concrete shape and edges hard enough to wound.

"I don't know," I say at last. My voice is croaky. "I'm asking . . . I'm asking if there's something else we should know before we go into that police interview."

"There is nothing else you need to know." Her voice is stony.

"There's nothing else we need to know, or there's nothing else, full stop?"

"There's nothing else you need to know."

"So there *is* something else? You're just not telling me what?"

"For fuck's sake, please stop asking me, Isa!" Her face is anguished, and she paces to the window, Shadow feeling her distress and pacing with her. "There's nothing else I can tell you—please, please believe me."

"Thea said—" I start, and then feel my courage almost fail, but I have to ask it. I have to know. "Kate, Thea said Ambrose was sending you away. Is that true? Why? Why would he do that?"

For a minute Kate stares at me, frozen, her face white.

And then she makes a noise like a sob and turns away, snatching up her coat and slinging it on over her pajamas, shoving her feet into the mud-spattered Wellingtons that stand beside the doorway. She grabs Shadow's lead, the dog anxiously following at her heels, his gaze turned up to Kate's, trying to understand her

When I go up to put Freya down for her nap, I can hear her, pacing about on the floor above, even see her shape occasionally through the bare gappy boards as her silhouette passes across a window, blocking out the slivers of gray light that filter down through the cracks.

Freya is hard to get to sleep, but at last she's slumbering, and I go back down to the living room to try to sit at the window, watching the restless waters of the Reach. It's not quite four o'clock, and the tide is almost at its height, an exceptionally high tide, one of the highest since we've been here. The jetty is awash, and when the wind blows off the Reach, water comes lapping in beneath the doors to the seaward side of the Mill.

The mist has lifted slightly, but the sky is still cloudy and chill, and it's hard to remember the heat of just a few weeks ago as I sit, watching the iron-gray water slapping at the boards outside. Did we really swim in that estuary earlier this month? It seems impossible that it could be the same place as the warm, balmy water where we floated and swam and laughed. Everything has changed.

I shiver, and wrap my jumper around myself. I packed badly—shoving stuff into my shoulder bag without looking, and I have too many pairs of jeans and lightweight tops, and not enough warm clothes for the weather, but I'm too cowardly to ask Kate to lend me something of hers. I can't face her, not now, not today. Tomorrow, perhaps, when all this has blown over.

There's a pile of books on the floor by the window, the covers curling with damp, and I walk across and pick one at random. Bill Bryson—*Notes from a Small Island*. The cover is neon-bright and incongruously cheerful against the muted colors of the Mill, damp-stained wood and bleached cottons. I go across to the light switch to try to brighten the place up—and it fizzes against my hand, making me jump. From somewhere behind me there is a loud bang, and the light flashes once, unnaturally bright, and then goes dead.

The fridge gives a shuddering groan and stops its imperceptible hum. *Shit*.

"Kate," I call cautiously, not wanting to wake Freya, but she doesn't answer. I hear her feet pacing back and forth, though, and a check in the movement as I call, so I think she has heard. "Kate, a fuse has blown."

No answer.

There's a cupboard under the stairs and I put my head inside, but it's pitch-black, and although there is something that looks like it could be a fuse box, it's not the modern installation Kate mentioned. It's black Bakelite mounted on wood, with what looks like a tar-stained hank of cord coming out of one side, and some Victorian lead wiring coming out of the other. I don't dare to touch it.

Fuck.

I pick up my mobile, and I am about to google "how to reset a fuse box" when I see something that makes my heart stutter. There's an e-mail from Owen.

I click, my heart in my mouth.

Please, please, please let it be an apology for our quarrel—anything would do, any kind of halfway house that would enable me to climb down from the high horse I'm on. He must know, in the cold light of day, that his accusations were ridiculous. A bunch of roses and a trip to see an old friend equating to an affair? It's paranoid, and he's surely realized that.

But it's not an apology. It's not even really an e-mail, and at first I don't understand what it's saying.

There's no *Hey, love*, or even *Dear Isa*. There's no self-justification or groveling, pleading. In fact there's no text at all, and for a minute I wonder if he's sent me an e-mail meant for someone else.

It's a list of offenses, dates, and locations, without any names or context attached. There's a shoplifting offense in Paris, joyriding in some French suburb I've never heard of, aggravated assault in a seaside resort in Normandy. At the beginning of the list the dates are twenty years ago, but they become more recent as I scan down, though there are long gaps, sometimes spanning several years. The later ones are all in southern England. Drunk driving near Hastings, a caution for possession in Brighton, taken into custody after a brawl somewhere in Kent but released without charge, more cautions. The last incident is just a couple of weeks ago—drunk and disorderly near Rye, a night spent in the cells, no charges. What *are* they?

And then suddenly I understand.

This is Luc's police record.

I feel sick. I don't even want to know how Owen got hold of all this, and so quickly. He knows people—police, MI5 officers—and has a senior position in the Home Office in his own right, with high-level security clearance, but this is a gross violation of professional conduct however you look at it.

But it's not just that. It's the fact that this shows he is not climbing down, he still believes Luc is the reason I've come down here. He still believes I am fucking another man.

I feel anger flood through me, making the skin on the back of my neck prickle and my fingers tingle with fury.

I want to scream. I want to phone him up and tell him he's a bastard, and that the trust he's broken may never be mended.

But I don't. Partly because I am so angry, I'm not sure if I can trust myself not to say something unforgivable.

But partly because I know, and a small part of me is ready to admit that fact, that he is not *completely* to blame.

Yes, he's to blame, of course he is. We've been together for almost ten years, and in that time I've never so much as kissed another man. I've done nothing to deserve being treated like this.

But Owen knows I am lying to him. He's not a fool. He knows it—and he's right.

He just doesn't know why.

I crush my phone in my fist until it makes a faint complaining buzzing sound to tell me I'm holding it too tight, and I force my grip on the plastic to relax, and flex my fingers.

Fuck. *Fuck.*

It's the insult I can't stand—the idea that I would reel straight from his bed to Luc's—and if he wasn't Freya's father, that alone would be enough for me to end it. I've had jealous boyfriends in the past, and they're poison—poison to the relationship and poison to your self-esteem. You end up looking over your shoulder, second-guessing your own motives. *Was* I flirting with that man? I didn't mean to. *Did* I look at his friend like I wanted some? *Was* my top too low, my skirt too short, my smile too bright?

You stop trusting yourself, self-doubt filling the place where love and confidence used to be.

I want to phone him up and tell him that's it—if he can't trust me, it's over. I won't live like this, suspected of something I haven't done, forced to deny infidelities that exist only in his mind.

But . . . even aside from my own part in all this, can I do that to Freya? I know what it's like, living without a parent. I know only too well, and I don't want that for her.

There is a thick blanket of cloud covering the sky, and the Mill feels dark and chilly, the stove burning low behind its little door, and suddenly, as I hear Freya stirring from above, her wakening whimper drifting down the stairs, I know I have to get out. I will go to the pub for dinner. Maybe I can find something out, talk to Mary Wren about the police investigation. Whatever, it's plain that Kate isn't about to come down anytime soon, and even if she did, I'm not sure if I could face her, if I could sit there over dinner, exchanging small talk, with the specter hanging between us, and Owen's e-mail like poison in my phone.

I run upstairs to the bedroom and wrestle Freya into a coat. Then I make sure the rain guard is packed beneath the pram and push her out onto the sandy shore, the wind in our faces as we turn to begin the walk to Salten.

I have a long time to think on the cold, windswept walk to Salten village, my feet eating up the distance mile by slow, chilly mile. My mind seesaws between dwelling resentfully on Owen's failings as a partner and the guilty consciousness that I haven't behaved perfectly to him. I tick off his faults in my head—his short-fused temper, his possessiveness, the way he plows ahead with plans without asking me what I think.

But other memories intrude. The curve of his spine as he bends over the bath, pouring warm water over our daughter's head. His kindness; his resourcefulness. His love for me. And Freya.

And beneath it all, like a bass counterpoint, is my own complicity in this. I have lied. I have lied and concealed and withheld from him. I've been keeping secrets since the day I met him, but these last few weeks have been on a different scale, and he knows something is wrong. Owen has always been possessive, but he was never jealous before—not like this. And that is down to me. I have made him like this. *We* have. Me, Fatima, Thea, and Kate.

I hardly notice the distance, so wrapped am I in my thoughts, but I am no nearer making any decisions by the time the far-off smudges in the mist resolve into houses and buildings.

As I round the corner towards the Salten Arms, flexing my cold fingers on the pram handle and brushing away the puddle of rainwater that has gathered in the hood, I can hear music. Not piped music, but the warm now that we're out of the cool bathroom. She manages to unpop the rain cover with one particularly bad-tempered shove, and gives a little squeal of triumph, and I pick her up, shushing her against my shoulder. "You don't mind babies in the bar, do you?"

"Not so long as they drink beer," Jerry says, and he grins his whiskery, gap-toothed grin. "What can I get you?"

"Are you serving food?"

"Not until six, but it's . . ." He glances up at the clock above the bar. "Well, it's all but now, here's the menu."

He pushes a grubby piece of dog-eared paper across the bar and I study it. Sandwiches . . . fish pie . . . dressed crab . . . burger and chips . . .

"I'll have the fish pie," I say at last. "And . . . and maybe a glass of white wine."

Well, why not. It is almost six.

"Want to start a tab?"

"Sure. Do you want a card?" I'm feeling in my hand-bag but he laughs and shakes his head.

"I knows where to find you."

I'm not sure how, but he manages to make the well-worn phrase sound faintly threatening, but I smile and nod towards the back room, which is quieter, with a couple of free tables.

"I'll sit through there, if that's okay?"

"You do that, I'll bring the drink across meself. You won't want to be carrying it with the little'un."

I nod, and make my way through the back room, where there are just two tables left empty. One is by the door and strewn with greasy pint glasses. Someone has knocked out their pipe on the wood and left the contents there. The other, in the corner, isn't much better. There is a wasp buzzing in a puddle of spilled beer, trapped beneath an upturned glass, and the blistered faux-leather seat is covered in dog hair, but it has space for Freya's pram, so I clear the debris to the other table, give the surface a cursory wipe with a beer mat, and settle us both down, wedging the pram in the gap. Freya is squirming in my arms and head-butting my chest, and I can see I'm not going to be able to stretch her feed until I get back; she has decided it's time, and is about to kick off any minute. It's not where I'd choose to feed her—I've fed in pubs before, often, but almost always with Owen present, and to be honest, in London no one would care if you breastfed a cat. Here, by myself, it feels very different and I'm not sure how Jerry and his regulars will react, but I don't really have a choice unless I want Freya exploding. I unbutton my coat and rearrange my layers for maximum modesty, then clamp her on as quickly as I can and let my coat fall to shield us both.

A few heads turn as she latches on, and one old man with a white beard stares with frank curiosity. I'm just thinking, with a little shift in my stomach, what Kate said about the salacious old men gossiping in the Salten Arms, when Jerry comes up with a glass of white on a tray and a knife and fork wrapped in a paper napkin.

"We ought to charge corkage on that," he says with a grin and a nod at my chest, and I feel the color rise in my cheeks. I manage a slightly thin laugh.

"Sorry, she was hungry. You don't mind, do you?"

"Not I. And I'm sure the rest of 'em won't mind an eyeful, neither." He cackles fruitily, a noise that's picked up like a wheezing echo by his cronies at the bar, and I feel my face begin to burn. More heads are turning, and the white-haired old man gives me a bleary wink and then guffaws, scratching at his crotch as he whispers something to his friend, nodding towards where I sit.

I am seriously considering telling Jerry to cancel the fish pie and walking out, when he slides the glass across the table and then nods back towards the bar. "Drink's on your friend, by the way."

My friend? I look up, and my eyes meet . . . Luc Rochefort's.

He is sitting by the bar, and as I watch, he raises his glass to me, his expression a little . . . rueful? I'm not sure.

I think of Owen. Of that e-mail he sent me. Of what he would say if he walked into the bar right now, and I feel again that unsettling shift in my stomach, but before I can think what to say, Jerry has gone, and I realize that Luc is standing up, walking towards me.

There's no escape. I'm penned in by the pram to my left and a group of people's chairs to my right, and I'm handicapped by Freya clamped to my bare breast beneath my coat. There's no way I can get out before he makes it across. I can't even rise to meet him without something going astray and Freya kicking off.

I think about the bloodied sheep.

I think about Freya in his arms, wailing.

I think about the drawings, about Owen's suspicions, and my cheeks flame, and I can't tell whether it's with anger . . . or something else.

"Look," I say as he comes closer, his pint in his hand. I want to be brave, confrontational, but I'm shrinking back against the padded bench almost in spite of myself. "Look, Luc—"

"I'm sorry," he says abruptly, cutting across me. "About what happened. With your baby." His face is set, his eyes dark in the dim light of the back room. "I was trying to help, but it was a stupid thing to do, I realize that now."

It is not what I was expecting him to say, and the

wind is taken out of my sails, so that my speech about keeping the hell away from me falters and I'm not sure what to say.

"The drink—I know, it's pointless, but I—it was a peace offering. I'm sorry. I won't bother you again."

He turns to go, something rises up inside me, a kind of desperation, and to my own astonishment I find myself blurting out, "Wait."

He turns back, his expression guarded. He's refusing to catch my eye, but there's something there . . . a sort of hope?

"You—you shouldn't have taken Freya," I say at last. "But I accept your apology."

He stands there, mutely, towering over the table and then he ducks his head in awkward acknowledgment and our eyes meet. Perhaps it's his uncertainty, the way he's standing with his shoulders hunched, like a child who has outgrown their own height. Or perhaps it's the expression in his eyes, the way they hold mine with a kind of painful vulnerability, but for a minute he looks so like his fifteen-year-old self that my heart seems to catch and skip.

I swallow against the pain in my throat, the pain that is always there, lately—my old symptom of stress and anxiety.

I think of Owen and his accusations, of the act he already thinks I've committed . . . and I feel a recklessness take hold.

"Luc, I—Do you want to sit down?"

He doesn't speak. For a minute I think he's going to pretend he didn't hear me, turn away.

But then he himself swallows, the muscles moving in his throat.

"Are you sure?" he asks.

I nod, and he pulls back a chair and sits, holding his

pint in one hand, staring down into the deep amber liquid.

There is a long silence, and the men at the bar turn away, as if Luc's presence is some sort of shield against their curiosity. I feel Freya's strong suck, her hands flexing against me. Luc sits, not looking at the two of us, his eyes averted.

"Did you . . . did you hear the news?" he asks at last.

"About the—" I stop. I want to say *about the bones*, but somehow I can't make myself say the words. He nods.

"They've identified the body. It's Ambrose."

"I heard." I swallow again. "Luc, I'm so, so sorry."

"Thanks," he says. His French accent is stronger, as it often is at moments of stress. He shakes his head, as if trying to push away unwanted thoughts. "I was . . . surprised how much it hurt."

My breath catches in my throat, and I realize afresh what we did—the life sentence that we inflicted not just on ourselves, but on Luc.

"Have . . . have you told your mother?" I manage.

"No. She wouldn't care anymore. And she doesn't deserve that name," Luc says, very quietly.

I take a gulp of wine, trying to calm my heart, which is hammering, and soothe the pain in my throat.

"She . . . she was an addict, right?"

"Yes. Heroin. And later méthadone."

He pronounces the word the French way, may-tadon, and for a moment I don't understand, then I realize and I bite my lip, wishing I had never brought up the subject. Luc is silent, staring down at his pint, and I don't know what to say, how to retrieve this. He came here to try to make things right between us, and all I've done is remind him of everything he lost.

I'm saved from speaking by the arrival of a young girl with a plate of steaming fish pie. She puts it down in front of me without preamble, and says, "Sauces?"

"No," I say, with difficulty. "No, thanks. I'm fine."

I put a spoonful of pie to my mouth. It's rich and creamy and the cheese on top is golden and bubbled, but it tastes of sawdust. The soft flakes in my mouth crumble, and I feel the scratch of a bone at the back of my throat as I force down the mouthful.

Luc says nothing; he just sits, in quiet thought. His big hands rest on the table, his fingers curled loosely, and I remember that morning in the post office, his contained fury, the cuts on his knuckles and the sense of fear I had at his presence. I think about the sheep, and about the blood on his hands . . . and I wonder.

Luc is angry, I know that. But if I were him, I would be angry, too.

IT IS MUCH LATER. FREYA is asleep, sprawled against my chest, and Luc and I have fallen silent after hours of talking. Now we are just sitting, side by side, watching her breathe, thinking our own thoughts.

When the bell goes for last orders I can't quite believe it, and have to get out my phone to check that, yes, it really is ten to eleven.

"Thank you," I say to Luc, as he stands and stretches, and he looks surprised.

"What for?"

"For tonight. I—I needed to get out, to forget everything for a little bit." I realize, as I say the words, that I have not thought of Owen for hours, nor Kate. I rub my face, stretch my cramped limbs.

"It was nothing." He stands, and then takes Freya from me, very gently, so that I can squeeze out from behind the little table. I watch as he cradles her inexpertly against his chest, and find myself smiling as she gives a little sigh and snuggles into his warmth.

"You're a natural. Do you want kids?"

"I won't have children." He says it matter-of-factly, and I look up in surprise.

"Really? Why not? Don't you like them?"

"It's not that. I didn't have the best childhood. You get fucked-up, you're liable to pass that on."

"Bullshit." I take Freya from him as he holds her out and put her tenderly into her pram, resting my hand gently on her chest as her eyelids flutter open and then close again in capitulation. "If that were true, none of us would ever reproduce. We've all got baggage. What about all the good qualities you've got to pass on?"

"There's nothing about me any child should have," he says, and for a minute I think he's joking, but he's not, his face is serious, and sad. "And I won't risk giving another kid an upbringing like mine."

"Luc . . ." I don't know what to say. "That—that's so sad. I'm sure you wouldn't be anything like your mother."

"You can't know that."

"No, but no one knows for sure what kind of parent they'll be. Crap people have babies every day—but the difference is they don't care. You do—that's what makes the difference."

He shrugs, puts his arms into his jacket, and then helps me into mine.

"It doesn't matter. I'm not having children. I don't want to bring a child into a world like this."

His words shock me in some way I can't define—it's not the first time I've heard people say things like that, but it's the first time I've heard it said so matter-of-factly. And tonight, full of wine and food and warmth and companionship—it's not something I can believe. It's not something I *want* to believe.

Out in the car park Luc pushes his hands in his pockets, hunches his shoulders.

"Can I walk you home?"

"It'll be miles out of your way."

But I realize as soon as I've said it that I have no idea where he lives. Still, the Mill can't possibly be on the way anywhere, can it?

"Not really out of my way," he says. "My rooms are on the coast road, out towards the school. The quickest way is across the marsh."

Oh. It explains a lot. Not least, why he was passing the Mill the night we went to the alumnae ball. I feel a faint twinge of guilt at disbelieving his story.

I don't know what to say.

Do I trust Luc? No, is the answer. But since my conversation with Kate this morning, the way she ran rather than answer my questions . . . I'm no longer sure if I trust anyone in this place.

I DIDN'T BRING A TORCH, and with the cloud cover the night is very dark. We walk slowly, me pushing the pram, Luc picking our route, both of us talking quietly. A truck passes in the darkness, its headlamps throwing our shadows long and black on the road ahead, and Luc raises a hand in greeting as it passes and disappears into the darkness.

". . . night, Luc . . ." comes faintly from one of the windows, and it strikes me that in a way, Luc has succeeded where Kate has not. He has made a life for himself here, become part of the community, while she is still an outsider, just as Mary said.

We are just at the bridge over the Reach when I find I have a stone in my shoe and we pause for me to get it out. While I hop on one leg and then wriggle the shoe back on my bare foot, Luc leans his elbows on the railings, looking out down the estuary towards the sea. The fog has lifted, but with the clouds so low and thick, the Reach is shrouded in darkness and there is nothing to see, not even the faint glimmer of lights from the Mill. His face is unreadable, but I am thinking of the little white tent, hidden in the darkness, and I wonder if he is, too.

When my shoe is back on, I move to stand beside him and rest my own arms on the bridge. Even though we're not touching, our forearms are so close I can feel the heat of his bare skin striking through the thin material of my coat.

"Luc," I begin, but suddenly and almost without warning, he turns, and then his lips are warm on mine and I feel a rush of desire so strong it almost blindsides me, a liquid heat, low in my belly.

For a moment I do nothing, just stand there with my fingers splayed against his ribs, and his mouth hot against mine, and my heart beating like a drum in my chest. And then the realization of what I'm doing breaks over me like a cold wave.

"Luc, no!"

"I'm sorry." His face is stricken. "I'm so sorry—I don't know what I was—"

He breaks off, and we stand, facing each other, our breath coming as quick and shallow as each other's, and I know the confusion and distress that's in his face must be mirrored in my own.

"*Merde*," he spits, suddenly, hitting his fist against the railing. "Why do I always fuck things up?"

"Luc, you didn't—you don't—"

The pain in my throat is back, hurting when I swallow.

"I'm married," I say, although it's not true, but it is in all the ways that matter. Whatever troubles we're having, Owen is the father of my child, and he and I are together—that's it. I'm not going to play around.

"I know," he says, his voice very low, and he doesn't look at me as he turns and begins to walk across the bridge, towards the Mill.

He is a few paces ahead when he speaks again, so softly that I'm not sure if I heard what he said right.

"I made such a mistake . . . I should have chosen you."

I should have chosen you.

What does it mean? I want to bring it up, as we walk slowly along the rutted path beside the Reach, but Luc's silence is unapproachable, and I can't find a way to ask the questions clamoring inside me.

What did he mean? What *happened* with him and Kate?

But I can't find a way of asking, and besides, I am afraid. Afraid of what he might ask me in return. I can't demand the truth when I'm hiding so many lies of my own.

Instead, I concentrate on wheeling Freya's pram around puddles and trenches in the rutted path. It has rained heavily while I was in the pub, and away from the tarmac, the track is soft.

I'm painfully aware of Luc beside me, measuring his pace to mine, and at last I make a halfhearted attempt at disengaging, letting him make his own way back.

"You don't have to walk me the whole way, you know, if you want to cut off here, save yourself the walk . . ."

But he shakes his head.

"You'll need a hand."

It's only when we get to the Mill that I realize what he means.

The tide is high—higher than I've ever seen it. The wooden walkway is invisible—fully submerged, and almost impossible to see in the pitch-blackness. Beyond the tract of sluggish dark water, the black silhouette of the Mill is cut off from the shore completely. The bridge can't be more than a few inches beneath the surface, but I can barely see where the shore ends and the water begins, let alone the dissolving shape of the dark planks in the water.

If it were just me, I might risk it, but with the pram? It's heavy, and if one of the wheels edges off the walkway in the darkness, I'm not sure I'll be strong enough to stop the whole thing from toppling into the water.

I can feel the dismay in my face as I turn to Luc.

"Shit, what do I do?"

He glances up at the darkened windows.

"Looks like Kate's out. She could have left a light on." His voice is bitter.

"There was a power cut," I say. Luc shrugs, an inexpressibly Gallic gesture that is halfway between resignation and contempt, and I feel like I should defend Kate, but there is nothing I can say to Luc's silent disapproval, especially when a little voice in the back of my head is whispering my own resentment. How could Kate have just gone out and left me to deal with this alone? She had no way of knowing I'd have Luc to help.

"Take your baby," he says, gesturing to the pram, and I pick up Freya. She is sleeping, and when I lift her she curls with compact heaviness against my shoulder like an ammonite made flesh.

"What are you—?"

But I break off, as Luc pulls off his shoes, picks up the pram, and splashes into the dark water. It closes above his ankles, halfway up his calves.

"Luc, be careful! You don't know—"

But he knows. I don't know how, but he knows exactly where the bridge is. He wades unerringly across the gap, with me holding my breath with every step in case he misses and stumbles off the edge into the deep water, but he doesn't. He reaches the other side, now a narrow slip of bank barely wide enough to rest the pram on, and tries the door.

It's unlocked, and it swings wide to show an empty blackness. Luc wheels the pram inside.

"Kate?" His voice echoes through the silent house. I hear a click as he tries the light switch, flicking it back and forth. Nothing happens. "Kate?"

He reemerges back on the bank, shrugs, and hitching up his jeans he begins to wade empty-handed to the shore.

On the bank, I try for a laugh.

"This is like one of those logic puzzles. You've got a duck, a fox, and a boat . . ."

He smiles, the tanned skin at the side of his eyes and mouth crinkling, and I realize with a shock how alien the expression looks on his face. How little I've seen him smile since I returned.

"So how do we do this?" he asks. "Do you trust me to take Freya?"

I hesitate, and the smile drops from his eyes as he sees.

"I—I do trust you," I say quickly, though it's not completely true. "It's not that. But she doesn't know you—I'm worried if she wakes up and starts trying to get free—she's surprisingly strong when she doesn't want to be held on to."

"Okay," he says. "So . . . what do you think? I could carry you, but I'm not sure the bridge would take the weight of us both."

I start laughing at that.

"I'm not letting you carry me, Luc. Bridge or no bridge."

He shrugs.

"I've done it before."

And I realize with a flicker of shock that he's right.

I had completely forgotten, but now that he says it, the picture is sharp in my mind—a sunbaked beach, high tide, my shoe got swept away. There was no way back except over the barnacled rocks, and after a quarter of an hour watching me hobble on bleeding feet, Kate and Thea and Fatima wincing in sympathy, offering me shoes I wouldn't accept and couldn't fit into, Luc had picked me up without a word and carried me, piggyback, the rest of the way to the Tide Mill.

I remember it so well—his hands on my thighs, the muscles in his back moving against my chest, the scent of his neck—warm skin and soap.

I feel myself flush.

"I was fifteen. I'm a bit heavier now."

"Take off your shoes," he says, and I hobble on one foot, trying to hold Freya with one hand while prying off my sandals with the other—and then, before I can protest, he's on his knees, his fingers working the straps. I step out of one shoe, blushing scarlet now, grateful for the darkness, and let him undo the other, before he straightens.

"Take my hand," he says, stepping into the water. "Follow me. Stay very close behind me, as close as you can."

I take his hand with my free one, the arm that's not holding Freya, and I step into the sea.

It's so cold it makes me gasp, but then my bare toes feel something warm—my feet are touching his in the water.

We stand for a moment, steadying each other, and then Luc says, "I'm going to take a big step, you follow me. This is where the rotten board is, we have to step over it."

I nod, remembering the gaps in the bridge, the way I edged the pram over the worst of them. But thank

God Luc was here—I would not have had any idea which boards were sound and where they fell. I watch as he takes a wide stride and then imitate him, but it's a bigger stretch for me than for him, and the boards beneath the waves are slippery. My foot slides on a piece of weed, and I feel myself start to lose balance.

I cry out, without meaning to, the sharp sound ringing across the water. But Luc has me, hard in his grip, his fingers so tight on my upper arm it hurts.

"You're all right," he's saying urgently. "You're all right."

I'm nodding, gasping, trying not to hurt Freya as I regain my balance and try to steady my breathing. A dog in the far distance lets out a volley of barks at my scream, but now it falls silent. Was it Shadow?

"I'm sorry," I say shakily. "It's the boards—they're so slippery."

"It's okay," he says, and his fingers loosen on my arm but don't quite let go. "You're all right."

I nod, and we edge across the last few boards, his grip on my arm firm, but no longer tight enough to hurt.

At the far side I find I'm panting, my heart thumping absurdly in my chest. Amazingly Freya is sleeping steadily.

"Th-thank you," I manage, and my voice is trembling in spite of myself, in spite of the fact I'm on firm ground and safe. "Thank you, Luc, I don't know what I would have done if you hadn't been here."

What *would* I have done? I imagine myself trying to guide the rocking pram across that slippery, treacherous bridge, the wheels sloshing in a foot of water—or sitting down in the cold drizzle to wait for Kate to return from wherever she's gone. Resentment flares again. How could she just disappear like that without so much as a text?

"Do you know where the candles are?" Luc asks, and I shake my head. He clicks his tongue, but whether in disgust or disapproval or what, I can't tell, and he pushes past me into the dark cavern of the Mill. I follow him, standing uncertainly in the middle of the floor. The hem of my sundress is damp and clinging to my legs, and I know I'm probably making a muddy puddle on the floor, and I realize, too, with a sense of chagrin, that my shoes are on the other side of the bridge. Well, never mind. The tide can't possibly get any higher, not without the Mill actually floating away. I'll collect them tomorrow when it subsides.

I'm shivering, too, the cold breeze from the open doorway chilling the wet cloth against my legs, but Luc is busy searching through cupboards, and I hear the rasp of a match, smell paraffin, and see a warm golden flare in the darkness by the sink. Luc is standing, an oil lamp in his hand, adjusting the wick so that the flame burns bright and clear in the little chimney. When it's steady, he slips a frosted glass globe over it, and suddenly the flickering, uncertain light is diffused into a golden glow.

He shuts the door, and we look at each other in the lamplight. The little circle of light is somehow more intimate even than darkness, holding us close in its narrow circle, and we stand just inches apart, suddenly unsure of each other. In the softly piercing light, I can see a vein in Luc's throat is pulsing as quick as my own heart is beating, and a kind of shiver runs through me. He is so hard to read, so impassive—but now I know that's just a surface, that beneath he is as shaken as me, and suddenly I can't bear to meet his eyes anymore, and I have to drop my own gaze, afraid of what he might find there.

He clears his throat, the sound unbearably loud in the quiet house, and we speak at the same time.

"Well, I should—"

"It's probably—"

We stop, laugh nervously.

"You first," I say. He shakes his head.

"No, what were you about to say?"

"Oh—nothing. I was just . . ." I nod down at Freya. "You know. This one. I should probably put her to bed."

"Where's she sleeping?"

"In—" I stop, swallow. "In your old room."

He looks up at that, but I'm not sure if it's surprise, or shock, or what. It must be so strange for him— seeing Kate reallocate his childhood home, and I'm struck again by the unfairness of what happened.

"Oh. I see." The light dips and wavers as if the hand holding the lamp shook a little, but it might have been a draft. "Well, I'll take the lamp up for you—you can't manage a light and a baby up those stairs." He nods at the rickety wooden staircase, spiraling upwards in the corner of the room. "If someone dropped a candle in here the whole place would be in flames in minutes."

"Thanks," I say, and he turns without another word and begins to climb, me following his retreating back, and the circle of light that is disappearing into the rafters.

At the door to his old room he stops, and I hear a sound like a caught breath, but when I draw level with him, his face is almost blank, and he is just staring at the room—at the bed that used to be his, now strewn with my clothes, and the cradle at the foot with Freya's comforter and stuffed elephant. I feel my face burn at my part in all this—at my case spread out across *his* floor, at my bottles and lotions on *his* old desk.

"Luc, I'm so sorry," I say, suddenly desperate.

"Sorry for what?" he asks, his voice as impassive as

his face, but I can see that vein in his throat, and he shakes his head, puts the lamp down on the bedside table, and then turns without a word and disappears into the darkness.

WHEN FREYA IS ASLEEP, I pick up the lamp and make my way cautiously back down the stairs, picking my way in the pool of golden light, which throws more shadows than it dispels.

I was more than half expecting him to be gone, and the ground floor is in darkness, but when I get to the foot of the stairs, I see a shape rise from the sofa, and when I hold the lamp high, it's him.

I put the lamp on the little table beside the sofa, and without a word, as if this is something we've agreed, he takes my face between his hands and kisses me, and this time I don't say anything—I don't protest, I don't push him away—I only kiss him back, running my fingers up beneath his shirt, feeling the smoothness of his skin, and the ridges of bone and muscle and scar and the heat of his mouth.

Outside, on the bridge, when Luc kissed me, I felt like I was betraying Owen, even though I didn't kiss him back, but here—here, I don't feel any guilt at all. This time, this moment, melds seamlessly into all the days and nights and hours I spent back then longing for Luc to kiss me, to touch me—a time before I ever met Owen, before I had Freya, before the drawings and Ambrose's overdose—before any of this.

I could marshal my resentments with Owen, ticking them off on my fingers: the false accusations, the lack of trust, and the crowning insult—that e-mailed list of Luc's criminal convictions, as though *that* of all things would be the one thing that would prevent me from fucking a man I have wanted—and yes, I'm not ashamed to admit it now—a man I have wanted since I was fifteen, and perhaps still do.

But I don't. I don't try to justify what I'm doing. I just let go of the present, let the current tug it from my fingers, and I let myself sink down, down into the past, like a body falling into deep water, and I feel myself drowning, the waters closing over my head as I sink, and I don't even care.

We fall backwards onto the sofa, our limbs entangled, and I help Luc pull his T-shirt over his head. There is an urgent need in the pit of my stomach to feel his skin against mine—a need that outstrips my self-consciousness about my stretch marks and the blue-white slackness of skin that was once tanned and taut.

I know I should be trying to make myself stop, but the truth is, I feel no guilt at all. Nothing else matters, as he begins to undo my dress, one button after another.

My fingers are at Luc's belt, when he stops suddenly and pulls away. My heart stills. My face feels stiff with shame as I sit up, ready to gather my dress around myself and begin the awkward justifications: no, you're right; it's fine—I don't know what I was thinking.

It's only when he goes to the front door and shoots the bolt that I understand, and a kind of dizzying heat washes over me—a realization that this is it, that we are really going to do this.

When he turns back to me, he smiles—a smile that transforms his serious face into the fifteen-year-old I once knew, and my heart seems to rise up inside me, making it hard to breathe, but the pain—the pain that has been there since I found those drawings on the mat, since Owen's angry accusations, since all of this began—that pain is gone.

The soft, saggy sofa sighs as Luc climbs onto it, and

I lie back and he takes me in his arms, and I feel his weight against me. My lips are on his throat, feeling the tenderness of the skin between my teeth, and tasting the salt of his sweat . . . and then suddenly I freeze.

For there, in the shadows at the top of the staircase, something is moving. A figure in the darkness.

Luc stops, raises himself up on his arms, feeling the sudden tense stillness of my muscles.

"Isa? Are you okay?"

I can't speak. My eyes are fixed on the dark space at the stairs. Something—some*one*—is up there.

Pictures flash through my head. A gutted sheep. A bloodstained note. An envelope full of drawings from the past . . .

Luc turns, looks over his shoulder in the direction of my gaze.

The draft of his movement makes the lamp gutter and flare, and for a moment, just the briefest of moments, the flame illuminates the face of the person standing in the darkness, silently watching.

It is Kate.

I make a sound—not a scream, but something close to it, and Kate turns and disappears into the silent upper floors.

Luc is scrabbling his T-shirt back over his head, buttoning his jeans, leaving his belt trailing in his haste. He takes the stairs two at a time, but Kate is too quick for him. She is already halfway up the second flight and I hear the attic door slam and a key turn in a lock, and then Luc hammering at the door.

"Kate. Kate! Let me in!"

No answer.

I begin to rebutton my dress with shaking fingers and then scramble to my feet.

Luc comes back down, his step slow, and his face,

when he comes back into the circle of lamplight, is grim.

"Shit."

"She was there?" I whisper. "All the time? Why didn't she come when we called?"

"Fuck knows." He puts his hands over his face, as if he can grind away the sight of Kate standing there, her face blank and still.

"How long was she standing there?"

"I don't know."

My cheeks burn.

We sit, side by side, on the sofa for a long, silent time. Luc's face is impassive. I don't know what my expression is like, but my thoughts are a confused jumble of emotion and suspicion and despair. What was she *doing* up there, spying on us like that?

I remember the moment the lamp flared, and her face—like a white mask in the darkness, eyes wide, mouth compressed as though she was trying not to cry out. It was the face of a stranger. What has happened to my friend, the woman I thought I knew?

"I should go," Luc says at last, but although he gets to his feet, he doesn't move towards the door. He just stands there, looking at me, his dark brows knitted in a frown, and the shadows beneath his wide cheekbones giving his face a gaunt, haunted look.

There is a noise from upstairs, a whimper from Freya, and I stand up, irresolute, but Luc speaks before I can.

"Don't stay here, Isa. It's not safe."

"*What?*" I stop at that, not trying to hide my shock. "What do you mean?"

"This place—" He waves a hand at the Mill, taking in the water outside, the dead light sockets, the rickety stairs. "But not just that—I—"

He stops, scrubs his free hand into his eyes, and then takes a deep breath.

"I don't want to leave you alone with her."

"Luc, she's your sister."

"She's not my sister, and I know you think she's your friend, but, Isa, you—you can't trust her."

He's lowered his voice to a whisper, even though it's impossible that Kate should hear us—three floors up, and behind a locked door.

I shake my head, refusing to believe it. Whatever Kate has done, whatever strain she's under right now, she is my friend. She has been my friend for almost twenty years. I won't—can't—listen to Luc.

"I don't expect you to believe me." He's speaking hurriedly now. Freya's wail from upstairs gets louder, and I glance at the stairs, wanting to go to her, but Luc is still holding my wrist, his grip gentle but firm. "But just—just please be careful, and listen, I think you should leave the Mill."

"I'll leave tomorrow." I say it with a heaviness, thinking of Owen and what's waiting for me back in London, but Luc shakes his head.

"Now. Tonight."

"Luc, I can't. There's no train until the morning."

"Then come back to my flat. Stay the night. I'll sleep on the sofa," he adds hurriedly, "if that's what you want. But I don't like to think of you here, alone."

I'm not alone, I think. *I have Kate.* But I know that's not what he means.

Freya wails again, and I make up my mind.

"I'm not leaving tonight, Luc. I'm not dragging Freya and my luggage halfway across the marsh in the middle of the night—"

"So get a cab—" he cuts in, but I'm still talking, ignoring his protests.

"I'll leave first thing tomorrow—I'll catch the eight a.m. train if you're really worried, but there is no way that I'm in danger from Kate. I'm just not. I've known her for seventeen years, Luc, and I can't believe it. I *trust* her."

"I've known her for longer than that," Luc says, so quietly that I can hardly hear him beneath Freya's choking wails. "And I don't."

Freya's cries are too loud for me to ignore now, and I pull my wrist gently out of his grip.

"Good night, Luc."

"Good night, Isa," he says. He watches as I retreat up the stairs with the oil lamp, leaving him in darkness. Upstairs, I pick up Freya, feeling her hot little body convulsing with angry sobs, and in the silence that follows I hear the click of the door latch and the sound of Luc's footsteps on gravel as he disappears into the night.

I don't sleep that night. I lie awake, words and phrases chasing around my head. Pictures Kate said she had destroyed. Lies she has told. Owen's face as I left. Luc's face as he walked towards me in the soft lamplight.

I try to piece it all together—the inconsistencies and the heartbreak—but it makes no sense. And through the whole thing, like maypole dancers, weave the ghosts of the girls we used to be, their faces flashing as they loop over and under, weaving truth with lies and suspicion with memory.

Towards dawn one phrase comes into my head, as clear as if someone whispered it into my ear.

It is Luc, saying *I should have chosen you.*

And I wonder again . . . what did he mean?

IT'S SIX THIRTY WHEN FREYA wakes, and we lie there, she feeding at my breast, me considering what I should do. Part of me knows I should go home to London, try to mend bridges with Owen. The longer I leave it, the harder it's going to be to salvage what's left of our relationship.

But I can't face the thought, and as I lie there, watching Freya's contented face, her eyes squeezed shut against the morning light, I try to work out why. It's not because of what happened with Luc, or not just because of that. It's not even because I'm angry with Owen, for I'm not anymore. What happened last night has somehow lanced my fury, made me face the ways I've been betraying him all these years.

It's because anything I say now will just be more lies. I can't tell him the truth, not now, and not just because of the risk to his career and the betrayal of the others. But to do that would be to admit to him what I've already admitted to myself—that our relationship was built on the lies I've been telling myself for the past seventeen years.

I need time. Time to work out what to do, how I feel about him. How I feel about *myself.*

But where do I go, while I figure this out? I have friends—plenty of them—but none where I could turn up with my baby and my bags and no end for my stay in sight.

Fatima would say yes in a heartbeat, I know she would. But I can't do that to her, in her crowded, chaotic house. For a week, maybe. Not longer.

And Thea's rented studio flat is out of the question.

My other friends are married, with babies of their own. Their spare rooms—if they have any—are needed for grandparents and au pairs and live-in nannies.

My brother, Will? But he lives in Manchester, and he has his own wife and twin boys, in a three-bedroom flat.

No. There is only one place I could go, if it's not home.

My mobile phone is beside me on the pillow, and I pick it up, and scroll through the numbers until my finger hovers over his contact. Dad.

He has room, God knows. In his six-bedroom place up near Aviemore, where he lives alone. I remember what Will said last time he came back from visiting. "He's lonely, Isa. He'd love for you and Owen to come and stay."

But somehow there was never time. It's too far for a weekend—the train journey alone is nine hours. And before I had Freya there was always something—work, annual leave, DIY on the flat. And then later, getting ready for the baby, and then after Freya was born, the logistics of traveling with a newborn . . . or a baby . . . or soon, a toddler.

He came down to meet Freya when she was born, of course. But I realize, with a pang that hurts my heart, I have not been up to see him for nearly . . . six years? Can that be right? It seems impossible, but I think it must be. And then only because a friend was getting married in Inverness, and it seemed rude not to call in when we were passing so close.

It's not him, that's what I want him to understand. I love him—I always have done. But his grief, the gaping hole left after my mother died—it's too close to my own. Seeing his grief, year after year, it only magnifies my own. My mother was the glue that held us together. Now, with her missing, there are only people in pain, unable to heal each other.

But he would say yes. And more than yes, I think. He—alone of everyone—would be glad.

IT'S GONE SEVEN WHEN I finally dress, pick up Freya, and go down to the kitchen. Through the tall windows overlooking the Reach, I can see the tide is low—almost as low as it will go. The Reach is just a deep runnel in the center of the channel, the wide banks exposed, the sand clicking and sucking as it dries and all the little creatures—the clams and oysters and lugworms—retreat and shore up until the tide turns.

Kate is still in bed—or at least she hasn't yet come down—and I can't help a shudder of relief when I realize Freya and I are alone. As I touch the coffeepot—checking for any vestigial warmth—I find myself looking up to the turn of the stair, where I saw her face last night, ghost white in the darkness. I'm not sure

I will ever forget it—the sight of her standing there, watching us. What *was* her expression? Anger? Horror? Something else?

I run my hands through my hair—try to attribute a motive I can understand to her actions. Kate neither likes nor trusts Luc—and it's plain now that that feeling is mutual. But why stand there in the dark like that? Why not call out, stop me from making whatever mistake she thought I was committing?

Why stand there in the shadows like she had something to hide?

One thing is plain: I can't stay here—not after last night. Not just because of Luc's warnings, but because the trust between me and Kate is gone. Whether I destroyed it with my actions last night, or whether it was Kate and her lies, it doesn't matter.

What matters is that part of the bedrock of my life has cracked and broken, and I feel the foundations I've built my adult self on shifting and creaking. I no longer know what to believe. I no longer know what to say if I'm questioned by police. The narrative I thought I knew has been ripped and broken—and there is nothing to take its place except doubt and mistrust.

Today is Wednesday. I will go back to London on the first train, pack my bags while Owen is at work, and leave for Scotland. I can call Fatima and Thea from there. They deserve an explanation.

It's only when a tear runs down my nose and splashes onto Freya's head that I realize I am crying.

NO ONE AT RICK'S RIDES picks up when I call, and at last I load the bags onto Freya's buggy and wheel her out into the cool sunshine. I bump the buggy barefooted across the rickety bridge, and shove my feet into my shoes, which are still there on the far side, like strange flotsam and jetsam. Beside them is a print of two larger soles—the imprint of Luc's shoes—and I can see his footprints trail across the shore, and disappear into the muddy confusion of the track.

I let myself out of the gate, and begin the long walk to the station, talking to Freya as I go—anything to distract myself from the reality of last night and the mess of what's facing me in London.

I'm just turning onto the main road, when I hear the hiss of gravel and a horn beeps from behind me, making me jump. I swing round, my heart thumping—and see an ancient black Renault, coming to a halt on the verge.

The driver's window winds slowly down, and an iron-gray head looks out, unsmiling.

"Mary!"

"Didn't mean to scare you." Her strong, bare arm rests on the window, the hairs dark against the pale skin. Her perpetually grubby nails tap the paintwork. "On your way to the station?"

I nod and she says, as a statement, without asking for my opinion, "I'll give you a lift."

"Thanks," I say awkwardly, "but—" I'm about to use the car seat as an excuse, but then my eyes drop to the pram, where Freya is snuggled into the car seat adaptor. Damn. Mary raises one eyebrow.

"But?"

"B-but . . . I don't want to put you to any trouble," I say weakly.

"Don't be soft," she says shortly, swinging open the back passenger door. "Get in."

Somehow I can't find another excuse, and I strap Freya into the rear seat and then walk around to the front passenger door and climb silently in. Mary puts the car into gear with a coughing rasp, and we begin to pick up speed.

We drive in silence for perhaps a quarter of a mile, but as we round the corner to the level crossing over the railway, I see the lights are flashing, and the barriers are coming down. A train is about to pass.

"Damn," Mary says, and lets the car glide to a halt in front of the barrier. She switches off the ignition.

"Oh no. Does this mean I'm going to miss the train?"

"This'll be the northbound train for London they've closed for. It'll be cutting it very fine to get there. But you might be lucky. Sometimes they wait, if they're ahead of themselves."

I bite my lip. I have nothing I need to get back for, but the thought of waiting at the station for half an hour with Mary is not a good one.

The silence in the car grows, broken only by Freya's snuffles from the backseat, and then Mary speaks, breaking the quiet.

"Terrible news, about the body."

I shift in my seat, moving the seat belt away from my throat where it has ridden up, and somehow grown tight.

"H-how do you mean? The identification?"

"Yes, although I don't think anyone round here was surprised. There wasn't many thought Ambrose would have left his children like that. He was devoted to those kids, would have walked through fire for them. A little local scandal? I don't think he'd have even cared, much less scarpered and left his kids to deal with the fall-out." She taps the rotting rubber of the steering wheel, and with an impatient gesture sweeps back a frond of iron-gray hair that's fallen out of her pigtail. "But it was more the postmortem I was thinking of."

"What do you mean?"

"Haven't you heard?" She casts me a quick glance, and then shrugs. "Maybe it's not in the papers yet. I hear stuff early sometimes, what with my Mark being one of the boys. Perhaps I shouldn't tell you, just in case."

She pauses, enjoying the moment of power, and I grit my teeth, knowing that she wants to be begged for her insider information. I don't want to give in to her. But I have to know. I must know.

"You can't leave me hanging like that," I say, doing my best to keep my voice light and casual. "I mean, I don't want you to break any confidences, but if Mark didn't tell you to keep it under wraps . . . ?"

"Well, it's true he normally only tells me things if it's about to be released anyway . . ." she drawls. She bites her fingernail, spits out a fragment, and then seems to make up her mind, or tire of playing with me. "The postmortem found traces of heroin in a bottle in his jacket. Oral overdose, they're saying."

"*Oral* overdose?" I frown. "But . . . that makes no sense."

"Exactly," Mary Wren says. Through her open window I can hear the sound of a distant train, growing closer. "Ex-addict like him? If he wanted to kill himself he'd have injected the stuff, of course he would. But then, like I said, I never did believe that Ambrose would leave those kids of his own accord—it makes no more sense for him to kill himself than run away. I'm not one for gossip"—she brings out the lie without so much as a blush—"so I've kept my thoughts to myself. But in my mind, I never thought it was anything else."

"Anything else than . . . what?" I say, and suddenly my voice is hoarse, sticking in my throat.

Mary smiles at me, a wide smile, showing her stained yellow teeth, like tombstones in her mouth. Then she leans closer, her cigarette breath hot and rank against my face, and whispers.

"I never thought it was anything but murder."

She sits back, watching my reaction, seeming almost to enjoy my floundering, and as I scrabble frantically for the right words to say in response to something like that, a thought flashes through my mind—has Mary known the truth all this time?

"I—I—"

She gives her slow, malicious smile, and then turns to glance up the track. The train is coming closer. It sounds its horn, and the lights at the level crossing blink with a maddening regularity.

My face is stiff with trying not to show my reaction, but I manage to speak.

"I find that . . . I find that hard to believe, though, don't you? Why would someone murder Ambrose?"

She shrugs, her huge shoulders rising and falling heavily.

"You tell me. But it's easier to believe than the idea of him killing his-self and leaving those kids to fend for themselves. Like I said, he would have walked through fire for them, especially that Kate. Not that she deserved it, little bitch."

My mouth falls open.

"What did you say?"

"I said he'd have walked through fire for his kids," she says. She is openly laughing at me. "What did you think I said?"

I feel anger flare, and suddenly the suspicions I've been having of Kate seem like vile gossip. I've known her for almost twenty years—am I really going to let rumor and innuendo turn me against one of my oldest friends?

"You've never liked her, have you?" I say flatly, crossing my arms over my chest. "You'd be delighted if she were questioned over this."

"Truth be told? I would," Mary says.

"Why?" It comes out like a plaintive cry, like the voice of the child I used to be. "Why do you hate her so much?"

"I don't hate her. But she's no better than she ought to be, the little slut. Nor are the rest of you."

Little *slut*? For a moment I'm not sure if I've heard right. But I know from her face that I have, and I find my tongue, my voice shaking with anger.

"What did you call her?"

"You heard me."

"You don't believe those disgusting rumors about Ambrose, do you? How can you think something like that? He was your friend!"

"About Ambrose?" She raises one eyebrow, and her lip curls. "Not him. He was trying to stop it. That's why he was trying to get them away from each other."

I feel suddenly cold all over. So it's true. Thea was right. Ambrose *was* sending Kate away.

"What—what do you mean? Stop what?"

"You mean you don't know?" She gives a short hacking laugh, quite mirthless, like the bark of a dog. "Ha. Your precious friend was sleeping with her own brother. *That's* what Ambrose knew, that's why he was trying to get them away from each other. I went over to the Mill the night he told her, but I could hear her outside the door, before I even knocked. Screaming at him, she was. Throwing things. Calling him names you wouldn't think a girl of that age would know. *Bastard* this and *heartless cunt* that. *Please don't do it,* she says, *think about what you're doing.* And then, when that doesn't work, that she'll make him regret it, a threat to his face, bold as you like. I got out of there as quick as I could and left them to it, hammer and tongs, but I heard that right enough. And then the very next night, he vanishes. You tell *me* what I should think, Miss Butter-Wouldn't-Melt-in-My-Mouth. What should I think, when my good friend disappears, and his daughter doesn't report him missing for weeks, and then his bones surface in a shallow grave? You tell me." But I can't tell her anything. I can't speak. I can only sit, gasping, and then suddenly blood rushes back into my fingers and I find myself scrabbling for my seat belt, yanking at the door, snatching Freya out of the backseat as the train thunders past, its speed like a scream in my face.

As I slam the car door with shaking hands she leans across, her deep, rasping voice carrying easily above the roar of the train.

"There's blood on that girl's hands, and not just sheep's blood, neither."

"How—" I manage, but my throat is stiff and closing, and the words choke me. But Mary doesn't wait for me to finish. The lights stop flashing and the barriers begin to lift, and even as I stand there, gaping, the car's engine roars into life, jolting across the tracks.

I can't let it go on . . . it's all wrong.

I am still standing there, trying to process what she's said, when the southbound train comes in, blocking the view between us, and when it pulls out of the station, she's gone, the platform empty, and it's just me and an old lady waiting for the train to Hampton's Lee.

Five minutes, says the board. Five minutes and I could be out of here with Freya, safe, forgetting about all of this.

It's all wrong.

There's blood on her hands.

Instead, I turn the pram around and I head back. Back to the Tide Mill.

Kate is out when I get back to the Mill, and this time I make sure of it. Shadow's lead is missing from the peg by the door, but I leave nothing to chance. I check every room, right up to the attic. Kate's room. Ambrose's room.

The door is unlocked, and when I push it open, my heart stutters in my chest for it is *just* like it was when Ambrose was here, barely a paintbrush out of place. It feels like him. It *smells* like him—a mix of turps and cigarettes and oil paints. Even the throw over the battered divan is the same as I remember, worn blue and white with a faded pattern like floral china. Only now it is fraying at the edges, and even more sun-bleached.

It is when I turn to go that I see it. There, above the desk, is the handwritten sign. *You're never an ex-addict, you're just an addict who hasn't had a fix in a while.*

Oh, Ambrose.

My throat tightens, and I feel a kind of furious determination flood through me, blotting out my selfish fear. I will find out the truth. And not just for my own self-protection, but to avenge a man I loved—a man who gave me shelter and comfort and compassion at a time in my life when I needed those things most.

I cannot say that Ambrose was the father I never had, because unlike Luc, I *had* a father—just one who was grieving and hurting and fighting his own battles. But Ambrose was the father I needed that year—present, loving, endlessly understanding.

I will always love him for that. And the thought of his death, and my part in it, makes me angry in a way that I have never felt before. Angry enough to ignore the voices in my head telling me to leave, turn around, go back to London. Angry enough to drag Freya back somewhere she may not be completely safe.

I am angry enough not to care about any of that anymore.

I am as angry as Luc.

When I've finished checking every room, I run back down the rickety stairs, and go to the dresser, praying that Kate hasn't thought of this and hidden it in my absence.

But she hasn't.

There, in the drawer where she took it out for me just yesterday, is the sheaf of papers tied with a red string.

I riffle through them, my hands shaking, until I get to the brown envelope, marked *Kate.*

I take it out. And for the first time in seventeen years, I read Ambrose Atagon's suicide note.

My darling Kate, it reads, in Ambrose's characteristic looping hand.

> *I am so sorry, I'm so very, very sorry to be leaving*
> *you like this—I wanted to see you grow up, to*
> *see you grow into the person I know you will be;*
> *strong, loving, responsible and selfless. I wanted*
> *to hold your child on my knee as I once held*
> *you—and I am so terribly sorry that I can't do*
> *any of these things. I was foolish not to see where*
> *my actions would lead, so now I am doing the*
> *only thing I can to make things right. I am doing*
> *this so that no one else will have to suffer.*
>
> *Don't blame anyone else, my sweet. I have*

*made my decision and I'm at peace with it, and
please know, darling Kate, that I am making this
decision with love—it's a father's role to protect
his children, and so I am doing the last thing, the
only thing, I can do to protect mine. I don't want
anyone to live in a prison of guilt, so go on: live,
love, be happy, never look back. And above all,
don't let this all be in vain.*

I love you.

Dad

There is a lump in my throat when I finish reading, a pain so hard and sharp that I can hardly bear
to swallow back the tears that are threatening to flood
the page.

Because at last, seventeen years too late, I think I
understand.

I understand what Ambrose was trying to tell Kate,
and the sacrifice that he made. *Don't blame yourself. I
am doing the only thing I can to protect you. I am making this decision with love. Don't let it be in vain.*

Oh God. Oh, Ambrose. None of this makes any
sense. What did you *do*?

My fingers are shaking as I take out my phone and
text Fatima and Thea.

I need you. Please come. Hampton's Lee, 6pm?

And then I put the letter into my pocket and I get
myself and Freya out of that place as fast as I can. And
I don't look back.

It is 6:38, and the little coffee shop on the London-bound platform at Hampton's Lee has shut up, drawing the curtains across the window and turning the sign to CLOSED. Freya is sheltered by her pram and the sensible emergency fleece I shoved into the basket underneath, but she is bored and grizzling, and I am shivering in my summer dress, my fingers wrapped around goose-bumped upper arms as I walk back and forth, back and forth, trying vainly to keep my blood moving.

Are they coming? They hadn't texted by 4:00 p.m., but then my phone ran out of charge—too long in the beachfront café at Westridge, nervously checking my messages, refreshing my e-mails, waiting for their response.

When I sent the text I had no doubt at all that they would come. But now . . . now I'm not sure. And yet I don't dare leave. Without my phone, I can't text them another meeting point. What if they come and I'm not here?

I have reached the far end of the platform, and I turn and walk back, really shivering now, trying to ignore Freya's increasingly fretful grousing. 18:44 reads the clock above the ticket office. When should I give up?

The platform is deserted, but a far-off sound makes me cock my head, listening. It's a train. A southbound train.

"The train stopping at platform . . . two . . . is the delayed eighteen thirty-two from London Victoria," says the robotic voice of the announcer. "The front seven carriages only will be continuing to West Bay Sands, stopping at Westridge, Salten, Riding, and West Bay Sands. Would passengers for Westridge, Salten, Riding, and West Bay Sands please use the front seven carriages only."

I make up my mind. If they're not on this train then I'll get on board and head south myself to Salten, and phone them from there.

My fingers close over the envelope in my pocket.

Oh, Kate. How could you lie to us like that?

The train is getting closer . . . and closer . . . and at last there is the hiss of pneumatic brakes and the noise of wheels on rails, and it grinds to a halt. Doors open, people are getting out, and I scan frantically up and down the platform, looking for the little-and-large combination of Fatima and Thea. Where *are* they?

There is a beeping noise and the doors slide shut. My heart is thumping in my chest. If I'm going to go back to Salten, I have to go now. There won't be another train for an hour. Where *are* they?

I hesitate a moment longer . . . and then I take a step forwards, press the DOOR OPEN button, just as the guard blows his whistle.

It doesn't respond. I press it harder, banging it with my fist. Nothing happens. The door stays closed.

"Stand well back," the guard calls, and the engine whine grows louder.

Shit. I have spent two long cold hours on this platform and they're not here, and now I'm stuck for another hour.

The train noise grows deafening, and it slides imperviously out of the station, ignoring my shout of "You absolute fucker!" to the guard, who wouldn't be able to hear it anyway above the sound of the engine.

There are hot tears on my face, chilling in the back

draft of the train's passing, and then I hear a voice from behind me.

"Fucker yourself, bitch."

I whip round, and then my jaw drops, and I begin laughing—a kind of hysterical combination of tears and relief. *Thea!*

For a minute I can't speak, I just hug her, gripping her neck. She smells of cigarettes . . . and gin, I realize, with a twinge of foreboding. I feel the crunch of a can in her coat pocket, and I know without looking it will be one of those premixed G&Ts you can buy at Marks and Spencer.

"Where's Fatima?" I ask.

"Didn't you get her text?"

I shake my head.

"My phone's out of charge."

"She can't get away from the surgery until half five, but she's coming down on the train after mine. I said we'd find a place to talk, text her where to come."

"Okay." I rub my arms. "Good plan. Oh, Thee, I'm so glad you're here. Where shall we go?"

"Let's go to the pub."

I look at Thea, at the way she's concentrating slightly too hard on articulating her words.

"Can we not?" I say at last. "I—it's not really fair on Fatima."

I feel a twinge of guilt at using her as an excuse, although it's true, I don't think she would want to hang out in a bar.

"Oh for fuck's sake." Thea rolls her eyes. "All right, then, we'll go and get fish and chips. Assuming the Fat Fryer is still there."

IT IS. IN FACT NOTHING has changed, from the lime-green melamine counter, to the stainless-steel display cabinets, where golden cod and battered sausages sit lined up in rows.

PICK A PUKKA PIE, reads the faded open-and-closed sign on the door, just as it always used to, seventeen years ago, and I wonder—do Pukka Pies still exist, even?

As we push open the door, a wave of warm, vinegar-scented air washes over me and I breathe it in, feeling the coldness begin to leach out of my bones. Freya has fallen asleep on the way to the chip shop, and I park the pram by one of the plastic tables and go and study the menu with Thea.

"Portion of chips, please," she says at last to the red-faced, sweating man behind the counter.

"Wrapped, or open?"

"To have here, please."

"Salt and vinegar?"

She nods, and the man shakes it on, a shower of salt that skitters across the melamine, like snow over the two-pound coins Thea has slid onto the counter.

"You can't have just chips, Thee," I say, knowing I'm sounding like a mum, but not able to help myself. "That's not a proper dinner."

"It's two of the major food groups," Thea says defiantly, taking the chips back to her table and pulling an unopened can of G&T out of her pocket.

"No alcohol," the man says crossly, and he points to a sign on the wall that reads, ONLY FOOD AND DRINK PURCHASED FROM THE FAT FRYER MAY BE CONSUMED ON THESE PREMISES. Thea sighs and slips the can back into her pocket.

"All right. I'll have a water. Can you pay for it, Isa? I'll give you the money."

"I think I can stretch to a water," I say. "I'll have . . . um . . . battered haddock, please. And a small chips.

And a side portion of mushy peas. Bottle of still water for my friend. Oh, and a Coke."

"Ugh," Thea says, as I slide into the seat opposite her and open up the peas. "Gross. Like snot in a pot."

The chips are perfect: hot and slightly limp with vinegar, zinging with salt. I dip one into the peas and then bite into it, feeling it squish creamily against the roof of my mouth.

"Oh my God, these are good. I mean, don't get me wrong, I like triple lard-cooked gastro chips as much as anyone . . . but proper seaside chips . . ."

Thea nods, but she's not really eating. She's picking at her chips, pushing them around, turning the paper wrapping translucent with fat as she presses them into the absorbent paper.

"Thea, you're not trying to soak the fat out of the chips, are you? You realize they're *chips*? They're fried. That's kind of the point."

"Nah," Thea says, but she doesn't look at me. "Just not that hungry."

I shut my mouth, and for a minute I'm back at school, watching helplessly as the school nurse calls Thea in for the weekly weight check, and she comes back spitting and raging about threats to call her dad if she loses any more weight.

I wish more than anything that Fatima were here. She would know what to say.

"Thee," I manage. "Thee . . . you have to eat."

"I'm not hungry," she says again, and this time she pushes the paper of chips away, and her jaw juts dangerously as she looks at me across the table. "I lost my job, okay?"

What? I'm not sure if I've said the words aloud, or just thought them, but Thea replies as if I have spoken.

"I lost my job. They sacked me."

"Because of . . . all this?"

She just shrugs, her mouth twisting unhappily.

"Because my mind wasn't on it, I guess. Fuck 'em."

I am groping for what I should say—what I *can* say—when Freya gulps, stirs, and wakens. She holds up her arms to be picked up and I pull her out of the buggy straps and into my lap, where she smiles up gummily at me and Thea, looking from one face to another, her eyes darting back and forth. I can see her little mind working . . . Mother . . . not Mother. Mother . . . not Mother.

Her eyes are wide, entranced by it all—the bright chrome counter, Thea's wide hoop earrings flashing in the fluorescent lights. Thea reaches out a tentative hand to touch her cheek—and then the bell above the shop door pings, and we turn to see Fatima slip inside, grinning, although she looks tired and worried beneath the smiles.

"Fatima!" I stand, giddy with relief, and give her a crushing hug. She hugs me back, and then leans down to hug Thea, and slides into the seat next to her.

"Have a chip," Thea says, pushing the paper across to her, but Fatima shakes her head, a little ruefully.

"Ramadan, innit? Started last week."

"So you're just going to sit there and watch us eat?" Thea says with incredulity. Fatima nods, and Thea rolls her eyes. I bite down the urge to tell her she can hardly talk. Now doesn't seem like the time, not after what's happened. I want to tell Fatima, but it doesn't feel like my right.

"Them's the breaks," Fatima says matter-of-factly. "Anyway . . . I have to get back for prayers and iftar," she looks at her watch as she speaks, "which doesn't give me much time before the train back, so can we cut to the chase?"

"Yeah, spit it out, Isa," Thea says. She takes a sip of water, eyeing me above the bottle. "I'm hoping it was something pretty fucking special to drag us down here."

I swallow.

"I don't know if *special* is the right word. But it's important."

I need you. Those three little words, that we never used except in direst straits. *She whistles, and you come running, like dogs.*

"It's this."

I shift Freya to my other arm, fish the envelope out of my pocket, and push it across the table towards them.

It's Fatima who picks it up, and her face is puzzled.

"This is addressed to Kate. Wait—" She slips a finger inside the ripped top, and checks inside, and her face pales as she looks up at me. "It's not . . . ?"

"It's not what?" Thea twitches it out of her fingers, and then when she recognizes the handwriting on the note inside her face changes. They are so unlike, so polar opposite in every way, rosy, birdlike little Fatima with her dark, watchful eyes and quick smile, and thin, sulky Thee, all bones and fags and heels. But their expressions, in that instant, are exactly the same—a mix of horror, shock, and foreboding.

I could almost laugh at the similarity—if it weren't for the fact that there is nothing, nothing funny about this situation at all.

"Read it," I say, keeping my voice low, and as they pull the thin, fragile sheet out of the envelope and begin to scan down the page, I tell them, very quietly, about what Mary Wren told me. About the argument. I even tell them—my face flushing with defiant shame—about that night with me and Luc, and looking over his shoulder to find Kate there in the darkness, silently watching us both, her face a stone mask of horror.

I tell them about what it was that Ambrose found so sick and wrong. About Kate sleeping with Luc.

And finally I tell them about the bottle. About what Mark told Mary. About the heroin they have found in the bottle.

"An oral overdose?" Fatima's voice is a whisper, even though the bubble of the fryers drowns our conversation. "But, that makes *no* sense. It's a stupid way to commit suicide, incredibly chancy—the dose would be really hard to calculate, and it'd take a long, long time. Plus it's easily reversible with naloxone. Why wouldn't he just inject it? With his tolerance down, he'd be dead within minutes, with no chance of being revived."

"Read that note," I whisper back. "Read it from the perspective of a man who has just been poisoned by his child. Now do you see what I'm saying?"

I'm hoping against hope that they will tell me I'm being crazy, paranoid. That Kate would never hurt Ambrose. That being separated from the boy you love and being sent away is an absurd motive for murder.

But they don't. They just stare at me, faces pale and frightened. And then Fatima manages to speak.

"Yes," she says, and there's a catch in her voice. "Yes. I see. What have we done?"

Y ou going to order something?"

We look up, all of us, at the man in the grease-stained apron standing with his hands on his hips at the end of the table.

"Pardon?" Thea says, in her best cut-glass accent.

"I says"—he enunciates his words with exaggerated care, as though for the hard of hearing—"are you ladies going to order any more food? Well over an hour, you've been sitting there taking up table space and she"—he jerks his thumb at Fatima—"ain't ordered so much as a cup of tea."

"Over an hour?" Fatima jumps up, looks at her watch with horror, and then her shoulders slump. "Oh no, I can't *believe* it. It's quarter to nine. I've missed the train. Excuse me," she pushes past the man in the greasy apron. "I'm sorry, I've got to phone Ali."

Outside the fish shop window she paces up and down, snatches of conversation filtering through the door as customers come and go, and Thee and I pick up our belongings. *So sorry*, I hear. *Emergency . . .* and *really didn't think it would take . . .*

We gather up our things, and I strap Freya into her pram. Thea scoops up Fatima's handbag along with her own, while I pick up the chips that Freya was playing with, gumming them mercilessly into pulp, before she threw them on the floor.

Outside Fatima is still talking.

"I know. I'm so sorry, hon. Tell Ammi I'm sorry, and kiss the kids for me. Love you."

She hangs up, her face twisted with disappointment. "Ugh, I'm such an idiot."

"You couldn't go back, though," Thea says, and Fatima sighs.

"I guess not. I suppose we're really going to do this?"

"Do what?" I ask, but I know, before she answers, what she's going to say.

"We have to put this to Kate, don't we? I mean, if we're wrong . . ."

"I bloody hope we are," Thea puts in grimly.

"*If* we're wrong," Fatima says again, "she has the right to defend herself. There could be a million ways to read that letter."

I nod, but in truth I'm not sure there *are* a million ways. With Mary's revelations fresh in my mind, the only way I can see it is a father trying to keep his child out of prison, knowing his own life is forfeit and doing the one thing he can do to keep her safe.

I've read the note again and again, more times than Fatima has, more times than I can count, watching the way the words trail away into illegibility, following the progress of the drug in Ambrose's straggling letters. I read it on the train up from Salten, and during the long wait at Hampton's Lee. I read it while my own daughter lolled against my breast, her rosebud mouth open, her halting breath cobweb-soft against my skin, and I can only see it one way.

It is a father saving his child, and telling her to make his sacrifice worthwhile.

It is nearly ten when we get to the Mill, a journey full of delays, of waiting for trains, of watching Fatima break her fast on a station platform, when I know she would rather be with her family.

At Salten there's more waiting while we call Rick and wait for him to complete another job, but at last we are ensconced in the back of his cab, Freya chewing her chubby knuckles in her car seat; Thea fidgeting beside me, biting at her bloodied nails; Fatima in the front, staring unseeingly into the night.

I know they are going through the same, disbelieving round-and-round I have been running all day. If this is true, what did we do? And what does it mean for us all?

Losing our jobs . . . that would be bad enough. But accessory to murder? We could be looking at custodial sentences. Fatima and I could lose our kids. If this is true, will anyone in their right minds believe that we didn't know what we were doing?

I try to imagine myself in a prison visiting room, Owen's pinched face as he hands Freya over to a mother she barely recognizes.

But my imagination fails—the only thing I know about prison is culled from *Orange Is the New Black*. I can't accept that this is happening. Not to me. Not to *us*.

Rick goes as far as he can down the track before the wheels begin to spin, and then he lets us out and backs carefully up to the road, while we make our long, slow way down the road towards the Mill.

My heart is thumping. It looks as if the electricity is still out, but I can see a light flickering in Kate's window. It's not the steady stream of a bulb, though, but the soft uncertainty of a lamp, flickering a little as the curtains blow in the breeze.

As we get closer I realize I'm holding my breath, half expecting a repeat of the flooded bridge, but high tide won't be for another few hours, and the walkway is still just clear of the rising waters. As we cross the rickety planks I see from Fatima's and Thea's faces what they are thinking—the knowledge that if the waters rise, we may be stuck here for the night.

At last, though, we are assembled on the shrinking strip of muddy sand outside the door of the Mill.

"Ready?" Thea says in a low voice, and I shrug.

"I'm not sure."

"Come on," Fatima says. She raises her fist, and for the first time since I can remember, we knock on the Mill door, and wait for Kate to come and let us in.

"YOU! WHAT ARE YOU ALL doing here?"

Kate's face, as she sees us all gathered on the doorstep, is surprised, but she stands back to let us in, and we file past into the darkness of the living room.

The only light is from the moonlight striking off the high waters outside the windows overlooking the Reach, and from the oil lamp in Kate's hand, and as I pass her I get a flashback to her white face peering out from the shadows, watching me and Luc on the couch, and I cannot help but flinch.

"The electricity's still out," she says, her voice strange and detached. "Let me find some candles."

I stand, watching her as she hunts through the dresser, and my hand on the handle of Freya's pram is trembling, I notice. Are we *really* going to do this? Accuse one of our oldest friends of killing her father?

"Do you want to put Freya down in the back bedroom?" Kate says over her shoulder, and I open my mouth to say no, but then nod. I don't suppose we will be staying the night—not after we say what we've come to say—but there will be a scene either way, and I don't want Freya mixed up in it.

I unclip the car seat attachment from the pram, and then tell Fatima in a low voice, "I'll be back down in a sec. Wait for me."

Freya slumbers on as I carry her carefully up the stairs to Luc's room, and stays asleep as I deposit her gently on the floor and pull the door so it's just ajar.

My heart is hammering as I walk back down to the ground floor.

The candles are lit, dotted around the place on saucers, and as I reach the sofa where Fatima and Thea are sitting, hands clasped anxiously around their knees, Kate straightens.

"What's all this in aid of?" she asks mildly.

I open my mouth—but I don't know what to say. My tongue is dry, sticking to the roof of my mouth, and my cheeks feel hot with shame, although I don't know what, exactly, I'm ashamed of. My own cowardice, maybe?

"Fuck, I'm getting a drink," Thea mutters. She picks up the bottle that's on the sideboard and fills a whiskey tumbler. The liquid glints, black as oil in the candlelight, as she knocks it back and wipes her mouth. "Isa? Kate?"

"Yes, please," I say, my voice shaking a little. Maybe it will help steady my nerves, help me to do this horrible necessary thing.

Thea pours a glass, and as I swallow it back, feeling the roughness against my throat, I realize, I don't know which is worse—the prospect that we're wrong, and about to betray two decades of friendship on a misguided hunch. Or the idea that we're right.

In the end it's Fatima who stands up. She takes Kate's hands, and I'm reminded once again of the steel beneath her compassion.

"Kate," she says, and her voice is very low. "Honey, we came here tonight to ask you something. Maybe you've already guessed what it is."

"I don't know." Kate's face is suddenly wary. She pulls her hands away from Fatima and draws up a chair to sit opposite the sofa. I have a sudden image of her as a plaintiff and us as a panel of judges, grilling her, passing sentence. "Why don't you tell me?"

"Kate." I force myself to speak. It was me who brought my suspicions to the others—the least I can do is say them to her face. "Kate, I met Mary Wren on the way to the station earlier. She—she told us something that the police have discovered. Something we didn't know." I swallow. Something is constricting my throat. "She—she said . . ." I swallow again, and then force myself to say it in a rush, like ripping off a bandage, stuck to a wound. "She said that the police have discovered heroin in the bottle Ambrose was drinking from. She said that the overdose was oral. She said they're not looking at suicide but—but—"

But I can't finish.

It's Thea who says it finally. She looks up at Kate from beneath the curtain of her long fringe, and the lamplight throws her face into shadows so that it looks so much like a skull, gleaming in the darkness, that I shudder.

"Kate," she says bluntly, "did you kill your father?"

"What makes you think that?" Kate says, still in that oddly calm voice. Her face in the circle of lamplight is blank, almost surreally so, compared to the naked pain on Fatima's and Thea's. "He overdosed."

"An oral overdose?" I burst out. "Kate, you know that's ridiculous. It's a stupid way to commit suicide. Why would he do it when he had his works right there, ready to inject? And—" And here my heart fails me, and I feel a stab of even greater guilt at what I've done, but I force myself on. "And there's this."

And I take the note out of my pocket, and throw it down on the table.

"We read it, Kate. We read it seventeen years ago but I didn't understand it until today. It's not a suicide note, is it? It's the note of a man who has been poisoned by his own child, and is trying to keep her out of prison. It's a note telling you what to do—to go on, not to look back, to make his final action worthwhile. How *could* you, Kate? Is it true you were sleeping with Luc? Is that why you did it, because Ambrose was splitting you up?"

Kate sighs. She shuts her eyes, and puts her long slim hands to her face, pressing them against her forehead. And then she looks up at us all, and her face is very sad.

"Yes," she says at last. "Yes, it's true. It's all true."

"*What?*" Thea explodes. She stands up, knocking over her glass so that it smashes on the floor, red wine seeping across the boards. "*What?* You're going to sit there and tell us that you dragged us into covering up a *murder*? I don't believe you!"

"What don't you believe?" Kate says. She looks up at Thea, her blue eyes very steady.

"I don't believe any of it! You were fucking Luc? Ambrose was sending you away? And you *killed* him for it?"

"It's true," Kate says. She looks away, out of the window, and I see the muscles in her throat move as she swallows convulsively. "Luc and I . . . I know Dad thought of us as brother and sister, but I barely remembered him. When he came back from France, it was like . . . it was like falling in love. And it seemed so *right*, that's what Dad couldn't get. He loved me; he *needed* me. And Dad—" She swallows again, and shuts her eyes. "You would have thought we really *were* brother and sister from the way he acted. The way he looked at me when he told me . . ." She is looking away, across the Reach, towards the headland, beyond which lies a tent surrounded by police tape. "I've never felt dirty before. And I felt it then."

"What did you *do*, Kate?" Fatima's voice is low and shaking, as if she can't believe what she's hearing. "I want to hear it from you, step by step."

Kate looks up at that. Her chin goes up, and she speaks almost defiantly, as if she's made up her mind, at last, to face the inevitable.

"I bunked off school that Friday and I went home. Dad was out, and Luc was at school, and I poured the whole of his stash into that red wine he kept beneath the sink. There was only one glass left in the bottle, and I knew Luc wouldn't drink it—he was out that night, in Hampton's Lee. And it was always the first thing Dad did on a Friday night—come home, pour himself a glass of wine, throw it back—do you remember?" She gives a shaking laugh. "And then I went back to school, and I waited."

"You dragged us into this"—Thea's voice is hoarse— "you got us to cover up a *murder*, and you're not even going to say *sorry*?"

"Of course I'm sorry!" Kate cries, and for the first time her weird calm cracks, and I get a glimpse of the girl I recognize beneath, as anguished as the rest of us. "You think I'm not sorry? You think I haven't spent seventeen years in agony over what I made you do?"

"How could you do it, Kate?" I say. My throat is raw with pain, and I think I may sob at any moment. "How *could* you? Not us—him. Ambrose. How *could* you? Not because he was sending you away, surely? I can't believe it!"

"Then don't believe it," Kate says. Her voice is shaking.

"We deserve to know," Fatima snarls. "We deserve to know the truth, Kate!"

"There's nothing else I can tell you," Kate says, but there's an edge of desperation in her voice now. Her chest is rising and falling and Shadow patters over, not understanding her distress, and butts his head against her. "I can't—" she says, and then seems to choke. "I—I can't—"

And then she jumps up and walks to the windows overlooking the Reach. She steps out with Shadow at her heels, and slams them behind her.

Thea makes as if to go after her, but Fatima catches at her arm.

"Leave her," she says urgently. "She's at the breaking point. If you go after her now, she's liable to do something stupid."

"What?" Thea spits. "Like throw me in the Reach, too? *Fuck.* How could we be so stupid? No wonder Luc hates her—he *knew* all along. He knew, and he said nothing!"

"He loved her," I say, thinking of his face that night when we saw Kate standing at the corner of the stairs— the mix of triumph and agony in his eyes. They both turn to me, as if they'd forgotten I was there, huddled in the corner of the sofa. "I think he still does, in spite of everything. But living with that—with that knowledge all these years—"

I stop. I put my hands to my face.

"She killed him," I say, trying to make myself believe it, understand it. "She killed her own father. She didn't even try to deny it."

WE ARE STILL SITTING THERE much later, when there is a noise from the window, and Kate comes back inside. Her feet are wet. The tide has risen, covering the jetty, and the wind has picked up, and I see that her hair is speckled with rain. A storm is coming.

Her face, though, is back to that unsettling calm as she clicks the window shut behind her and puts a sandbag against the frame.

"You'd better stay," she says, as if nothing has happened. "The walkway has been cut off, and there's a storm coming."

"I'm pretty sure I can wade through two feet of water," Thea snaps, but Fatima puts a warning hand on her arm.

"We'll stay," she says. "But Kate, we have to—"

I don't know what she was about to finish. We have to say something? Talk about this? Whatever it was, Kate interrupts.

"Don't worry." Her voice is weary. "I've made up my mind. I'll call Mark Wren in the morning. I'll tell him everything."

"Everything?" I manage. Kate's mouth twists in a wry, tired smile.

"Not everything. I'm going to tell him I acted alone. I won't bring you into it."

"He'll never believe you," Fatima says uncertainly. "How could you have dragged Ambrose all that way?"

"I'll make him believe," Kate says flatly, and I think

of the drawings, the way Kate made the school believe what she wanted them to, in the face of all the evidence. "It's not that far. I think with a tarp someone could—could drag a—" But here she chokes. She cannot say the words. *A body.* Someone could drag a body.

I feel a sob rise in my throat.

"Kate, you don't have to do this!"

"Yes," she says, "I do." And she comes across the room, and puts her hand on my cheek, looking into my eyes. And her mouth flickers in a little sad smile, just for a moment. "I want you to know this, I love you all. I love you so much, all of you. And I am so, so sorry, more than I can express, that I dragged you all into this. But it's time I ended it, for all our sakes. It's time I made it right."

"Kate—"

Thea looks shaken, her face is white. Fatima is standing, and she rubs her hand over her face as if she cannot believe it has come to this, that our friendship—the four of us—is going to end this way.

"Is this it?" she asks uncertainly. And Kate nods.

"Yes. This is it. This is the end. You don't need to be afraid anymore. I'm sorry," she says again, and she looks from Fatima, to me, and last of all to Thea. "I want you to know that. I'm so, so sorry."

I think of the lines from Ambrose's letter. *I am so sorry, I'm so very, very sorry to be leaving you like this . . .*

And as Kate picks up the lamp and walks up the stairs, into the darkness, with Shadow a glimmer of white at her heels, I feel the tears begin, falling down my face like the rain that is spattering the windows, for I know she is right. This is it. This is the end. And I can't bear for it to be so.

When I eventually make my way up the stairs to Luc's room, I'm not expecting to sleep. I'm expecting another night of lying there, questions churning in my head as Freya slumbers beside me. But I'm tired—more than tired, exhausted. I climb into bed fully clothed and as soon as my head touches the pillow, I fall into uneasy dreams.

It's sometime later—I'm not sure how late—that I am jerked awake by the sound of voices in the room above my head. They are arguing, and there is something about the voices that prickles at the back of my neck.

I lie for a moment, dragging myself out of disturbing dreams of Kate and Ambrose and Luc, trying to orientate myself, and then my eyes adjust. Light is filtering through the gaps in the floorboards of the room above, flickering as someone prowls back and forth, voices rising and falling, and a thud that makes the water in my glass ripple, as if of someone hitting a wall in barely contained frustration.

I reach out for the bedside light, but the switch clicks uselessly before I remember about the electricity. Damn. Fatima took the lamp to bed with her, but in any case, I have no matches. No means of lighting a candle.

I lie still, listening, trying to work out who is speaking. Is it Kate, ranting to herself, or has Fatima or Thea gone up to confront her for some reason?

"I don't understand, isn't this what you wanted all along?" I hear. It's Kate, hoarse and ragged with weeping.

I sit up in the darkness, holding my breath, trying to hear. Is she on the phone?

"You wanted me to be punished, didn't you?" Her voice cracks.

And then the answer comes. But not in words, not at first.

It's a sob, a low groan that filters through the darkness, making my heart leap into my throat.

"It wasn't supposed to be like this."

The voice is Luc's, and he sounds beside himself with grief.

I don't think. I slip out of bed and go to Fatima's door, rattling the handle. It's locked, and I whisper through the keyhole, "Fati, wake up, wake up."

She's there in a moment, her dark eyes wide in the blackness, listening as I point to the creaking boards above. We hold our breaths, trying to listen, trying to make out who's speaking.

"What did you want, then?" I can hardly understand Kate, she's crying, her words blurred with tears. "What did you want if not this?"

Fatima's fingers close on my arm, and I hear her intake of breath.

"Luc's up there?" she whispers, and I nod, but I'm trying to hear Luc's words, between the sobs.

"I never hated you . . ." I hear. "How can you say that? I love you . . . I've always loved you."

"What's going on?" Fatima whispers frantically.

I shake my head, trying to replay everything from last night in my mind. Oh God; oh Kate. Please tell me you weren't . . .

Luc says something, Kate's voice rising above in anger, and then there's a crash, and a cry from Kate—

of pain or alarm, I can't tell, and I hear Luc's voice, too choked for me to make out words. He sounds on the verge of losing it.

"We need to help her," I whisper to Fatima. She nods.

"Let's get Thea, and we'll go up together. Strength in numbers. He sounds drunk."

I listen as I follow Fatima down the landing, and I think perhaps she's right. Luc is beside himself, barely coherent now. He's ranting at Kate, and I can't make out her terrified sobbing replies.

"It was only ever you," I hear as we run down the stairs. His words are anguished. "I wish to God it wasn't, but it's true. I would have done anything to be with you."

"I would have come for you!" Kate sobs. "I would have waited, made him change his mind. Why couldn't you have trusted him? Why couldn't you have trusted *me*?"

"I couldn't—" Luc chokes, and I hear his words come faintly as I run down the corridor to Thea's room. "I couldn't let him do it. I couldn't let him send me back."

Thea's door is not locked, and she starts up from bed as we burst in, her face wild with fear, changing to shock as she sees Fatima and me standing there.

"What's going on?" she gasps.

"It's Luc," I manage. "He's here. We think—oh God, I don't know. I think we might have got it all wrong, Thea."

"What?" She's out of bed in an instant, pulling her T-shirt over her head. "Fuck. Is Kate okay?"

"I don't know. He's up there now. It sounds like they're fighting. I think one of them just threw something."

But she's already out of the room, running towards the stairs.

She's barely reached the bottom when there is another crash—this one much louder. It sounds like someone pulling over a piece of furniture and we all freeze, just for a moment. Then there is a scream, and the sound of a door opening, running footsteps.

And then I smell something. Something that makes my heart seem to clench in my chest. It's the smell of paraffin. And there's a strange, alien noise as well. A noise I can't place, but it fills me with a dread I can't explain.

It's only when Kate comes running down the stairs, her face full of horror, that I realize what I can hear. It's the crackle of flames.

K ate?" Fatima says. "What's going on?"

"Get out!" Kate pushes past her to the front door, flings it open. And then, when we don't move, she shouts it again. "Didn't you hear me? Get out, now! There's a lamp broken—there's paraffin everywhere."

Fuck. Freya.

I bolt for the stairs, but Kate grabs my wrist, yanking me back.

"Didn't you hear me? Get out, *now*, Isa! You can't go up there, it's dripping through the floorboards."

"Let me go!" I snarl, twisting my wrist out of her grip. Somewhere, Shadow has begun barking, a high repetitive sound of fear and alarm. "Freya's up there."

Kate goes white, and she lets me go.

I'm halfway up the stairs, coughing already at the smoke. Burning drops of paraffin are falling through the gaps in the boards above, and I cover my head with my arms, though I can hardly feel the pain in comparison with the stinging in my eyes and throat. The smoke is already thick and acrid, and it hurts to breathe—but I can't think about that—all I can think of is getting to Freya.

I'm almost at the landing, when a figure appears above me, blocking my route.

Luc. His hands are burned and bleeding, and he is bare-chested where he has ripped off his shirt to smother the flames on his skin.

His face changes as he sees me, shock and horror twisting his features.

"What are you doing here?" he shouts hoarsely, coughing against the fumes.

There's the sound of breaking glass from above, and I smell the raw, volatile stink of turps. My stomach turns over, thinking of the rows of bottles in the attic, the vat of linseed oil, the white spirit. All of them dripping through the boards into the bedrooms below.

"Get out of my way," I pant. "I've got to get Freya."

His face changes at that.

"She's in the house?"

"She's in *your room*. Get out of my *way*!"

There is a corridor of flame behind him now, between me and Freya, and I'm sobbing as I try to push past him, but he's too strong. "Luc, *please*, what are you doing?"

And then, he pushes me. Not gently, but a proper shove that sends me stumbling down the staircase to fall at the bottom, my knees and elbows raw and scraped.

"Go," he shouts. "Go outside. Stand beneath the window."

And then he turns, puts his bloodied shirt over his head, and he runs back down the corridor towards Freya's room.

I scramble up, about to go after him, when a floorboard from the attic above falls with a crash, blocking the corridor. I am looking around for something, anything, to wrap around my hands, or something I can use to push the burning wood out of the way, when I hear a noise. It is the sound of Freya crying.

"Isa, the goddamn window!" I hear, above the roaring sound of the flames, and then I realize. He can't get Freya back through that inferno. He is going to drop her into the Reach.

I run, hoping I am right. Hoping I will be fast enough.

Outside Thea, Fatima, and Shadow have retreated to the bank, but I don't follow them across the little bridge, instead I splash into the water, gasping at the coldness, feeling the heat coming from the Mill against my face and the freezing chill of the Reach against my thighs.

"Luc!" I scream, wading through the water until I am waist-deep, beneath his window. My clothes drag against the current. "Luc, I'm here!"

I see his face, lit by flames behind the glass. He's struggling with the little window, warped by damp from the recent rain and stuck fast. My heart is in my mouth as he thumps his shoulder against the frame.

"Break it!" Kate shouts. She is struggling through the water towards me, but just as she says it, the window flies open with a bang, and Luc disappears back into the smoky darkness of the room.

For a minute I think he's changed his mind, but then I hear a sobbing, bubbling cry, and I see his silhouette, and he's holding something, and it's Freya—Freya screaming and bucking against him, coughing and screaming and choking.

"Now!" I'm shouting. "Drop her now, Luc, *hurry.*" His shoulders barely fit through the narrow frame, but he forces one arm and then his head out, and then somehow squeezes the other arm through the narrow space. And then he is leaning out as far as he can, holding Freya precariously at arm's length as she flails.

"Drop her!" I scream.

And Luc lets go.

IN THE MOMENT OF FALLING, Freya is completely silent—mute with shock as she feels herself go.

There is the flutter of garments, and a brief flash of a round startled face—and then an almighty splash as she hits my arms and we both fall into the water.

I am scrabbling for her beneath the surface of the Reach, my fingers hooking on her face, her hair, her clutching arms . . . my feet slipping beneath me as the waters tug.

And then Kate is hauling me upright with Freya in my arms, and we are both choking and spluttering, and Freya's thin scream of fury pierces the night, a choking shriek of outrage at the cold and the salt water stinging her eyes and her lungs—but her fury and pain is beautiful: she is alive, alive, alive—and that is all that matters.

I stagger to the far bank, my feet sinking into the sucking mud, and Fatima snatches Freya from my arms while Thea hauls me up the bank, my clothes dripping water and mud, and I am laughing or sobbing, I am not sure which.

"Freya," I'm saying, "is she okay? Fatima, is she okay?"

Fatima is checking Freya as best she can, between Freya's steam-engine shrieks.

"She's okay," I hear. "I think she's okay. Thea, call 999, quick."

She hands me back my near-hysterical baby, and then turns to help Kate up the bank.

But she is not there. She is still standing in the water, beneath Luc's window, and holding her arms up.

"Jump!"

Luc looks at her, and at the water. For a minute I think he is about to do it, about to leap. But then he shakes his head; his expression is peaceful, resigned.

"I'm sorry," he says. "For everything."

And he takes a step back, a step away from the window, into the smoky depths of the room.

"Luc!" Kate bellows. She splashes along the shore, looking from window to window, desperately seeking the shape of Luc's silhouette against the flames as he runs the gauntlet of the flaming corridor. But there is nothing there. He is not moving.

I picture him—curling on his bed, closing his eyes. Home at last . . .

"Luc!" Kate screams.

And then, before I realize what is happening, before any of us can stop her, she splashes through the water towards the door of the Mill, and hauls herself up.

"Yes, the old tide mill," Thea is saying. "Please hurry. Fire and ambulance."

"Kate?" Fatima cries, her voice alarmed. "Kate, what are you—"

But Kate has reached the door of the mill. She wraps her wet sleeves around her hands to protect them from the heat of the doorknob, and then she disappears inside, closing the door behind her.

Fatima darts forward, and for a second I think she is going after her. I grab her wrist with my free hand, but she stops at the edge of the jetty, and we stand, all three of us, Shadow whining at Thea's heels, barely breathing as the smoke from the Mill billows out across the Reach.

I see a shadow flash past one of the tall windows— Kate on the stairs, hunched against the heat, and then nothing—until Thea points up at the window of Luc's old room.

"Look!" she says, her voice strangled with fear, and we see, against a sudden burst of flame, two figures, dark against the red-gold of the inferno.

"Kate!" I cry, my voice hoarse with smoke. But I know it's no use. I know she can't hear me. "Kate, please!"

And then there is a sound like an avalanche—a roaring crash that makes us all cover our ears, and cover our eyes against the blast of sparks, broken glass, and burning wood that bursts from every window of the Mill.

Some vital beam in the roof has given way, and the whole thing tumbles in on itself, a bonfire collapsing under its own weight, shards of glass and flaming splinters spattering the shore as we hunch against the explosion. I feel the heat of cinders scalding my back as I huddle over Freya in an effort to protect her.

When the noise subsides and we stand at last, there is no need for any of us to say what we already know.

The Mill is a shell, with burning beams poking like ribs into the sky. There is no roof, no floors, no staircase anymore. There are only the tongues of flames, lapping from broken window frames, consuming everything.

The Mill is destroyed, utterly destroyed.

And Kate is gone.

I wake with a start, and for a long minute I have no idea where I am—the room is dimly lit and filled with the bleep of equipment and the sound of low voices and there is a smell of disinfectant and soap and smoke in my nostrils.

Then it comes back to me.

I am in the hospital, on the pediatric ward. Freya is slumbering in the cot in front of me, her small fingers wrapped tightly around mine.

I rub my free hand across my eyes, raw with tears and smoke, and try to make sense of the last twelve hours. There are pictures in my head—Thea throwing herself across the narrow slip of water to try to make it to the Mill, Fatima holding her back. The huddle of police and firemen who arrived to try to deal with the blaze, and their faces when we told them there were people still inside.

The image of Freya, her chubby face smudged with ash and soot, her eyes wide and filled with the reflection of flickering flames as she watched the blaze, hypnotized by its beauty.

And, most of all, that last glimpse of Kate and Luc, silhouetted against the flames.

She went back for him.

"Why?" Thea kept asking hoarsely, as we waited for the ambulance, her arms wrapped tightly around a shaking, bewildered Shadow. *"Why?"*

I shook my head. But in truth, I think I know. And at last I understand Ambrose's letter, *really* understand it.

It's strange, but in the last few days and hours I have begun to realize that I never really knew Ambrose at all. I have spent so long trapped inside my fifteen-year-old self, seeing him with the uncritical eyes of a child. But I am an adult myself now, approaching the age Ambrose was when we first met him—and for the first time I have been forced to consider him as an adult—equal to equal, and he seems suddenly very different: flawed, full of human faults, and wrestling with demons I never even noticed, though his struggle was written, quite literally, upon the wall.

His addictions, his drinking, his dreams and fears—I realize now, with a kind of shame, that I never even thought about them. None of us did, except for maybe Kate. We were too wrapped up in our own story to see his. I never noticed the sacrifices he had made for Kate and Luc, the career he had given up to be an art master at Salten, for her sake. I never thought about what it had taken to kick his addiction, and stay clean—I was, quite simply, not interested.

Even when his problems were shoved under our noses—that agonized conversation Thea reported to us in the café—we only saw them through the lens of our own concerns. We wanted to stay together, we wanted to keep using the Mill as our private refuge and playground—and so we heard his words only as far as they threatened our happiness.

The truth is, I did not know Ambrose, not really. Our lives collided for a summer, that's all, and I loved him for what he gave *me*: affection, freedom, a moment's escape from the nightmare that had become my home life. Not for who he was. I know this now. And yet, in this same moment, I think I finally understand him, and I understand what he did.

I was right, in a way. It *was* the letter of a man who

had been poisoned by his own child and was doing the only thing he could to spare his child the consequences. But the child wasn't Kate. It was Luc.

We had it all backwards, that is what I have realized at last. Not just the letter, but everything. It wasn't Kate who Ambrose was sending away. It was Luc. *Why couldn't you have trusted him?* Kate had said. But Luc had had his trust broken too many times. He thought, I suppose, that what he had always feared was coming true—that Ambrose had repented of his generosity in taking this boy into his home, loving him, caring for him. He had tested Ambrose's love so many times—pushing him away, trying, desperately, to make sure that *this* person would not betray him, that *this* person's love wouldn't waver.

Mary was not the only person who overheard Kate fighting with Ambrose. Luc must have heard them, too, and he must have understood what Thea and I had not—that *he* was the one to be sent away, not Kate. I don't know where—to boarding school most likely, from what Ambrose said to Thea. But Luc, betrayed too many times, must have jumped to the conclusion he had always feared. He thought Ambrose was sending him back to his mother.

And he did something utterly, utterly stupid—the act of a fifteen-year-old, painfully in love, and desperate not to be sent back to the hell he had escaped from.

Did he mean to kill Ambrose? I don't know. As I sit there, my eyes locked on Freya's cherubic, sleeping face, I wonder, and I can believe both scenarios. Perhaps he did want to kill Ambrose—a moment's fury, bitterly regretted when it was too late to undo. Perhaps he just wanted to punish him, disgrace him. Or perhaps he wasn't thinking at all—just acting out the anger and despair burning inside him.

I want to believe that it was all a mistake. That he never meant to kill, that he only wanted to humiliate Ambrose, to have him dial 999 and be found in a pool of heroin-tainted vomit, sacked from his job, suffering the way Luc was about to suffer in return. He was the child of an addict, who had grown up around heroin, and he must have known the unreliability of an oral overdose, the time it would take for Ambrose to die, the possibility of reversing the effects.

But I'm not certain.

In a way, it doesn't really matter anymore. What matters . . . what matters is what he did.

He did just as Kate had told us in her strange, cold, step-by-step account of actions she was taking responsibility for. He bunked off school, making his way back to the Mill in the daytime when he was sure that Kate and Ambrose would both be at Salten House. There he poured Ambrose's stash into a screw-top bottle of wine and left it on the table for him to find when he came home from school that evening, and then he gathered up the most incriminating drawings he could find, and sent them to the school.

Oh, Ambrose. I try to imagine his feelings when he realized what Luc had done. Was it the odd taste of the wine that alerted him? Or the strange sleepiness that began to steal over him? It would have taken time . . . time for Ambrose to notice what was happening . . . time to put two and two together as the heroin filtered through his stomach lining and into his blood.

I sit there, holding Freya's hand, and in my mind's eye, I see it all, unreeling like a sepia film. Ambrose examining the bottle, and then getting up, his feet unsteady. Walking to the dresser, where the tin was concealed. Opening it up . . . and realizing then what

Luc had done, and the size of the dose he had swallowed. A dose that might not have been fatal once, to a seasoned addict, but now, after years of not using, most certainly could be.

What did he think, what did he feel as his crabbed hands scratched out those wavering letters, begging Kate to protect her brother from the consequences of what he had done?

I don't know. I can't begin to imagine the pain of realizing what had happened, the magnitude of the mistake that Luc had made, and the bitter impulsive revenge he had taken. But there is one thing I am sure of, as I look down at Freya, and feel her fingers tight on mine. For the first time, I understand Ambrose's actions. I understand them completely, and it all makes sense at last.

His first thought was not to save himself, but to protect his child. The boy he had raised and loved and tried and failed to protect.

He had let Luc go back to that hell, the sweet trusting toddler he had saved from the Reach as a baby, and whose nappies he had changed, and whose mother he had loved, before she fell apart.

He had let Luc go once, and now he understood that from Luc's perspective, he had been planning to betray him once again. *I was foolish not to see where my actions would lead. . . . I am doing this so that no one else will have to suffer. . . .*

He wrote that note to make sure that only one life would be forfeit—his own. And he wrote it to Kate, not Luc, knowing that she, who knew her father better than any other person in the world, would understand and know what he was saying—that he was asking her to protect her brother.

Don't blame anyone else, my sweet. I have made my

decision and I'm at peace with it. . . . Above all, don't let my actions be in vain.

And Kate . . . Kate carried out her father's wishes as best she could. She protected Luc, she lied for him, year after year after year. But one part of Ambrose's letter she could not fulfill. She did blame Luc. She blamed him bitterly, for what he had done. And she never forgave him.

Luc was right after all. She could have waited until they were both sixteen before she told the police that Ambrose had disappeared. But she did not. And so he was taken away, back to the life he thought he had escaped.

And Luc, who had killed the only real parent he ever had for love of his sister, saw her turn cold, and turn away from him. When he was sent back to France, he knew it was Kate's doing—Kate punishing him for the murder only she knew he committed.

I remember his cry, sobbing out in the night, *It was only ever you . . .*

And I think my heart might break.

RULE FIVE

KNOW WHEN TO STOP LYING

It is not Owen who comes to collect Freya and me from the hospital—I still haven't called him when, in true NHS style, Freya and I are abruptly discharged at 9:00 a.m. the next day because they need the bed.

My phone was burned up in the house, like everything else, and they let me ring from the nurses' station, but even as my fingers hover over his number, something inside me fails, and I can't face the conversation we must have. I tell myself my reluctance is down to practicalities—it would take him hours to traverse rush-hour London and the snarled-up grid of motorways between us. But it's not that—or not only that. The truth is that last night, as Freya's life flashed before my eyes, something inside me shifted. I just don't know exactly how, and what it means.

Instead, it is Fatima who I call, and as I stand outside the pediatric wing, Freya huddled in a borrowed blanket, I see a taxi pulling up, and Fatima's and Thea's pale faces at the windows.

When I climb in, buckling Freya into the seat Fatima has sensibly organized, I see Shadow lying, flattened on the floor, at Thea's feet, her hand on his collar.

"We were discharged earlier this morning," Fatima says over her shoulder from the front seat. There are dark circles under her eyes. "I've booked us into a B and B on the coast road. I think Mark Wren will want us to stick around, at least until the police have spoken to us."

I nod. And my fingers close over the note in my pocket. Ambrose's note.

"I still can't believe it." Thea's face is white, her fingers move nervously in Shadow's fur. "That he . . . Do you think it was him? The sheep?"

I know what she means. Was it Luc? Did he do that, as well as everything else? I know they must have spent the night as I did. Thinking. Puzzling. Trying to work out the truth from the lies.

I look at Fatima, meeting her eyes in the rearview mirror.

"I don't know," I say at last. "I don't think so."

But there I stop. Because I don't want to say what I really think. Not in front of the taxi driver. He's not Rick—I don't recognize him. But he must be a local. And the truth is, of all the things Luc did or didn't do, I think that we were mistaken in suspecting him of that.

I thought that he wrote that note because he hated Kate, and suspected her of covering up Ambrose's death. I thought he wanted to scare us into confessing. I thought he wanted the truth to come out.

But later, when Kate told me about the blackmail and the money, I started to wonder. It didn't seem like Luc, somehow. Not that cold-blooded calculated draining of her resources. I couldn't imagine Luc giving a damn about the money, but trying to even up the scores—make Kate pay for the suffering she had caused him . . . yes, that felt like something he might do.

Now, though, after last night, I don't believe it anymore. It makes no sense. Luc, alone of all of us, except Kate, knew the truth, and he was lying as much as the rest of us. He was part of the Game just as much as we were and he had more to lose than any of us if the truth came out. And besides, in that long night in the hospital I have had time to think, to remember that list of convictions that Owen sent me, and one date on it sticks in my mind.

No. I think someone else wrote that note.

I remember her fingers in the post office, strong fingers, with blood under the nails.

And I am certain, in a way that I wasn't with Luc, that she is capable of this.

WHEN I GET TO THE B and B I crawl into bed with Freya, and then we both fall into sleep like bodies sinking into deep water. I surface, hours later, and for a moment I have the strangest sense of disconnection.

The B and B is on the coast road, just a few miles up from the school, and the view from my room as I sit up, adjusting my disheveled, salt-stained clothes and smoothing Freya's sweaty hair away from her face, is exactly the same as the view from Tower Two B, all those years ago.

For a second, even though my daughter is asleep beside me, I am fifteen again and I am back there— the sound of the gulls in my ears, the strange clear light splashing across the wooden windowsill, my best friend in bed beside me.

I close my eyes, listening to the sound of the past, imagining myself back into the skin of the girl I once was, a girl whose friends were still around her, whose mistakes were ahead of her.

I am happy.

And then Freya stirs and squawks and the illusion is broken, and I am thirty-two and a lawyer and a mother again. And the knowledge in the back of my mind that I have been wrestling with all night comes down upon me like a weight.

Kate and Luc are dead.

I scoop Freya up and we make our way downstairs, yawning, to where Fatima and Thea are sitting in the glassed-in sunporch overlooking the sea.

It is July, but the day is chilly and gray, and the clouds threaten rain, their dark streaks the exact shade of the gray fur that ripples along Shadow's spine. He is curled at Thea's feet, his black nose in her hand, but he looks up as I come in, his eyes bright for a moment, and then he sinks back. I know the person he was looking for. How do you explain the finality and unfairness of Kate's death to a dog? I barely understand it myself.

"We got a call from the police station," Fatima says. She draws her knees up in the chair, hugging them to herself. "They want us to come in at four this afternoon. We need to work out what to say."

"I know." I sigh and rub my eyes, and then put Freya down on the floor to play with some old magazines left there for guests to read. She tears at the cover of one with a little shriek, and I know I should stop her, but I am just too tired. I don't care anymore.

We sit for a long moment in silence, watching her, and I know without asking that the others have spent the night as I did: struggling to understand, struggling to *believe* what has happened. I feel as if yesterday I had four limbs, and today I have woken with only three.

"She broke the rules," Thea says. Her voice is low, bewildered. "She lied to us. She lied to *us*. If only she'd told us. Didn't she trust us?"

"It wasn't her secret to tell," I say. I am thinking not just of Kate, but of Owen. Of the way I have lied to him all these years, betraying our own unwritten rules. Because there is no right answer, is there? Just a trade—one betrayal for another. Kate had the choice of protecting Luc's secret, or lying to her friends. And she chose to lie. She chose to break the rules. She chose . . . I swallow at the realization. She chose to protect Luc. But she chose, too, to protect us.

"I just don't get it," Fatima bursts out. Her fists on the chintz cover of the armchair are clenched. "I don't get why Ambrose let it happen! An oral overdose takes time, and even if he didn't realize what was happening straightaway, he clearly knew what was happening in time to write that note. He could have dialed 999! Why the hell did he spend his last moments telling Kate to save Luc, instead of trying to save himself?"

"Maybe he didn't have a choice," Thea says. She shifts in her chair, pulls the cuffs of her woolen sweater down over her ragged fingers. "There's no landline at the Mill, remember? I don't even know if Ambrose had a mobile in those days. Kate did, but I never saw him with one."

"Or maybe . . ." I say, and then stop. I look down at Freya, playing on the rug.

"What?" Thea demands.

"Maybe saving himself wasn't the most important thing to him," I say. There is no answer to that. Fatima only bites her lip, and Thea looks away, out of the window towards the restless sea. I wonder if she is thinking of her own father, wondering if he would have made the same choice. Somehow I doubt it.

I think of Mary Wren, of her words at the station. *He'd have walked through fire for his kids. . . .*

And then I remember something else she said, and my stomach shifts.

"There's something I need to tell you," I say. Thea looks up.

"Sorry?"

"You were asking in the car, about the sheep, and I couldn't tell you then, but—" I stop, trying to marshal my thoughts, trying to explain the conviction that has been spreading like a shadow across my mind since that meeting at the station. "We thought it was Luc because it fit with what we knew, but I think we were wrong. He had as much to lose as us, with the truth coming out. More. And anyway, I'm fairly sure he was in custody that night in Rye." They don't ask me to explain, and I don't volunteer to. "And there's something else—something Kate told me when I came down without you both."

"Spit it out," Thea says gruffly.

"She was being blackmailed," I say flatly. "It had been going on for years. That's what the sheep was about, and the drawings. It was a way of suggesting that she start bleeding us, too."

"*No!*" Fatima says. Her face is pale against the dark head scarf. "No! How could she not tell us?"

"She didn't want us to worry," I say helplessly. It seems so futile now. How I wish she had told us. "But it just doesn't seem like something Luc would do—and besides, it started years back, while he was still in France."

"Then who?" Thea demands.

"Mary Wren."

There is a long silence. For a minute they both just sit, and then, slowly, Fatima nods.

"She's always hated Kate."

"But where's this come from?" Thea asks. Her fingers move restlessly in Shadow's fur, smoothing his ears, the smoke-colored hairs catching on her rough, bitten skin.

"It was on the way to the station," I say. I press my fingers to my forehead, trying to remember her words. My head is aching and Freya's joyous shrieks as she shreds the magazine are making it worse. "Mary gave me a lift, and she said something . . . I didn't pay attention at the time, I was too shocked about what she'd said about Kate and Luc . . . but she said something about Kate and the sheep, she said, *She's got blood on her hands, and not just sheep's blood, either.* But how would she know about the sheep?"

"Mark?" Fatima guesses, but Thea shakes her head.

"Kate didn't call the police, remember? Though I guess the farmer could have called it in."

"He could," I say. "But I'm pretty sure Kate paid him to keep quiet. That was the point of the two hundred pounds. But it's not just what Mary said, it—it was the *way* she said it. It was—" I break off, struggling to find the words to explain. "It was . . . *personal*. Gloating. Like she was pleased Kate's chickens were coming home to roost. That note, it was venomous, do you know what I mean? It reeked of hate, and I got the same feeling from Mary when she said those words. She wrote that note, I'm sure she did. And I think she sent the pictures, too. She's the only person who could have got hold of all our addresses."

"So what do we do?" Fatima asks.

Thea shrugs.

"Do? What can we do? Nothing. We say nothing. We can't tell Mark, can we?"

"So we just let it go? We let her threaten us and get away with it?"

"We keep lying," Thea says grimly. "Only this time, we get it right. We sort out a story and we stick to it, and we tell it to everyone. To the police, to our partners—everyone. We've *got* to get them to believe that Ambrose committed suicide; it's what he wanted, after all. It's what Kate wanted. But I just wish we had *something* to back up our story."

"Well . . ." I put my hand in my pocket, and I draw it out—an envelope, with Kate's name on it, very old and much folded, and now salt-stained and watermarked as well.

It is readable, though—just. The Biro ink has bloomed,

but not washed away, and you can still make out Ambrose's words to his daughter: *go on: live, love, be happy, never look back. And above all, don't let this all be in vain.*

Only now it feels like he is speaking to us.

The taxi drops us off on the promenade at Salten, and as Fatima pays the driver, I get out and stretch my legs, looking not towards the police station, squat and concrete next to the seawall, but out—towards the harbor and the sea beyond.

It is the same sea that greeted me at the window of my room at Salten House, the sea of my childhood, unchanging, implacable, and that thought is somehow reassuring. I think of all that it has witnessed, and all that it has accepted into its vastness. The way that it is taking the ashes of the Tide Mill back for its own—Kate and Luc with it. Everything we did—all our mistakes, all our lies—they are being slowly washed away.

Thea appears at my elbow, looking at her watch.

"It's nearly four," she says. "Are you ready?"

I nod, but I don't move.

"I was thinking," I say, as Fatima steps back from the cab, and it pulls away.

"About what?" she asks.

"About . . ." The word comes to me almost unbidden, and I say it with a sense of surprise. "About guilt."

"Guilt?" Fatima's brow furrows.

"I realized, last night, I've spent seventeen years thinking that what happened with Ambrose was our fault, in a way. That he died because of us—because of those drawings, because we kept coming back."

"We didn't ask to be drawn," Fatima says, her voice low. "We didn't *ask* for any of this."

But Thea nods.

"I know what you mean," she says. "However irrational it was, I felt the same."

"But I realized . . ." I stop, feeling for the right words, groping to pin down a realization only half formed in my own mind. "Last night, I realized . . . his death was nothing to do with that. It was never about the drawings. It was never about us. It was never our fault."

Thea nods slowly. And then Fatima puts her arm through both of ours.

"We have nothing to feel ashamed of," she says. "We never did."

We are turning to walk towards the police station when a figure comes out of one of the narrow twittens that wind between the stone-built houses. A massive figure, swathed in layers of clothes, with an iron-gray pigtail that flutters in the sea breeze.

It is Mary Wren.

She stops when she sees us, and then she smiles, and it is not a pleasant smile—it's the smile of someone who has power, and intends to use it. And then she begins to walk across the quay towards us.

But we begin to walk, too, the three of us, arm in arm. Mary changes her course, ready to cut us off, and I feel Fatima's arm tighten in mine, and hear the pace of Thea's heels on the cobbles quicken.

Mary is grinning now, as we draw closer, her big yellow teeth bared, like a creature ready to fight, and my heart is thumping in my chest.

But I meet her gaze, and for the first time since I came back to Salten I am without guilt. I am without fear. And I know the truth.

And Mary Wren falters. She breaks stride, and the three of us push past her, arm in arm. I feel Fatima's arm, firm in mine, and I see Thea smile. The sun breaks through the clouds, turning the gray sea bright.

Behind us, Mary Wren calls out something inarticulate.

But we keep walking, the three of us.

And we do not look back.

here is a story I will tell Freya when she is older. It's the story of a house fire, an accident caused by faulty wiring, and a lamp knocked over in the night.

It's the story of a man who risked his life to save her, and my best friend, who loved him, and went back for him when she knew it was hopeless.

It's a story about bravery, and selflessness, and sacrifice—about a father's suicide and his children's grief.

And it's a story about hope—about how we have to go on, after the unbearable has happened. Make the most of our lives, for the sake of the people who gave theirs.

It's the story that Thea, Fatima, and I told Sergeant Wren when we went to the station, and he believed us, because it was true.

It's also a lie.

We have been lying for almost twenty years, the three of us. But now, at last, we know why. Now, at last, we know the truth.

IT IS TWO WEEKS LATER, and once again, Freya and I are on a train, to Aviemore this time, almost as far from Salten as you can get without crossing the North Sea.

I think about the lies I have told, as the train hurtles north, and Freya sleeps in my arms. I think about those lies, the lies that poisoned my life and my relationship with a good and loving man. I think about the price that Kate paid for them, and how they put Freya in danger, and my fingers tighten on her, so that she stirs in her sleep.

Perhaps it is time to stop lying. Perhaps . . . perhaps we should tell the truth, all of us.

But then I look down at Freya. And I know one thing—I never, never want her to have to go through what I did. I never want her to have to check a story against the lies that she has told, testing it for holes, trying to remember what she said last time and guess what her friends might have told.

I never want her to have to look over her shoulder, to protect others.

I think about the sacrifice that Ambrose made for Kate, for Luc, and I know—I will never tell Freya the truth. Because to do that would be to pass on my burden to her.

I can do this. *We* can do this, Fatima, Thea, and I. We can keep our secrets. And I know they will do it. They will stick to the story we cooked up in whispers in our bedrooms at the B and B—of vague timings and mutual alibis. It's the last thing we can do for Kate, after all.

MY PHONE BLEEPS AROUND YORK, making Freya stir in my arms before she settles. It's Owen.

How's it going—did you make the train ok?

I have been thinking of him, all journey. Of how he looked as I waved him good-bye this morning as Freya and I set off to King's Cross.

And further back, to the way his hands were trembling when he got out of the car in the car park of the B and B at Salten, the way he took Freya in his arms as if they'd been apart for weeks, as if he'd have swum an ocean to save her. He pressed his lips to the top of her head and when he looked up, there were tears in his eyes.

And further back still, to the light that seemed to illuminate him from within when he held her that very first time, the night she was born. He looked down at her face and up at me with a kind of wonder, and I knew then what I know now—that he would walk through fire for her.

I take a breath and hold it for a long time, looking down at Freya's slumbering face. And then I text back.

Everything's fine. Dad's meeting us at Aviemore. I love you.

It's a lie; I know that now. But for her, for Freya, I can keep lying. And maybe one day I can make it true.

ACKNOWLEDGMENTS

I'm very lucky in all my publishers, but particularly lucky in the fantastic team at Scout Press, who have astounded me every single time with their care, attention, and cracking jackets.

My US editor, Alison Callahan, is fearsome, brilliant, and nurturing in exactly the right measures, and along with Liz, Jade, and Alison in the UK, has worked to make each of my books at least 50 percent better than I could have achieved alone.

As for everyone at Simon & Schuster—Nina Cordes, Meagan Harris, Jen Bergstrom, Liz Psaltis, Melanie Mitzman, Carolyn Reidy, Louise Burke, Wendy Sheanin, Erica Nelson, Jennifer Robinson, and everyone else—I'm in awe of what you achieve and so happy to be on team Scout.

My agent, Eve White, and her team always have my back, and I'm constantly grateful for the support and cheer of the vast community of writers, both online and off, who provide laughs, advice, and technical help. The list of the people I ought to thank in that respect would fill a book on its own, so please know that I love you and value you! However, particular thanks needs to go to my dear friend Ayisha Malik for taking time out of writing her own books to advise on *The Lying Game*. Needless to say, any bloopers are my own fault, but there would have been a lot more without her help. . . .

I would also like to thank Marc Hopgood for his generous bid in the CLIC Sargent children's cancer charity auction, and for lending his name to a guest at that Salten House dinner. I hope you like your character, Marc!

Finally to my dear friends and family, I love you, and I (quite literally) couldn't do it without you, so thank you, always. xxx

3rd September 2017

Dear Mr. Wrexham,
   I know you don't know me but please, please, please
you have to help me

Dear Mr. Wrexham,

You don't know me, but you may have seen coverage of my case in the newspapers. The reason I am writing to you is to ask you please

Dear Mr. Wrexham,

I hope that's the right way to address you. I have never written to a barrister before.

The first thing I have to say is that I know this is unconventional. I know I should have gone via my solicitor, but he's

5th September 2017

Dear Mr. Wrexham,
    Are you a father? An uncle? If so, let me appeal

Dear Mr. Wrexham,
    Please help me. I *didn't* kill anyone.

Dear Mr. Wrexham,

You have no idea how many times I've started this letter and screwed up the resulting mess, but I've realized there is no magic formula here. There is no way I can *make* you listen to my case. So I'm just going to have to do my best to set things out. However long it takes, however much I mess this up, I'm just going to keep going and tell the truth.

My name is . . . And here I stop, wanting to tear up the page again.

Because if I tell you my name, you will know why I am writing to you. My case has been all over the papers, my name in every headline, my agonized face staring out of every front page—and every single article insinuating my guilt in a way that falls only just short of contempt of court. If I tell you my name, I have a horrible feeling you might write me off as a lost cause and throw my letter away. I wouldn't entirely blame you, but please—before you do that, hear me out.

I am a young woman, twenty-seven years old, and as you'll have seen from the return address above, I am currently at the Scottish women's prison HMP Charnworth. I've never received a letter from anyone in prison, so I don't know what they look like when they come through the door, but I imagine my current living arrangements were pretty obvious even before you opened the envelope.

What you probably don't know is that I'm on remand.

And what you cannot know is that I'm innocent.

I know, I know. They all say that. Every single person I've met here is innocent—according to them, anyway. But in my case it's true.

You may have guessed what's coming next. I'm writing to ask you to represent me as my solicitor advocate at my trial.

I realize that this is unconventional and not how defendants are supposed to approach advocates. (I accidentally called you a barrister in an earlier draft of this letter—I know nothing about the law, and even less about the Scottish system. Everything I do know I have picked up from the women I'm in prison with, including your name.)

I have a solicitor already—Mr. Gates—and from what I understand, he is the person who should be appointing an advocate for the actual trial. But he is also the person who landed me here in the first place. I didn't choose him—the police picked him for me when I began to get scared and finally had the sense to shut up and refuse to answer questions until they found me a lawyer.

I thought that he would straighten everything out— help me to make my case. But when he arrived—I don't know, I can't explain it. He just made everything worse. He didn't let me *speak*. Everything I tried to say he was cutting in with "My client has no comment at this time," and it just made me look so much more guilty. I feel like if only I could have explained properly, it would never have got this far. But somehow the facts kept twisting in my mouth, and the police, they made everything sound so bad, so incriminating.

It's not that Mr. Gates hasn't heard my side of the story exactly. He has, of course—but somehow— Oh God, this is so hard to explain in writing. He's sat down and talked to me, but he doesn't *listen*. Or if he does, he doesn't believe me. Every time I try to tell him what happened, starting from the beginning, he cuts in with these questions that muddle me up and my story gets all tangled and I want to scream at him to just *shut the fuck up*.

And he keeps talking to me about what I said in the transcripts from that awful first night at the police station, when they grilled me and grilled me and I said— God, I don't know what I said. I'm sorry, I'm crying now. I'm sorry—I'm so sorry for the stains on the paper. I hope you can read my writing through the blotches.

What I said, what I said then, there's no undoing that. I know that. They have all that on tape. And it's bad—it's really bad. But it came out wrong; I feel like if only I could be given a chance to get my case across, to someone who would really listen . . . do you see what I'm saying?

Oh God, maybe you don't. You've never been here, after all. You've never sat across a desk feeling so exhausted you want to drop and so scared you want to vomit, with the police asking and asking and asking until you don't know what you're saying anymore.

I guess it comes down to this in the end.

I am the nanny in the Elincourt case, Mr. Wrexham. And I *didn't* kill that child.

I started writing to you last night, Mr. Wrexham, and when I woke up this morning and looked at the crumpled pages covered with my pleading scrawl, my first instinct was to rip them up and start again, just like I had a dozen times before. I had meant to be so cool, so calm and collected—I had meant to set everything out so clearly and *make* you see. And instead I ended up crying onto the page in a mess of recrimination.

But then I reread what I'd written and I thought, *No. I can't start again. I just have to keep going.*

All this time I have been telling myself that if only someone would let me clear my head and get my side of the story straight, without interrupting, maybe this whole awful mess would get sorted out.

And here I am. This is my chance, right?

140 days, they can hold you in Scotland before a trial. Though there's a woman here who has been waiting almost ten months. Ten months! Do you know how long that is, Mr. Wrexham? You probably think you do, but let me tell you. In her case that's 297 days. She's missed Christmas with her kids. She's missed all their birthdays. She's missed Mother's Day and Easter and first days at school.

297 days. And they still keep pushing back the date of her trial.

Mr. Gates says he doesn't think mine will take that long because of all the publicity, but I don't see how he can be sure.

Either way, 100 days, 140 days, 297 days . . . that's a lot of writing time, Mr. Wrexham. A lot of time to think, and remember, and try to work out what really happened. Because there's so much I don't understand, but there's one thing I know. I did not kill that little girl. I *didn't*. However hard the police try to twist the facts and trip me up, they can't change that.

I didn't kill her. Which means someone else did. And they are out there.

While I am in here, rotting.

I will finish now, because I know I can't make this letter too long—you're a busy man; you'll just stop reading.

But please, you have to believe me. You're the only person who can help.

Please, come and see me, Mr. Wrexham. Let me explain the situation to you and how I got tangled into this nightmare. If anyone can make the jury understand, it's you.

I have put your name down for a visitor's pass—or you can write to me here if you have more questions. It's not like I'm going anywhere. Ha.

Sorry, I didn't mean to end on a joke. It's not a laughing matter, I know that. If I'm convicted, I'm facing—

But no. I can't think about that. Not right now. I won't be. I won't be convicted, because I'm innocent. I just have to make everyone understand that. Starting with you.

Please, Mr. Wrexham, please say you'll help. Please write back. I don't want to be melodramatic about this, but I feel like you're my only hope.

Mr. Gates doesn't believe me; I see it in his eyes.

But I think that you might.

Dear Mr. Wrexham,

It's been three days since I wrote to you, and I'm not going to lie, I've been waiting for a reply with my heart in my mouth. Every day the post comes round and I feel my pulse speed up, with a kind of painful hope, and every day (so far) you've let me down.

I'm sorry. That sounds like emotional blackmail. I don't mean it like that. I get it. You're a busy man, and it's been only three days since I sent my letter but . . . I guess I half hoped that if the publicity surrounding the case had done nothing else, it would have given me a certain twisted celebrity—made you pick out my letter from among all the others you presumably get from clients and would-be clients and nutters.

Don't you want to know what happened, Mr. Wrexham? I would.

Anyway, it's three days now (did I mention that already?) and . . . well, I'm beginning to worry. There's not much to do in here, and there's a lot of time to think and fret and start to build up catastrophes inside your head.

I've spent the last few days and nights doing that. Worrying that you didn't get the letter. Worrying that the prison authorities didn't pass it on (can they do that without telling me? I honestly don't know). Worrying that I didn't *explain* right.

It's the last one that has been keeping me awake. Because if it's that, then it's my fault.

I was trying to keep it short and snappy, but now I'm thinking, I shouldn't have stopped so quickly. I should have put in more of the facts, tried to show you *why* I'm innocent. Because you can't just take my word for it—I get that.

When I came here, the other women—I can be honest with you, Mr. Wrexham—they felt like another species. It's not that I think I'm better than them. But they all seemed . . . they all seemed to fit in here. Even the frightened ones, the self-harmers and the ones who screamed and banged their heads against their cell walls and cried at night, even the girls barely out of school. They looked . . . I don't know. They looked like they belonged here, with their pale, gaunt faces and their pulled-back hair and their blurred tattoos. They looked . . . well, they looked *guilty*.

But I was different.

I'm English, for a start, of course, which didn't help. I couldn't understand them when they got angry and started shouting and all up in my face. I had no idea what half the slang meant. And I was visibly middle-class, in a way that I can't put my finger on but which might as well have been written across my forehead as far as the other women were concerned.

But the main thing was, I had never been in prison. I don't think I'd ever even met someone who had, before I came here. There were secret codes I couldn't decipher, and currents I had no way of navigating. I didn't understand what was going on when one woman passed something to another in the corridor and all of a sudden the wardens came barreling out, shouting. I didn't see the fights coming; I didn't know who was off her meds, or who was coming down from a high and might lash out. I didn't know the ones to avoid or the ones with permanent PMS. I didn't know what to wear or what to do, or what would get you spat on or punched by the other inmates, or what would provoke the wardens to come down hard on you.

I sounded different. I looked different. I *felt* different.

And then one day I went into the bathroom and I caught a glimpse of a woman walking towards me from the far corner. She had her hair scraped back like all the others, her eyes were like chips of granite, and her face was set, hard and white. My first thought was, *Oh God, she looks pissed off; I wonder what she's in for.*

My second thought was, *Maybe I'd better use the other bathroom.*

And then I realized.

It was a mirror on the far wall. The woman was me.

It should have been a shock—the realization that I wasn't different at all but just another woman sucked into this soulless system. But in a strange way it helped.

I still don't fit in completely. I'm still the English girl—and they all know what I'm in for. In prison they don't like people who harm children, Mr. Wrexham; you probably know that. I've told them it's not true, of course—what I'm accused of. But they look at me and I know what they're thinking—*They all say that.*

And I know—I know that's what you'll be thinking too. That's what I wanted to say. I understand if you're skeptical. I didn't manage to convince the police, after all. I'm here. Without bail. I must be guilty.

But it's not true.

I have 140 days to convince you. All I have to do is tell the truth, right? I just have to start at the beginning and set it all out, clearly and calmly, until I get to the end.

And the beginning was the advert.

WANTED:
LARGE FAMILY SEEKS
EXPERIENCED LIVE-IN NANNY

ABOUT US: *We are a busy family of four children, living in a beautiful (but remote!) house in the Highlands. Mum and Dad co-run the family architecture practice.*

ABOUT YOU: *We are seeking an experienced nanny, used to working with children of all ages, from babyhood to teens. You must be practical, unflappable, and comfortable looking after children on your own. Excellent references, background check, first aid certificate, and clean driving license are a must.*

ABOUT THE POST: *Mum and Dad work mainly from home, and during those periods you will have a simple eight-to-five post, with one night a week babysitting and weekends off. As far as possible we arrange our schedule so that one parent is always around. However, there are times when we may both need to be away (very occasionally for up to a fortnight), and when this occurs, you will be in loco parentis.*

In return we can offer a highly competitive remuneration package totaling £55,000 per annum (gross, including bonus), use of a car, and eight weeks' holiday a year.

Applications to Sandra and Bill Elincourt, Heatherbrae House, Carn Bridge.

I remember it nearly word for word. The funny thing was, I wasn't even looking for a job when it came up on my Google results—I was searching for . . . well, it doesn't really matter what I was looking for. But something completely different. And then there it was—like a gift thrown into my hands so unexpectedly I almost didn't catch it.

I read it through once, and then again, my heart beating faster the second time, because it was *perfect*. It was almost too perfect.

When I read it a third time I was scared to look at the closing date for applications—convinced I would have missed it.

But it was that very evening.

It was unbelievable. Not just the salary—though God knows, that was a pretty startling sum. Not just the post. But the luck of it. The whole package—just falling in my lap, right when I was in the perfect position to apply.

You see, my flatmate was away, traveling. We'd met at the Little Nippers nursery in Peckham, working side by side in the baby room, laughing about our terrible boss and the pushy, faddy parents, with their fucking fabric nappies and their homemade—

Sorry. I shouldn't have sworn. I've scribbled it out, but you can probably see the word through the paper and, God knows, maybe you've got kids, maybe you even put them in Little Plushy Bottoms or whatever the fashionable brand was at the time.

And I get it, I do. They're your babies. Nothing is too much trouble. I understand that. It's just that when you're the one having to stockpile a whole day's worth of pissy, shitty bits of cloth and hand them back to the parent at collection time with your eyes watering from the ammonia . . . it's not that I *mind* exactly, you know?

It's part of the job. I get that. But we all deserve a moan, don't we? We all need to let off steam, or we'd explode with frustration.

Sorry. I'm rambling. Maybe this is why Mr. Gates is always trying to shut me up. Because I dig myself a hole with my words and instead of knowing when to stop, I keep digging. You're probably adding two and two together right now. *Doesn't seem to like kids much. Freely admits to frustration with role. What would happen when she was cooped up with four kids and no adults to "let off steam" with?*

That's exactly what the police did. All those little throwaway remarks—all those unedifying facts. I could see the triumph on their faces every time I dropped one, and I watched them picking them up like bread crumbs, adding them to the weight of arguments against me.

But that's the thing, Mr. Wrexham. I could spin you a web of bullshit about what a perfect, caring, saintly person I am—but it would be just that. Bullshit. And I am not here to bullshit you. I want you to believe that—I want it more than anything in the world.

I am telling you the *truth*. The unvarnished, ugly truth. And it is all that. It *is* unpolished and unpleasant, and I don't pretend I acted like an angel. But *I didn't kill anyone*. I just fucking didn't.

I'm sorry. I didn't mean to swear again.

God, I am messing this up so badly. I have to keep a clear head—get this all straight in my head. It's like Mr. Gates says—I should stick to the facts.

Okay then. Fact. The advert. The advert is a fact, right?

The advert . . . with its amazing, dizzying, fabulous salary.

That should have been my first warning signal, you

know. The salary. Because it was *stupidly* generous. I mean it would have been generous even for London, even for a live-out nanny. But for a nanny in someone's house, with free accommodation provided and all bills paid, even down to the car, it was ridiculous.

It was so ridiculous, in fact, that I half wondered if there had been a typo. Or something that they weren't saying—a child with significant behavioral needs maybe? But wouldn't they have mentioned that in the ad?

Six months ago I probably would have paused, frowned a little, and then passed on without thinking too much more about it. But then, six months ago I wouldn't have been looking at that web page in the first place. Six months ago I had a flatmate and a job I liked, and even the prospect of promotion. Six months ago I was in a pretty good place. But now . . . well, things were a bit different now.

My friend, the girl at Little Nippers I mentioned, had left to go traveling a couple of months ago. It hadn't seemed like the end of the world when she told me—to be honest, I found her quite annoying, her habit of loading the dishwasher but never actually switching it on, her endless Euro-pop disco hits, hissing through my bedroom wall when I was trying to sleep. I mean, I knew I'd miss her, but I didn't realize how much.

She had left her stuff in her room, and we'd agreed she'd pay half rent and I'd keep the room open for her. It seemed like a good compromise—I'd had a series of terrible flatmates before we found each other, and I wasn't keen to return to posting on Facebook Local and trying to weed out weirdos by text message and email, and it felt, in some small way, like an anchor—like a guarantee that she would come back.

But when the first flush of freedom wore off, and the novelty of having the whole place to myself and watching whatever I liked on the shared TV in the living room had started to fade a little, I found I was lonely. I missed the way she'd say "Wine o'clock, darling?" when we rolled in together from work. I missed sounding off to her about Val, the owner of Little Nippers, and sharing anecdotes about the worst of the parents. When I applied for a promotion and didn't get it, I went to the pub alone to drown my sorrows and ended up crying into my beer, thinking how different it would have been if she had still been here. We could have laughed about it together, she would have flipped Val the bird behind her back at work, and given her earthy belly laugh when Val turned around to almost catch her in the act.

I am not very good at failing, Mr. Wrexham, that's the thing. Exams. Dating. Jobs. Any kind of test, really. My instinct is always to aim low, save myself some pain. Or, in the case of dating, just don't aim at all, rather than risk being rejected. It's why I didn't go to university in the end. I had the grades, but I couldn't bear the idea of being turned down, the thought of them reading my applications with a scornful snigger. "Who does she think she is?"

Better to achieve perfect marks on an easy test than flunk a hard one, that was my motto. I've always known that about myself. But what I didn't know, until my flatmate left, was that I am also not very good at being alone. And I think it was that, more than anything, that pushed me out of my comfort zone and made me scroll down that advert, holding my breath, imagining what lay at the other end of it.

The police made a lot out of the salary when they first questioned me. But the truth is, the money wasn't the reason I applied for the post. It wasn't even really about my flatmate, though I can't deny, if she hadn't left, none of it would have happened. No, the real reason . . . well, you probably know what the real reason was. It was all over the papers, after all.

I called in sick to Little Nippers and spent the entire day working on a CV and getting together everything that I knew I would need to convince the Elincourts that I was the person they were looking for. Background check—check. First aid certificate—check. Spotless references—check, check, and check.

The only problem was the driving license. But I pushed the issue aside for the moment. I could cross that bridge when I came to it—if I got that far. Right now, I wasn't thinking past the interview.

I added a note to the cover letter, asking the Elincourts not to contact Little Nippers for a reference— I told them that I didn't want my current employers knowing that I was casting about for another job, which was true—and then I emailed it off to the address provided and held my breath and waited.

I had given myself the best possible chance of meeting them face-to-face. There was nothing else I could do now.

Those next few days were hard, Mr. Wrexham. Not as hard as the time I've spent in here, but hard enough. Because—God—I wanted that interview *so much*. I was only just beginning to realize how much. With every day that passed, my hopes ebbed a little more, and I had to fight off the urge to contact them again and beg for an answer. The only thing that stopped me was the knowledge that looking so desperate would certainly not help my case if they were still deciding.

But six days later it came, pinging into my email inbox.

To: supernanny1990@ymail.com
From: sandra.elincourt@elincourtandelincourt.com
Subject: Nanny position.

Elincourt. The surname alone was enough to make my stomach start churning like a washing machine. My fingers were shaking almost too much to open it, and my heart was hammering in my throat. Surely, surely they didn't often contact unsuccessful applicants. Surely an email must mean . . . ?

I clicked.

Hi, Rowan! Thank you so much for your application, and apologies for taking so long to get back to you. I have to admit, we were slightly taken by surprise at the volume of applications. Your CV was very impressive, and we would like to invite you to interview. Our house is rather remote, so we are happy to pay your train fare and can offer you a room in our house overnight, as you will not be able to make the trip from London in one day.

However, there is one thing I must make you aware of up front, in case it affects your enthusiasm for the post.

Since we bought Heatherbrae we have become aware of various superstitions surrounding the house's history. It is an old building and has had no more than the usual number of deaths and tragedies in its past, but for some reason these have resulted in some local tales of hauntings, etc. Unfortunately, this fact has upset some of our recent nannies, to the extent that four have resigned in the past fourteen months.

As you can imagine, this has been very disruptive for the children, not to mention extremely awkward for myself and my husband professionally.

For that reason we wanted to be completely honest about our predicament, and we are offering a generous salary in the hopes of attracting someone who can really commit to staying with our family for the long term—at least a year.

If you do not feel that is you, or if you feel at all concerned about the history of the house, please say so now, as we are very keen to minimize further disruption to the children. With that in mind, the salary will be made up of a basic stipend, paid monthly, and then a generous year-end bonus on the anniversary of employment.

If you are still keen to attend the interview, please let me know your availability for the forthcoming week.

Best wishes, and I look forward to meeting you.

Sandra Elincourt

I closed down the email and for a moment just sat there staring at the screen. Then I got up and did a little silent scream, punching the air in jubilation.

I had done it. I had *done* it.

I should have known it was too good to be true.

I had done it, Mr. Wrexham. I had cleared the first hurdle. But it *was* only the first hurdle. I had to get through the interview next—and without slipping up.

Almost exactly one week after I had opened the email from Sandra Elincourt, I was on a train up to Scotland, doing my very best impression of Rowan the Perfect Nanny. My normally bushy hair was brushed to a shine and tamed into a neat, jaunty ponytail, my nails were buffed, and my makeup unobtrusively on point, and I was wearing my best "approachable yet responsible, fun yet hardworking, professional yet not too proud to get down on my knees and clear up vomit" outfit—a neat tweed skirt and a white cotton fitted shirt with a cashmere cardigan over the top. Not quite a Norland nanny, but definitely a nod in that direction.

My stomach was flipping with butterflies. I had never done anything like this before. Not the nannying, I mean. Obviously. I had done that for nearly ten years, though mostly in nurseries rather than private homes.

But . . . *this*. Putting myself on the line. Setting myself up for rejection like this.

I wanted this *so* much. So much that I was almost scared of what I was going to find.

Much to my annoyance, the train was delayed, so it took nearly six hours to get to Edinburgh instead of the time-tabled four and a half, and when I got off the train at Waverley, stiffly flexing my legs, I found it was past five o'clock, and I had missed my connection by a good hour. Fortunately there was another train due, and while I waited, I texted Mrs. Elincourt, apologizing profusely and warning her that I would be late into Carn Bridge.

At last the train arrived—much smaller than the big intercity, and older too. I settled myself in a window seat, and as the train headed north I watched the countryside change from rolling green fields to the smoke-blue and purples of heathered moors, mountains rising behind, darker and bleaker with every station we passed. It was so beautiful it made me forget my irritation at being late. The sight of the huge hills rising inexorably around us somehow put everything else into perspective. I felt the hard lump of trepidation lodged in my gut start to soften. And something inside me began . . . I don't know, Mr. Wrexham. It was like I began to *hope*. To hope that this could truly be real.

I felt, in some twisted kind of way, like I was coming home.

We passed through stations with half-familiar names, Perth, Pitlochry, Aviemore, the sky growing darker all the time. At last I heard "Carn Bridge, next stop Carn Bridge," and the train pulled into a little Victorian station, and I got out. I stood on the platform, jumpy with nerves, wondering what to do.

Someone will meet you, Mrs. Elincourt's email had said. What did that mean? A taxi? Someone holding up a sign with my name?

I followed the small straggle of travelers to the exit and stood awkwardly while the other passengers dispersed to cars and waiting friends and relatives. My case was heavy, and I set it down by my feet as I looked up and down the dusky platform. The shadows were lengthening into evening, and the fleeting optimism I had felt on the train was starting to fade. What if Mrs. Elincourt hadn't got my text? She hadn't replied. Perhaps a prebooked taxi had come and gone hours ago and I'd been marked up as a no-show.

Suddenly the butterflies were back—and badly.

It was early June, but we were pretty far north, and the night air was surprisingly cold after the fuggy summer warmth of London. I found I was shivering as I pulled my coat around me, a cool wind whipping down from the hills. The platform had emptied, and I was all alone.

I felt a strong urge for a cigarette, but I knew from experience that turning up to an interview stinking of fags was not a great start. Instead, I looked at my phone. The train had arrived exactly on time—at least, exactly at the revised time I had told Mrs. Elincourt in my text. I would give it five minutes and then call her.

Five minutes passed, but I told myself I'd give it just five minutes more. I didn't want to start off on the wrong foot, badgering them if they were stuck in traffic.

Five more minutes ticked away, and I was just digging in my bag, looking for the printout of Mrs. Elincourt's email, when I saw a man walking down the platform, hands in pockets.

For a moment something seemed to stutter in my chest, but then he got closer and he looked up, his eyes meeting mine, and I realized, it couldn't possibly be *him*. He was much too young. Thirty, thirty-five at the outside. He was also—and even in my nervousness I couldn't help but clock it—extremely good-looking, in a scrubby unshaven kind of way, with tangled dark hair and a tall, lean frame.

He was wearing overalls, and as he came up to me he took his hands out of his pockets and I saw they were grained with something—soil, or engine oil, though he'd made an attempt to clean them. For a moment I thought perhaps he was an employee of the railway, but as he drew level with me he spoke.

"Rowan Caine?"

I nodded.

"I'm Jack Grant." He grinned, his mouth curling disarmingly at the edges, as though appreciating a private joke. His accent was Scottish but softer and more distinct than the Glaswegian girl I'd worked with after school. He pronounced his surname with a lilt, to rhyme with *ant*, not the longer English *aunt*. "I work up at Heatherbrae House. Sandra asked me to pick you up. Sorry I'm late."

"Hi," I said, suddenly shy for no reason I could pin down. I coughed, trying to think of something to say. "Um, it's fine. No problem."

"It's why I'm in such a state." He looked ruefully down at his hands. "She didn't tell me you'd be wanting a lift until half an hour ago. I was halfway through fixing the mower, but I was worried I'd miss your train, so I just set out, dirt and all. Can I take your case?"

"Honestly, it's fine." I picked up my case. "It's not heavy. Thank you for coming out."

He shrugged.

"No need to thank me; it's my job."

"You work for the Elincourts?"

"For Bill and Sandra, aye. I'm . . . well I don't know quite what my job title would be. I think Bill's got me on his company payroll as a driver, but odd-job man would cover it better. I do the gardening, fix the cars, run them in and out of Carn Bridge. You'll be the nanny?"

"Not yet," I said nervously, but he grinned sideways at me, and I smiled in spite of myself. There was something infectious about his expression. "I mean, that's the position I'm going for, yes. Have they had many other interviewees?"

"Two or three. You're doing better than the first one. She didn't speak much English; I don't know who she got to write her application, but from what Sandra said it wasnae her."

"Oh." Somehow his words made me feel better. I'd been imagining a parade of starched and fiercely competent Mary Poppins types. I stood straighter, smoothing the wrinkles out of my tweed skirt. "Good. I mean, not good for her, I suppose. Good for me."

We were outside the station now, walking across the little sparsely populated car park, towards a long black car on the opposite side of the road. Jack clicked something on a fob in his pocket and the lights flashed and the doors opened, shooting up like bat wings, making my jaw drop involuntarily. I thought of my stepfather's bland gray Volvo, his pride and joy, and gave a short laugh. Jack grinned again.

"It's a bit conspicuous, isn't it? It's a Tesla. Electric. I don't know if it would have been my choice of vehicle, but Bill . . . well, you'll see. He's into technology."

"Is he?" The words were meaningless as a response, but somehow . . . just the knowledge of this small thing was a little nugget, a connection to this faceless man.

Jack stood back as I put my case into the rear of the car.

"Do you want to ride in the back, or up front?" he asked, and I felt my face color up.

"Oh, in front, please!"

The thought of sitting regally in the back, treating him like a chauffeur, was enough to make me squirm.

"The views are better anyway" was all he said, but he clicked something that made the batwing doors at the rear of the car swing closed, and then held open the front passenger door.

"After you, Rowan."

For a moment I didn't move, almost forgetting who he was speaking to. Then, with a start, I pulled myself together and climbed into the car.

BOOK CLUB FAVORITES

READER'S GUIDE

THE LYING GAME

RUTH WARE

INTRODUCTION

On a cool June morning, a woman is walking her dog in the idyllic coastal village of Salten along a tidal estuary known as the Reach. Before she can stop him, the dog charges into the water to retrieve what first appears to be a wayward stick, but to her horror, turns out to be a human bone.

The next morning, three women in and around London—Fatima, Thea, and Isa—receive the text they had always hoped would never come, from the fourth in their formerly inseparable clique, Kate. It says only "I need you."

The four girls were best friends at Salten, a second-rate boarding school set near the cliffs of the English Channel. Each different in their own way, the four became inseparable and were notorious for playing the Lying Game, telling lies at every turn to both fellow boarders and faculty. The rules of the game are strict: no lying to each other—ever. Bail on the lie when it becomes clear it is about to be found out. But their little game had consequences . . . and as the four converge in present-day Salten, they realize their shared past was not as safely buried as they had once thought.

Atmospheric, twisty, and with just the right amount of chill to keep you wrong-footed, *The Lying Game* is told in Ruth Ware's signature suspenseful style, lending itself to become another unputdownable thriller from the Agatha Christie of our time.

TOPICS AND QUESTIONS
FOR DISCUSSION

1. Describe the Lying Game and its rules. What inspired Thea originally to come up with the idea for the game? Why do she and Kate decide to include Fatima and Isa in the Lying Game? What about the game is appealing to the girls?

2. Isa says that Kate "knows what we'll say—what we've always said, whenever we got that text" (p. 5). Were you surprised by how quickly Isa, Fatima, and Thea rushed down to Salten upon receiving Kate's text? Why do they rush to her aid so quickly? Do you have any friends for whom you would do the same?

3. Describe the Tide Mill. What role has it played in the adolescence of the girls in the clique, and why is it so important to Kate, in particular? Isa is convinced that Kate will never leave the Tide Mill or Salten. Did you think she was correct in her assessment as the novel progressed? Why might Kate be unwilling or unable to leave?

4. When Isa and her friends reunite at Salten seventeen years after they have been dismissed from school there, Thea gives the same toast that she gave when they were students: "To us . . . May we never grow old" (p. 64). What

is Isa's reaction to Thea's toast? Were you surprised by it? Why do you think Isa reacts the way she does? How has she changed since leaving Salten as a student?

5. Each section of *The Lying Game* begins with a rule from the game. What's the effect of having the rules as chapter headings? How do they inform your reading of the story?

6. Isa says, "I once tried to describe Ambrose to an old boyfriend . . . but I found it almost impossible" (p. 84). How would you describe Ambrose? What kind of a teacher and parent was he? Mary Wren says that Ambrose would have done anything for his children whereas Fatima describes him as "an irresponsible fool" (p. 280). Why do each of the women feel so differently about Ambrose? What did you think of him?

7. Isa's housemistress tells her, "I'm very glad you've found friends. But remember, part of being a well-rounded young woman is having a wide *variety* of friends" (p. 114). Do you agree with the housemistress? What were some of the benefits of having such close friends? Mary describes Isa and her friends as a "little clique" (p. 120). Is that an accurate description? How does Isa feel about Mary's description and the clique itself as an adult? Were there any disadvantages to being part of it?

8. Rick praises Kate for staying in Salten, telling her, "Your dad was a good man, no matter what others in this place say, and you done well to stick it out here with the gossips" (p. 27). Do you think that Kate is brave for staying in Salten? Why or why not? Discuss some of the rumors about Kate and her father. What are they? Why might the townspeople find them plausible? Were there any rumors that you thought had merit? Which ones and why?

9. On Isa's first morning back at the Mill, Kate discovers a dead sheep. Who or what did you think was responsible for the sheep's death? Why? Describe the note that Isa finds in Kate's pocket. What does it say? Although Isa's initial impulse is to tell Fatima, "a kind of instinct takes over" (p. 120). Why doesn't Isa tell Fatima about the note? Would you?

10. When Isa reflects upon the events that took place, she muses that she will tell Freya "a story about bravery, and selflessness, and sacrifice" (p. 420). Do you agree with Isa? Do any of the characters in *The Lying Game* embody the traits that Isa enumerates? If so, who? How would you characterize the events that have taken place at Salten both during Isa's school days and at the friends' reunion?

11. When describing the events that happened shortly before their expulsion from Salten, Thea proclaims that the girls had no choice but to take the actions that they did. Do you agree with Isa when she cries, "Of *course* we had a choice!" (p. 229). Why or why not? Why might the girls have felt that they had no other options in the moment? Do you think that Kate took advantage of her friends when she asked for their help? If so, how?

12. Although Isa wants to tell Owen what she and her friends did while they were students at Salten, she feels she "can't. Because it's not only my secret—it's theirs, too. And I have no right to betray them" (p. 258). Do you agree with Isa's decision to withhold this information from Owen? Explain your answer. Do you think that there are any instances when it is permissible to betray a shared secret? If so, what are they?

13. Isa says that she and her friends "have spent seventeen years running and hiding, in our different ways" (p. 107–108). What are they hiding from? Describe the ways that each of the women has attempted to run from their shared past. Have any of their attempts been successful? Why or why not?

14. What were your initial impressions of Luc? Did you trust him? Why or why not? Describe his relationship with Ambrose and Kate. Were you surprised by his anger as an adult? Why does he harbor such resentment toward Kate? Do you think he is justified in doing so?

ENHANCE YOUR BOOK CLUB

1. When Isa is on the way to Salten, she muses, "It is heart-stoppingly familiar. London, in all the years I've lived there, has been constantly changing . . . But this line, this journey—it hasn't changed at all" (p. 17). Are there any places in your life that remain unchanged? What are they? Tell your book club about them.

2. Of Kate, Fatima, and Thea, Isa says, "I can't tell where I end and the others begin" (p. 166). Do you have friends like Isa's? Share some details with your book club.

3. When you were in school, did you play any games like the Lying Game with your friends? If so, what did you call them? Tell your book club about the games you played, explaining the rules.

4. Owen treats Isa to a day at a spa and, although she doesn't think it will help her relax, when she gives herself "over to the practiced hands of the spa therapist . . . somehow all the obsessive thoughts are pummeled out of me" (p. 298). Have you ever been to a spa? Did you find it similarly relaxing? Plan a spa day with your book club and unwind together.

5. To learn more about Ruth Ware, read excerpts from her books, and find out if she will be in a city near you; visit her official site at ruthware.com. You can also follow Ruth Ware on Twitter at @ruthwarewriter for regular updates on her writing.

A CONVERSATION WITH
RUTH WARE

Q: Both of your previous novels have been *New York Times* bestsellers. Given the success of your earlier books, did you feel any added pressure when writing *The Lying Game*? If so, how did you deal with it while you were writing?

A: I found the success of *In a Dark, Dark Wood* really distracting when I was writing *The Woman in Cabin 10*, but in a way the fact that *Cabin 10* was doing well felt quite freeing while I was writing *The Lying Game*. I suppose my biggest worry was proving a "one-hit wonder." The fact that *Cabin 10* was giving *Wood* a run for its money made me feel like I was (hopefully) not just going to be a flash in the pan as a writer.

Q: As a *New York Times* bestselling novelist, do you have any advice for aspiring writers? Is there anything that you wish you had known when you first began your career as a professional writer?

A: Oh, I wish there was a magic fix or some piece of advice that would smooth everything out—I'd bottle it and make a fortune! The only advice I can give to aspiring writers is to write the book that you would want to read, and hope other people agree. As for the publishing side . . . I guess one can do worse than follow the advice Rudyard Kipling gave in his poem "If—", particularly meeting with triumph and disaster just the same (which I interpret as good and bad reviews!).

Q: You describe Salten and the girls' experiences there so vividly. Was Salten based on a real place? How did you come up with it?

A: The landscape around Salten is sort of loosely based on Romney Marsh on the south coast, which is eerily beautiful and very isolated. But the Tide Mill is based on one I drove past one misty morning in northern France, in Brittany. It's near a place called Saint-Suliac. The place I saw is definitely not habitable—it was quite clearly dilapidated beyond repair—but I was completely entranced by the landscape—the bleak, wide salt marshes, the bleached blue skies, and this black crumbling hulk slowly disappearing into the sea. I knew there and then I would end up putting it into a book.

Q: *The Lying Game* is intricately plotted and filled with unexpected twists. When you began writing, did you know how the story would end?

A: I had the bones of the story in place from the outset, and the final cataclysmic scene at the Mill was in my mind from the beginning. But the exact twists and turns (including who was responsible for some of the creepier happenings) only revealed themselves in the writing.

Q: There are so many memorable scenes in *The Lying Game*, from Isa's train ride down to Salten, where she meets Kate and Thea, to the girls' weekends at the Tide Mill. What were your favorite scenes to write? Why?

A: Ooh . . . hard question! Possibly my favorite was the scene where Isa meets Mary Wren at the post office for the first time. I love writing a scene with a good measure of conflict. But I also love the scenes where all the women are together, figuring stuff out. I really enjoy writing about female friendship. It's an endlessly interesting dynamic for me.

Q: In *The Lying Game*, the action alternates between the past when the girls were in school at Salten and present day. Was it difficult to switch between time periods while you were writing? Can you tell us about your writing process?

A: I write as if I'm someone reading the book—often people ask if I write one strand first, and then go back and seed in the other, but I don't think I could keep track of who knows what, and the tension would come out wrong, so the answer is no—I write it more or less in the order you read it. (The more or less part being because sometimes my editors will ask me to go back and add an extra scene here or there.) I didn't find it hard at all to switch back and forth; it felt very natural because the present strand is in the present tense, and the past strand is all linked to Isa's memories. It did make it hard to edit, however. Normally you can move scenes around if you need to, to preserve a reveal for later in the book, or prolong the tension for some reason. But because all the past scenes are triggered by Isa's memories—often by specific things that happen in the present-day narrative—it meant that it was really hard to change things.

Q: *Kirkus Reviews*, *Bustle*, and *Metro* have all compared your writing to Agatha Christie's. Were you influenced by Christie's novels? Are there any other authors who have inspired you? Who are they?

A: I love Christie. I read her a huge amount as a teen and I still think there's little more satisfying than curling up in front of the fire with a sumptuous Christie adaptation on the TV! But for this book, I think I was maybe more influenced by all the boarding school stories I read as a child. There's maybe a bit of *The Secret History* in there, too.

Q: Is there anything that has been particularly rewarding about publishing *The Lying Game*? If so, what?

A: Well, as I'm writing this, it hasn't yet come out—so I'm still waiting for the most rewarding part, which is talking to readers and finding out what they made of my characters.

Q: What would you like your readers to take away from *The Lying Game*? What compelled you to write it?

A: I'm quite resistant to telling people what they are supposed to find in a book—I don't like it as a reader, and so I try not to tell people how they should react, although I'm always interested in the different things people pick up on. But I suppose what compelled me to write it was thinking about the priorities in our lives and how our loyalties shift throughout our lifetimes—how we go from being small children, completely focused on our parents, to teens wrapped up in our friends, to love affairs, and then finally we become parents ourselves and that focus moves to our own children, and we would sacrifice almost anything to keep them safe. I'm not sure if I realized that's what I was writing about until I'd finished, though!

Q: Are you working on anything now? Can you tell us about it?

A: I'm about to start my fourth book! It's way too early to say very much about it, because I'm not sure if I've figured it out myself yet, but I think it might feature a bequest. . . .